FIERCE
COWBOY WOLF

KAIT BALLENGER

sourcebooks
casablanca

WOLF PACK RUN: BOOK 4

← FARMLAND

TRAINING FIELD

Training Gym
(Underground)

PASTURE

Reception Hall
(Refurbished Barn)

Medical Facility

Tunnels (Underground)

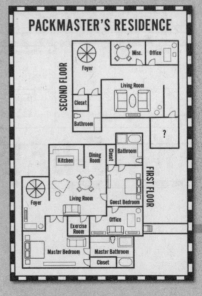

PACKMASTER'S RESIDENCE

SECOND FLOOR

Foyer · Misc. · Office · Living Room · Closet · Bathroom · ?

FIRST FLOOR

Kitchen · Dining Room · Bathroom · Closet · Foyer · Living Room · Guest Bedroom · Exercise Room · Office · Master Bedroom · Master Bathroom · Closet

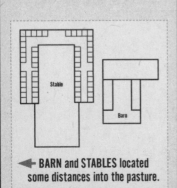

Stable

Barn

← BARN and STABLES located some distances into the pasture.

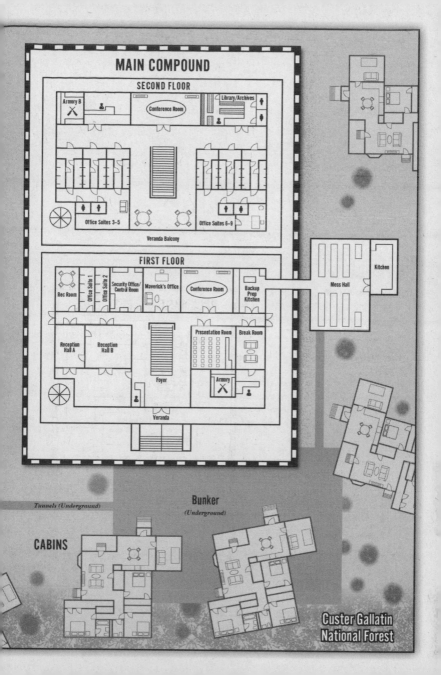

For all the fierce females who pave the way

Published by Sourcebooks Casablanca, an imprint of Sourcebooks
P.O. Box 4410, Naperville, Illinois 60567-4410
(630) 961-3900
sourcebooks.com

Printed and bound in Canada.
MBP 10 9 8 7 6 5 4 3 2 1

Chapter 1

Sierra Cavanaugh's fist collided with her opponent's cheekbone. A sting raked her knuckles despite the cloth sparring gear that padded her hands. Two more punches, a kick, and a sweep of her leg. Within seconds, her opponent was laid flat, panting for breath in the mountain dirt beside Sierra's cowgirl boots. Sierra smiled in satisfaction. Tonight was her night, and she intended to claim her victory.

Dakota raised up onto her elbows from where Sierra had annihilated her. "You're unstoppable," the other she-wolf slurred around her mouth guard. "You've got this." Dakota ripped the guard from between her lips, sending an unladylike spray of spit into the dirt.

Sierra didn't so much as blink. None of them did. Ladylike be damned. They didn't owe a thing to anyone. Sierra extended a hand, helping Dakota to her feet. The other she-wolf let out a soft groan muffled by the thrum of feminine voices around them and the crackle of the roaring fire. The Grey Wolf female warriors had taken over the pack firepit tonight, driving out their male counterparts by sheer force of will, and okay…*maybe* a bit of friendly intimidation.

"You pack a hard wallop." Dakota pawed at her jaw.

She was barely half Sierra's size, but her stature made her formidably fast on her feet. Sierra had won by brute force.

"I'd say I'm sorry, but you know I'm not." Sierra grinned.

Fierce and fiery, Dakota playfully punched her in the arm, muttering a few teasing, choice words.

They were all there with her, every one of the pack's females. A swell of pride grew in Sierra's chest. She couldn't believe how lucky she was to call these strong women her sisters, not by blood but by choice.

"You're so good the elders can't ignore you." The praise came from Naomi Calhoun, their second-in-command's human mate, a former biologist turned rancher, as she pushed a cold bottle of Coors into Sierra's hand. "Cheers." She clinked the neck of her beer bottle with Sierra's. "You'll make an excellent elite warrior."

Elite warrior. Sierra smiled. She intended to claim the title for herself tonight. Which of the current elite warriors had nominated her for the council's consideration was confidential, but that failed to matter. She would be the first female of their kind to hold the title. Tonight, she was their fearless leader.

Sierra cast Naomi a teasing smile. "You're only impressed because you're a human."

"Who you callin' human?" Dakota's eyes flashed to her wolf as she cast Sierra an impish grin. She tipped her Stetson back on her head to cover her mussed, dark hair. "Now when are you going to open the letter? I'm dying for you to open it."

"Me too." Cheyenne grabbed a Coors from the cooler, wiping the moisture that remained on the bottle across her track pants. Sierra shook her head. Cheyenne was always ready for a run. The other she-wolf's endurance and drive were unstoppable.

Sierra wouldn't have reached this moment without their support, without every time strong, fierce little Dakota reassured her, or every morning energetic Cheyenne woke her up at the ass crack of dawn and forced her to run all the way out past the stables. The other she-wolves raised their drinks as another round of howling ensued. Cowgirls didn't take no for an answer.

"Okay, okay." Sierra removed the letter from her back pocket. She'd been itching to open it, but she'd wanted to wait until they were all together.

The envelope had arrived in her ranch mailbox this morning, only two days after the Elder Council meeting, which meant their decision had been a quick one. Tentatively, she stared down at the cream-colored paper glowing orange in the firelight. Silence fell over the warriors as the air buzzed with quiet anticipation.

With a deep breath, Sierra ripped open the envelope and unfolded the letter, her eyes scanning over the block of text. She'd known from the start she had to be stronger, faster, *better* than all the males for the pack to even have her name put forth to the elders for consideration.

And she had been.

But still, it wasn't enough.

Her stomach churned as the message sank in. Desperately, she fought to keep her hands from shaking as she forced herself to look up at her fellow females. Her eyes scanned over the crowd of women around her. She'd been their best chance, the leader upon whom they'd hung their collective hopes.

And she'd failed them.

Shame built in her chest, a sinking feeling that pulled at her stomach as she felt hot tears catch in her throat, too large for her to swallow, but she would hold them in anyway. She *refused* to cry, because Sierra Cavanaugh did not cry. She hadn't shed a single tear in years. Not since the last time she'd allowed her emotions, her fear and weakness, to get the best of her.

When she finally managed to speak, she was distant, calm, measured, not showing any of the tumultuous feelings raging inside her. "They denied my application."

A murmur of righteous outrage broke out among the women.

"For what reason?" Dakota snarled.

Sierra knew her next words would only spark their anger further because as far as she was concerned, as far as they *all* were concerned, there was no adequate explanation.

"Because I don't have a mate."

The silence was deafening.

The collective disappointment mixed with fury in her packmates' expressions cut her worse than a thousand knives, worse than the words or decisions of any group of sexist elders ever could.

They'd all known the pack's unspoken expectation of alpha females of pure bloodline: to mate with an alpha male and further the pack's longevity. It was a narrative born of evolutionary necessity as old as the true wolves from which they'd descended, and yet, they'd thought they had moved beyond that. They thought if they played by every one of the pack's ridiculous rules to prove themselves, and if they forced the elders to speak those archaic expectations aloud, the pack's ancient ways would bend to the will of progress.

But they hadn't.

Without another word, Sierra ripped the letter in two and threw the remnants into the firepit. The paper burned and blackened, quickly turning to ash. "Where is he?" She didn't need to specify which *he* for her fellow warriors to instantly know who she meant.

"He was in his office when Wes—" Naomi answered.

Sierra didn't pay attention to the rest of the statement. She was too focused on her goal to care. She was already striding toward the compound, the epicenter of the ranch.

"What are you going to do?" Dakota called after her.

For a moment, Sierra paused. Slowly, she inhaled a deep breath before she turned back toward them, looking from face to face of each woman around her who'd put their faith in her, trusted her with their dream. She'd never forget their righteous anger—and she would use it as fuel. "I'm going to do what I always do. I'm going to fight, and I'm going to win."

And she knew exactly the alpha upon whom she planned to lay siege.

———

"Packmaster or not, it's unheard of."

Maverick Grey tipped his Stetson low over his brow, fighting to mask the look of disgust in his eyes. One would think after nearly two hundred years of existence, the Council of Grey Wolf Elders, whose membership changed every several decades, would have become more progressive in their policy. Unfortunately, that couldn't be further from the truth.

"First, you expect us to approve when you choose to keep company with outlaws, and now we're considering a *female* as an elite warrior?"

Maverick didn't fight the growl that escaped his throat. As if the candidacy of a highly qualified female alpha wolf was anything as controversial as when he'd named his former enemy turned packmate Wes Calhoun to second-in-command. He'd never once regretted that decision, despite the council's disapproval.

The company he kept was of no concern, so long as the pack remained safe.

He met the gaze of Rex Johnson, the council's leader, head-on. "That *female* could rip out any alpha wolf's organs and tie their intestines into knots with little more than her teeth."

The statement sounded as threatening as he intended it.

Because at the moment, he would have welcomed Sierra Cavanaugh, the *female* in question, doing exactly that to the council wolves before him. The Grey Wolf elite warriors were the best the pack had to offer, and as the first female appointed, Sierra would set a precedent that would resonate for generations to follow.

"Be that as it may, it's not in the best interest of the pack," Rex announced as if his word were the final decision.

Maverick scowled. A retired alpha warrior from one of the western subpacks, Rex and the council he represented served the sole purpose of upholding the Grey Wolf pack's ancient traditions by acting as a counterbalance to Maverick's power as packmaster. As the elder members of the pack, many of them former elite warriors themselves, the council ensured that Maverick always kept the pack's best interests at heart. Perhaps two decades ago, when Rex and his peers had still been out on the front lines of battle, Maverick would have said that they knew what was best for the pack.

Now, the tables had obviously turned—considerably.

Rex shuffled the stack of papers in front of him. From where he sat at the conference-room table, beneath the large mounted skull of a long-horned bull that one of Maverick's great-grandfathers had placed on the wall, the frown on his lips made Rex look more like an angry bullfrog than a retired alpha wolf.

What about retirement made former fierce warriors into old curmudgeonly bastards?

Maverick had stood against the worst of the pack's enemies and still maintained a level head, yet if he managed to make it through this conversation without strangling someone, he might deserve an award. "What *exactly* about naming one of Wolf Pack Run's most formidable warriors to the elite ranks, where we've had an open position, is *not* in the best interest of the pack?" He didn't hide the bite of cynicism in his tone.

Rex bristled. "I think you know."

Maverick crossed his arms over his chest. Even if he wanted to, he couldn't have hidden his disapproval of the council's opposition. It didn't help matters that most days he had little taste for anything, or *anyone* for that matter—the council in particular. He lived to protect the pack and little more, and the old bastards were constantly getting in his way.

His lip twitched with a barely contained snarl. "No, I don't," he challenged.

If the council was going to play that card, he was going to make them say it.

On the record.

Anderson, one of the other retired warriors, cleared his throat. "I think Rex has a fair point that a female elite warrior is unprecedented, and considering the current condition of your cousin…"

Maverick's jaw clenched. Yes, because ignoring the true threats against them in favor of being highly concerned with the inner goings-on of all the packmembers' bedrooms was *clearly* the best course of action. His cousin and her pregnancy were irrelevant to this.

Birth rates were typically low among their kind, serving as built-in population control, but since his cousin Belle had announced that she and Sierra's older brother, Colt Cavanaugh, the Grey Wolf high commander and Maverick's closest friend, were expecting a pup of their own, there had barely been a moment where one of the pack wasn't fussing over Belle's growing bump. The pack tended to produce young in waves, with many pairs of mates giving birth within a few years' time. To the pack, if Belle successfully carried to term, that meant many more births would follow.

Maverick's frown only deepened. "The tentative state of the treaty is a far greater threat. The renegotiation with the rogue wolves nullified our immunity from the Execution Underground. We needed to renegotiate the terms with the human hunters *yesterday*. Hell, last *week*," he growled, "not waste valuable time with useless pack politics."

Several of the council members mumbled their disapproval.

"Renegotiation will be safest for the pack if *all* our elite warrior positions are filled. Sierra Cavanaugh is an unrivaled candidate. She's supremely and uniquely qualified, and there are other pure-blooded alpha females who will *choose* to mate," Maverick said, reminding them of the facts. Let the bastards think what they like of him, but he refused to beat around the bush. He glowered at the council, daring any one of the members to suggest otherwise. "I speak from experience when I say her lack of a mate has no bearing on her abilities as a warrior."

Maverick had complicated feelings when it came to Sierra Cavanaugh, but doubt in her abilities wasn't one of them.

Anderson cleared his throat. "We're aware that being a widower hasn't impeded you on the battlefield, Packmaster, but you'd do well to be more concerned about the current situation. If birth rates continue at this stagnated rate, the pack is one good war from being extinct within a hundred years. Now's not the time to be renegotiating with long-standing enemies." The old wolf hesitated before he finally added, "It's been six years, Maverick. You could take a mate yourself. Set an example."

Maverick grunted. He couldn't think of Rose. Not now. Not with everything that was at stake.

Six years and still the wound felt fresh, open, as if it would bleed him.

He forced the dark memories aside. They only stayed at bay for so long.

"I'm aware of the *projections*." He emphasized the word.

And they were exactly that—projections. Not true threats like the broken treaty was. The birth rates would rise again when the pack needed them to, and it would happen without any meddling as it had for thousands of years before. He refused to allow speculation to get in the way of renegotiating the treaty and appointing a warrior who was more than worthy of the open position, regardless of her gender.

"There will be a revote." Like it or not, the council would get on board. He'd make sure of it. Entertaining anything else would be a waste of time and a threat to them all.

Rex readjusted his position in his chair. "All things considered, now is not the time to be making any radical decisions, especially since you've developed a certain reputation as of late."

Maverick released a feral snarl.

So that was what this was about? Not Sierra's gender, though the council would use that to their advantage to deny his requests. This was about him. The council had never been fond of his tendency to break tradition and circumvent their restrictions when necessary, yet their negative opinions had never held any legitimacy.

Until now.

Until the sins of the father had become the sins of the son.

Maverick had earned many names over his years as packmaster. At first, they'd been the whispers of his enemies, meant to denote the terror he wrought when he came for them. He'd destroyed every one of the pack's opponents with a cold ferocity the likes of which the pack had never known. But considering the revelations that had been made about his father in the past few months, the once harmless rumors about him had taken on a new meaning.

And now they called him the Monster of Montana.

Along with his demand that the pack provide protection for the rogue wolves, the recent reappearance of a former Grey Wolf named Jared Black had revealed that Maverick's father had committed crimes against the young wolf to ensure Jared never had the opportunity to challenge the Grey family line for packmaster. His father's illegal actions had ended talks of another founding family taking over the pack before they'd even truly began.

Since then, despite the fact that Maverick had been young and as manipulated by his father's lies as the rest of the pack and that he had *always* been next in line for the throne even before his father's crime had been committed, his father's sins had become his own. Now, every past decision he'd ever made was being drawn into question, every time he'd ever gone around the council vilified. The greater pack was scrutinizing his every move.

He scowled. He didn't need to be liked. Hell, he'd never expected the pack's thanks, let alone their appreciation. He fulfilled his role because it was his duty to protect them. He lived for little more. But now, the whispers of his critics were no longer whispers. Never mind the legitimacy of his birthright, the loyalty he inspired among his warriors, his years of dedicated service, and every sacrifice he'd ever made on behalf of *his* pack. All that was forgotten in the face of a council who'd been eager to oppose him from day one, who planned to force him to behave. They thought he was a rebel, a renegade, an outlaw.

Monster. The memory of the harsh accusation ripped through him.

If only they knew the truth...

"My *father's* sins are of no concern in this consideration," Maverick growled.

At the blunt mention of the previous packmaster's crimes, the council members bristled.

Rex grabbed the stack of papers in front of him and shuffled them pointedly. "Be that as it may, the vote remains."

Maverick shoved back his chair and stood. Supporting the weight of his torso with his hands, he leaned over the tabletop, his eyes flashing to his wolf. "The treaty *will* be renegotiated. I won't deny a wolf of her caliber based on a *hope* of furthering the pack's young."

Rex grinned, like the viper he truly was. "Fortunately for you, Packmaster, you don't have to. We already notified the candidate on your behalf."

Son of a bitch.

Maverick growled. "You're undermining my authority?"

They had challenged him in the past, delayed him considerably, but this would be the first time they'd ever outright gone *against* him.

Rex shook his head as he rose from the table. "Don't consider it undermining. We're guiding you in the direction of your ancestors. The original vote remains."

Which meant they *were* undermining him, and as far as the old bastards were concerned, the meeting was over.

But Maverick wasn't done yet.

Collectively, the other elders followed Rex's lead, rising from their seats, and filtered out of the conference room, but Maverick prowled straight toward Rex. The few who lingered in his path scattered out of his way, rushing and bumping into one another like scared newborn calves first weaned from their mothers in the cattle chute. Maverick snarled. They truly believed their own hype. That he was a beast, a monster that needed to be tamed. Like his father.

If it was a monster they wanted, then that was what they'd get.

To Rex's credit, he didn't back down as Maverick approached. Instead, a smirk curled the old wolf's lips. "The days of you side-stepping the council are done. You'll thank me when your legacy as packmaster is long and fruitful."

Maverick drew so close to the old wolf that he towered over him. He lowered his voice to a threatening growl. "This isn't over."

Leaving on that final warning, Maverick tore out of the compound. He wasn't his father and he never would be. He could give two flying fucks about his legacy. All he cared about was what was best for the pack: protecting those he cared for most. Naming Sierra to the role of elite warrior before they renegotiated with the Execution Underground *was* best. No one could convince him otherwise.

When he reached the stables, he brushed past the stall housing his temporary steed and headed straight toward Trigger. He'd recently been forced to retire the old horse from regular work, but every time he rode another, it was no replacement. He hadn't broken the others, trained them. Not in the way he had Trigger.

Saddling up the mare, Maverick led her from the stables, hooking his foot into the stirrup and swinging into seat before they galloped across the mountainside. He rode hard and fast, pushing the beast to her limit. As the wind whipped past him, the clouds overcast the mountainside with a gray hue, highlighting the bright orange, red, and yellow autumn leaves in stark contrast. Maverick inhaled a deep breath of chilled mountain air.

Monster or not, he was their packmaster, their king.

And he refused to be denied.

Chapter 2

THE ABANDONED STABLE ON THE FRINGES OF THE GREY Wolves' ranch had seen better days. Moonlight streamed through the open stable doors, highlighting the age of the old wooden planks and the dust-covered stone floor on which Maverick stood. The metal of a rusty stall gate creaked as a howl of autumn wind whipped through. He often came here when he needed to think, to clear his head, and by all expectation, he *should* have been alone.

But he wasn't.

Off in the distance, Trigger nickered.

Maverick stiffened, his muscles coiled and prepared to fight. He sensed it, too. The mountain air around them crackled with silent tension, and the elongated shadows of the pines shivered with awareness. He'd hoped the promise of violence lingering in the night air would disappear once the heady feeling of rage at the council's defiance subsided, yet still it remained. A sharp whinny pierced through the night.

Maverick drew his blade. The horse had been grazing in the forest brush just beyond the abandoned stable. With lethal stealth, Maverick prowled toward the source of the noise, his wolf senses primed with awareness. But as he drew closer, it soon became evident that the old mare wasn't in imminent distress as he'd anticipated.

As he stepped into the adjacent clearing, a large stallion came into view. The newly arrived Appaloosa sidled up behind the mare, while Trigger cast Maverick a familiar look that said *Not this fool again*. Maverick scowled and let out a frustrated curse under his breath. He recognized the other horse instantly.

A hard-working ranch horse who'd been recently made into a

gelding, Randy, was appropriately named, considering when he was left to his own devices, he was an uncontrollably horny beast who'd run off with the nearest willing mare as soon as look at her, and he belonged to none other than…

A feminine voice growled at Maverick from behind. "You pompous, arrogant bastard."

Maverick turned to find Sierra Cavanaugh, the horse owner in question, charging through the underbrush toward him with all the force of a raging bull, and from the spark of angry fire in her eyes, she was as dangerous as one to boot. Her gaze locked on him, boring straight through him with such intense focus that she didn't appear to notice her gelding was using his teeth to repeatedly nudge at his mare's tether with a mischievous look in his eyes that meant intended escape.

Or maybe she did notice, and she simply didn't care.

Another feral growl ripped from her throat. "How dare you?" She stabbed an accusatory finger toward Maverick as if it were a sword. From the fiery look in her eye, that single finger might have been lethal. Even for a wolf as dangerous as him.

"You've been harder on me than every other warrior since day one," she accused, "and to what end—to let the council reject me on the grounds of not having a *goddamn mate*?" She snarled the last words as if they were the most abhorrent phrase she'd ever spoken.

He battled the urge to point out that her horse was currently about to make a *goddamn mate* of his if the two beasts managed to elope together. His mare's suddenly intrigued huffs and Randy's pleasured grunting as he pranced around her, trying to chew her free from the rope she was tied with, were getting downright noisy.

Maverick remained silent, welcoming Sierra's rage. He'd gladly serve as her target. He understood the depths of her need to serve the pack, her internal drive to protect their own. In that way, he and Sierra Cavanaugh had always been more alike than he cared to admit. But despite their similarities and the fact that *he* had been the one who put forth her candidacy to the council, he'd never expected her thanks.

Hell, he not only welcomed her rage, he'd anticipated it. She might have been his best friend's little sister since as far back as he could remember, but ever since he'd assumed his role as packmaster, Sierra Cavanaugh had hated him with a passionate fury rivaled only by some of his worst enemies.

And he needed it to stay that way.

Because the feeling had never been mutual.

He drank in the raw energy she put into every word, every gesture and movement as if he were a starving man in the middle of the desert and she was his only drink of water. She and her fiery temper were unbridled passion compared to his every cold, calculated move. He envied that fire as much as he both disliked and craved it. He always had.

Sierra was a problem, that was for certain. The havoc she wreaked on his day-to-day was never-ending, and he disliked every ounce of chaos she and her challenging nature stood for. But he didn't dislike *her*. Not like he should.

And that was precisely the heart of the issue, wasn't it?

Still ranting, she stomped through the underbrush toward him, her long, blond braid swinging about behind her like a whip. "You pushed me to be stronger, faster, better than all the others."

"I did." He grumbled the words, low and feral, despite the equal rage he felt inside, because her anger was warranted—and it matched his own. He wouldn't deny it. He *had* been harder on her because he had to be. He and her brother had warned her of that from the start when she'd first declared her intent to earn the position. Though admittedly over time, he'd taken pleasure in pushing her to her limits. Hell, if he hadn't wanted...fuck, no, *needed* to see that look of fiery defiance in her eyes every time he'd demanded more of her.

He'd damn near ached for it.

"It's not right. It isn't fair."

"It isn't."

"I *earned* that position." She growled the words with confidence. She stomped one of her cowgirl boots hard into the mountain dirt. "I deserve it, damn it."

"Then we're in agreement." Maverick crossed his arms over his chest, leaning against a nearby tree with a smirk. She seemed completely unaware of the increasingly loud sounds of their horses attempting to escape a mere ten feet away or of the fact that he was affirming every statement she made.

Chaos followed her like the damn plague.

She threw up her hands in exasperation. "And even if I wanted to appease those old, decrepit assholes, where the hell would I find a mate on this godforsaken ranch?"

Despite his better judgment, his body had a few ideas about that, considering the growing pressure against the fly of his jeans. Every time that braid of hers whipped about, he smelled the warm scent of cinnamon and clove in her hair. She'd always smelled like the warmer elements of autumn, and it made his wolf come alive, like he was prowling through the forest, the cold wind prickling at his back. She made him want to nibble his human canines across the skin of her neck as he claimed her like the animal he truly was…

He hadn't felt so awake in years.

In an instant, the solution to their mutual problem barreled through him.

She needed a mate, and he needed to appease the Elder Council.

As quickly as the solution came, his protective instinct flared, reminding him of all that was at stake. *Monster.* The dark memory of the accusation pierced through him again.

No, he couldn't allow a woman close to him. Not again. Not even a woman as formidable and lethal as Sierra Cavanaugh. He'd always done what was best for the pack, even when it nearly destroyed him, and he'd sworn to himself never to take another wife. Period. Let alone a woman who, despite how she vexed him, was *supposed* to be like a little sister to him, even though there'd never been anything remotely sibling-like between them, save for their constant bickering, and...

He quirked a brow. Was that a rooster pecking in the brush behind her?

"Are you even listening anymore?" she snapped.

He grunted. He was, but he wasn't about to argue the point.

Sierra let out one final angry snarl. She didn't seem to care that he was her packmaster or that despite how impressive she was on the battlefield, *he* was considered by their kind to be the most dangerous wolf to have ever lived. Had she not been one of his pack, her disrespect of him would have gotten her killed. He'd seen her angry before, but never like this, never outright defiant. Petulant even.

He liked it more than he should.

Her hands clenched into fists as she drew closer to him, her long, blond braid still swinging behind her. He wanted to grip those strands of hair in his fist, use it to pull her even closer. They were practically nose to nose now. Close enough that he could smell the earthy scent of her wolf on her skin. Close enough that if he wanted to, which he *did*, he could have kissed the righteous anger straight off her perfectly plump lips.

If that wouldn't have made her a thousand times angrier...

Somehow, that made him want to do it even more.

"What do you have to say for yourself, *Packmaster*?" she growled.

And that alone sealed his decision.

He needed a wife of convenience, with no attachments or love—and who better than a she-wolf who hated him?

Maverick never backed down from a challenge.

His eyes flashed to his wolf as he met Sierra's gaze head-on. "Marry me."

Chapter 3

SOMEONE HAD TAKEN ALL THE WIND OUT OF HER SAILS. SIERRA blinked, trying to digest the moment. She was suddenly and acutely aware of the fact that she was standing in the middle of the forest, inches away from the face of the Grey Wolf packmaster himself, a man who held unprecedented power over her, and not only had he *agreed* with everything she'd said, but he had asked her to *marry* him. If there'd ever been a time she'd been caught off guard…

This was it.

Packmaster or not, inside she was ready to throttle him, but instead she only managed to gape, and as if she couldn't have looked like any more of a fool, Randy chose that exact moment to let out an exceedingly pleased nicker, and it was then that she realized her gelding had managed to get the packmaster's enthusiastic mare free from her hold—and he was leading her off into the darkness.

She didn't want to consider the act that might follow.

"Are you going to take care of that?" Maverick grumbled, more than a hint of amusement in his voice.

An embarrassed blush crept down her neck. "You damn horny bastard," she swore at Randy. Sidestepping around Maverick, she grabbed onto her horse's reins, hauling him away from Trigger with every ounce of her strength. It took more than a few tugs and a fair bit of grunting and growling—both from her and the now pissed-off, horny gelding—but finally with a flash of her wolf eyes, she managed to remind Randy who was in charge and wrangle him away from the old mare.

Once she'd finished subduing her horse, she turned back toward the packmaster, a layer of sweat coating her brow despite the cold autumn wind. Maverick was still watching her, his cold, harsh eyes assessing as if he saw straight through her. Since he'd become pack-master, she'd always hated that about him, and for a moment, from the gruff, impenetrable coldness in his face, she could almost convince herself he hadn't just proposed to her.

Almost.

"I guess Randy was a little Trigger-happy?" She wiped the sweat from her brow with a feeble, unamused laugh. "Trigger-happy. Get it?" Considering the embarrassed blush coloring her cheeks, the badly timed pun was the best attempt at levity she had to offer.

The stone-faced packmaster didn't so much as grin.

Of course. He'd never been a fan of her jokes, no matter how clever. The blush in her cheeks deepened. Lord help her.

When he didn't respond, she swept back the stray strands of hair that had come loose from her braid, but they rebelled again before she chose to feign a deep interest in the color of her new boots. They were brown. Normal leather brown. Just like every other pair of cowgirl boots she'd owned. Ever.

She cleared her throat. "So Wes finally decided to go back to the dark side and drugged your afternoon coffee. I can't say I'm surprised." The comment sounded as ridiculous and inane as she felt, but all things considered, he couldn't possibly be serious.

"Sierra." The deep, biting thrum of his voice vibrated through her. Maverick's voice was so low and graveled, it often sounded as if he were growling, even when he wasn't.

A shiver rolled down her spine.

His voice always had a visceral effect on her. As their leader, Maverick was concise, only speaking when it was necessary. Especially since the death of his wife, Rose, he was anything but vocal unless he was addressing the pack, handing out orders. Even in private, he was grumbly, taciturn, an impenetrably cold wall of ice. But on the rare occasions Maverick spoke her name, his voice wrapped around her with a warm heat that took her thoughts to places she only dared venture to in her most private dreams. She *couldn't* want her packmaster, a man who angered her nearly as much as she admired him.

And yet she did.

Perhaps more than she'd ever wanted anything.

He was her alpha, and he'd addressed her directly. She had to look up. She couldn't *not* look at him. When she did, the severity of his harsh, handsome features coupled with that delicious voice and those piercing green eyes shook her. The puckered scar that severed the hair of his left eyebrow drew low. From the harsh look in his dark features, the Grey Wolf packmaster was serious.

Her breath caught.

No. No.

Her heart thumped hard against her chest. He *couldn't* be serious.

She knew that without a doubt—because ten years earlier, he'd chosen another. So he *couldn't* want to marry her, at least not for the reasons her younger self would have hoped, which meant this long-dreamed-of moment she'd built up in her head as a girl was about to go horribly, terribly wrong…

On a night in which she'd already been gutted by disappointment.

Maverick cleared his throat. "It would be to our mutual benefit."

Mutual benefit.

A business deal…

That was all she needed to hear for the moment to go instantly south.

"We need a full team of elite warriors to protect the pack, not to mention the council has been blocking me from renegotiating with the Execution Underground at every turn. Each passing day is a danger to all of us. I need to throw them a bone, or they'll continue to oppose me, and they've been begging me to take a mate again for years…" His deep voice trailed off.

A sharp intake of breath caught in Sierra's throat. He was asking her out of obligation, a drive to protect the pack and little more.

The packmaster of the Grey Wolves had found a way to accomplish all he wanted in one swift, daring move. It was so quintessential to his leadership style that she almost laughed at the sheer, cruel irony of it. Maverick destroyed their enemies with such ease even his predecessors failed to compare. He would sacrifice *anything* in the name of protecting the pack.

Even her heart.

"It won't be an easy position, but you'll do." He spoke the words with such gruff disinterest that any excitement she would have once felt at his proposal dissipated.

"For the position of elite warrior or your wife?" she snapped.

He held her gaze, refusing to look away. "Both," he offered. "I don't see how that matters."

Of course the distinction mattered. It mattered to *her*.

Sierra scowled, fighting the snarl that threatened to rip from her throat.

Nothing in that moment would have satisfied her, short of shifting into her wolf and tearing out his cold, distant heart. He'd already shamed her once. The hurt of his rejection when he'd chosen Rose instead of her had haunted her for years. And now, he was the one wolf who stood in the way of everything she wanted. And still, he had the nerve to ask her to *marry* him?

No. Not ask. Demand. *Marry me* wasn't exactly a request, was it?

He cleared his throat. "I need a wife of convenience. Love is a price I can't afford, so who better than a woman who..." He raked his gaze over her, assessing.

A prickle of heat coursed through her, and she hated it.

"Loathes you?" she finished for him. She'd worked hard over the years to make him think that was her opinion of him because the truth that she'd once, long ago, been madly in love with him would have made her look weak, and she couldn't allow that. She'd only allowed Maverick Grey to see her at her weakest once before, and she would never allow it again.

If love was a price he couldn't afford, then she wasn't a pawn for sale. She wouldn't let him use her in his ridiculous game with the council.

She squared her shoulders, summoning what remaining pride she could muster as she held her head high. "No." She said the word with every ounce of venom she felt for him in that moment.

"No?" He raised a brow.

"No," she repeated. This time, louder.

Maverick eased away from the old maple upon which he'd been leaning. With pale green-yellow eyes the color of a true wolf's, skin a dark, tanned brown from all the hours he spent working on the ranch, and long, untamable hair pulled into a ponytail at his nape, the packmaster of the Grey Wolves was a large, dark, hairy brute of a man with canine teeth so sharp that he looked part beast even when he was in human form. He uncrossed his large arms from over top his chest. In the moonlit shadows of the forest, the movement highlighted the sheer massive size of him. Sierra was taller and more muscular than most of the females in the pack, yet his presence dwarfed her. She may have been lethal in her own right, but even she was no match. Not for him.

He prowled toward her, his gait smooth and predatory. In the moonlight, the onyx tribal tattoos across his forearms, which marked him as packmaster while in human form, looked like gnarled shadows cast from the tall mountain pines above them. The gold of his wolf eyes glowed beneath the brim of his Stetson, and coupled with the scar over his brow, he looked as terrifying and dangerous as he did handsome.

Until he grinned.

The slightest hint of a smirk curled his lips as if he were amused by her and the fact that she would dare challenge him, and suddenly, despite the cowboy's more alarming features, he was so ruggedly handsome and masculine, it was damn near unreasonable.

Sierra inhaled another sharp breath.

She was certain she hadn't seen the packmaster look amused since he'd been a boy, back when their constant banter had made him feel about as *un*brotherly to her as possible, despite everyone thinking he was like a sibling to her. When they'd been young, their families had always been close, often leaving them alone together. Back then, he'd been adventurous, playful even, just…different. These days, he wore a permanent scowl, but now a hint of a smirk quirked his lips all the same.

"Are you rejecting me?" His low, husky voice hummed through her again.

When he grinned like that, reminding her of everything he'd once been to her, she *wished* he were growling at her—horribly dirty, naughty things preferred.

"Yes." She placed her hands on her hips to fortify herself. "Yes, I *am* rejecting you." She sounded uncertain. Try as she might, she never had an iron will when it came to him.

That amused grin of his widened ever so slightly, and that single look coupled with the deep thrum of his voice still buzzing through her nearly did her in. He was the most powerful wolf to have ever lived, and her packmaster to boot. Any woman who didn't want him would have been a fool. *She* was being a fool.

And he damn well knew it.

But she refused to back down now.

"I won't marry you." She held her head high with every ounce of pride she felt. "You may be packmaster, Maverick Grey, but you forget that I knew you *before* you became king of these godforsaken mountains, and handsome or not, while other she-wolves may swoon at your feet, I wouldn't marry you if you were the last alpha on earth." She sounded unconvincing even to her own ears.

He quirked a brow like he didn't believe her. "Are you sure?"

The question caught her off guard. "Why wouldn't I be?"

That damn amused smirk widened. "You just called me handsome, warrior."

Warrior. When he said it like that, it didn't make her ready for battle. Instead, it made her nipples tighten and a rush of heat flood between her legs.

Damn him.

When had she—? Her brow furrowed, retracing her words. *Damn. Damn. Double damn.* She *had* just called him handsome. It had been an unintentional slip, but of course, he noticed. He noticed everything.

"*That* was the part you heard?" She let out an exasperated sigh.

He adjusted his Stetson, his eyes darting toward the horses. "Among other things."

Color filled her cheeks. "It was a statement of fact, not affect. Anyone with eyes can see it." She waved a hand in dismissal.

He sauntered closer with every bit of swagger he'd earned being *her* packmaster. "And you're certain of this?"

"Why is that so hard to believe?"

He drew nearer, close enough that in the dark like this, with her wolf senses on high alert, she could smell the woodsy scent of his aftershave. "Correct me if I'm wrong, but there was a time in which you would have welcomed my attention."

"That time has passed." He wasn't wrong, but she would never admit it. Not to him.

"Is that so?"

He was challenging her, and she didn't like it.

Not one damn bit.

"It is. And I'll prove it to you."

Before Sierra could think twice about what she was doing, she grabbed the packmaster by the lapel of his shirt and kissed him.

———————————

Maverick was certain Sierra Cavanaugh was the only woman who'd ever rejected him. And yet, she was kissing him.

Christ, yes.

He'd seen the spark of challenge and intrigue in her eyes, but fortunately, despite his better judgment, he'd been too late to stop her. In an instant, Sierra's lips were on his, soft and gentle, as she pulled him in toward her. Her lithe, muscled body pressed against his, the curve of her breasts brushing against the wide expanse of his chest. She braced one of her hands against his pectorals, and in response, his cock gave a heady throb.

Fuck.

Despite the force with which she'd grabbed him, her kiss was tentative, inexperienced, almost…innocent. A growl rumbled in his throat. He wanted to take her innocent kisses and make them as filthy as everything he'd always longed to do to her, and nothing could have stopped him from doing as much…

Short of an enemy's dagger.

He'd sensed the other wolf's presence only moments earlier. Breaking their kiss, Maverick shoved Sierra out of the way, blocking her with his body as the blade sank into his side. Pain seared through him, the initial instinct to stiffen in defense nearly overwhelming him. But he fought to control it, forcing himself to fall limp into the attacker as if the dagger had pierced an internal organ…

He'd taken so many blades in his life, he knew by now that it hadn't.

"For the Seven Range Pact," the other wolf growled into his ear. The shifter's scent was unfamiliar. Not a known enemy. But that didn't matter.

Whoever he was, when Maverick slumped against him, he felt the other wolf's tension ease. For a brief beat, Maverick stared up into his attacker's face, slowly watching his guard lower and his pride overtake his sense. How easy he must have thought it had been to bring down the almighty Maverick Grey, packmaster of the Grey Wolves, with no more than a single dagger.

His hubris would be his fatal mistake.

Maverick's eyes flashed to his wolf. "My turn," he snarled.

Seizing the momentary advantage, he ripped his dagger from his belt, plunging it behind him into the other wolf's thigh. With a howl of pain, the other wolf reared back, but Maverick twisted the blade, locking him in place and forcing the wound further open. He dragged the weapon downward with all his strength, flaying the length of his enemy's thigh within seconds. His attacker dropped into a howling, incapacitated heap.

Free of further threat, Maverick sank to his knees beside his wailing enemy. Hands trembling, he ripped the other wolf's weapon from his side, dropping it to the ground before he shifted into his wolf. He'd survived worse before, and his wolf form would aid that. Bones shifted and cracked as his fur sprang forth. Despite his wounds, a sense of calm overtook him as he felt his four paws connect with the dirt and ground beneath him. He was still injured, but he'd live.

Now in wolf form, he tried to ignore the sharp pitch of his enemy's keening human cries, but it pounded against his wolf senses, seeming to thud in time with his weakening pulse. The keening would stop soon. He would ensure that. He didn't allow his enemies to live. Not without a price.

Maverick surged forward, using his teeth to finish his opponent off. Somewhere, in the back of his mind, as the iron-filled taste of his enemy's blood coated his muzzle, he was faintly aware of the sound of Sierra shouting for the other warriors in the distance. Maverick watched as his enemy drew his final breath, but he couldn't bring himself to savor the triumph. As his own blood pooled in the mountain dirt beneath him, one singular thought shook him.

Someone wanted him dead.

And it was one of his own.

Chapter 4

"DID YOU *HAVE* TO KILL HIM?"

Maverick glared at Blaze in response to the inane question. His patience was growing thin with each additional stitch being threaded through his side. Austin, the Grey Wolf medic stitching him, had a steady, sure hand. The Grey Wolf was able to save a life as easily as he could end it on the battlefield, but that didn't mean having a needle shoved through an already bleeding knife wound didn't hurt like a son-of-a—

"What?" Blaze said in response to Maverick's glaring, interrupting his thoughts. Blaze spoke around a mouthful of the barbecue chips he'd been snacking on throughout the entire discussion. "I'm just saying it would've made our job a helluva lot easier."

Maverick shook his head. At the moment, he couldn't even begin to take Blaze seriously, despite knowing how truly lethal the wolf was. The elite warrior's black ops tech savvy and fighting skills were nearly as incomparable as his poor taste in clothing. Tonight, his plain white T-shirt boasted the bright-red words SUSPICIOUS PACKAGE in the U.S. Mail emblem followed by a large arrow that pointed toward his belt.

If only the pack had such a thing as a dress code.

Following the attack, a handful of the Grey Wolf elite warriors had gathered in Maverick's office as Austin had tried to halt Maverick's bleeding. With his blood loss slowed and Austin now stitching the wound closed, the conversation had quickly turned to strategy. Austin threaded another stitch through the wound, and Maverick let out a pained hiss. If he'd had any sense, he'd would have sent them all away and milked the injury for all it was worth.

Austin muttered something under his breath in Spanish. His

slow Texas drawl as he chose his next words served as a mild distraction from the sutures wiggling beneath Maverick's skin. "I think what Blaze is likely gettin' at is that the short list of our enemies who want to kill you ain't exactly…"

"Short?" Wes offered. The former Wild Eight packmaster turned Grey Wolf second-in-command leaned against Maverick's bookshelf. Though Wes was now as loyal as any to the Grey Wolves, that never stopped him from taking pleasure in provoking Maverick.

Frequently.

Maverick scowled. "I'm aware, considering you were once on it."

Wes grinned. "Who said I'm off it?"

Maverick's closest friend and Sierra's brother, Colt Cavanaugh, the Grey Wolf high commander, jerked a thumb toward Wes from where he lounged in Maverick's desk chair. "You know it's not too late to reverse the decision to make him second, don't you?"

Maverick grumbled a vague response. His choice to make Wes his second had caused the council to nearly have a collective heart attack, but unfortunately, he didn't regret the decision. Wes was the only wolf who'd ever proved a true challenge to Maverick in a fight. Fierce bastard that he was. Should Wes ever assume the role, he'd make a formidable packmaster, and as a previous leader himself, albeit a helluva misguided one, Maverick trusted that his former enemy understood the dark choices being packmaster would compel him to make, and more importantly, what the role would force him to sacrifice.

Heavy hangs the crown…

His father had once warned him of that, and now he lived the unfortunate truth of that statement with every borrowed breath he drew.

Never one to parse words, Colt cleared his throat. "The question remains… Aside from the human hunters, which of our enemies has a stake in the Seven Range Pact?"

"Our enemies wouldn't. But our allies would," Maverick

growled, finally giving voice to what his elite warriors refused to say.

One of their allies wanted him dead.

Silence fell over the group, highlighting the unspoken tension in the room. The council, the treaty, and the attempt on his life, which by proxy, was an attack on the pack. The mess was related. He supposed he had his sister, Maeve, and her beau, Rogue, to thank for the pack's current situation.

Years ago, the Grey Wolves had formed a treaty with the Billings division of the Execution Underground, an enemy human organization hell-bent on hunting supernaturals under the guise of protecting humanity. Their arrangement with the pesky humans had been simple: led by the Grey Wolves, the Seven Range Pact, an alliance among the seven Montana shifter clans, would protect the human population throughout Big Sky Country by keeping their and the Execution Underground's mutual enemy at bay: the vampires. In exchange, as long as the treaty continued, the Execution Underground would never hunt any of the Seven Range shifters.

It had never pleased Maverick to partner with the self-righteous human bastards, but it'd been an ill-fated necessity. At best, the agreement had kept them safe for a time. But it had been contingent on the packless rogue shifters of their varied species serving as fodder for Execution Underground Headquarters, the governing branch of the vast human organization, which would never approve of the local division's backroom deals with any shifter, let alone Maverick.

Only recently, the rogue wolves had ensured a deal to put them under the Grey Wolves' and the Seven Range Pact's protection. Thus, the local division of the Execution Underground would need an alternative scapegoat, and like it or not, thanks to the blustering delays of the old fools on the Elder Council, Maverick was long overdue to renegotiate the treaty, lest the human organization declare open season on hunting the Seven Range Pact.

The lives of his packmates depended on it.

"It's process of elimination at this point. We can't rule anyone out until we have more information," Colt said, coming to his aid.

Colt was ever loyal to him. Almost to a damn fault.

"It makes sense." Blaze tossed another barbecue chip into his mouth, talking as he chewed. Despite all the hours behind a computer, the other shifter was a massive wall of lean muscle with the constant appetite to prove it. "The deal with the rogues has made the treaty with the Execution Underground tenuous. If that deal ends, it affects not only us, but all our allies in the Seven Range Pact."

"Can we be certain it's not the bloodsuckers though? They coulda hired a wolf to do the job for 'em," Austin drawled.

Over the past year, they'd fielded several battles with their parasitic enemies. Their kind and the vamps had never seen eye to eye, having centuries of distrust sown between them, but any thin pretenses of civility had been lost years ago when the Seven Range Pact negotiated their treaty with the Execution Underground and vowed to keep the bloodsuckers in line.

Colt shook his head to Austin's question. "Not likely. The bloodsuckers still haven't recouped their legions yet. They're hiding with their tails between their legs. For now..." The grim expression on his face promised future resurgence on that front.

"It's sheer dumb luck that the ceremony's two nights from now, but it could prove useful." Blaze lifted a brow in question.

Maverick nodded in agreement. The pack's calendar year ended with the transition from fall to winter, and on the last full moon of their lunar year, the Grey Wolves came together as one in order to remember the history from which they came while looking toward their future. An integral part of that process was receiving guidance from their ancestors.

It had saved them before. More than once.

"The ceremony is our best chance at this point." Colt nodded. "But in the meantime, how would one of our allies attacking the leader of the Pact prove fruitful when Maverick's trying to get the council to approve enough warriors to renegotiate the deal?"

"It's simple." Wes shrugged a shoulder. Considering his dark past, Maverick's second was always keenly aware of their enemies' motivations. "Whoever's doing this wants the treaty to remain the same. To keep the treaty intact, one of our allies in the Seven Range Pact would do the one thing Maverick won't: betray the rogue wolves." He cast Maverick a pointed look. "And now they're after your position as Pact leader to do it."

"If there were no deal with them, there would be no need to renegotiate the treaty." Colt raised a brow at Maverick, as if to question the possibility.

Maverick shook his head. No. He wouldn't even consider it. He couldn't betray the rogue wolves. Not a chance. The effects for the Grey Wolves would be devastating. Jared would never sit by if the deal for the rogues wasn't honored. Not only would going back on his word spark a civil war the likes of which the pack had never known, but Maverick's own sister would be caught in the cross fire. He had far more integrity than that. He was a man of his word.

That was all he had left these days.

But keeping that word made him a target, a singular opportunity to seize power.

With him dead and the deal with the rogue wolves nullified, not only would the treaty with the Execution Underground remain intact for their allies, but that would pave the way for new leadership to rise among the Montana shifter clans. The Grey Wolves would no longer be the leaders of the Seven Range Pact. Another of the shifter clans would take over, which meant...

His pack would be at the mercy of another's leadership.

A familiar thrum of rage built inside Maverick as his gut instinct to protect his pack, his family flared. He would never allow that to happen. He would do whatever it took to protect them. All costs be damned.

"Ignore the council's protests and renegotiate the deal now, despite the extra danger it poses." Wes eased forward. "We can stop this before it gets out of hand."

Maverick grumbled. "Unfortunately, I'm held to a higher standard than you." The damage of that move would impact his relations with the council for years. They'd use the action to block him at every future turn. It'd render him a useless figurehead of a packmaster. Not to mention, he'd be risking the lives of the pack, should negotiations go south. Without the council's support, the pack wouldn't be unified. He wouldn't risk a war with the human hunters while their leadership was divided.

"But assumin' Mav kicked the bucket, wouldn't you be the default leader of the Seven Range Pact?" Austin shook several strands of dark curls back from his face as he paused to look at Wes. He was nearly finished with his work on Maverick's wound and had begun the final stitch.

"No." Blaze had finally abandoned the damn bag of barbecue chips and cleaned his hands with a nearby napkin before he whipped out his laptop. His fingers flew across the keyboard. "Wes would become packmaster, but according to the Seven Range Pact bylaws, Pact leadership wouldn't go to him. It follows a sort of primogeniture. It has to default to another Grey family member, regardless of who's in line for packmaster." He turned the screen toward them and pointed to a specific subsection of the document.

Maverick clenched his fists. He guessed he had his own father to thank for that rule.

"So if Maverick kicks the bucket, it defaults to Maeve?" Wes asked.

Maverick's sister, Maeve, may have run off with one of their former enemies, but wayward as she was now, she'd still do what was right for the pack. It was what had caused her to run off with the criminal bastard in the first place.

Blaze winced. "Actually...not that simple."

Maverick growled. He didn't like the sound of this. Not for one second. "What do you mean, *not that simple*?"

Colt shot Blaze a shut-up-now look.

Blaze flashed Colt an unapologetic grin like he was a small child with a secret he couldn't wait to tell rather than one lethal mother-fucker. "He's going to find out eventually."

Maverick raised a brow.

Colt released a short sigh. "Belle spoke with Maeve over the phone the other day. She and Jared were somewhere in India and apparently...they decided to elope."

Maverick snarled. "In India?" He wasn't sure why the location mattered, but somehow it seemed to.

"Good move on Jared's part." Blaze raised both brows and nodded as if he were impressed. "I hear the weddings there are top-notch." He made an okay sign with his thumb and forefinger.

Maverick's sister had always had a soft spot for wounded animals. In this case, a *feral* wounded animal. To say he wasn't his new brother-in-law's biggest fan was an understatement.

Maverick gripped the sides of his temples, rubbing in slow circles. "It wasn't enough to be mated to the bastard, she had to go and marry him?"

Blaze shrugged. "Apparently, yes."

Maverick swore.

"Personally, I like him." Wes grinned.

Colt shook his head. "You would, Brother."

Maverick inhaled a deep breath through his nose, fighting to remain levelheaded despite the surmounting mess. Someone wanted him dead, and considering Maeve was the only other living member of the Grey family and no longer shared the family name, in the event of his death, the Grey Wolves would no longer be the leaders of the Seven Range Pact.

Which meant...

He *did* need a wife. Far more than he'd initially anticipated.

At that moment, the door to his office flew open, and Sierra charged in as if she owned the place. How the damn thing hadn't fallen off its hinges by now from the countless times she'd kicked it in, he'd never know. There was a cut on her temple from where he'd shoved her away from the attacker's blade, and she'd hit a hard bit of tree stump. When he spotted her wound, Maverick stiffened. Minor or not, he didn't care for the sight of her injured, and the fact that he'd been the cause ate away at his insides. Austin had reported that she'd momentarily lost consciousness, though she had been fine afterward. The Grey Wolf medic had suggested she rest, but from the glare of anger in her eyes, she hadn't taken that advice to heart.

If Maverick had thought she'd been angry before, it was nothing compared to this.

"First you demand I marry you, and now *this*?"

Maverick wasn't exactly certain what *this* meant, considering he had taken a blade to protect her. Was it too much to hope she might thank him? If not for him, she'd have been little more than fodder.

"Wait. What?" Colt's eyes went wide, and he glanced between them. "Maverick asked you to *marry* him?" The high commander looked as if his sister had announced the most ludicrous thing he'd ever heard, which all things considered, probably wasn't far from the truth.

Sierra shot him a disapproving glare. "Don't act like it's so surprising. He did, and all while my stupid horse was busy trying to run off and dry-hump his no less."

Austin quirked a brow from where he was now collecting the remains of his medical equipment. "Is that some kinda euphemism for somethin'?"

Blaze shook his head. "Nah. If it was, I would know."

Maverick had little doubt on that point.

Wes, who was watching Colt's emerging reaction to the situation with more than a hint of amusement, clicked his tongue. "Wait till I tell Naomi there's now an unrulier horse on this ranch than Black Jack."

Sierra waved a hand. "Don't be ridiculous. Randy is a saint compared to Black Jack. Just not an abstinent one."

Maverick couldn't disagree on that point. Wes's monstrous black mustang had bit him on more than one occasion. Wes was lucky he had extra patience, at least when it came to the ranch's horses. Maverick still hadn't decided if his second's amusement following the last incident had been a sign that Black Jack's bite had been provoked by his master, rather than incidental.

Disregarding the turn of conversation, Colt cast an uncharacteristic glare at Maverick. "Did you at least get down on one knee?" The words were half question, half growl.

Maverick shot his friend an impatient look. The high commander hadn't taken such a harsh tone with him in years.

Colt's frown only deepened. "Don't give me that look. You're the one who proposed to my *sister*. Packmaster or not, you could have bothered to ask me for her hand first."

"I'm not property to be given away." From the gleam in Sierra's eye, that distinction was vitally important.

As Sierra and Colt devolved into a sidebar of bickering while Sierra recounted his proposal, Blaze was busy enticing Wes and Austin into looking at satellite images he'd found on his laptop that would no doubt forever serve as Maeve's only wedding photos. Maverick leaned back against his desk amid the chaos, the pain of his newly stitched wound throbbing. By now, he was accustomed to the level of insanity that usually ensued when his packmates—who, for all intents and purposes, were his family—were left to their own devices. Everyone knew that was what family was for after all, making a person miserable.

Though he rarely enjoyed the insanity, most of the time, Maverick expected it. So many hotheaded wolves living in proximity, even on a ranch as large as the Grey Wolves', were bound to give way to lunacy. But as their packmaster, it was his job to draw the line—and that line was crossed the moment a rooster crowed in the hall outside his office.

"What the hell was that?" he snarled.

Immediately, the room fell silent.

Sierra groaned in frustration. "Elvis."

As if on cue, the Polish rooster in question flapped his way into the office, ridiculous mess of crested feathers atop his head, bobbing with each step.

Sierra tsked at the animal. "Why have you been following me everywhere?" She shook her head before turning back toward the crowded office. "Since I nursed him back to health from an infected wing, Elvis is practically family now."

As if that were a perfectly reasonable explanation…

She was a madwoman. He was sure.

And yet, she was going to be his wife, even if it killed him. He'd make certain of it.

Chapter 5

"ALL OF YOU OUT."

The packmaster snarled the words with such forceful command that Sierra nearly turned tail herself, but from the incline of his head toward the rooster now flapping about her feet, she realized she wasn't fortunate enough to be included in his order.

Maverick leaned against his one-of-a-kind executive desk, the dim lighting of the sizable office casting shadows across his face. The polished dark maple of the unique piece he perched upon, coupled with the sheen of the coffered wooden ceilings overhead, looked too polished to belong to the hardened, rough cowboy who owned them.

Because if looks could kill...

"Out." He growled again. "And take the damn rooster with you."

Sierra snorted, covering her mouth with her hand as she fought to hold in a laugh.

The elite warriors exchanged glances before finally Blaze muttered a few displeased curses under his breath and corralled Elvis out of the office. Soon, nearly all the crew had made their exit. Only her brother lingered.

"Your orders about the attack?"

At the reminder, any humor Sierra had felt was gone.

The thought of what happened in the woods sent a shiver down her spine. Someone was trying to kill their packmaster. Had Maverick not shielded her, the attacker would have killed her, too. It was a blatant attack on the pack, and if she had any say in the matter, she'd find out who'd orchestrated it. Then, she'd prove exactly how much she deserved the position he and his damn council had denied her.

Maverick's response to Colt was as decisive as it was cryptic. "Intel only. No one moves until we know what we're facing."

Colt nodded before he made his exit, though not before his gaze darted between her and his friend with more than a hint of skepticism. Finally, as the door closed behind her brother, the goose bumps on Sierra's skin intensified. This time, she couldn't blame the cold autumn wind of the Montana mountainside. Deep down, she was aware of the source of her nerves.

She was alone with Maverick again, and not only had he proposed to her, but then she'd stupidly gone and kissed him. Why in the world had she kissed him?

Whatever point she'd intended to make at that moment, it was lost to her now. Not that it mattered. She'd come here with a purpose, and if she didn't state it before he turned those piercing eyes on her, she might make a fool of herself again.

The packmaster crossed his large arms over his chest, waiting for her to say her piece. He was shirtless from where Austin had stitched the knife wound in his side closed, and she was highly aware of it. Several stitches ran along the side of his muscled abdomen, interrupting the curving black tattoos that marked him as packmaster. The ancient markings covered the wide span of his back and wrapped around the chiseled muscles of his obliques.

She still remembered what he'd looked like before the tattoos were there. Before he had made the idea of *them* an impossibility.

But she didn't dislike how they looked on him. That much was certain.

She cleared her throat. "You owe me an apology."

He looked at her as if she'd lost her mind. "I saved your life, warrior."

Warrior.

There was that title again. On his lips, it did things to her, things it shouldn't have.

And now to make matters worse, he'd saved her.

That unfortunate fact hadn't escaped her. He'd been valiant, brave, fierce. She'd only blacked out momentarily, courtesy of that godforsaken tree stump, which meant she'd seen most of what he'd done for her. He hadn't even hesitated. His life, the state of the pack, his title: he'd risked all of it. As she'd watched him eviscerate their enemy with such lethal precision, it had stolen her breath away to know that he'd risked everything for *her*.

And it wasn't the first time he'd done as much.

To pretend she hadn't been moved by his noble actions would have been disingenuous. Watching him risk his life to defend her had awakened something primal inside her, and of course, she was grateful she hadn't had to suffer the wound herself, but he failed to see the obvious. She hadn't needed him to be noble.

She could have defended herself.

"Of course you saved me, and I'm obviously grateful, but when word of that gets out to the pack, especially with the last moon of the lunar year being only a few nights from now and every damn packmember we have coming home to the ranch, you'll have also made me look weak…and after the council already denied me."

"I think you and I have different definitions of the word 'obviously,' warrior." He couldn't have appeared less interested in her or her silly problems. "And as for the ceremony, I'm aware of it."

As packmaster, it was a tradition in which Maverick led them, so of course he was *aware of it*. She frowned. What he didn't understand was that meant she'd have to face the whole pack, all from their own large, extended families—and being a female who didn't walk the expected path… Lord, the endless questions. She could already feel the frustration and hurt building in her.

Still chasing that long-shot warrior position? And now the council denied you? And you're still not mated? What a shame.

If she had to hear even one comment about why she still hadn't found a mate, particularly *this* year, she might forcibly vomit on the unsuspecting culprit's boots and use that as an excuse to skip out on the whole event. And now, on top of the usual, she'd have to deal with questions about the packmaster saving her.

"That doesn't change what you did," she said.

"Would you have rather I let you take an enemy's blade?"

"Yes," she snapped.

How could he be so obtuse?

Maverick grumbled something unintelligible about chaos under his breath as he rounded his desk. "I'll try to remember that the next time I plan to throw myself on a knife for you."

"Please do. I don't need you to save me." She tried to inhale a sharp breath, but it ended up sounding more like a sniffle. "Not anymore."

This hadn't been the first time, and that only irked her more. Back then, she'd been barely a woman and she *had* been weak, so weak that she'd frozen, and it had cost her everything. In that moment, she'd sworn to herself things would change, that *she* would change, and she had, because she would never be weak again.

"Besides, it won't help the matter when word gets out about your proposal. If you can call *demanding* that I marry you a proposal…"

It could only reflect poorly on her. The world was all too eager to find any reason it could to bring strong women like her down. How often had she been told to remain on the sidelines, as if that were her rightful place? Had she and all the other women in her life not proven themselves to be equal, to matter, despite the fact that they should never have been asked to prove themselves to begin with?

They deserved better than the role the world tried to force them into.

Maverick pegged her with a hard stare, his words cutting through her. "What are you afraid of, warrior?"

She shook her head, being more than a bit petulant. "I don't know what you mean."

Most days, he would have left it at that, but he didn't. "This isn't about me asking to marry you, so what is it about?"

She couldn't tell whether it was the graveled quality of his voice shaking her or whether he'd laced the words with a coaxing growl.

Of course, it wasn't about his proposal.

It was about all the ways she'd failed the women who'd placed their hopes in her, all the ways she'd proved every one of her critics right. She knew the council's decision was unfair, but that didn't stop her from questioning if she could have done something, anything, to make herself good enough. She'd have to own up to those failings, no matter how unfair they were, sooner rather than later.

She crossed her arms over her chest, shielding herself as she fixed her eyes on his bookshelf. She couldn't look at him when he was watching her like that. Like he saw *everything*. "I should have gotten the position."

He didn't say anything at first. He simply watched her. With one look, he seemed to be able to recognize all the words she left unspoken. It'd always been that way, hadn't it? At times, he seemed to know her better than the back of his own hand.

Rounding his desk again, he eased closer. So close that she couldn't force herself to stare at the bookshelf anymore.

"Then marry me." To her surprise, Maverick reached out and captured the end of her braid between his fingers. He toyed with the golden strands with the pad of his thumb, gentle and reverent, so unlike the grumbly beast of a man she now knew him to be that she felt the caress all the way to her toes. "All behavior is excusable for a fool in love."

Sierra's breath caught, because for a moment, the gruff, impenetrable mask he wore faltered, and once again, he was Maverick. Just Maverick. Not the man, myth, and legend who had stood before her for the past ten years but the friend who'd once meant the world to her. Loyal. Noble. Brave. All the things he kept hidden from her now behind walls and scars so impenetrable she could scarcely see the real man beneath.

But despite the longing in his eyes, she couldn't bring herself to believe him.

It couldn't be her he spoke of.

It was Rose. He'd loved Rose. His wife.

So why did she get the feeling he was speaking in the present?

"I'm no fool." She pulled her braid from between his fingers. She couldn't look at him now. If she did, he would see straight through her. "And I can't marry you."

Mate separation among their kind was unheard of, which meant even if she had the mind to entertain the idea, once she committed, there was no turning back.

In an instant, the vulnerability she'd glimpsed was lost, and the stone-faced packmaster returned. The cold look in his eyes hurt more than it should have.

"It's a simple negotiation. We'd both get everything we want."

A simple negotiation? She almost let out a pained laugh. There was nothing simple about it. Yet he said it as if he knew the inner workings of her heart.

A cowboy like him *would* likely assume he knew all a woman desired. But he couldn't know her desires, because he'd never so much as bothered to ask.

Filled with renewed frustration, she rounded on him again. "Did it ever occur to you that I might want a mate who loves me, maybe even a family someday, in *addition* to the position of elite warrior?" She wanted to have her cake and eat it, too, damn it. How could he not see that?

"You may want those things, but not *more* than being an elite warrior," he challenged.

Her hands clenched into fists. He was right, of course, and she hated that he saw through her. There was nothing she wanted more. Yes, she wanted a mate who loved her, a family and children to call her own in the future, but those things alone wouldn't fulfill her. Her drive to protect and serve the pack was the singular goal she'd based her identity around. She was a warrior first and foremost. She defined herself by it, and everything else came second.

"And if it's children you want, that part I can give you," he said, interrupting her thoughts. He raked his gaze over her so thoroughly that heat prickled beneath her skin. "It wouldn't be a problem."

Sierra blinked. "Are you suggesting that we...?" She couldn't even bring herself to say it.

"For a packmaster, the point of mating is to produce an heir, so yes, I am suggesting *that*," he said, saving her from the mortification of exactly what *that* entailed. "Eventually."

Heat flushed through her cheeks.

"For now, all you need to do is say 'I do.' Then we spend a single night together to convince the council we're fully mated. We both know they'll expect to scent that we've slept together. Then, after the mating ceremony, we can live our separate lives while you get everything you wish. The position of elite warrior that you rightfully earned, and the power, privilege, and prestige that come with it. Not to mention all the benefits of being the packmaster's wife."

She was aware of the benefits. When Rose had been alive, no one dared look twice at her. Not without risking the censure of the packmaster himself. He was offering her an unprecedented level of power, more than her role as elite warrior would ever afford her.

But power wasn't what she was after.

"I understand, but I'm not willing to lose my sense of dignity. I won't sleep my way to the top—and certainly not with you." She wrinkled her nose as if the thought of sleeping with him displeased her. She *wished* that were the truth. "Why play into the council's hands? Why not disband them and call it a day? You've defied them before." He'd gone against tradition at more than one turn. It was what the council hated most about him. So why bow to their will now?

"I can't do that."

"Can't or won't?"

"Both," he grumbled.

He was nothing if not honest.

Yet why did she get the feeling there was something he wasn't saying?

"The council proved an invaluable resource to every packmaster before me. They serve a greater purpose for the Grey Wolves, and the strength of a wolf is his pack."

It was the practiced answer, the measured one that befit a man in his role. Not all of what *he* really thought, or at least that was what she suspected. Most of the time, she couldn't see where he and his role began and ended anymore.

She nearly scoffed. Even when it benefited him, she knew Maverick wouldn't do anything that would hurt the Grey Wolves, or even anything that could be construed as such. He was too loyal for it. Despite all the judgment from his critics about his lack of respect for tradition, he always did what was best for the pack.

It was something she'd always admired about him.

Even when it frustrated her.

"You deserve the position. The pack wouldn't question it," he said.

"Don't patronize me." He may not have ever stood in her way, but he hadn't exactly helped her as she once would have hoped either. She didn't expect a handout or a favor, just for someone to unlock the door to let her in, to take their foot off her neck.

"Marrying me is a formality, a way to get around the council for both of us. If it's your pride you're concerned with, I'll petition them to reverse their decision before we announce the proposal. They'll be thrilled I'm taking a mate. They won't hesitate."

"There's only one problem with that plan, Packmaster." She shook her head. "You don't love me." She forced a laugh. "Hell, we don't even like each other."

His gaze darkened. "You don't have to like someone to want to sleep with them, Sierra."

Her name on his tongue sent an instant wave of heat to her core. "If you're referring to when I kissed you, I was only trying to make a point, to show you there's nothing between us."

It was a blatant lie. When she'd kissed him, there hadn't been a single part of her that hadn't been affected. She still felt the ache it'd sparked low in her belly. The longing.

The sides of his lips quirked into that damn amused grin again. "And did you succeed?" he taunted.

"Yes. You may be boss of this godforsaken ranch and packmaster of the most powerful wolf pack to ever exist, Maverick Grey, but not every she-wolf swoons in your presence."

"Not every she-wolf throws herself into my arms, warrior."

This time, the use of the title only made her bristle.

"You'd asked me to marry you, and you're the packmaster. I couldn't have told you no if I hadn't fully considered my options. It was curiosity. Nothing more." It was a feeble excuse, but it was the best she had to offer.

His eyes flashed to his wolf. "And was your curiosity satisfied?"

She raked her gaze over him.

No. It hadn't been. Not in the slightest.

"My answer is still no."

"Then we're at an impasse." He stepped behind his desk, lowering himself into his executive chair. Behind it, he was the image of authority. She'd never much had a taste for authority figures, for being bossed around or told what to do and yet…

"Go home, warrior. Rest assured I won't allow your reputation to be damaged. Our conversation doesn't leave this room." The smoldering fire that flashed in his wolf eyes caused a rush of heat between her legs. "But my offer still stands."

Before she lost all her will to refuse, she turned to leave. But as she did, she gripped the door handle and turned back toward him. "What about the attempt on your life?"

He watched her for a long beat before he finally answered. "My role forces me to do many things that don't bear repeating." He cast her a dark grin. "But if I do my job right, the pack will be none the wiser."

Sierra had little doubt about that.

Without another word, she left his office. When she stepped outside the main building, the cold air hitting her face, her careful steps developed into a run. The last vestiges of night were fading over the horizon, and the pale yellows of the early Montana sunrise stretched across the vast open sky. Before she could stop herself, she shifted into her wolf, the cold autumn air whipping through her with such force she felt the cold beneath her fur, deep within her bones.

She didn't stop running or shift back to human form until she finally reached the safety of her house on the far end of the compound. Her mind had been too busy pondering what dark deeds the packmaster's role had forced him to make, things she couldn't even begin to fathom. Yet as she did, despite being alone and with most of the packmembers long since settled into sleep, she couldn't shake the feeling that she was being watched.

Logically, Maverick had a long list of enemies who would be happy to claim his life.

Yet she'd been denied by the council, Maverick Grey had asked her to marry him, and now someone wanted him killed. All in the same night. They were three separate events she'd never expected to happen, and now, despite her logical judgment, she couldn't shake the instinct that those three events were inexplicably linked.

Chapter 6

"WHAT DO YOU MEAN YOU TOLD HIM *NO*?"

To say that wasn't the reaction Sierra expected from Dakota would be an understatement. They'd been out on the training field since midmorning, and despite the gray overcast of the wide-open skies, the damp, frostbitten mountainside had finally given way to a hint of warmth as afternoon approached.

"Not so loud." Sierra nodded for Dakota to follow her as they made their rounds across the thawing grass.

From the edge of the field, Randy let out a frustrated whinny, stomping a hoof on the frozen grass as he nibbled at a few brown bits. He paused only to huff at Elvis who, despite the cold, had followed them from the chicken coop and was pecking about Randy's legs.

Fortunately, they hadn't yet gotten snow this season—an unusual turn of events—which meant the few straggling calves that had recently hit the ground would likely make it through. The treacherous Montana autumn often gave way to plummeting icy temperatures. Welcome weather for a wolf, but not so much for the cattle they raised.

Dakota was shaking her head, her lips pursed as she monitored one of the new trainees. Whether the distaste twisting her features was due to Sierra's recounting of the previous evening or the bad form of the trainee they were monitoring, Sierra wasn't certain.

Sierra glanced toward the trainee and fought back a cringe. "Shoulders back, Amaya. You can't slouch while swinging a sword."

Ever since her application had been put forth to the council several months prior, they'd had an influx of female trainees. Sierra's candidacy had inspired a spark of hope in them. But once word of the council's rejection got out, she feared their ambition would be doused. The thought of any young woman on the ranch hearing that she'd been denied for not having a mate twisted her stomach into knots. Thank goodness most of the established female warriors had been too disappointed for it to become a point of discussion yet. The last thing she needed as she grieved that loss was to feel their disappointment in the situation...in her.

Finally, when she and Dakota were a safe distance away from the trainees again, Sierra turned toward the other female. "Go on."

"I really can't believe you. He offered to give you *everything* you've been working for, and you said no?" Her dark brows drew low as she muttered a curse in Vietnamese, her family's native language. "I mean really, Sierra?"

Elvis chose that moment to stop pestering Randy, only to start pecking at Sierra's feet, the ridiculous mop of feathers on his head flopping.

"Okay, okay." She reached into the inside pocket of her Carhartt jacket and removed the pouch of chicken feed she kept there. She'd started carrying it since lately it seemed there was no way to get the bird to stop following her.

Dakota shook her head. "You're encouraging him."

Sierra shrugged. "Maybe. But the King waits for no one." She tossed another handful to Elvis before she placed the satchel into her pocket. "You're wrong about Maverick though. He offered me a trade for the position, not what I've been working for. I want to be recognized for my contributions, to pave the way for the rest of you."

"Exactly." Dakota crossed her arms with an exasperated huff. "He held out the opportunity for you to pave the way on a damn plate, and you turned it down. And for what? The sake of your pride?"

As if Sierra's pride wasn't an entirely important and valid reason. Of course, she wanted to feel pride in her accomplishment. She'd worked hard for this, and she didn't want that accomplishment undermined.

"I didn't think this would be your reaction." Sierra had expected her friend to feel like she had. At first confused, and then filled with outrage at the injustice of it all. She shouldn't have to marry anyone to get what she wanted, especially not when she'd deserved the position.

"Sierra, I understand," Dakota said, practically reading her thoughts. "But for once, he's right. Everyone knows you deserve the position, and anyone who thinks otherwise isn't worth your time. We both know that those who don't want to see change in the pack will find any reason not to support you."

Sierra nodded. "Don't I know it." She'd found plenty of anonymous disapproving messages in her pack mailbox before. Hell, she'd even discovered one last night once she'd returned home, and that'd only been the most recent. It'd been written in anger and read like a thinly veiled death threat. It'd likely been from only one or two begrudged beta males who'd felt threatened by the existence of an alpha she-wolf who could best them.

As much as she loved the Grey Wolf pack, every family had a few bad apples.

Dakota paced several steps to the left, craning her neck to see one of the trainees in the back row. "If not this, it would be something else. If you were a man, you wouldn't think twice about claiming the title you rightfully deserve by any means necessary. You say you want recognition, and you *did* achieve recognition. One of the elite warriors put your name forth. That's never happened before in the history of this pack."

Dakota had a point. In that way, she had achieved her goal, at least in part. Pack policy dictated that an elite warrior could only be appointed via anonymous nomination by an already established member. Then, the nomination moved forth to the council for a vote.

She'd warned her brother that they could both be accused of nepotism, so he was out of the question. She and Dakota had a sneaking suspicion that Wes or Austin had nominated her, or maybe even Blaze, since he and Dakota had always been close friends, and Sierra and Blaze once served together outside the pack. In any case, she'd never be certain who had submitted the nomination unless she assumed the role. But while Maverick may have presented the nomination to the council as his role dictated, he was no obvious fan of hers.

Unsatisfied that the trainee was not about to slice one of her own fingers off, Dakota glanced over her shoulder again. "But let's be real. Without you getting the position, the recognition makes little difference. Maverick offered you a path that will pave the way for the rest of us. It's only been so hard for you because you're the first, but once you're through, it sets a precedent. Who cares what means you use to get it if the council refuses to play fair? You'll be so good you'll blow them away, and then years from now, there won't just be a first, but a second, a third, hell, a hundredth."

When Dakota said it like that, Sierra felt a tinge of guilt. She was aware that for some, she was a role model, but in this instance, that responsibility was a double-edged sword.

The kind Amaya was still slouching over top of.

Sierra cupped her hands in the shape of a megaphone over her mouth to amplify her voice against the autumn wind. "Shoulders back, Amaya, or you'll have to fight *me* with that sword."

The young trainee blanched and immediately corrected her posture.

Sierra lowered her hands and glanced back toward Dakota. "But he offered me the position only if I'd marry him and…fulfill my wifely duties for a night."

"It's the council whose requiring you to take a mate, not Maverick, and now he's offering to help you get it in spite of them, even if it's not the most favorable of terms." Dakota's lips curled into a devious grin. "And please, like those wifely duties aren't one of the many reasons you *should* have agreed."

Sierra's cheeks turned a fiery red. "Dakota," she hissed.

Dakota rolled her eyes. "Don't 'Dakota' me. I know the intimate details of your little predicament, and I also know that despite how you're always growling at him, you want to climb that tree like a friggin' monkey. Don't even try to deny it."

Sierra groaned. Dakota wasn't wrong. She *did* want Maverick—or the old him at least. She had since she'd been a teenage girl, despite how she disliked the power of the position he now held, and Dakota was also intimately familiar with the details of Sierra's *predicament* as she called it, a.k.a. Sierra's sex experience… or more accurately, her lack thereof.

She wasn't totally naive. As a teenager, she'd once snuck away from Wolf Pack Run and tried to sleep with a human male who lived on a nearby ranch. That experience had ended in tears before it'd even really begun when she'd made the mistake of thinking that humans enjoyed biting each other on the scruff during the act like wolves did. She'd been young and had only seen other wolves mating while in their true form, so she'd had no frame of reference. Needless to say, that hadn't ended well.

Fast-forward to the years since, and she'd never been afforded the opportunity of sexual exploration, considering she'd declared her intent to become one of the pack's elite warriors shortly thereafter. She couldn't have slept with anyone in the pack without gaining an unfair reputation. Then after Maverick had chosen Rose as his mate, she'd briefly left Wolf Pack Run to train in a shifters-only branch of the human military. Considering her rank and the position of power she'd held there, she hadn't wanted to open herself to the harassment that often came with being the only female in the barracks by sleeping around. Then, upon her return to the pack, doing so would likely have injured her candidacy as a warrior.

Not that there were any males on this godforsaken ranch who weren't already like her brothers. Save for one.

Dakota's face softened at the hint of embarrassment on Sierra's face. She knew Sierra's remaining virginity was a sore point. Sierra had been dying to be rid of it for years. "I'm your best friend, Sierra. You can't lie to me. If it were anyone else, any other man, it would be different, but I know you want Maverick, at least physically, and my speculation is that Maverick's sexual prowess is likely insanely skilled, if the fact that he's your *brother's* closest friend is any indication."

Sierra groaned. She'd thought she had escaped the shadow of her brother's ladies' man reputation when he'd finally married Belle. He'd once been known as Commander Casanova among the females of the pack.

Dakota continued, "So not only do you get to finally lose your virginity to a man you've wanted your whole life, but as an added cherry on top, you get the position you've been working toward for years, along with a place in pack history—all while telling the council to take their asinine sexist rejection and shove it. Then after the deed is done, all you have to do is say you're married to him." Dakota rolled her eyes again. "Cry me a river, Sierra."

When she put it like that, telling Maverick no *did* seem ridiculous.

"It seems like a non-choice to me." Dakota shrugged. "Plus, did you ever stop to consider that maybe he's trying to help you?"

Sierra shook her head. "That's not the case. He offered to marry me out of necessity for the game he's playing with the council."

"Maybe, or maybe that's just his excuse. He *does* want you. According to you, he practically said as much."

Sierra scoffed. "Saying you don't have to like someone to want to sleep with them doesn't count as a romantic confession. Plus, there's one problem with the lovely little fantasy you've painted."

Dakota quirked a brow. "And what's that?"

"He doesn't love me." Of that, Sierra was certain.

And Dakota knew that as well. She'd been there the day he'd become packmaster, the day he'd chosen Rose. It'd been Dakota who'd held Sierra together, who'd helped pick her up when she'd fallen to pieces.

"Simple details." Dakota waved a hand in dismissal. "The past is the past, and if it's love that you want, then there's only one thing you can do."

Sierra quirked a brow.

A grin spread across Dakota's face. "*Make* him fall in love with you."

Sierra let out a harsh bark of a laugh. "And how exactly am I supposed to do that, all things considered?" Her sexual prowess was the one area of her life where she *wasn't* the most qualified and experienced woman in the room. Not to mention that as a young girl, she'd sought out Maverick's attention for years, only to be thoroughly disappointed that not only did he not want her, but he'd never so much as noticed her. At least not in that way.

"That's easy. You'll use your feminine wiles, that's how. You're the most badass female warrior this pack has to offer, and even with all your poorly timed, corny jokes, any man would be lucky to have you, Sierra."

Sierra smiled. "We both know you secretly love my jokes," she teased. "They're *punny*. Punny, get it?" If only she was equally as confident in her feminine wiles as she was in her poor comedic timing. "And my crazy growing menagerie of animals."

Elvis chose that moment to let out a loud, earsplitting crow, causing them both to wince.

Dakota shook her head yet smiled. "I've told you a thousand times, we could all make do without you being so *punny*, and I'm sure Maverick could, too." A far-too-pleased nicker came from Randy's direction, and Dakota leaned to the side, her eyes trained over Sierra's shoulder. "Speak of the devil."

Sierra followed Dakota's line of sight to the other side of the training field and the source of Randy's excitement. In the distance, Maverick dismounted from a less-than-docile-looking mare before he strode toward them. They'd been anticipating the arrival of her brother, not the packmaster himself. As the leader of the pack's warriors, the high commander often came to monitor the various training sessions, scouting out those who held the potential to advance up the ranks, but Colt must have been otherwise preoccupied and asked Maverick to serve in his place.

An evil band of fluttering butterflies invaded Sierra's stomach. How could she act normal after the events of last night? After she'd kissed him? After her horse had almost mounted his? And from the look in Randy's eye, he was planning a repeat. She groaned.

"No better time to start than now." Dakota shoved her between the shoulders, pushing her into Maverick's footpath as the other she-wolf grinned with uncharacteristic friendliness. "Packmaster, how nice of you to join us. Sierra was just speaking fondly of you."

Sierra scowled. Oh, her friend was going to pay for this one day. In spades.

Thankfully, always the conversationalist, Maverick only grunted in acknowledgment of Dakota's greeting. Small talk had never been one of his strong suits.

Sierra eyed him wearily. "Where's Colt?"

"With Belle." Maverick grumbled under his breath as the sole means of explanation.

Dakota let out a small *eep* of excitement. "Is she in labor?"

Maverick shook his head.

Sierra sighed. Which meant her brother was at the bedside of his mate needlessly worrying once again. Despite Belle, a talented orthopedic surgeon and physician, telling Colt herself that the false, practice contractions she'd been having were no cause for alarm, Sierra's brother was too hell-bent on supporting her through every moment of her pregnancy to listen.

"Perfect, then we have you at our disposal for the foreseeable future." Dakota rubbed her hands together as her impish grin widened. "Sierra and I were just talking to the trainees about demonstrating proper posture while wielding a sword, even when they're training in the early no-blood stage. Considering you and Sierra are the best swordsman on the ranch, instead of Sierra and me, I think it'd be more valuable to the new recruits if the two of you demonstrated—*together*."

Sierra shot Dakota a chastising glare. They'd been talking about no such thing, and Sierra had been friends with Dakota long enough to know exactly what sort of cockamamie plan the other she-wolf was concocting. In no-blood, the winner wasn't declared until one of the opponents landed flat on the ground or tapped out, and Dakota knew full well that both Sierra and Maverick would never tap out, especially against each other. They were both too stubborn, which meant the only way to win the fight would be for either one of them to get their opponent on the ground, and with two masters at sword work, that wouldn't happen unless one of them swept the other opponent's leg.

That move required a level of proximity that was damn near close to an embrace.

Fortunately, Sierra had something in her arsenal Dakota didn't—the truth—that would instantly douse the plans of one well-meaning but meddlesome friend.

"That's a great idea, Dakota, but unfortunately, the packmaster is still healing from—"

A quiet yet rumbling growl sounded low in Maverick's throat as he shot her a look, instantly silencing her.

Intrinsically, she knew what that growl meant. Save for the elite warriors and herself, the packmaster didn't intend to make the attempt on his life known to the whole pack, which meant not only would she be spared the embarrassment of having been saved by him, but no one would know how he'd risked his life for her or the peril he was currently facing on behalf of them all. She doubted this was the first time the pack wouldn't know the weight of the torch he'd been forced to bear. Saving her had been noble, but somehow, subsequently not claiming credit transformed the situation entirely.

He wasn't only noble. He was selfless. Grumbly exterior or not.

Sierra swallowed the lump that instantly formed in her throat from her gratitude.

Perhaps Dakota had been right. Maybe he *did* understand the weight of her disappointment. Maybe his offer to marry her had been out of a willingness to take on the pain of the pack, her pain, and bear it as his own. Even if it was misguided.

"Thank you," she mouthed silently.

At her gratitude, she expected to see his gaze soften, but it didn't. Instead, his features hardened, but for a moment, she could have sworn she saw a hint of pain flash through the packmaster's eyes. Silently, he nodded. *Think nothing of it*, his gaze seemed to say as he stepped away from her.

Their kind healed quickly, but she didn't want him to risk tearing open a fresh wound. He may have thwarted his attacker with minimal damage this time, but whoever had ordered the hit had been bold enough not only to attack the pack, but to make an attempt on the life of the Grey Wolf packmaster himself. They wouldn't be pleased with the result of their initial effort. If they were out for his life, she had no doubt they'd come for him again. It was only a matter of when…

"You're sure you're at your best?" she whispered.

Catching the subtext of her question, he cast her a dark look. Clearly, he didn't like her attempt to coddle him. "Our enemies don't wait for my best."

Dakota, who was already busy rounding up the trainees, didn't appear to have noticed the exchange between them. The trainees crowded around them in a large circle, forming a makeshift sparring ring.

Maverick went to the nearby weapon rack at the edge of the training field, the trainees quickly parting out of his way as he claimed a sword. "Are you still *curious*, warrior?" That seemingly innocent question, which to all other ears sounded like a friendly battle challenge, held an entirely different meaning to her ears. Maverick swung the weighted weapon in a large circling arc with ease, as if it weighed little more than a toothpick, before he cast her a grin.

That grin.

The one that sent a hot wave of moisture between her legs, and from the sheer look of amusement in his eyes, he damn well knew it. That dark, smoldering look said it all. He hadn't forgotten how she'd kissed him last night, and more importantly, he wouldn't allow *her* to forget it either. He was still the same frustrating, infuriating friend of her brother he'd always been, eager to relentlessly toy with her. And now he was challenging her.

She growled. So much for thinking she could play nice with him.

She squared her shoulders. "Not in the slightest, *Packmaster*." She said his title with more than a hint of distaste. Dakota may have softened her to the idea of his proposal, but noble packmaster or not, Sierra would fight him with everything she had.

Had she not been looking for it, she might have missed the spark of pleasure that twitched in his scarred brow at her response, if only for a brief second. Apparently, she wasn't the only one who appreciated a good challenge.

Two could play at that game.

At least they'd give the trainees something to talk about.

Taking his lead, Sierra strode to the weapons rack where she'd stored her own sword, a custom claymore with a silver handle, which was inscribed with the words that she'd heard her mother often whisper to her father about her. Before they'd both passed, her mother had whispered it every time her father had expressed concern that she shouldn't try to emulate him in his role as high commander, that she should be more like the other girls, *normal* girls. Those same words had fueled her and forced her to rise every morning, continuing to train, even when the grief of her mother's death had hit her full force.

There's fire in her.

And she wouldn't allow that fire to be easily snuffed out.

Sierra gripped the handle of the claymore. She may not have swung her sword with the ease of her muscled brute of an opponent, but she could wield a lethal blow all the same.

She and Maverick stood at the opposite ends of the makeshift ring the trainees had formed around them, both clutching their weapons. Though Dakota hadn't called time yet, Sierra knew better than to take her eyes off him, even for a second.

She'd never faced a more formidable opponent.

Once Dakota had finished reminding the trainees to pay attention to Sierra's and Maverick's posture, Dakota turned toward them as referee. "You both know the rules. No blood. First one to tap out or hit the ground loses."

"Intimidated?" That hint of a grin still lingered on his lips.

Sierra didn't blink. She refused to let her eyes leave his. "Not a chance, *Maverick.*"

From the quirk of his scarred brow, the use of his given name in a public arena caught him off guard, exactly as she intended. Dakota let out a quick whistle as Sierra surged forward. But the packmaster recovered quickly. Their weapons cut through the air and their swords clashed, both moving with a practiced, unrivaled skill that was more impressive than that of their predecessors.

Sierra's heart raced as she pushed herself to her limit. She didn't have time to think, to hear the reaction of the trainees, or even to notice the growing shouts cheering them both on. She simply was there. Present. In the moment.

Her attention focused singularly on her opponent.

Maverick moved with a lethal grace even the pack's other elite warriors had never managed to master. Each movement belied a calm ferocity that stole her breath away. The dedication and training it would have taken were stunning. This was a man who'd spent his life pushing his body to its limits with one singular purpose.

To protect those that he loved.

Sierra sliced her claymore in a downward arc, barely missing the scruffy hair of his beard. It'd been all she could do to mitigate the intensity of his onslaught. He must have recognized that, because he chose that moment to ease in a way she hadn't anticipated. As a result, the weight of her sword came down hard, too hard, catching her off-balance.

Any other opponent wouldn't have been fast enough. She could have channeled the counterbalance of gravity and then fallen into a roll, recovering to begin fighting again. But not with him. Maverick caught her in his arms, wrapping her close against him to stop her from falling, even as his sword pressed against the skin of her neck. Had she been a true enemy, he could have slit her throat. But of course, she wasn't his enemy.

Not really.

With the length of her body clutched against him, save for the arm that held on to her claymore, she could feel every muscled ridge of his chest, the heavy weight of his hips pressing against her, and more importantly, the thick, hard length between his legs. To onlookers, Sierra assumed they both looked as if they were struggling to catch their breath from the heat of their battle, but she knew better.

Even through his worn ranch jeans, she felt the deep, throbbing pulse of his erection against the heat of her core as he held her. A wave of delicious moisture flooded between her legs. All she needed to do to stop him from winning was to take one good swing at the side of his head. Then, he'd be forced to release her as he guarded his temple. It would allow her the opening she needed to gain her victory.

But she couldn't.

At the start of the fight, she'd wanted to best the pompous, arrogant packmaster, but now that the opportunity stared her straight in the face, she found that her singular path to victory wasn't so singular. His eyes flashed to the gold of his wolf beneath the brim of his Stetson. Sierra would have given anything not to move from that position, to fulfill the heady tension and desire that electrified the air between them.

Dakota had been right. She *could* have her victory. Every delectable bit of it. Even if that meant giving up on the original path she'd intended. She didn't owe anyone an explanation. This was *her* victory, and hers alone, and she intended to claim all her spoils and then some…

"Yes." She breathed all the desire she felt into that one word before she could stop herself. It was barely more than a whisper. Loud enough for Maverick's ears alone.

He seemed to immediately catch her meaning, because for a moment, his impenetrable gaze faltered, and what she saw there both frightened and thrilled her more than the threat of his blade at her neck ever could.

Desire. Pure and raw.

She saw it in the eyes of his wolf clear as day.

Which meant she could claim her victory, perhaps in *every* way she intended. Perhaps she *would* make him fall in love with her, even if it meant risking everything.

With the tension between them clouding her head, she didn't recognize the initial fault in her logic, because as quickly as the moment came, it passed, and any fanciful notion she had of love was gone with it. In an instant, the mask he wore was back again, the flicker of passion she'd seen replaced by the same gruff, impenetrable leader she'd come to expect over the years. As it did, the true extent of her mistake hit her full force. Love was something that would never be between them. Of that, she was certain, because it was at that moment, the packmaster swept her leg, causing her to land flat on her ass and defeated in the mountain dirt.

As turned on and full of desire as she was furious.

Chapter 7

SHE'D SAID YES. MAVERICK WASN'T CERTAIN HE'D EVER ACTU-ally expected her to say yes. The weight of that single word refused to escape him as leaned against the paddock gate outside the stables. Dean, one of their elite warriors and the head of the Grey Wolf front-of-house, stood at the gate of one of the horse trailers they'd backed up to the open paddock. Though he was the friendly face of their ranch to the human world, their enemies had learned the hard way to fear him.

"You ready?" Dean asked.

Maverick nodded.

In response, Dean released the latch on the ramped trailer gate.

The gate burst open with a loud metal *thwack* as one bucking brute of an untamed mustang barreled out into the paddock. Maverick crouched low, rope in hand, on the far side near the gate, prepared to dive out of the way if necessary. He'd give the beast a moment to settle, to get used to the pen and the fact that he was in it. He wasn't about to try to put a rope around the horse's neck when it was still fresh out of the gate and reeling from transport.

The horse kicked and bucked, thrashing about the pen in a display that was equal parts impressive strength and intimidating fury. Wolf shifter or not, no cowboy wanted to be on the wrong end of one of those hooves.

Dean wrenched the trailer gate closed, whistling for Malcolm to pull the truck forward before he slammed the paddock shut and hopped over the fence to safety.

Leaving Maverick alone in the pen with the wild mustang.

Maverick crouched in quiet stillness, his eyes only occasionally darting away from the magnificent, powerful horse before him and toward Dean. Dean removed his Stetson momentarily, readjusting the dreads tied back at the base of his neck as he rounded the paddock on the outside of the gate to where Maverick stood. "This one's feisty. You've got your work cut out for you." Dean kicked a buildup of cold mountain slush from his boots.

They'd had plenty of snow flurries, rain, and hail this fall, but so far none of it had stuck to the ground other than as a persistent, damp coldness.

Maverick grunted in agreement. This bucking, spirited beast was intended to be Trigger's young successor, as soon as Mav managed to break him in, at least.

It'd take more than a few days with this one.

The Grey Wolves had plenty of horses, between the regular working horses they kept in the stable and the wild-horse contract they managed out in the far sections of their lands. Enough that, at times, during a particularly hard calving season where they lost a lot more heads than they birthed, if they had subsisted as a normal *human* operation, they would have occasionally risked becoming horse poor. But the pack's private monetary reserves, built up over the centuries of their existence, always kept them on the right side of wrong, and this particular horse was coming out of Maverick's own private funds. Sure, he could have used one of the spare work horses as his own after retiring Trigger, but that would have robbed him of this.

Maverick never shied away from the thrill of a challenge.

Slowly, he moved one of his boots to the right. The horse watched him with weary eyes as it flitted around the paddock. It was calmer now but still skittish as hell and ready to bolt should he approach too quickly.

"Are you sure I should leave you alone?" Dean asked. "All things considered."

All things considered being the looming threat on Maverick's life and thus the pack. Blaze and the other elite warriors had begun gathering intel, but at this stage, it would be a game of patience. They'd confirmed that the attempted assassin had been a rogue wolf shifter, likely hired by someone to complete the task, but they couldn't be certain who had cashed out the now-dead bastard.

In the past, Maverick's new brother-in-law, Rogue, would have been his first suspect. It wasn't as if he and Rogue hadn't squared off before. Though they'd been on different sides, they'd both only been trying to protect their own. The decision Maverick had made to throw the rogue wolves to the Execution Underground had never sat well with him, but it'd been a choice between following his own moral compass or risking the lives of his pack.

And the pack always came first.

Nevertheless, he and Rogue, criminal bastard that he was, were on the same side now, despite the many problems and threats that was causing the pack, and while Maverick might not like his new brother-in-law, he knew Rogue would never do anything to jeopardize their deal for his kind—or worse, hurt someone close to his sister.

Dean had reason to worry. Whoever was out for Maverick's life would come for him again. The packleader had little doubt of that. But this time, he anticipated them.

"I'll be fine, Dean. I always am," Maverick said, his eyes still thoroughly pinned to the wild horse before him. This wouldn't be the first time someone had attempted to kill him, though admittedly, it'd been the first time they'd dared come for him *here*, on his own territory.

Recognizing that his attention was elsewhere, Dean tipped his Stetson. "I'll leave you to it then. Aaliyah's waiting," he said, referring to his mate. The Grey Wolf front-of-house director sauntered back to the still-heated truck, hitting the roof of the cab twice as he climbed into the driver's side.

As Dean drove off, leaving Maverick alone with the unruly and angered horse, Maverick surveyed the scene before him. When he stood with the stables at his back like this, looking outward toward the ranchlands of Wolf Pack Run, there was nothing as far as the eye could see. Only frozen pastures, the silent sway of the mountain pines against the backdrop of the midday sun, and him, here with this horse.

He released a hefty sigh of the tension he'd been holding.

This was what he craved.

This little bit of peace. The solitude and quiet of the mountains. The sting of the fresh autumn wind on his face. This was the life he'd have chosen had he ever been given a choice. Not the paperwork. Not the desk. Not the meetings with other packmasters and diplomats, representatives from other packs around the globe. Not the settling of pack disputes or the constant push and pull with the council. That was a never-ending, always-present grind.

But all that was his life, as much as this was, and it always would be.

For years, it'd been his job to suppress his more human desires, his sense of self. That was his singular burden: to protect the pack as he bore the weight of their collective expectations. He had to be more than himself. Not Maverick Grey the man, the cowboy, but Maverick Grey, packmaster of the Grey Wolves, a mixture of man, wolf, and legend.

As packmaster, it was his duty to be reserved in everything— his emotions, his actions, his choices—in a way that lived up to the myth of his existence. But over the years, he had forced himself to remain so cold, so distant, that now it came as second nature, because his role had changed him.

He barely recognized himself anymore.

Save for rare moments like this.

Fully present in the moment, he circled the paddock. The stallion watched his every move with wary, skittish movements. Slowly, Maverick bunched the rope in his hands. He swung the lasso, drawing close enough several times only for the beast to jump just out of his reach. If he could either get the rope around the horse's neck at the right angle or draw close enough…

This dance continued for a while, a back-and-forth push and pull. Just him, the horse, and the gray-blue sky. An hour later, he heard one of the pack's grapple forks approaching from behind. Frustrated and tiring, he cast his rope out one last time.

The stallion released an angered whinny before it kicked its front hooves hard against the cold mountain dirt. The flash of fury in the horse's dark eyes told Maverick all he needed to know.

The beast was about to charge him.

Maverick leaped over the paddock fence just as the weight of the mustang's heavy front legs came down in the exact spot where he'd been standing.

Bending over, he rested his hands on his knees as he caught his breath, grumbling a few choice curses.

"I think he doesn't like you."

Maverick recognized the voice immediately. He straightened, rope still in hand. Sierra was staring down at him from behind the wheel of the grapple fork, that ridiculous rooster that'd been following her nestled in the seat beside her as if he were a damn cat.

"Course he doesn't like me. There isn't a horse in his right mind who'd trust a wolf, at least not until I show him he can," he called back to her over the heavy winds.

Sierra gathered the rooster in her arms as she hopped down from the cab, the massive pile of crested feathers on the animal's head flopping as she adjusted her Carhartt. She raised her voice slightly over the gusts of wind. "I'm supposed to be headed out to do my chores for the day. The cows won't feed themselves, and Cheyenne's supposed to meet me with the hay truck, but Colt mentioned you were out here and I…" Her voice trailed off, cut off in part by the wind but also by her own reluctance.

Maverick couldn't put his finger on it, but she didn't seem her usual chaotic self. Instead of confidence, there was a hesitation about her, as if she had something to say but couldn't find the words to say it, and after her surprise "yes" earlier, he'd be damned if he wouldn't find out exactly what was on her mind.

The wind picked up speed, whipping through the open ranch-lands with enough force that they both had to bend their knees to stay upright against it.

"Come inside." Maverick nodded toward the stable, signaling for her to follow him.

She frowned at the authoritative tone but didn't protest.

Inside the stables, the gray hue of the skies overhead dimmed the natural lighting, casting the long rows of stalls in the glowing orange hue of the horses' heat lamps. With most of the pack-members out working their chores for the day, the stable was surprisingly empty, save for the horses. Maverick closed the door behind him, blocking out the sound of the wind as he turned toward Sierra.

The rooster she held let out a screeching crow, causing several of the horses to stir.

"Yes, we're all aware the King has arrived." She set the rooster down and waved him away, but Elvis didn't so much as move. He simply bobbed his head several times before attempting to peck at her boots. Sierra sighed and shook her head as if he were a hindrance, but then leaned down and gingerly patted his feathers.

Maverick released a long, slow breath through his nose as he shook his head. He still remembered the summer everything had changed between them, because his wolf had suddenly *noticed* her. Where she'd once been all straight lines and muscle, there had been new feminine curves. Her hips had widened, better balancing the thick corded muscles of her legs, and there had suddenly been soft, full breasts bulging beneath her sports bra. Breasts he *still* wanted to lick, to tease, to suck until he captured the taut pink tips of her nipples between his canines and toyed with them until she screamed his name. Back then, he'd been young and practically salivating over her, and it'd taken everything in him not to bend her over and mount her like the animal he was.

But he'd kept his hands to himself, because Colt would have *murdered* him if he hadn't made an honest woman of her first, and they'd been young enough that marriage and mating seemed like a far-off distant future. Pursuing her hadn't been something Maverick had been willing to risk. It would have changed everything. Between him, her, Colt, their families.

Nevertheless, he'd always planned her for to be his eventually.

Years later, when his father died and it'd been time for him to assume his role as packmaster, it'd been her he wanted to claim as his mate, though circumstance had other plans…

But now, ten years later, life had left him a lonely widower with more regrets and guilt than any cowboy could bear. Yet still, despite the fact that she now hated him and the power he represented, and it was years too late for him to ever have her in the way he truly wanted, God help him…

He'd never stopped wanting Sierra Cavanaugh.

He'd need to tread lightly. This marriage was a necessity for them both—and for the protection of the pack. He didn't have anything more to give. It could never be anything more than that. Even if he'd once wanted it to be.

Silently, Maverick waited for her to start. She'd come to him after all, and like her older brother, Sierra didn't parse words. But as she stood before him now, something was off, different. Several feet away from him, she toyed with the edge of her horse's stall gate, refusing to look at him. Where was the confident, outspoken she-wolf he was so accustomed to?

Finally, he cleared his throat. He wasn't one for making conversation, yet one of them would need to speak eventually. "Here to talk about the flowers?" he asked, latching on to the first ludicrous question to come to mind. He sounded ridiculous. Small talk had never been his strong suit. But wasn't that the sort of thing future brides cared about?

She stopped toying with the stall gate hinge and raised a brow. "Flowers?"

The wind outside whistled. Even inside the shelter of the stable, the occasional gusts against the old wood of the building roared. "Yes, the flowers," he grumbled.

Her brow furrowed in confusion. "I've heard it called that before, but I think I'd prefer to use anatomically correct verbiage."

Anatomically correct verbiage? He quirked a brow. What in the blazing hell was she talking about?

She must have realized his confusion, because suddenly, her eyes widened in horror. "Oh boy. You didn't say *de*flower, did you?"

Deflower? Who the hell even used words like *deflower*? And what in the world was she...

"*The* flowers," he corrected. "For the ceremony."

She bit her lower lip, drawing his attention there.

He growled. *Christ.* Why did she have to do that? Whenever she did, his thoughts strayed in a direction that was far too forbidden for them. If they were going to marry, one night was more than enough to convince the council. Yet when she did that, considering all the scenarios that ran through his mind, he'd need far more than a single night before he was through with her. He'd claim her as his in every way she'd allow, in any *place* she'd allow.

On his bed. On his desk. On the mountainside. In the showers of the training gym.

Hell, in this very damn stable atop a fucking haystack if she wanted.

She stopped worrying her lower lip in favor of cupping her hand over her chin as if deep in thought. "That makes a lot more sense. I wondered how you knew what I'd come here to say to you."

Maverick shook his head. He couldn't even pretend that he was following this conversation, but no one had ever argued that Sierra wasn't eccentric. Hell, she'd have to be to take on the pack's traditions and the council with no power other than the hope and spirit she inspired in the other women.

It was lunacy really. Brave, valiant lunacy.

And he'd be a damned liar if he didn't admit that he admired it.

He continued to watch her as she flitted between the stall gates, pacing and fidgeting to a near-excessive degree. She looked every bit as skittish as the horse he'd left in the corral.

He lowered his voice to a rumbling growl. "Out with it, warrior," he ordered.

She sighed. "Well, I guess there's no better segue than that." She stopped her pacing and finally turned toward him. "I want you to tutor me."

The statement caught him off guard. He'd known she would grieve the loss of not getting the position in the way she'd intended, but he hadn't expected it to shake her confidence like this. "Sierra, your name wouldn't have been put forth if you weren't quali—"

"That's not what I mean," she snapped, her tone filled with a hint of annoyance.

Maverick fought back a grin. There she was. The Sierra he'd known as far back as he could remember, the one who'd always been so quick to point out when he'd made a misstep or gone too far. He'd always secretly appreciated that honesty and their bickering. When they'd been young, their constant back-and-forth banter had been the battle of legends, both always trying to best the other with a smarter quip.

She might have been eccentric and wild, but Sierra Cavanaugh possessed more than a bit of sharp wit. He'd never enjoyed the challenge of another opponent as much as her.

Until his role, his duties, and Rose had come along, changing everything.

Sierra continued, her tone more than a bit saucy, though at least that rooster had finally wandered off. "I *know* I'm qualified for my position, and I don't need your validation." She hesitated. "For *that*."

Maverick crossed his arms over his chest, leaning against the closed stable door. He wasn't certain what she was getting at. "I don't follow."

She let out an exasperated huff, as if *he* were the one always being difficult. "I don't want you to tutor me for my position as warrior. I want you to tutor me in something else." Clenching her hands into fists as if she were prepared for battle, she met his gaze head-on, those glowing honey-brown eyes filled with the renewed confidence he knew so well.

She cleared her throat. "I want you to teach me how to pleasure a man."

Chapter 8

"COME AGAIN?" IT WAS SEVERAL BEATS BEFORE MAVERICK MANaged to say anything.

"I said that I want you to teach me how to pleasure a man," she repeated. "And with what I have in mind, hopefully you'll be enough of a gentleman that if anyone is going to *come again*, it would be me." She'd obviously intended for the play on words to be funny, but Maverick couldn't have laughed even if he'd tried. She wanted him to...

No. He couldn't have heard her correctly. "I still don't follow."

She momentarily buried her face in her hands. When she removed them, her cheeks had transitioned from a lovely shade of pink to crimson. "Jesus, Maverick, do I have to spell out every detail of it for you? I'm inexperienced."

"Inexperienced?" For some reason, he could only repeat her exact words. But in his defense, with each additional phrase that passed her gorgeous lips, he seemed to be less capable of thinking about anything other than all the things he wanted to do to her.

Sexually experienced?

Christ.

She might as well as have asked him in no uncertain terms to mount her as furiously as that still-horny gelding of hers, because if the length throbbing between his legs was any indication...

He turned away from her. He couldn't look at her. This conversation ended now.

Because if it didn't...

"Yes, inexperienced," she said, echoing the words back to him.

From the corner of his eye, he could see her trying to draw his attention as she stepped into his line of view again.

"Inexperienced. Unpracticed. Ignorant. Untried. Do I have to break out a thesaurus for you? Whatever you want to call it, when it comes to sexual experiences, I'm a…"

"Virgin?" he finally growled.

"Yes, I'm a virgin." She breathed out another long-exasperated huff as if she hated that single word and all the baggage that came with it. "My V-card is still unfortunately intact with a big capital V."

Maverick swallowed down the aroused growl building in his throat. He could think of a few things he could make into a big capital V. Namely, her legs. She'd be naked and bare, and he'd spread her wide beneath him as he buried his face in her…

No, he couldn't allow himself to think that way.

"How is that possible?"

"Well, it's simple anatomy really, despite the fact that virginity is actually only a social construct. But I've never had a man put his—"

"That's not what I mean," he snarled. He let out a frustrated curse.

How the hell the woman standing before him was still a virgin he'd never begin to guess. He raked his gaze over her. She was taller than many of the other females of the pack, all lean, muscled athleticism. At quick glance, from the ways she tried to hide her looks, many might have overlooked her as dull, plain even, save for her obvious physical strength. But as far as he was concerned, when a man had the patience to look beneath it all, it wasn't an exaggeration to say she was the most gorgeous woman in the pack.

Did she *have* to have grown up to be so breathtaking? It would have made his life considerably easier had she been unsightly. But clearly nature hadn't seen it fit enough for her to only be the smartest, the boldest, the bravest, the strongest, the craziest. The most *everything*.

It was a fucking nuisance, really.

But he couldn't think of that. Not now. Because if he did, there would soon be a lot less talking and a lot more fuc—

"King of these mountains isn't your title," Sierra declared, interrupting his thoughts. "The only king on this ranch is Elvis, so you may be packmaster, but you're not the only one who gets to make proposals. You need to hear me out."

Considering his life was currently at risk for the entire pack, hers included, he didn't appreciate having his title compared to that of a damn rooster, but he wasn't about to interrupt her. He was too busy hanging on her every word. Hell, practically salivating like the wolf he was.

"You said you want a marriage of convenience. One night together and then we'll have what we both want."

He *had* said that. In that way, he supposed their goals weren't opposed, but he didn't see how proposing one night out of obligation to convince the council translated into him teaching her pleasure…

Pleasure.

That word stirred something low in his belly. In his mind, he was in the forest again, her lithe figure pressed against him. Her confidence and muscles were hard as steel, but beneath all the armor, she was soft, feminine curves in all the right places. Curves he hadn't known existed until she pressed against him.

Sure, he'd seen her naked, technically speaking, on the occasions when all the pack shifted beneath the full moon, but that was different. During those times, he was so close to changing form that he was more wolf than man, and then he didn't care about the gentle curve of human hips, soft swells of full breasts, or handfuls of firm ass that for a woman who spent every day training was too mouthwateringly full and round to be reasonable.

Until she'd kissed him in the damn forest. Then, all he'd known, all he'd been able to think about were those curves beneath her baggy clothes, or the way his tongue parted her, dipping inside the moist, wet cove of her lips until her breathing hitched, until she was moving and writhing against him.

His cock gave an eager throb and his mouth watered.

Clearly, he wasn't thinking only about kissing anymore. He'd moved far beyond that the moment she'd haphazardly thrown herself into his arms.

"Well, you're wrong," she said, drawing his attention again. "One night doesn't get us both what we want. At least not me anyway. I want more."

Of course she did. Didn't she always demand more of him? "And what do you want, warrior?"

"Commitment. Passion. Loyalty." She paused. "Love."

He shook his head. "I can't give you those things."

"I never expected you would, which is why, if I have to marry you to claim my position, I have a proposal of my own to make."

He didn't like the sound of that. Not one damn bit. Maverick had never envisioned himself being proposed to. He was the kind of man who did the proposing, not received it.

"In a marriage of convenience, your plan is for us to live separate lives. Am I right?"

He grunted in acknowledgment. That *had* been in the initial plan. Until she'd uttered the word *pleasure* and thrown a massive wrench into it. That was her way of course. Thwarting, delaying, complicating everything he did. Now he felt that plan crumbling before his eyes. He shouldn't have been surprised. He was a damn fool.

"In that case, it wouldn't matter if I was in love with another, would it?"

The question caught him off guard. By that logic, it wouldn't, but the idea bothered him, though he didn't dare admit it. He'd already made it clear love wasn't on the table, and he would never place his own pride above her happiness.

"Go on." He regretted the encouragement in those words the moment he said them.

She plucked a stray piece of hay from one of the nearby stacks. "I want to have love in my life. I don't just want my position. I want someone to share it with, someone to enjoy and spend my life with,

but you're right. Without the position, I *know* I won't be happy."
She turned her gaze toward him. "Which is why after our marriage
night, it's my plan to take a lover."

He snarled in response. The thought of her calling any other
wolf, any other man a lover when *he* was supposed to be her husband angered him in a way it shouldn't have. "Your plan is to cuckold
me?" The question was filled with every bit of rage he felt at the idea.

"It wouldn't be another packmember or anyone else at Wolf
Pack Run," she said quickly, as if that ludicrous amendment made
anything she was asking of him better. "It'd be someone outside
the pack. Maybe a rogue shifter or a wolf from another pack? Who
knows. In any case, one night of you taking my virginity won't be
enough. I want to be able to have whoever I choose to love. I want
to know how to seduce and pleasure a man, so I need to be experienced, which means…"

She needed him to seduce her, to give her that experience.

Christ.

She was chaos. Pure, fucking chaos. That was what she was.

He knew he had no right, no place to feel frustrated about the
whole damn ridiculous situation. She wasn't his, and even once
they were married, he'd made clear it was a marriage of convenience only. She wouldn't be his property to control. They were
just words, ideas, *projections*. They were marrying out of necessity,
nothing more, but despite that, he already *felt* cuckolded. And he
didn't like the idea one damn bit.

One night with him and she'd never want another man. He'd
make certain of it.

He straightened from where he'd leaned against the door, his
limbs wrought with tension as if he were a coiled viper prepared to
strike. "And I'm your choice for such a task?"

"You're my brother's best friend, Maverick. You may have lived
like a monk since Rose passed, but before you became packmaster,
you had a bit of a reputation yourself."

He growled. There was that word again. He'd had enough of his apparent tendency to collect reputations as of late, and he didn't like hearing Rose's name on her lips. Somehow, it felt wrong. He'd dreamed of this, of her. More than once.

Rose was never supposed to have been part of the equation.

"You're a safe choice for me, someone I can trust to have honorable intentions. We may not see eye to eye all the time, and you may be a total grump, but I know you won't hurt me."

Him? A grump? He quirked a brow. No one had ever dared call him grumpy before...

And of course, he wouldn't hurt her, but him? A safe choice?

No one had ever dared consider him a *safe* anything. Unless they had a death wish.

He growled. "There's nothing honorable about my intentions, Sierra."

Not to mention for him, there was nothing safe about this. He'd never been in more dangerous territory...

He shook his head. Sierra was Colt's younger sister. He wasn't supposed to want her at all. Period. End of story. He'd also sworn he would never marry again. His role didn't make him an ideal romantic partner. He had to place the needs of the pack first at all times. For the sake of the pack, he was best off alone, his judgment unclouded, yet here he was, standing here with Sierra Cavanaugh, a woman who was now his fiancée in name alone, and not only was she proposing someday taking another man into her bed, but she wanted him, her future husband, to tutor her in pleasure as she'd so plainly put it.

She wasn't just a madwoman. She was certifiably insane.

And apparently so was he, considering he wanted to take her up on her ridiculous offer. Far more than he should. In fact, he was so tempted, he had half a mind to suggest they start right now, which as far as he was concerned was the very definition of a marriage of *in*convenience. Which meant he needed to end this. Fast.

This time, it was his turn to turn down her proposal. "No."

Chapter 9

"No?" Sierra's eyes shot to Maverick's and locked there. She hadn't been certain what to expect from him. But she'd never considered he would say no.

It stung her pride more than she cared to admit.

Maverick stood on the opposite side of the stall row, towering over her, his corded muscles primed with tension. His scarred brow twitched, making him look ruggedly masculine, but that wasn't what held her captive. It was his eyes. They told a different story than the cold disinterest etched across his face. They flashed to the gold of his wolf, burning with a fire that kissed her with a thrill of danger, of pleasure, because whatever it was, despite how he tried to hide it, she'd made the growly, grumbling packmaster feel *something*.

And *something* she could work with.

"What do you mean no?"

"Sierra," he growled in warning as she drew closer. His voice was low, feral.

But she'd be damned if she'd drop the conversation now.

She placed her hands on her hips. "I deserve an answer."

"It means exactly that. No," he snarled. He turned away, prowling the length of the stall block as he distanced himself from her. "Isn't that an important distinction these days?" he tossed over his shoulder.

She blinked. Was he *mansplaining* consent to her? She let out a frustrated growl, charging after him as she caught up to his quick pace. She knew her proposal was a little...unusual, but she failed to see how it was all that different from sleeping together for a night to convince the council, and she'd make him understand that much.

One way or another.

When she caught up to him, he stood in the saddle room, surveying the leather equipment in search of a saddle he'd likely place on that bucking beast in the hold that wanted nothing to do with him. He was good at that. Agitating things, animals, *people* who wanted nothing to do with him—only to walk away when he was through.

That'd been exactly what he'd done to her years ago.

She should've said something then, made her feelings known, but she'd been young and too destroyed by his decision to marry Rose to tell him exactly how much he'd hurt her.

Not that it would have made a difference...

But now, she was older and a hell of a lot angrier, life having filled her with years of righteous feminine fury, and she wasn't letting him off the hook so easily. Not this time.

She gripped a hand on the doorframe, blocking his only exit. "You said yourself you don't have to like someone to want to sleep with them."

His back was to her, and he didn't bother to look over his shoulder as he answered. "That much is apparent."

She frowned. The comment stung, though in her mind, it was also evidence he did want her, a least a little. If one could call the erection that had strained his jeans during their battle a little anything. There'd been nothing *little* about it.

"If you can suggest we have sex for obligation, why can't I suggest that for instructional purposes, a few times we do..." She struggled to find the words. "Other things," she finally supplied.

He quirked a brow at her choice of words, though he still refused to look at her. "'Other things'? You'll need to be more specific than that, warrior."

She crossed her arms over her chest. "Could you stop repeating everything I'm saying like it's so confusing?"

This time, he did look at her. "I will when you stop saying things that damn well warrant confused repeating," he snarled.

She guessed he had a point there. "Yes, 'other things.' Obviously, considering your reaction, I'm not very good at this whole seducing-a-man thing, and we've already discussed that I have no idea what I'm doing when it comes to sex, so to be fully clear, I figured why not make a list?"

"Logically," he grumbled, picking up one of the saddles and testing its weight before he laid it back in place. "Why *wouldn't* you make a list?"

She suspected he didn't appreciate what a superior idea it was. Despite that, she removed the folded paper, a torn-out piece from her old leather-bound diary, and extended it toward him. He glanced down at the quivering note she held out. Her hands were shaking, and the gesture highlighted exactly how much. She may have seemed confident, but she wasn't fully confident when it came to this. She was nervous, and he had to see it. But at least her head was held high and she was daring to ask for what she wanted.

He hesitated, watching her with those penetrating, judging eyes of his.

For a moment, she wasn't certain he would take the paper, but finally he did.

He snatched it from her hand, though he didn't unfold it. Instead, he stared at it for a long beat before muttering a string of colorful curses. He rested an arm on the wall of the saddle room, leaning his forehead against it, the silence highlighting the mounting tension between them.

"Well?" she prompted.

When he still didn't respond, she sighed.

"If you're not going to read it, at least say something, damn it."

He rounded on her then, beating one large fist against his chest. "You think so little of me?" He brandished the list at her. "That I would use you like this?"

"Isn't that already what you're doing? Using me as a means to an end?"

"It's not like that, Sierra, and you know it."

This time, her name on his lips didn't have the effect it usually did. Instead, it only reminded her of all the distance he'd placed between them over the years. All the ways he'd hurt her, intentional or not.

"Isn't it? I'm the means you need to appease the Elder Council, to get your approval to negotiate with the Execution Underground. Isn't that the heart of it, Packmaster?" She hurled his title at him as if it were a weapon. "You don't have a problem using me if it benefits *you*."

His nose wrinkled in distaste. "My job is to protect the pack."

She laughed. As if his motivation gave him any right. If she married him, she'd never be able to escape him. He would constantly invade her mind, her body, her heart. Everything she'd offered him years ago that he'd refused to take. And he expected all that in exchange for what? A title she'd already *earned*?

He could find other ways to deal with the council. Sure, they'd take longer, potentially risking the lives of the pack and the deterioration of negotiations with the Execution Underground. But for her, there was no alternative. At all.

"Of course it's your duty to protect the pack. Unfortunately for you, that includes me."

"I *am* protecting you, which is why I won't even begin to consider this." He brandished the list again, crumpling it in his massive fist. He could've thrown it into the muck in one of the horse's stalls or, hell, even burned it with one of the heat lamps.

But he didn't.

Instead, he stared down at it for another long beat. With an intense, almost reverent focus, he gently placed the paper in the back pocket of his work jeans. She could only see a hint of his expression beneath his Stetson, but his wolf eyes had faded now, and it was almost as if her request had pained him.

If her pride had any say, she would have turned tail and left, but she had more important things to consider. She thought of all the women coming up after her. If she got the position, she'd forge the way, create a legacy they could follow, but thanks to the Elder Council, the only way she could do that was to marry the man who stood before her.

She was going to do this for all of them, so she'd be damned if she'd cater to her own sense of pride and walk away, and since she was making this sacrifice, she refused to limit herself to a lonely life for the rest of her days. No one was going to fight for her, her happiness, her needs, if not her.

"How is this any different from you proposing we sleep together for a single night?"

"That was to appease the council. Nothing more." He paced the floor of the saddle room as if he were a caged animal. Considering that she blocked the only entrance and his irises were once again the gold of his wolf's, it wasn't too far from the truth. "I made my offer to benefit us *both*, but I refuse to treat you like some naughty plaything."

She blushed at the words. If her damaged pride wouldn't stop her, she wouldn't allow embarrassment to do so either. "I'm *asking* you to treat me like some naughty plaything," she said, "but apparently, what I want doesn't matter."

Using two fingers to massage his temples, he stopped pacing. "You're Colt's sister. I can't treat you that way. Doing so would make me even more of a beast, a—"

"Monster," she finished for him.

Immediately, he stiffened.

She'd known that would hit a nerve, but with the pain of his rejection building in her chest, she intended it to. "What? You thought I hadn't heard the nickname? Monster of Montana. That's what they've been calling you, isn't it?"

For a long beat, he remained still, the gold of his wolf eyes boring into her, before finally he growled, "Is that what you think of me?"

She glanced away. She didn't think that of him. Not really, but with all the pain and hurt of years being overlooked bubbling to the surface, she wasn't about to stroke his fragile male ego. From the look in his eye, he was primed for a fight, and if that was what he wanted, she'd give it to him. They'd always been good at that—fighting.

It wasn't as painful as whatever *this* was between them.

"You're willing to use me for your own means but won't even consider *my* needs." Easing inside the saddle room, she took one of the riding crops down from the hook on the wall to toy with it. She'd never liked not having something to do with her hands. She swatted it gently against her palm, testing the snap against her skin. "So if the shoe fits." She dared to glance up at him.

He stood only a foot away from her, looking more infuriated than she'd ever seen him. "I can't give you what you want," he growled.

She stepped closer. "You're right. Clearly you can't. You're too protective and brotherly to do that."

The gold of his wolf eyes flared. In the dim light of the saddle room, they glowed with an ethereal intensity. "There's nothing *brotherly* about how I feel about you, Sierra."

"Then prove it." Her eyes flashed to her wolf as she drew near, so close that they were almost chest to chest, like they'd been in the forest. The memory of what passed between them was so heady, so fresh and visceral that her body buzzed with the electricity of it. She could practically feel his lips on hers again, savor the spiced masculine taste of him.

And from the look in the packmaster's gaze, so could he.

"If that's true, show me," she challenged. She placed the riding crop on his chest, tracing the looped leather tip over his heart. "I don't need protection. Not even from you."

He stiffened as a low growl rumbled from his throat, but he didn't dare move.

Which meant she'd won this round.

She removed the riding tool, casting him a satisfied grin. "That's what I thought." She turned away, but turning her back on him was a mistake, because it meant she missed the fiery look in his eye as he made his onslaught.

In seconds, Maverick was on her, one hand gripping her chest as the other roughly palmed her rear. He bent her over one of the mounted saddles as he drew her behind flush against him. The thick length of his erection pressed between her ass cheeks, causing her to let out a squeak in surprise. Even through their jeans, she felt the hard, throbbing length of him.

"This is no way to treat a virgin," he purred against her ear. The heat of his breath caused a shiver to run down her spine, making its way lower until a pool of heat gathered between her legs. Slowly, he eased the hand atop her chest lower, unzipping her Carhartt and continuing downward until he cupped the weight of her left breast in his hand. His fingertips rolled over the rough material of her work shirt, expertly locating the taut peak of her nipple as he began toying, playing with her. "If I were any sort of decent man, I wouldn't…"

A small moan tore from her lips in response, instantly singeing her cheeks with heated embarrassment. She'd never made a sound like that before, not even when she'd taken care of herself with her own hand, and yet he didn't seem to dislike it.

The length of his cock stiffened, rubbing against her behind. Slowly, he eased his hand lower, trailing down the length of her stomach until he located the button of her jeans. "But I'm nothing close to decent."

She opened her mouth to respond, but he chose that moment to unbutton her jeans with expert precision, tugging down the zipper until her underwear was exposed. The warm heat of his palm cupped over her, her moisture soaking through the thin material of her panties. She thought he would pull the material aside and touch her there, at the aching bud of her clit, but suddenly, his hand was gone.

Instead, he plucked the riding crop from her hand, surprising her as he slowly trailed it over her body, drawing lower with each stroke. Each part of her he touched with the cool leather burned with dark erotic promise as if it were his hand stroking her, feeling her, caressing her, though he didn't dare.

Her body came alive with awareness. She couldn't guess what he was going to do with the taboo tool until suddenly the leather loop of the crop's head slipped beneath the hem of her underwear, brushing against the sensitive skin of her clit.

She cried out as he massaged slow, rhythmic circles over her tender flesh. Unable to stop herself, she pushed harder against the riding crop, seeking out the pressure and pleasure he gave her with it.

"Is this what you want?" The words were purred on an aroused growl. "For me to use you like the monster you think I am?"

Unable to form words, she moaned again, barely managing to nod her head in affirmation. Yes. This *was* what she wanted. Him, wild and feral, caught off guard like when she'd kissed him in the forest, everything he'd refused to be to her since he'd become packmaster. She could feel the length of him still pressed against the cheeks of her ass, and in response to her yes, his cock gave a receptive throb.

Pressure and pleasure built inside her with an intensity she'd never experienced before, so much that she felt if he continued, she would break into a thousand pieces, yet she didn't want him to stop, not by a long shot. On the contrary, she wished they were both rid of their clothes, naked, so he would drive his hard length into her. It didn't matter that she was a virgin. She knew what her body wanted, and she ached for him there, deep inside. She felt a needy pulse for the feeling of fullness that she expected having him claim her would bring.

As he edged her closer and closer to the brink, she finally managed to pant the words she wanted to say. "You're not a monster. Not really." She'd only said as much to goad him, to challenge him.

At that, he let out a dark chuckle. "There's no point in attempting to reform me. I'm a lost cause." He increased the speed and pressure, massaging against her clit until she was bucking and rocking against it.

She was close to the brink now. She could feel it.

"And when being a monster means I get to fuck innocent virgins with a riding crop…" He leaned over her, nipping at the sensitive skin of her ear with his sharp canines. "Who says I give a damn?"

Abruptly, he stopped, withdrawing the crop only long enough to turn her to face him. He pinned her against the saddle mount.

"Why did you st—?" He slid his hand between them, cutting her off as he replaced the riding crop's presence with the heat of his own palm.

"Because I want to watch your pleasure." The words fell from his lips with ease. It felt as if he'd spoken more naughty things to her in the past few minutes than all the words he'd grunted and grumbled to her in the past several years. He flicked his thumb over her clit with a heated, sensual stroke. His hands were those of a cowboy, rough and worn, but the hard contrast to the smooth leather of the riding crop and the sudden return of sensation caused her to cry out.

"Fuck," he swore. The hand that was still gripping her ass tightened as he ran his index finger along the length of her slit. "You need to come now, warrior," he purred.

He plunged a single finger deep inside her, curling it in a way that hit a spot deep inside.

As if her body were under his command, she came apart, trembling and shattering in his arms as waves of pleasure rolled through her. The walls of her pussy shook. It was ecstasy. Her own explorations of her body couldn't begin to compare. As the last throes of her orgasm rolled through her, she was left gasping for air, panting against the heat of him.

As she came down from her pleasured haze, in an instant, any hint of tenderness she'd felt in his touch was gone. Instead, he released her and stepped back as he looked down at her with that same distant gaze she loathed. He turned away from her, grabbing the riding crop from where he'd abandoned it only to hang it back on its rightful hook.

She was still panting, catching her breath from all that he'd made her feel. Inside, her wolf was howling in pleasure. She reached out to touch him. "That was—"

"Don't," he warned. He stepped out of her reach. He didn't turn to look at her, but she watched as the muscles beneath his jacket writhed with tension. "Not now, warrior."

There was something in that deep, biting voice, a lingering dark promise. For once, she obeyed him, because from the heat that'd been burning in his eyes as she came, if she didn't…

He stood like that for several beats, refusing to look at her before finally he inhaled a deep breath. When he spoke, his voice was graveled, strained. "Consider that your first lesson."

Without another word, he tore out of the saddle room, leaving her breathless and panting.

But she wasn't done with him yet. Though her legs trembled, she found her footing and stepped out into the stall block, calling after him. "I have one other request."

He froze, his back toward her. "What more could you possibly ask of me, woman?"

There was pain in his voice that she didn't understand, but she didn't dare step closer. "I want to be involved in finding out who's orchestrating the attacks on your life."

He tossed her a dark look over his shoulder as she gestured to his midsection where he'd been injured. The wound would be long since gone, but the scars often lingered.

The tension in his body eased, as if he were grateful for the change in conversation. "Done," he said without hesitation. Turning away, he started toward the door again.

"Really?" She jogged to catch up with him.

"Why not? Once I notify the council of our engagement, as of the lunar ceremony tomorrow, you'll be an elite warrior, and you handled your last assignment with ease."

As he said the words, a swell of pride grew in her chest. She *would* be an elite warrior, wouldn't she? And she *had* handled her last assignment well. She'd been tasked with capturing two of the remaining at-large members of the Wild Eight, a former enemy wolf pack, and she'd done so not only faster but more efficiently than any of her male counterparts.

He gripped the door handle. "You should have led with that request."

"Why?"

Maverick paused, glancing back toward her. "You're new. Green in more ways than one." His hot gaze raked over her, scorching every inch of skin he'd touched. He now knew exactly all the ways in which she was *new*—intimately. "You'll learn to lead with the request most likely to get a yes."

"I didn't think you'd say no to my arrangement, considering that after the sword fight you were..." Her voice trailed off.

"Aroused?" he offered.

A blush flooded her cheeks, and she bit her lower lip. She should be able to say it after what had passed between them, but somehow that only made it more difficult.

"As the tenth and only female of the elite warriors, by observation, you'll find soon enough that adrenaline and battle will cause that in men more often than not."

"So you weren't"—she swallowed before forcing herself to say the word—"aroused by me?"

"I didn't say that." That devilish smirk curved his lips. "And unless you want your second lesson to start now, warrior, I suggest you don't continue biting your lip like some delicious little tease."

Her eyes widened. Had she been in wolf form, her ears would have perked up.

Delicious tease? Her?

No one had ever called her a delicious anything. Hell, half the males of the pack were intimidated by her.

But not him.

Her eyes locked momentarily with his, and to her surprise, she was the first to look away. Perhaps he was the only alpha male on this ranch who was man enough for her. She'd always suspected as much.

With that, he pulled open the stable doors, heading out into the whistling wind and leaving her alone, her mind reeling.

Several minutes later, she was still pacing around the stable in circles, grinning like a fool, her wolf feeling ready to howl as she determined every instance where she could worry her lower lip with her canine teeth.

Chapter 10

MAVERICK REMOVED THE LIST FROM HIS POCKET, STARING AT the folded paper for perhaps the hundredth time since she'd given it to him. The word *List* was written on the outside in large, looping letters, and the *i* was dotted with a small heart. Sierra had never struck him as the type of woman to dot her *i*'s with hearts, but as he was learning, there was *a lot* he didn't know about her. Like the fact that she was a virgin and she didn't want to be any longer, or that she was so responsive to his touch that when he'd commanded her to come, she'd melted into his hand.

Christ.

He rubbed his fingers over his temple to release the tension there. He'd thought being near her had made him and his wolf feel alive again, but that'd been before he'd seen the gold of her wolf eyes filled with desire as she came. He swore under his breath. Lord help him.

He placed the list in his back pocket again without opening it, fighting to maintain what little sense of self-control he had left. Out of sight, out of mind, or so he kept trying to convince himself. Thus far, that hadn't been the case. Since he'd last seen her yesterday afternoon, he'd spent the whole day in meetings, planning the security measures for the evening's events alongside the other warriors. As they'd done so, he'd struggled to focus on the fine details. He'd been distracted to say the least.

By the memory of the sounds she'd made. The scent of sex on her skin.

Not to mention that every time Colt looked at him, he was certain his friend saw straight through him to all the filthy things he'd done. It didn't matter that she was a grown woman, fully capable of making her own decisions; she was Colt's *sister* for fuck's sake. Maverick shook his head as he stared out the window. The landscape blurred before his eyes. He knew how protective he felt of his own younger sister, even though she too could make her own choices. What would he have done if he'd known Rogue had been seducing her?

Seducing her.

The weight of those words hit him.

Inhaling a sharp breath, he looked out over the pastures. He hadn't seduced anyone since long before Rose had passed, though he supposed he'd faced worse situations. They both knew the terms. Marriage of convenience. No love. He'd been very clear about what he couldn't be to Sierra. All he had to do was soldier through their little agreement, delicious and torturous as it would be. A few of their little lessons and he'd work her out of his system once and for all. Then after their wedding night, they'd be done with it. Live their separate lives. Maybe then, after years of wanting her from a distance, the itch would be scratched and he could finally move on with his life.

Maybe then he could find some peace.

He replayed everything she'd said, all she'd asked him. Fuck, he hadn't stood much of a chance of saying no. But he'd need to tread lightly—for both their sakes. Pushing her out of his mind, Maverick watched the last rays of sun disappear behind the snow-capped mountains. It wouldn't be long before the ceremony began.

Every year on the last full moon of their lunar calendar that marked the shift of season from autumn to winter, the Grey Wolf pack gathered as one to shift beneath the full moon. It was a ceremony as ancient as the true wolves from which they'd descended, designed for remembering their past while they navigated their future, which meant they'd be joined by the full pack. The council, the subpacks, the wolves of Wolf Pack Run. They'd all be in attendance.

Tonight, they existed as one. *Past, present, future.*

The evening would be a mingling of those concepts in more ways than one.

"We're ready for you."

The calm comment interrupted his thoughts. Maverick turned away from the window.

Blaze stood in the doorway, dwarfing the frame and looking pleasantly abnormal in a black T-shirt and a pair of worn work jeans. It was strange seeing him dressed so plain. There wasn't so much as a single flamingo, palm tree, pineapple, or other kitschy image or raunchy phrase in sight. Maverick gave an appreciative grunt and nodded toward Blaze's attire. Thankfully, even Blaze knew better than to press Maverick's patience on an evening like this.

"I figured you'd approve." Blaze shrugged. "Colt and Wes figured out what to do with the prisoners and the rogues."

Maverick struggled to hold back a grin. "You can't keep calling them that now that they're integrating into the pack."

Over a year ago, following the dissolution of the Wild Eight, the remaining at-large members had been captured and brought to Wolf Pack Run. As an opportunity to prove herself, Sierra had spearheaded the project, leading the elite warriors to bring the remaining members to justice. Since then, Wes and Colt had been working to reintegrate the bastards into pack life. Wes had insisted that like him, the two former Wild Eight members were worth saving. Tonight, they, among several rogue wolves who'd petitioned for pack membership, would officially swear loyalty to the Grey Wolves.

"I know. Wes says they're loyal." Blaze hesitated. "For now."

Blaze had never been a fan of Wes, at least not initially, and he was equally distrustful of the newly integrated Wild Eight members as well as the handful of former rogue shifters who planned to join the pack tonight. After serving in MAC-V-Alpha, a shifters-only special ops team that worked alongside the human military and the CIA, beneath his sarcastic, comedic exterior, Blaze was as lethal as they came. The Grey Wolf information security specialist had spent enough time searching out dual identities in their enemies and threats hidden behind humanity's anonymous black mirrors to be cynical, if a little impatient with anyone he perceived could be two-faced. It'd taken him considerable time to warm to Wes.

But who could blame him? Considering all he'd seen and done abroad, all the things he *still* did off the record on behalf of the pack, he carried more darkness than most on his shoulders. With a unique blend of strategic intelligence, lethal physicality, and the confidence and charm to pull the wool over the eyes of all who knew him, Blaze answered to no one. Not even Maverick, unless he chose to, which thankfully he did. If they knew the truth, perhaps the part of Blaze that would terrify both his friends and enemies the most was...

He knew how to cover his tracks.

Maverick cleared his throat. "I'm thankful for what you do for this pack. I likely don't say it enough."

Blaze shrugged. "You've never said it, and I would know. I monitor all your emails and messages, but who's counting?" He cast Maverick a wry grin.

"Add it to the ever-growing list of things I need to apologize for."

"So the Monster of Montana has an apology list now, huh?"

Maverick stiffened.

"I see and hear everything," Blaze said as a means of explanation. "You know that."

It was part of what made Blaze a valued member of the elite warriors. He protected them, all of them, even when he'd seen every one of them at their worst.

"You're not a monster, even if some of them believe it. Even if Rose believed it."

Maverick didn't respond. He couldn't find the words. They were caught in the swirl of dark memories that lived in his chest.

Blaze must have sensed his unease, because he cleared his throat. "We should head down there now, Packmaster."

They'd meet with only the elite warriors first, and then once the worst part was finished, the rest of the pack would be waiting. Maverick nodded and moved to step past him, but Blaze caught him by the shoulder. "The situation is under control, but I wanted to warn you," he said quickly.

Maverick grunted to encourage him to continue.

"One of the foot soldiers traced an unfamiliar scent near the edge of the territory. A wolf, but not pack. We followed the scent, but the trail went cold. Whoever it is, he passed the boundary lines and guards with ease, so he's either trained or likely had help…"

Which meant they had a traitor in their midst.

Maverick's upper lip twitched with unchecked rage.

"We don't have eyes on him yet," Blaze continued, "but I wanted your word before…"

Before they took the bastard out. One word from him and the insurgent wolf's life would be snuffed out in an instant. Maverick would never lose an ounce of sleep. Never even give it a second thought. That kind of power isolated a man.

All the more reason he was better off alone.

Closing his eyes, he inhaled a steadying breath.

This was all he had now. Years of dedicating himself to this pack, to his role had ensured that was all he'd ever have for himself. And yet…

Would he give it up? If he had the chance?

He'd never been certain.

Maverick cleared his throat. "Find him. His death is mine."

Blaze nodded. Silently, the elite warrior trailed Maverick as they headed out of the compound. As they stepped outside, the wind whipped past them, the dropping temperatures promising to bring an increasing number of chills throughout the night. They headed across the pastures.

"Are you worried?" Blaze broke the silence.

Maverick quirked a brow.

"About tonight?"

They both knew the outsider was here with only one purpose.

Maverick released a long breath. Perhaps he should be worried. Years ago, when he'd first became packmaster, he might have been. But now, after so many battles and wounds had left him a seasoned warrior, worry wasn't worth his time.

"I can't live in fear of the moment I draw my last breath. I wouldn't function if I did."

Blaze huffed a laugh with a small smile as if he understood the feeling, but Maverick didn't press further. They headed out toward the forest. As they did, Maverick glanced over his shoulder, the lights of the compound fading into the distance.

He would die someday. They all would.

The only thing he feared was that when death claimed him, he wouldn't have the will to fight against it.

Chapter 11

THE SIGNIFICANCE OF THIS MOMENT DIDN'T ESCAPE HER. A PERsistent dampness hung in the air, the earthy smell of running water against rock filling Sierra's nose as she reached the caves. She ducked inside the cavern, her bones instantly appreciating the shield from the freezing Montana winds. An arctic front had begun spilling over the Milk River Ridge in the north, causing the temperature to steadily drop throughout the state by twenty degrees within an hour.

They'd gotten snow by midday, and even now with evening set in, the fluffy white stuff still hadn't quit coming down. Thankfully, they'd arranged their pasture rotation to anticipate the dropping temperatures and the timing of the ceremony earlier in the year, because the Montana weather waited for no one.

By Sierra's guess, the inside of the cave was a fair fifty degrees Fahrenheit, balmy in comparison to what her packmates would endure waiting out on the mountainside. Inside, Maverick and Blaze waited for her.

The packmaster spoke first. "Tell me you left that damn horse of yours in the stable, or at least tied to a tree." He didn't look amused at the prospect of Randy roaming about.

She sighed. "Yes."

"And the rooster?"

Sierra frowned. When he asked it like that, she supposed it *did* highlight how silly her menagerie of pets was coming to be. "Yes, and the rooster," she huffed. "But his name is Elvis—the King to you—and that *damn horse* has a name, too. It's Randy."

Maverick grumbled in response before he turned away.

A grin curled Blaze's lips as he cast a glance toward where their surly packmaster descended the stone staircase. "You have to admit, Randy's really more of a descriptor than a name though, isn't it?"

Sierra cast him a hard look. After having served with him in MAC-V-Alpha and considering that he was one of Dakota's best friends, Sierra had never known Blaze to thwart her before. "Traitor," she mumbled under her breath with a smile.

To her surprise, Maverick stopped on one of the lower steps. His gaze narrowed on her. "Be careful tossing that word around, warrior." The biting order in his tone caught her off guard.

Without another word, Maverick eased his way farther down the carved, damp steps, clearly expecting her and Blaze to follow as Blaze filled her in on the news of the insurgent and the assistance he'd likely had in making it onto the ranch. As he finished, Sierra released a long breath. She appreciated that she was now in the know alongside the other elite warriors, but that didn't make the news sit any easier. She watched Maverick descending the steps ahead of them, contemplating strategies she and the others could use to ensure their packmaster's safety. In truth, she was more than a bit afraid for him.

They needed to end this threat against him and fast.

Hopefully, the ceremony would do just that, or so the other warriors had hinted, though how she wasn't certain.

She followed the other two wolves down the narrow stone-carved staircase. Over the past fifty years, since Maverick's grandfather's days as packmaster, the pack had installed a network of artificial lighting, making it easier to see the several hundred-foot drops inside the mountain cave. Sierra still recalled stories Maverick's mother had told her of his great-grandfather using chicken wire as a ladder to the depths below.

Since the four founding families of the Grey Wolf Pack—the Greys, the Blacks, the Cavanaughs, and the Calhouns—had first formed the pack in 1857 when Manifest Destiny had brought an influx of humans out west, Wolf Den Caverns had been a safe haven, a hideaway from human eyes that harkened back to the cave homes of the true wolves from which they descended and now, hundreds of years later, served as a temple for their ancestors. Originally descendants of the Clovis people, their current heritage was a mixture of various Native American tribal ancestry blended with the mixed-race settlers of Manifest Destiny's claim for the West, all before mating with humans had been against pack law. But their original kind had made their home here since the Pleistocene period, and since as far back as their oral history went, the cave had been used for those purposes—the ceremony and their burial grounds.

She'd be the first female ever to witness what happened each year within its depths.

Maverick and Blaze reached the bottom of the cavern stairs first, and she joined them a moment later at Maverick's side. Spinning in a slow circle, she glanced around her, taking in the breathtaking view. The twenty-foot stalagmites and stalactites told a beautiful, intimidating story of natural battles waged and millennia past. It was a reminder that this ground had been here before them and still would be long after them. It was both their privilege and responsibility to be good stewards of the Earth, the Mother Wolf, which had birthed them. Sierra inhaled a deep breath, her ears pricked to the slightest noise in the darkness.

Maverick turned toward her, the vibrant green of his eyes flecked with the gold of the wolf within. "Are you ready?"

She nodded, unable to form words courtesy of the nervous anticipation twisting her insides.

"They're waiting." Blaze tilted his chin toward the darkness up ahead.

Over the uneven rock, they followed the trail every packmaster in their history had for the last hundred and fifty years. Sierra had been in the caves before, for the burial of both her mother and father, but never this deep. Never here. The sound of the running stream and the din of hushed voices echoed off the cavern walls. They navigated several smaller drops and uneven climbs before they finally reached their destination. The last drop-off led to a grotto, culminating in a small waterfall, where in the dim orange of the cave lights, the other Grey Wolf elite warriors waited.

Sierra lingered behind a few steps.

"Not even the Duke of Windsor makes so grand an entrance." Jasper's thickly accented words cut through the silence as he set eyes on Maverick.

Maverick reached out a hand to pull Jasper and then Ace into a brotherly hug. Ace was the skilled Grey Wolf carpenter, who when he didn't have a hammer in his hand was a cowboy who loved to work with his hands as methodically as he killed with them on the battlefield. Ace had been out in the western subpacks for the past several months in an attempt to help restore the Missoula ranch the vampires had previously ravaged, but Jasper on the other hand hadn't set foot on the pastures of Wolf Pack Run in more than a few months.

The Indian British-born Grey Wolf liaison was an international jet-setter responsible for handling the pack's international business interests, and as such, Jasper hadn't been in the States in well over a year. He was the kind of wolf who traded a Stetson and cowboy boots for Armani loafers. He didn't live the life of a billion-dollar business mogul; he embodied it. He could cut a deal with that sharp tongue of his as quickly as he cut their enemy's throats.

Maverick clapped the other wolf on the shoulder. "It's been too long, brother."

"You'd be right 'bout that." Jasper flashed a charming, white-toothed grin.

Sierra smiled. "Where's your next stop? Dubai?"

At the sound of Sierra's voice, Jasper turned toward her. "Well, would you look at that." Jasper pulled Sierra in for a quick hug as she waved over his shoulder at Ace.

Ace tipped his Stetson.

"Singapore, actually," Jasper answered. When he pulled back, his dark eyes cut to Maverick as he ran a hand through his silky midnight hair, deferring to his alpha on how to react further to having Sierra present in their little fraternity powwow.

Maverick beckoned her forward to join the group as he addressed them. "Sierra is one of you now. Treat her with the same respect and loyalty you would any brother-in-arms."

All the men nodded, none of them daring to question his word.

Her brother cleared his throat, coming to her rescue in the awkward silence that followed. "The pack will be waiting." It was a reminder of the task that lay ahead of them. The timing of the moon waited for no one.

"Before we get started, I've got something new I want to try this year," Blaze said.

All the elite warriors, save for Sierra, let out a collective groan.

"What's that?" She quirked a brow as she watched Blaze dig out what appeared to be ten small microchips from his pocket. Watching him do so reminded her far too much of a particular mission they'd served on together in MAC-V-Alpha. Not only had the technology he'd developed led them straight to their enemies, but when she and the rest of the soldiers had gotten held up by a pipe bomb in the midst of their storm raid, Blaze, whose duty it'd been to swoop in from an alternative route, had taken out every one of those lethal m-fers.

Single-handedly.

After that, she'd never questioned his capabilities again.

"Every year, Blaze makes us wear some newfangled contraption he's rigged up to try to record what happens," Austin drawled. The Texan ran his fingers through his dark, curly hair.

"The adhesive from last year's gave me a rash." Malcolm scowled.

Dean leaned in and whispered to her, the ends of several of his dreads brushing her shoulder. "And there's never anything to show for it."

Blaze frowned. "This year will be different."

"He says that every year," Dean mumbled to her.

"Blaze's technology in MAC-V-Alpha saved our lives. More than once," Sierra said, coming to his defense. There was more to Blaze than met the eye, more than his kitschy flamingo shirts. Though the other warriors were clearly just joking with their friend to get a rise out of him.

Blaze fiddled with the equipment, using a pair of pliers he'd pulled from his back pocket to connect each chip to a thin wire. "Humans have managed to get rudimentary versions of thoughts and dreams projected onto a screen. It's the same technology, only more advanced."

"Or so he says," Dean added.

"New technologies take trial and error." Blaze shot Dean an annoyed glare. "And we're in a cave. It echoes. I can hear you."

"I'm aware." Dean cast Blaze a charming grin.

"Can it with the bickering." Malcolm, the Grey Wolf executioner, snarled. "You idiots are already giving me a headache."

Sierra's brow furrowed while she watched Blaze make his rounds, using rounded yellow pads that he appeared to be hooking up to the microchips before fastening the first one to poor Austin's forehead. The Texan stood patiently, likely the only amiable subject Blaze would find for his experiment all evening.

Sierra watched with genuine interest. "If you want to record it, why not use a video camera?"

Blaze laughed. "I don't really care to watch what we all look like writhing on the ground in an unconscious state, if you catch my drift. I care to capture what's up here." He tapped his forehead.

Now she was well and truly confused. "Beg your pardon?"

"The memory transfer."

Her brow drew low. "Memory transfer?"

At her confusion, Wes shook his head as if he were disappointed before his gaze darted to Colt. "Damn, brother, you really are tight lipped, aren't you?"

Maverick shot a glance in Colt's direction. "You never told her?" The graveled question was spoken with more than a hint of disapproval.

"You've expressly ordered us not to," Colt said in way of defense.

Sierra rolled her eyes. He may have once been a ladies' man, but when it came to serving the pack, her brother was such a golden boy. At least when it suited him.

Maverick growled. "I've ordered all of you to do lots of things you never listen to. Wes in particular."

Wes frowned. "Hey, now, I wasn't even a part of this, but you roped me into it."

Ace fiddled with the edge of his Stetson. "That's because you're always the one roping everyone else into it."

"Into refusing to be obedient zombies who follow every order?" Sierra asked.

Wes grinned. "See, she gets it." He punched Colt in the arm playfully. "I always knew I wanted a sister more than a brother."

Sierra smiled as she shook her head. Was this what being an elite warrior would be like? Verbal sparring with this motley crew of alpha males for the rest of her career? She'd didn't mind it as much as she should. Hadn't she always played this role with them? Only now she was finally being recognized as their equal rather than as Colt's little sister. She still loved them all as her brothers.

Save for one.

Her thoughts turned to Maverick's words in the stables, to the things they'd done. No one had ever touched her like that before, made her feel like that.

There's nothing brotherly about how I feel about you.

Heat filled her face, and she made a show of scraping some dirt off one of her boots to hide the sudden blush burning her cheeks. Pushing the thoughts aside, she cleared her throat. "In any case, someone needs to fill me in."

"The reason we come down here every year is because since the founding of our pack, we've found a way to communicate with our ancestral roots," Colt elaborated.

Her breath caught. "So it's true then? The magic?"

More than a few rumors had been passed among her packmates about what happened down here every year.

Colt shook his head. "Not exactly. It's a form of genetic memory that seems to exist only in the absence of a sensory experience. It's been incorporated into the pack's genetic genome over the course of our existence."

"And as packmaster, that big lothario over there is the conduit to accessing it, of course." Blaze nodded toward Maverick, who snarled in response to Blaze's descriptor.

Wes shrugged. "Maverick goes into this weird, wolfy voodoo trance, and we can all see inside his head."

Sierra's jaw dropped. "What?"

Colt gestured to her expression. "That's *exactly* why I hadn't told her."

Maverick frowned. "The guidance gained from this is what has given the pack such longevity. It helps us survive." From the grim look on his face, she recognized how important that survival was to him. The weight of the pack's existence rested on his shoulders.

She inhaled a sharp breath. She wasn't unmoved by everything that continued sacrifice cost him. At least in that way, she understood him, perhaps better than most. That same drive to protect everyone they both cared for had driven her to this moment.

"How does it work?" she asked.

Blaze shrugged as he twisted the pliers to connect a wire for use on his next victim, this time Malcolm, who was glaring at the adhesive in Blaze's hand as if it were the devil itself. "Well, we're never certain what exactly will pop up inside that thick skull of his. Usually, we have to put up with a few random bits of Mav's memory before we get to any pertinent information about whatever existential crisis we're facing, and typically we have to decipher or interpret it, but how do you think we all came to a consensus about allowing that asshole into the pack?" Blaze nodded toward Wes.

Wes rolled his eyes before he cast Maverick a wry smirk. "And to think I always thought you just had a soft spot for me."

Maverick grumbled a dismissive response under his breath that Sierra didn't fully hear. Something about luck and duty and disappointment that he hadn't been able to take Wes out *before* he'd become one of them.

Sierra fought to hide her grin. She wasn't certain she believed any of that for a second. Despite the packmaster's insistence otherwise, she had a feeling that Wes's statement wasn't entirely off the mark.

"Based on that year's genetic memory," Blaze continued, "we all agreed that one of our enemies was going to fall and their leader would ask to join us, and when they did, Maverick should let them because that would strengthen the pack. The information gathered from this has always proved relevant, though some years better than others." Blaze now stood beside Maverick, positioning the chip he was attaching to Maverick's temple. With each additional repositioning of the adhesive, Maverick bared his canines further.

She smiled. *Always more wolf than man.*

"So this year, that pertinent information would be…?"

"Who wants me dead." Mav's gaze shot to hers and locked there.

The grim warning in his voice shot a chill down her spine, but it was more than that. He held her gaze. It was the first time he'd truly looked at her since they'd been alone in the stable together, and though nothing in his expression indicated any intimacy between them, it was as if his wolf was barely contained within his skin. She could feel his presence as her alpha and the heat that simmered beneath the gold eyes of his wolf, and more importantly, she had a feeling the other warriors, her brother included, could see it too.

She forced herself to tear her gaze away, clearing her throat. Had she been in wolf form, her tail might have wagged, and she may have panted with anticipation.

Down, girl, she scolded herself.

"Why don't we use this all the time then?" Her voice cracked slightly at the end of the question.

Thankfully, her brother came to her verbal rescue once again. "It only works on this one moon every year. We know the change in lunar cycle and tides has always had a profound impact on all wildlife, the pack in particular, but if Maverick goes into an unconscious state while he's wolf during this period, it seems to unlock something primal in our genetic makeup."

Austin gestured to his medical kit, indicating he was prepared. "Not to mention, it's probably a good idea to have all the pack on standby should our enemies attack while all of our elite warriors are otherwise incapacitated."

Sierra breathed out a long breath. "That's the reason for the secrecy. Because if any of our enemies ever found out what happened down here…"

"It'd be a prime opportunity to attack while our strongest men were down," her brother finished.

In the brief silence that followed, several of the warriors cast their eyes toward the rock above them, as if to question the safety of their pack above. With an unknown insurgent on their land, each passing minute risked a greater threat to the pack.

"Men *and* women," Sierra added, drawing their attention back to the task at hand.

"And women," Colt amended.

Blaze was nearly finished attaching the last of his devices to Jasper and Ace. Now that she understood the process, Sierra recognized why the packmaster and elite warriors indulged him each year. In the event the technology worked, being able to access even that brief experience of the pack's genetic memory would prove invaluable. Otherwise, their own conscious memories of the experience would be their only guide.

Jasper leaned against the cave wall, relaxing as Blaze moved on to Ace. "It's doubtful Mav 'ere would want to do it more than once a year anyway, considering it puts 'im through the wringer."

Her brows shot up. "It hurts him?" She didn't like the idea of that.

"Not the memory sharing," Jasper answered.

Wes shrugged. "The nearly killing him part."

Her eyes went wide again. "What?" Tonight was full of more twists than she cared for.

Maverick snarled. "You could stop talking about me as if I'm not in the room."

Austin shook his head. "It doesn't nearly kill him. It just puts his body in a state of distress. When he shifts into his wolf, it must be out of survival necessity, or it won't work."

Sierra wrinkled her nose in distaste. "That's archaic."

Blaze finished fastening the chip to Ace's head and then made his way toward her. Apparently, she was his next victim.

Jasper shot her a skeptical glare. "We do what works." There was more meaning in that statement than she cared to decipher.

Ace shoved his hands into the pockets of his worn work jeans. "And this time, it could save his life."

"Is it safe to be doing this when we know someone's on the ranch hunting you?" This time, she addressed the question directly to Maverick.

"It goes quickly, warrior."

She knew it was an attempt to reassure her, but she didn't feel reassured in the slightest.

"Though it's never been done with a female present before." Blaze's offhand comment caused her to stiffen as he attached the adhesive to her temple.

Of course. The Elder Council's resistance to her appointment suddenly made sense. They'd feared if a female warrior was present that perhaps the ceremony wouldn't work. Not that those old, curmudgeonly bastards making decisions that blocked pack progress out of pure fear made their choices any better.

Colt glanced at his watch. "We do this now or we miss the opportunity."

Sierra hadn't intended to question the tradition in her first moments as an elite warrior, but her instinctive unease with the situation wouldn't be silenced. "Couldn't we get information from the insurgent?"

"Not as trustworthy as this," her brother answered.

The looks on all the other warriors' faces were grim, and she understood instantly.

There was no other way.

Maverick turned toward Austin. The Grey Wolf medic already had his medical kit in hand. Austin removed a small vial from inside, and she recognized the substance inside instantly.

Liquid silver.

It was poison to their kind. As Austin passed the vial to Maverick, who promptly uncorked it, she stepped forward, filled with the instinct to protect him.

Her brother caught hold of her hand and gave it a quick squeeze. Apparently, she wasn't the only person in the room who didn't feel right about the idea of their packmaster in pain.

Maverick tossed back the contents of the vial, swallowing the liquid silver without so much as a second thought. Sierra's breath caught. She wasn't certain even her brother or Wes would ever do anything so brave without hesitation. But that was what Maverick did, wasn't it? Put his life on the line with ease.

All in the name of protecting those he loved.

"She has a point." Wes cleared his throat. "Maybe next year it won't be necessary?"

Colt shot him a disapproving look, never one to question tradition.

Wes gestured toward her. "What? It's been less than a week since he threw himself on a blade for your sister."

Maverick met Wes's eyes. His irises glowed with the gold of his wolf reacting to the silver in his system. "Going to miss me if something goes wrong?"

Wes frowned. Sierra half expected some rebellious or sarcastic retort, but instead the Grey Wolf second-in-command resisted. "Yes. You've made me into the man I am today. Your leadership makes us *all* better, and I don't say it enough, but I'm grateful."

A round of affirmations followed as the other elite warriors expressed their agreement, though Sierra remained silent, her fear for Maverick caught in her throat.

"It's true," Dean echoed. "It's never felt right to me."

Maverick waded his way into the shallow depths of the river springs, the icy water drenching the hems of his jeans. "I'm no more important than the rest of you. No more integral or needed to this pack."

A lump formed inside Sierra's throat. His words didn't ring true. Not at all. He *was* important. Even before he'd become packmaster.

To her, he always had been.

Maverick reached down into the water, scooping a handful of graveled dirt into his hand. He smeared the earth across his face and chest as if it were war paint.

As his second, Wes stepped forward to join him.

"At least you don't have to get his blood all over you like Bo used to." Blaze shrugged.

Malcolm's gaze darkened at the mention of Maverick's fallen second-in-command. Sierra had little doubt that there had been more to Malcolm and Bo's relationship than mere friendship. Malcolm had never quite been the same since then.

"Poor bastard," Jasper said, referencing the fallen soldier.

Wes nodded at Austin, who'd clearly been responsible for discovering they could use liquid silver to force Maverick into the right state instead of drawing blood. "Thanks for that."

Maverick knelt in the water, leaning backward. Sierra's heart pounded in her chest as Wes placed a hand on Maverick's shoulder. The two men exchanged glances.

She wanted to be stoic. To blend in with the other warriors and not look weak, pretend as if watching him place himself in mortal peril on their behalf didn't faze her, like she was as hardened and callous as the men were, but she couldn't.

"I've always hated this part," Maverick growled. To her surprise, the packmaster cast a reluctant glance toward her, the molten gold of his wolf eyes scorching through her.

"I know." Wes flicked a glance toward her, too, then back to Maverick. As Wes's eyes met the packmaster's again, he nodded, a sense of understanding in his face.

Fuck looking weak. Let them think what they wanted of her. She was female. She could be as strong as the rest of them *and* care for the man they called their leader.

She stepped forward again, but her brother caught her by the wrist again, harder this time. She tore her hand away from him, overpowering his strength. But the momentary pause was long enough. She couldn't watch this. She couldn't. Her heart lurched.

"See you in hell, Packmaster." Wes shoved Maverick backward, submerging him in the water's depths.

Chapter 12

BOTH MAVERICK AND THE PACK STILL WEREN'T SURE WHAT DID the trick. Whether it was the mix of water and earth, the close brush with death, or the suggestive psychology of over a hundred years' tradition, they weren't certain. But every year, in Wolf Den Caverns, something happened…and for the briefest of moments, the veil between the land of the living and the land of the dead stretched thin and the elite warriors of the pack reached a collective consciousness.

Maverick opened his eyes. Beneath the surface of the water, he could scarcely decipher the blurred details of Wes's face. He lingered there for a moment, the air seeping from his lungs until there was none left, and then, against his will, he thrashed, his wolf fighting for survival until he was forced to shift into his true form. There was always violence when brushing elbows with death. There was nothing peaceful about it. Even the memories and visions came as quick flashes at first, faster and more painful than the slash of a dagger. All of it somehow separate but still a part of him, until finally one lingered.

James had been right. The expectation on their faces changed everything. Maverick stood inside the entryway of the packmaster's apartment, feeling as out of place and awkward as the newly placed furniture. The air smelled of fresh paint and peeled plastic wrap, the combination of which was quickly giving his wolf a headache. He'd forgotten exactly how this memory had felt in the moment until now…

Until now that he was experiencing it anew.

He was only vaguely aware of that separate part of himself, the part that was questioning why here, why now, why this memory.

He glanced around the fresh decorations, trying to make sense of the turmoil shaking him. He'd never spent much time in this place. His father had retreated here during times of peril for the pack, but he'd always returned to their family home. He supposed that was one minor detail Thomas Maverick Sr. hadn't taken painstaking lengths to prepare him for: that his first task as packmaster of the Grey Wolves would be something as dull as picking out furniture.

Maverick dropped into one of the armchairs he'd chosen. His older consciousness sank into the familiar memory with ease, as if the memory were the present. Doing so was as simple as sinking deeper into the cushions of the armchair. He supposed the pack figured that picking furniture was all he could handle at this point in the wake of grief over his father's death and the frenzy of expectation and tradition that followed thereafter. He'd been preparing for this moment his whole life, yet now that it was here, it seemed a little anticlimactic.

The entry door to the apartment opened with a loud creak.

He didn't bother to glance over his shoulder, but suddenly he was speaking. It was his voice, his memory. They were words he'd once said, but he hadn't recollected them until now. "I never wanted this. The role, the pomp and circumstance. I thought none of it would matter, but now that I'm here, you were right. His legacy, it . . ." He inhaled a long, slow breath. "It weighs on me."

A moment of silence followed as he waited for James's response, but it never came.

"You'll be more than worthy." The feminine voice that answered sent an immediate jolt of awareness through his body.

No.

He recalled the memory in full detail now, struggling to change its course and push past it to what the pack needed him to see, beyond this moment that he didn't want his men or, more importantly, her to see, but he couldn't.

Maverick stood and faced the door. Instead of James Cavanaugh, then high commander, standing in the doorway, he knew the face he'd find there.

"Sierra." He breathed her name half as a question, half as recognition. That was the only person this young woman who was standing there could be. She had the same warm, honey eyes, the same golden-blond hair, the same curve of full lips, square jaw, and slightly upturned nose, and yet she was different; everything about her was different. Because this wasn't a young girl who stood before him. This was a woman, with curves and hips and mouthwatering breasts that made him want to...

Maverick averted his eyes. What in the blazing fuck was wrong with him? Sierra was practically his sister, or at least he'd always thought of her as such...until now. There was nothing even close to sisterly about the thoughts running through his head or the suddenly raging hard-on he sported between his legs. Sweet Jesus, if Colt ever found out he'd even looked twice at her...

"Maverick, are you okay?" she asked. Her voice was different, too, no longer girlish and young but huskier and more...sultry. Fuck, there was no other word for it.

"Don't you think you should put some...some clothes on?" he managed to sputter out. He sounded like a complete imbecile, which, at the moment, he probably was. He made some sort of awkward gesture to the sports bra and well-fitted workout pants she was wearing before he made the mistake of glancing up at her, just in time to watch her smooth a hand over the dramatic curve of her hip.

"Oh, I just came from the gym." She shrugged as if he couldn't tell.

He was well aware of that, considering he was trying hard not to focus on a tantalizing bead of sweat that trailed from her neck down into a crevice of her cleavage. Cleavage that had never been there before...

"Yes, and someone might...see you."

"See me?" she echoed back. It sounded even more absurd when she repeated it. Shit, if he wasn't making himself into a complete tool. She frowned. "I didn't think I looked that bad."

"You don't." He wanted to tell her she looked good, so good he didn't want any other man, wolf or otherwise, to ever lay eyes on her again. The thought of anyone looking at her and even thinking similar thoughts to the array of scenarios running through his mind caused a feral growl to nearly escape his throat. He shook his head, trying to chase the thoughts away, before he waved a hand in dismissal. "Forget I said anything. I'm just surprised to see you, that's all. I thought you were—"

"My dad," she finished for him. A sly smile crossed her lips. "I had to argue my case pretty thoroughly to get him to yield his time to me, but as I told him, he'll have plenty of time to bend your ear and give you advice now that you'll be packmaster."

"And that's what brought you all the way back home? Giving me advice?"

Sierra was smart, wickedly so, and a fierce fighter to boot. From the time she'd been a young girl first able to give voice to her opinions, she'd made it clear that she wanted nothing more than to be a trailblazer— the first female elite warrior the pack had ever seen. She'd spent her whole life training for it, despite her father's half-hearted protests, even to the point that for the past few years, she'd been off serving in MAC-V-Alpha, a shifters-only special ops team that, for all intents and purposes, didn't exist on paper. He'd waited for letters from her and brief visits home with bated breath.

When she left, she'd still been a girl, barely a day over eighteen, but now…he couldn't imagine what advice this she-wolf, this woman had come to give him.

"I guess you could call it advice." She paused to consider that before changing the subject. "Did you mean what you said when I came in? That you don't want to be packmaster?"

He wasn't certain how to answer that. He was going to be pack-master, whether he wanted to or not. It was his birthright, his duty, his destiny as he'd been told so many times before. It had been since the moment of his birth, and yet…would he have chosen it for himself?

He wasn't sure.

"I don't want it to change me," he confessed. "My mother always said it changed my father, and the way she said it made me think…"

"That she didn't like the change it brought about in him?"

He nodded.

"For what it's worth, I think it will only change you as much as you let it."

"I don't know that I'll have much of a choice." Not when that choice would be between his own selfishness and the lives of those he cared for. From somewhere distant, he was vaguely aware that statement had proved truer than he'd known in that moment.

He swallowed the lump forming in his throat and forced himself to turn away from her, focusing instead on straightening a nearby frame on the wall. A portrait of his father.

Just his father. Alone.

He was vaguely aware that in the true memory, his younger self hadn't been able to turn away from her, which meant perhaps he could gain control, curb this memory for the better.

Before it revealed too much…

"So what piece of advice brought you all the way home from basic training? Must be a doozy." He sounded so much younger, even to his own ears. Now, he would've grumbled a vague response. He wouldn't have bothered to ask her or push further.

Because as a young man, he hadn't known better.

He hadn't yet learned of all the things he couldn't have.

Though he was about to.

"Well, I guess I'm breaking tradition again, because it's not really advice as much as it is a…confession."

His breath caught. He couldn't bring himself to breathe.

Older him wanted to keep looking at the portrait, to save her the embarrassment of her brother, all her fellow warriors knowing the secrets between them, but try as he might, he couldn't stop himself.

He turned toward her, the hopeful look in her eye and the visible blush on her cheeks more obvious than if she'd said the words outright.

She cared for him…or she once had. At least until…

She inhaled a deep breath. "I wanted to tell you that I—"

The door to the apartment flew open, causing them both to jump as her father came striding into the room. "Time's up."

Sierra blinked at him, shaken by the sudden intrusion on what she'd clearly intended to be an intimate moment, before she gathered her wits and glanced down at her watch. "It's been less than four minutes. You told me I had—"

"Plans have changed." James's words were spoken with the calm, steady authority of a soldier who didn't allow room for questions. Not when the pack was at stake. In retrospect, it was a tone so like what his oldest son would later adopt that it was almost eerie.

"But…" Sierra glanced back toward Maverick as if hoping that he, too, would protest.

His older self would have. He wanted to hear everything she had to say, everything he regretted never hearing when he had the chance, but his younger self had been too intimidated by James's presence and the weight of the crown soon to be laid upon his head.

Of everything he was supposed to do. Of all he was supposed to be.

James nodded toward the door again, a silent order.

With her indignant huff, Sierra's hands clenched into fists, her obvious embarrassment clearly driving her from the room as much as her father's order. As she left, she paused near the doorway, casting a quick glance toward him.

A part of himself, even then, had been vaguely aware that'd be the last time she'd ever look at him that way, as if there was hope for something more between them.

That hopeful look pierced him deeper than any blade that had ever wounded him.

The moment passed as quickly as it came, leaving him with an aching feeling gripping his chest. Sierra left, pulling the door shut behind her. As she did, Maverick felt himself stiffen.

No. If allowing her former feelings to be broadcast to the other elite warriors of the pack hadn't been bad enough, this would be worse. He *fought to go after her, to change the course of the memory and escape the harsh reality of James's next words, but he couldn't.*

Not without coming back to himself completely. Not without risking everything. The pack. The intel. His own life.

Monster, *his current conscious hissed.*

"Did something happen?" The grim look on James's face put him on edge.

"No." James shook his head. Though the high commander's tense stance relaxed, the tone of his gaze remained dark. "But I couldn't allow that conversation with my daughter to continue."

Maverick shifted his weight from one foot to the other. "Sir, I..."

James shook his head, his tone shifting back to stern command. "You no longer address me as 'sir.' I may be your senior by more than a few moons, but you are alpha now."

Maverick swallowed hard. "James, I know I'm older than Sierra, but..."

"It's not about the age difference, Maverick."

The use of his name surprised him, even now as it had then. Since the moment his father had passed, James had referred to him as nothing other than Packmaster. He knew it had been meant to reinforce the inevitable changes that followed in the flurry of his father's death, but the sudden reversion to his given name caught him off guard.

It was a reminder of everything James was and had been to him. His father's high commander and friend. To Maverick, a role model, a surrogate father that often had replaced his own. His own father had been too consumed by his duty to the pack to play that role to him.

Or too consumed with the power that had corrupted him, Maverick's awareness whispered.

Maverick struggled to reroute the memory, to mitigate the damage of the words about to come.

James gripped the back of the armchair, his fingers flexing over the fabric of the chair. "You can't choose Sierra as your mate."

Maverick sputtered. "I—"

James raised a hand. "Have more respect for me than that. I've known a long time that was where the two of you were headed. I may be an old man to you, but she's my daughter, and I know the way you look at her. But for the sake of the pack, you have to choose another."

Maverick remained silent, unable to find the words, though inside he was shouting, snarling. With every ounce of his being, he urged the memory away, trying desperately to push beyond his past before the memory progressed too far.

To a place he wasn't certain he could come back from.

James dropped his hand from the armchair, as if accepting Maverick's lack of outward protest as a sign of his acceptance. "Your mate will be Rose Everleigh."

"Rose?" The name felt as wrong on his tongue then as it did now. He'd barely exchanged more than a handful of words with Rose. She was quiet, unassuming, practically demure. There was nothing wrong with her, but she was...

Everything Sierra wasn't.

James crossed the room, gripping the door handle as if he not only anticipated Maverick's acceptance of this reality, he expected it. "She's the cousin of Alexander Caron, the young wolf who will be packmaster of the Yellowknife Pack."

Their Arctic wolf brethren in the Canadian north.

"Marrying her will cement an alliance with their pack. With the Wild Eight's power growing every day and the vampires constantly at our heels, it's in the best interest of all of us that we maintain as many allies as we can get."

All of us.

The weight of that phrase didn't escape him.

He had more than his own happiness to think about.

He opened his mouth, but still the memory persisted.

No.

Maverick tore through the veil, fighting his way back to himself. He shifted into human form, abruptly coming up from the water depths with a harsh gasp. The other elite warriors lay in various states across the cave floor, having clearly been jolted from the sudden and premature awakening. From appearance, no more than a few seconds of time had passed, yet in his mind, it had felt like an eternity.

An eternity of fighting, hoping, praying that none of them saw or heard the words that had been about to come.

He slicked his hair back, throwing the water from his nape as he gripped the long strands at the base of his skull. Fuck. The intel. They hadn't even gotten close, but if he'd held on any longer, they would have known, *she* would have known, and considering their agreement...

His gaze darted toward where Sierra had stood only moments before. She lay on the cave floor in wolf form, the gold of her wolf eyes swirled white and cloudy.

She was still there, locked in the memory, though the rest of them had always been forced to exit when he had, which meant...

"Sierra," he breathed.

He didn't think. He tore through the water, rushing to her side.

Having come to, Wes swore from beside him. "Shit," he said, looking toward Sierra and clearly realizing that something was wrong.

Terribly wrong.

As Maverick reached her, he gripped her by the scruff. He'd shake her awake as her alpha, as her protector, if that was what it took...

Before he could do so, a harsh grip on his shoulder tore him back.

Blaze growled. "The chip is working. If you pull her out now, then..."

Then they would lose everything.

He snarled at Blaze, snapping his teeth even though he was in human form and refusing to listen. Lethal warrior or not, the action instantly drove Blaze back into his place in the pack hierarchy. In the quivering reflection of the water's edge, Maverick saw the bright intensity as his own wolf eyes glowed. There was no point in trying to hide it from them now. They all knew.

The message in the single look he gave them all was clearer than the words he'd whispered in a painful, dark memory.

I love her.

Or at least, he once had. Long ago.

He wasn't certain he was capable of the emotion anymore.

But he felt it then as he once had years ago and maybe always had, even if he couldn't have her any more now than he could then. He'd be damned if he risked her life for anything. But the risk wasn't to the pack.

The only risk was his own.

He turned toward Sierra, pulling her into his arms by the scruff of her fur as he dropped to his knees, the words of her father echoing in his head.

Love is something a packmaster can't afford.

He gripped her hard by her thick gray fur. He knew that now. He'd learned that lesson, perhaps more intimately than any other lesson he'd learned in his life. The moment he'd lost Rose, his one jilted chance at happiness.

My daughter deserves better than a life with a man who will never be able to choose her.

Sierra did deserve better, and so had Rose.

Your life and the life of the pack are inextricably linked.

Which was why though he now held Sierra in his arms, wanting to shake her awake, as his calloused, ranch-worn fingers worked through the coarse hair of her fur, he was unable to do so.

She deserves better than a man who will never be able to put her first.

He'd known that then as he still knew that now.

Monster, his internal critic hissed.

And if you do love her, James's voice echoed, *you'll remember that.*

Throwing back his head, Maverick held Sierra unconscious in his arms as he released a long howl, a haunting, pain-filled sound that rang and echoed off the walls of the cave. He would remember that lesson, now more than ever.

Because if he didn't, it would be more than her life at stake.

Chapter 13

THERE WAS NO SUCH THING AS MERCY WHEN THE PACK'S SHE-wolves were on the prowl. In her mind's eye, Sierra was in the forest, hunting for the insurgent. She was close now. So close she could practically smell him, taste his filthy blood on her tongue. She rounded a tree, sword in hand, but suddenly she wasn't alone anymore.

This part of the forest was...familiar and the deep voice that thrummed through her even more comforting.

"Sneaking around with your father's spare sword again, I see."

She turned to find Maverick standing behind her, but instead of the packmaster she now knew, he was younger by years, the same Maverick she visited often in her memories—before everything had changed between them. There was a playful grin on his face, a far easier, more relaxed expression than she'd seen from him in years. Lord, how she'd missed that smile, that intense look in his eyes that could melt her heart and set a fire burning in her belly all with one crook of his white-toothed grin.

And the sound of her name on his lips...

"Sierra." He tipped his Stetson in greeting like the true cowboy he was. He'd always worn one, since he'd been a boy. He'd been so eager to be like the men on the ranch, like his father and hers. But as he was now, in this memory, he was already a man in all the ways that mattered. But a younger one. She remembered this moment, now that it was playing out before her. Though weren't the memories supposed to be his? Not hers? Somehow, she couldn't think straight about that. Every time she did, her conscious felt clouded, muddied.

All she knew was she was here now, when he'd been young and moving up the pack's warrior ranks with incredible ease, as if they all didn't already know that someday he would be their leader, their king.

She glanced down at the sword in her hand. Sure enough, it wasn't her own but the spare sword her father kept hidden in the back of his weapons closet. He'd never noticed it missing on the occasions she'd thought to steal it away, since he favored his claymore. She glanced down at her hand, noticing that the scar on her left thumb she'd once received from wielding this weapon was nowhere to be seen.

"Sneaking is what you do when you're doing something wrong," she said. "I'm not doing anything wrong."

The words surprised her. Although they came from her own mouth, she hadn't cued her brain to speak. But that was what she'd said then, in this distant, long-forgotten memory, and it was what she still felt now, wasn't it?

With a grin, Maverick sauntered toward her, all long limbs and lean muscle. In her mind, she brought a hand to her mouth to choke down tears at the sight of him, but in the memory, her hand didn't so much as move. Everything about him—the way he walked, the way he smiled, the set of his shoulders—was familiar yet so…different. He'd filled out his long limbs in the years since, the muscled width of his shoulders spreading wider to make him a formidable brute of a man. She'd never considered him baby-faced when they were younger, though he seemed to be now with age clouding her vision. Older Maverick was so much harsher, so much crueler and lethal looking that…

It made her chest ache.

She'd never realized how much the years had worn on him.

Inside, she choked down a sob.

Though not everything had changed, had it? When he'd found her in the forest like this, she'd feared he'd tell her father, that he'd scold her for not listening to the rules. She thought so many things of him then…

That you wouldn't support me.

That you would be like them.

That you think I'm unworthy.

All because I was born a girl, she thought.

All her doubts and fears simmered to the surface.

They were both the thoughts of her younger self and herself now.

He may not have championed her candidacy, but the memory was a reminder that in this moment she was living again, he hadn't told her father. In fact, he'd taken her by the hand, and instead of removing the weapon from it, he'd taught her how to use it. He'd inspired her, recognized her in a way no one else ever had…in what felt like a lifetime ago. Even if he only did so now because of their deal.

Inside, she felt a lump form in her throat. If only she could have warned her younger self then.

He'll never truly be yours. Not really.

But there was some of that young man still left in him somewhere, she was certain. This packmaster who'd become the leader of misfits, rebels, outlaws. It was only up to her to help him reclaim it.

She opened her mouth to say as much, expecting the memory to play out, but as she blinked, he was gone, the memory dissipating as if it'd never been there to begin with. But it had been there. Once. Long ago. She still remembered his heart, real and beating against her as he'd helped her wield the sword in her hands, and seeing him standing there moments ago had been so real it hadn't felt like a memory. It'd been…visceral.

Then she saw them.

She stopped in her tracks.

In the light, in the shadow of the moon, the silhouette of a woman walked toward her, forging a path through the underbrush. Intrinsically, Sierra knew she came of her own authority without the permission of any man or wolf who was her king. She came to her as she opened her dark mouth and all the lamentations of her sisters came forth. Each cry a call to all their feminine ancestors who came before. Their message increasingly clear.

We were.

We are.

The lifeblood.

Their chorus filled her ears, echoing and ringing until the cries transitioned into a sharp, haunting howl.

The howl of her alpha.

Sierra woke with a jolt, abruptly shifting into human form, her arms and legs kicking and flailing as if she were still her wolf, fighting to right herself from where she lay supine.

"Easy, easy." The voice was her brother's, but the arms holding her, cradling her, were most definitely not his, though the other elite warriors were gathered around them.

"Sierra."

The deep thrum of Maverick's voice instantly stilled her, his presence as her alpha both calming her and arousing her instantly. Her eyes shot to his. In the dim glow of the cave lights, the concern in the gold of his wolf eyes, the deep lines of worry on his face stole her breath away. The puckered scar above his left brow drew low as he searched her face.

In an instant, he knew.

She could see it in the way the muscles in his throat strained, how the edge of his nose flared. She'd seen *everything* from his memory and more, and she knew he could tell as much from the look in her eyes.

Rose had never been his choice.

And still, that didn't change anything. She knew that without a doubt.

The pain of that reality seared through her, reminding her of the loss of everything that could have been. Everything that *should* have been.

But there wasn't time for that now.

"Sierra," he said again. This time less of a prayer and more of a plea.

Have mercy on me, his plea seemed to say.

For never telling her. For stopping anything that could have been between them before there was ever so much as a chance for them.

Love is a price I can't afford. His previous words echoed back to her.

That was clearer to her now than it had ever been, and any

feelings he might have felt for her back then had been long since buried beneath the weight of a crown he'd never wanted to begin with. But she couldn't address that now.

She moved to push to standing, but he drew her closer, refusing to let her go not out of force but in gentle protection of her.

Gentleness that, considering all that had passed between them, she couldn't handle right now. She growled. "Let me go."

It was her brother who came to her assistance. Surprisingly, he didn't seem to care that Maverick was holding her. "Sierra, you stayed under longer than the rest of us. We don't know why or what that means. But—"

"There's no time for that now," she snapped.

Pushing away from them both, she rose to her feet. Her legs quivered with the sudden, abrupt change in balance from wolf form to human, and Blaze tried to grab her, to steady her, but she quickly found her footing and waved them all back.

Maverick and the other elite warriors stood around her, their faces all etched with concern and, if she looked deeper, more than a hint of admiration as she bent down and picked up her blade from where it had fallen onto the cave floor.

She clutched her knife in her hand. "I know how to find the insurgent."

Chapter 14

THE MOMENT SIERRA LEFT THE CAVE, SHE WENT TO WORK. SHE waited among the other female warriors, her friends and sisters flanking her in their support. The ceremony was nearly halfway over, and the pack buzzed with nervous energy, waiting, anticipating the hunt that lay ahead, though she hunted a different kind of prey. It'd been her brother who had given the orders, but she'd orchestrated the plans. The packmaster hadn't so much as questioned her. Maverick had simply nodded his complete support and approval of her, welcoming her input in a way she hadn't anticipated.

As the male elite warriors guarded Maverick's back, it would be the female warriors' duty to protect the packmembers, while *she* searched for him…

She lingered in the crowd, slowly moving among her packmates as she searched for the scent, the one that had come to her in what had felt like a dream. There were so many faces on the mountainside. Most of the Grey Wolf pack remained out west, the major subpacks all located within Montana and the surrounding states, but there were smaller subpacks, micro versions of what they had here at Wolf Pack Run, as far east as New York.

Inhaling a sharp breath, she scented the air. She knew the insurgent was male both from the memory of the scent and experience. Not to mention, she'd learned well over the years that an unrestrained male's anger resulted in violence while a woman's resulted in justice. She and her fellow female warriors understood that intrinsically, because even lethal women rarely threw the first punch. Theirs was a game of patience, courage, defense. Every kill was righteous. Every swipe of their blade warranted by a feminine power to love and protect their own by any means or method necessary. They were survivors, because that was what women did. They survived.

Even in the face of a world that threatened to destroy them.

Briefly, she turned her gaze toward the ceremony. She had to blend in, to look as if she were paying attention as she slowly navigated the crowd. She couldn't risk alerting the insurgent to her presence. Each movement she made was paramount.

She pretended to watch the ceremony with rapt eyes. But with each passing moment, the anxiety in her chest built, reminding her far too much of a night so much like this one ten years prior, a night in which she'd expected Maverick's acknowledgment at the very least, if not his love, his friendship, but instead, he'd chosen another.

She fought back a cringe as the memory gripped her.

That night, as all the other packmembers had stepped back, she'd stepped forward, not only wanting his acknowledgment but expecting it. Slowly, he'd approached, but he'd not nuzzled against her, marking her as a mate as she'd anticipated. Instead, he'd snarled at her. He'd urged her back to her rightful place, shaming her, before it'd been Rose he'd marked instead.

She fought to keep her focus as the weight of the memory hit her. Even with the fresh knowledge that the choice hadn't been his burning in her mind, she could still feel the sting of his rejection, of her own embarrassment.

Because he'd had a choice, hadn't he? And he'd made it.

It hadn't been Rose he'd chosen over her.

It'd been tradition, expectation, his role.

Dakota must have sensed her growing unease, because her friend chose that moment to reach over and grip Sierra's hand, giving it a tight, reassuring squeeze.

"It's almost over now," her friend reassured. "You'll find him."

They'd made it through the longest historical subsection, the past, which detailed the lengthy history of the pack via a series of oral stories presented by some of the pack's eldest members. The evolution of their species dated back to the Pleistocene period at the time wolf and canine held a common ancestor. According to the pack's historians, somehow in the evolutionary tumult, man and beast had become one. For their species, one question would always remain...

Were they more wolf or man?

Once she faced the insurgent, she had no doubt which side of her own nature would win.

"Spread out and search wide," Sierra whispered to Dakota. With the ceremony ending and the insurgent's window of opportunity narrowing, the risk of attack grew with each passing moment. If not her, then she intended for one of her warriors, her sister in arms, to find the insurgent, and when they did, they'd show the whole pack exactly what a female of their kind could do.

Dakota nodded, silently disappearing into the array of bodies as she signaled to the others to do the same. Slowly, they fanned out across the crowded mountainside, prowling through the crowd. Sierra chose the path west, heading through the sea of other shifters in the direction that led to the edge of their lands in the mountains.

Had she been trying to sneak an outsider onto Wolf Pack Run, this would have been the direction she'd choose. The boundaries of their land stretched onward for miles into the borders of Yellowstone. The public nature of those lands restricted access to the pack's territory by simply how deep into the park a tourist or ranger would have to venture to gain access to the packlands from that direction. It wasn't impossible, just unlikely.

Unless someone knew to specifically search for the ranch.

She feared the insurgent would.

A familiar protective instinct flared inside her. She would gladly lay down her life for her pack, her family, if it came to that. Her internal drive to protect them, to care for them in the only way she knew how was born of the deep love, the sense of belonging and home she felt every time her feet connected with this small patch of earth they called Wolf Pack Run.

Ears pricked to the slightest hint of movement, she waded through the packmates.

Maverick's deep voice rose and carried over the mountainside.

"Brent Remington and Silas Buck."

Sierra froze, temporarily turning her attention back toward the ceremony. Brent approached from the far side of the crowd, blending in with ease. He'd assimilated quickly among them, adopting their ways as if he held little loyalty to his former life. Sierra watched him with suspicious attention. Assimilated or not, something about him still set her instincts on alert.

But it was Silas who concerned her more.

A large hand brushed her shoulder, gently easing her to the side. Silas's proximity and scent clouded her senses. Unable to stop herself, she bared her teeth as she faced him but stopped short of letting out a feral growl. She couldn't draw attention to herself right now, even though she didn't approve of either man, wolf shifters or not, joining the pack.

Silas nodded to her, a spark of distaste in his eyes. "If you'll excuse me, warrior."

On his lips, the words sounded like a threat, a promise to repay how she'd bested him.

Her gaze raked over him, assessing the risk he posed. The former Wild Eight rivaled the male elite warriors in size and strength, which only heightened her suspicion. Both he and Brent had once been warriors for the now-dissolved enemy wolf pack, though vicious street thugs seemed a more appropriate description to her.

When she'd brought them to justice, Brent had been easy, considering she'd knocked him unconscious. Even once he'd awakened at Wolf Pack Run, he'd been oddly accepting of his new situation, angry yet resigned to it, but Silas had been a different story. He'd fought her every step of the way. The alpha male was nearly as feral as any she'd ever met, and now she was supposed to call him packmate?

She swallowed a feral growl, stepping aside so he could move past her.

Could it be him? Someone had helped the insurgent pass the guards, someone with knowledge of the pack's security but no loyalty to it. Silas moved past her, he and Brent coming to stand before Maverick as they swore their oaths to the pack.

As they did, Silas dared a glance in her direction. The spark in his eyes underlined his fury with her. But she couldn't call him out now. Not until she was certain.

Without turning, she stepped back, ready to resume her search, but a wrinkled hand clutched her arm, causing her to turn toward who held her elbow.

She schooled her features, forcing herself not to frown. Rex Johnson, the retired Grey Wolf warrior who now spearheaded the council. He'd been one of the most ardently opposed to her appointment. Anderson, another Elder Council member, stood beside him.

"Rex," she said in curt greeting. "Anderson." Rex's aged hand on her elbow made her feel more than a bit uncomfortable.

"We're so pleased to see you finally fulfilling your duty to the pack," Rex said.

Her duty being mating with Maverick, not fulfilling her position as warrior. The double meaning of those words didn't escape her. From the threatening look in Rex's baggy eyes, he wasn't too pleased she and Maverick had found a way around them.

"Yes, very pleased," Anderson echoed, seemingly unaware of the disapproval in Rex's words. From Anderson, she could *maybe* believe it was the truth.

"Thank you." She gave a stiff nod.

Rex's grip on her arm tightened. "Just remember to stay humble, warrior."

The thinly veiled threat in those words was evident. One wrong move and Rex would use any excuse to demote her again.

"I'll do that." Tearing her elbow away from him, Sierra mumbled a vague excuse before navigating through the crowd away from them. Let him try to take her position away from her. She and Maverick would cover their tracks, be more than convincing in their marriage.

And she had more urgent enemies to fight.

A few minutes later, after prowling the outskirts of the crowd, she found what she searched for. Had she not been looking for it, she'd have missed the faint trace of his scent.

She had him now.

With the smell of so many wolves in the air, it was only the scent of the city, the human smells of gasoline and concrete and construction and piss that tipped her off. Most of the pack made their home in the west, in the rural heartland. They had never been city dwellers. Moving westward of where the pack gathered, she prowled away from the crowd. Her suspicion was confirmed when she found several tracks in the snow, leading down toward the base of the mountain. All the tracks from her packmates should lead up the mountainside, radiating outward from the center compound at Wolf Pack Run.

Latching on to the scent, she circled back, following the snowy trail.

Now that she had his scent, she would find him, and when she did, God help the wolf who threatened the lives of those she loved.

The full moon was unusually bright tonight. Maverick leaned against a towering mountain pine with his Stetson tipped low over his brow. With his portion of the ceremony now over, he'd retreated to the outskirts of the crowd, looking onward as each member of the pack gathered around his cousin, Belle, taking their turns marking her and her pregnant belly, a custom to show that she and the pup she'd soon deliver were the responsibility of the whole pack. It was a ritual that would be repeated once the babe was born in a few weeks' time.

Somewhere in the dark forest behind him, an owl hooted, drawing his attention to a quiet brush in the mountain undergrowth. Someone approaching at his back. The hand tucked in the pocket of his jeans slowly eased toward his blade, gripping the hilt in anticipation. Had he been in his true form, his hackles would have raised in alert.

The wolf who approached cleared his throat. "Men behave differently when they smell death on you." The cool words were spoken as much to announce the other wolf's presence as they likely were to stop Maverick from drawing his blade.

Maverick glanced over his shoulder toward the wolf in the darkness. Silas, one of the pack's newest members, lingered in the shadows, watching him with knowing eyes that seemed to see too much. There was a coolness about the other wolf, a chill to the fiery spark of rage behind the former Wild Eight's eyes that reminded Maverick of every time he looked in the mirror. He knew firsthand there was danger in a man whose anger was cold, who wielded his rage as a weapon of calm fury, separate and distant from himself.

For a man like that, nothing was personal, little sacred.

He moved his hand back toward his pocket, no longer reaching toward his dagger. For now. "They circle like sharks. One drop of blood and they swarm," he answered. He'd experienced it before, but not like this. The vampires. The human hunters. His fellow shifters.

And now, one of his own…

He'd felt death lingering beside him before, but never this close.

"Vultures," Silas whispered, turning his eyes toward the crowd. "They'll pick the meat from your bones before your body goes cold."

"Some, but not all." Without intention, Maverick's eyes fell to his high commander. From where Colt stood across the mountainside, his arm wrapped around his mate, the commander's eyes found his as if he felt Maverick's gaze on him. Colt's steeled-gray irises hesitated on his for a moment before he turned back to his mate.

Maverick inhaled a sharp breath.

No, it wasn't the vultures that fazed him. It was the men he trusted and believed in.

None of the elite warriors would dare show it, but he felt the doubt there.

In him. In his skills and leadership.

He couldn't blame them. He'd been the sole cause of that. He should have known better than to end things as he had in the cave. Even if Blaze's technology came through this time, he'd risked the lives of them all by stopping the genetic memory before they'd gone deep enough, because he'd chosen his own needs over their own. Their skepticism was warranted.

Monster. The harsh criticism ripped through him.

He'd be certain it wouldn't happen again.

Silas nodded toward Wes. His former packmaster stood not far to Colt's left. "I remember the same before Wes fell."

The thinly veiled warning didn't escape Maverick.

One wrong move, Packmaster, and you'll face the same fate.

Maverick's gaze narrowed, his upper lip curling both in security for his own position and protective instinct for a man who, like the one beside him, was never supposed to be one of his own.

"If I recall, you were one of the vultures." Maverick pinned Silas with a hard stare, his distrust evident. He might have extended the invitation to join the pack toward him, but that was because he trusted Wes's judgment. Maverick hadn't remained packmaster this long by giving his trust freely. Even Wes himself had been forced to earn it.

And Silas would have to as well.

Silas dropped his head in respectful acknowledgment, but the action was underscored by the slight curve at the seam of his lips. "We all do what we need to survive."

Maverick grunted, facing his attention back toward the ceremony.

But Silas refused to take the hint.

"And what will you do to survive, Packmaster?"

Maverick stiffened. The words shivered through him as if they'd been whispered by the Devil himself. If not for the sake of the pack, would he care if he lost it all? His position? His life?

He wasn't certain.

Maverick cast a glance toward the other wolf.

This was a cowboy who'd seen the worst of him, because he'd once been his enemy. Maverick's primal instincts raised on high alert.

And perhaps he still was...

The insurgent hadn't made it onto their lands alone. Someone in the pack had betrayed him. And only time would tell.

A stir rippled through the far side of the crowd, bringing their conversation to a halt.

A moment later, the sea of packmembers parted to reveal a small group of the female warriors led by Sierra, bringing the last of the ceremony to a halt. Maverick's gaze instantly locked on her, assessing. Her hair was disheveled, and several scrapes marred her arms from the fight, but she was otherwise unharmed. She could take care of herself, and from the look in her eyes, anyone who dared to insinuate otherwise would face their own death.

The expression on her face was more dangerous than righteous fury. It was well-deserved and earned pride, plain and simple.

Dakota and Cheyenne flanked her, clutching the arms of the rogue wolf Sierra had clearly captured on his behalf. The rogue assassin was in human form, and his hands had been zip-tied behind his back as he struggled and fought against the women who held him. As they drew closer, the other she-wolves moved through the crowd, gathering behind Sierra in a sign of solidarity as she delivered their enemy to him.

"To protect the pack, you need to protect yourself, to be selfish in a way they'll never understand." Silas's gaze darted between him and Sierra, and his grin widened. "That's why you chose Wes as your second. He understands that. As do I. You don't need to play the selfless leader, Packmaster. Not with me."

The unspoken implication in those words was clear.

I know the truth.

Maverick straightened his Stetson, drawing up to his full height. "That's why they call me the Monster of Montana, or so I hear."

Silas chuckled. "People create legends of the things they fear most." His hand reached into the pocket of his leather jacket, and he removed an engraved metallic flask. From the peaty scent of the container, whiskey. Even wolves like them used it to stave off the cold. Silas threw back a quick swig before extending the flask toward him. "If it's a monster they want, I think you should give it to them."

Maverick accepted the flask, drawing it up to his lips. The fiery taste burned across his tongue as his eyes locked on his enemy held captive in Sierra's hands. The second wolf who'd come for him. And not likely the last. Maverick's gaze fell back to the woman who'd captured him, the woman who had saved his life even while the hope in her eyes as she looked at him threatened to destroy him.

"I think you're right." He passed the flask back toward Silas and strode across the cold mountain ground.

Maverick prowled toward Sierra and their prisoner, the rogue wolf thrashing against Cheyenne and Dakota's hold, a reminder of himself, of what he was about to do.

This was the part where he would have told Rose to look away. Sensitive and tender as she'd been, she'd never had a taste for bloodshed. For years, he'd tried hard to shield that part of himself from her, to protect her from the darker side of himself, one of the necessities of his role, which for her sake, he'd told himself he didn't enjoy.

But in the end, it'd been that same distance that had caused her to resent him.

He didn't blame her. How could he?

"Release him," he ordered.

As Cheyenne and Dakota let go of the prisoner, Sierra grabbed him and shoved the rogue wolf down into the snow at Maverick's feet. Hands still bound behind his back, the rogue fell to his knees without much resistance. But that didn't stop him from turning toward Sierra with a threatening snarl.

A spark of protective rage thrummed through Maverick.

That lone provocation was all he needed.

Palming the other wolf's hair, he dragged the assassin into his arms, yanking back the other wolf's skull as he drew his blade to his enemy's throat. A feral snarl rumbled up from deep in his chest. "I will ask only once. Who sent you?"

The rogue wolf growled in response. He bared his teeth and twisted just enough to spit in Maverick's face. "Fuck you and the horse you rode in on. I'm no snitch."

Slowly Maverick removed his blade from the other wolf's throat, only long enough to wipe the spittle from his face. "Even if you had been, it wouldn't have saved you."

Without warning, he drew his blade across the other wolf's throat, painting the white snow beneath them crimson. The assassin coughed and sputtered in his arms, choking on his own blood as several alarmed gasps came from the pack. He didn't often make a spectacle of warning off his enemies, but when he did, he let brutality reign.

He held the now-dead insurgent out for all the pack to see. His voice was a dark graveled promise as he growled. Whoever had helped this assassin onto the ranch would hear him, and for whatever enemy they worked for, the message would be clear. "You've come for my life twice now, and each time you've failed. Make no mistake. I will come for you, and when I do, I won't have to come twice."

Roughly, he dropped the dead wolf from his hold. As he did, he hung his head. The heat of his breath swirled about his face as it hit the cold mountain air. With the body of his enemy laid at his feet, he felt the weight of every packmember's eyes on him.

Their expectations. Their judgments. Their doubts and fears.

Fear of him.

But it was only the judgment of one he truly cared about.

Maverick lifted his gaze.

He watched Sierra as she stood still clutching her own blade in her hand. Moonlight reflected off the iron hilt. She was majestic, powerful, and to his shock, there was no hint of disgust on her face. No distaste for this small glimpse of who he truly was. Instead, she held his gaze, almost reverent, almost defiant. As if she saw every part of him, and she dared him to try to use it to push her away.

He'd saved her life before. But this time, she had saved him.

Maybe there was hope for them yet.

If only for a single evening...

A gust of wind whipped through the forest, and on it, he scented himself...on her. His wolf's response was instinctual, but even in his human form, in an instant, he was salivating. His cock stiffened, and he could only think of the sounds she'd make as he'd fucked her with that damn riding crop...

Lord help him.

He prowled toward her, unable to stop himself even if he'd tried.

Had she been one of the others, he'd have placed a hand on her shoulder in acknowledgment of her accomplishment, of how she'd served him and the pack. But she wasn't like the others. She was more.

To him, she always had been.

Instead, he gently cupped her cheek in his hand. Her eyes flared wide, flitting to the packmembers surrounding them with unease before her gaze found his again. As it did, the tension in her body softened, and to his surprise, her eyelids fluttered closed as she leaned into his touch. The ache that single action created in his chest was enough that had they been alone, he could have fallen to his knees in want and worship of this woman he'd never be worthy of.

If you love her…

"For tonight," he said, before he could stop himself.

She blinked, glancing up at him. From the surprised look in her eyes, she instantly gathered what he meant.

For tonight, you are mine.

His thumb caressed the line of her jaw. "*Mé nótahshême.*"

Not warrior, as he should have said.

My warrior.

He whispered the words in the Old Tongue, a language that for most of the pack was dead. But with the smooth touch of her skin beneath his palm, how could it be? These mountains, the pack, their home was alive with her beauty and strength, and had he been a different man, he would have laid it all at her feet.

But he wasn't any other man.

It was the truth. He knew that. Still, he infused that singular phrase with every bit of emotion he'd felt for her over the years.

Friend. Rival. Lover.

All the things he wanted them to be but that would always hang just beyond his grasp, because the life he'd been born into forbid him from it.

He traced the line of her jaw with his thumb again, wanting yet unable to draw her closer, and for the first time since he'd brought her name forth to the council, he questioned his own judgment, because having this fierce, beautiful, courageous woman by his side when he knew he could never truly have her might prove to be the death of him.

Chapter 15

THIS ISN'T REAL.

Sierra repeated that mantra to herself, trying to remember that whatever this seductive magic was that seemed to charge the air between them, it wasn't true. It couldn't be.

Yet she felt herself falling victim to it.

Maverick held the attention of the entire pack. But *she* held his attention. Slowly, he drew his hand away from where he cupped her cheek. As he did, she felt the loss of his touch as he eased away from her. Stepping back, he stood before her as wild and feral as she'd ever seen him. In the pale moonlight, the cold chill in the mountain air highlighted the jagged white scar that cut through his brow in stark relief against the golden hues of his skin. The pale green of his human eyes was nowhere to be found.

He raised his voice for all the pack to hear as his gaze remained on her. "The future of this pack is female."

A shiver shook through her as a chorus of approving shouts sounded behind her. A sense of pride filled her chest.

It was no surprise when Maverick shifted into wolf form, his clothes falling to the ground beneath him. At his cue, the whole pack followed suit.

Leaning into her true self, she found the wild part inside her and urged it forward. She fell to the ground on all fours. Bones shifted and cracked as her fur sprang forth in a satisfying release. When she was fully changed, she shook out her fur before she looked back toward him.

Slowly, he prowled toward her again, his paws sinking into the damp drifts of pure white snow still falling around them. Immediately, Sierra lowered her gaze. In their true forms like this, when they had no words, only actions, only sensation and feeling, it was a challenge to meet his eyes, a sign of outward aggression and not the kind she so carelessly wielded in human form.

She felt the weight of his stare on her, causing the fur on her back to prickle. As he drew nearer, she hunched lower, attempting to make herself smaller in deference. It was something she'd never consider in human form. But she wasn't human, she was wolf. She felt that deep in the marrow of her bones, the reminder gripping her as his shadow approached in the moonlit snow.

He drew neck to neck with her, and for the briefest of moments, she worried she'd pushed him too far. She didn't dare move. Positioned like this, his muzzle at her throat, he could easily bite her scruff or even take her life, punishing her for all the times she'd been haughty with him. Pack law gave him that power, while she was afforded none. But he didn't choose to wield that power against her. Instead, he stepped back, lifting and exposing his throat to her with a harsh, alerting bark. It wasn't without significance. It said so many things that any attempt to place it into human words in her mind lessened it.

I trust you. With my life. I yield my power to you. You are strong. You are alpha. I acknowledge you. I respect you. I am you. We are one.

She was supposed to place her jaws on the skin of his neck, accepting the power over him that he offered. It was what the male elite warriors before her had done, but she wasn't them. She was female, and there was power in that. Instead, she leaned forward, licking and nipping at the fur of his neck up to his muzzle. His ears perked up in surprise, but she knew from the look in his wolf eyes and the relaxed position of his stance that he understood.

I don't accept your power. I have my own. We are one. Friends. Equals.

She licked feverishly at his muzzle, savoring the taste of his wolf scent. He smelled like water birch, pine, and juniper.

He chuffed a hot breath, a swirl of heat in the air, and suddenly the tension between them changed. He drew up beside her again, pawing at her scruff until one of his front paws caught the fur and rested there. He snapped his jaws playfully, jumping back with spry, sharp movements as he wagged his tail and barked. The invitation was clear.

Run with me. Hunt with me.

Like when they'd been young, when they'd been friends. Had she not been in wolf form, a lump would have formed in her throat, holding the pain of all the years of distance between them, the relief that now that distance seemed to have disappeared. He barked again, snapping and nudging at her front paws until she realized what he was doing. He wanted her to initiate their hunt, to lead.

She puffed her chest forward, shaking off a layer of snow that had gathered on her fur before she threw back her head and howled. Her sisters joined in the chorus. All the females of the pack howling as the packmaster hopped around her like a playful pup.

And then they ran.

The pack divided into small units and hierarchies. It was tradition for the alpha to take the first kill, but he'd gifted that privilege to her, and she wanted not just to take the kill but to find the prey. She and Maverick raced up the mountainside. She knew these mountains, these lands.

Home.

A quiet ridge, bounding through the snow with Maverick flanking her. From the openmouthed panting coming from his jowls, he smelled it, too. When they located the buck, they waited in silent watch.

They followed the animal for some time. Sensing their presence but unable to shake them off his trail, the buck became disoriented with fear. Increasingly sloppy, he stumbled about, looking for escape and finding none. Sierra's heart pounded in anticipation as she exchanged glances with Maverick, and then they descended. He took the animal from the front, fielding the dangerous antlers as she lunged from the back, only narrowly avoiding the blow of a back hoof.

The deer died in the silent glow of the moonlight. Sierra reveled in the gamy taste of it in her jaws. She tore open the carcass, savoring the fatty liver for herself before ripping out the animal's still beating heart. Covered in blood, dirt, and snow, she laid it at the feet of her alpha before she nipped playfully at his ear, followed by a quick yip.

I give you my heart.

She'd meant for it to be funny. Even in wolf form, the human side of her could still appreciate a good pun. She expected him to growl and nose it away in disapproval of her antics before he devoured it. But he didn't so much as sniff it. Instead, his golden wolf eyes turned toward her, pinning her in place. She lowered her eyes, but as he stepped toward her, he bumped the underside of her muzzle more than once, forcing her to look toward him.

And then, he did the unthinkable. There, with the other elite warriors who'd fallen into ranks surrounding them, he marked her. Rubbing his neck against hers, he spread his scent over her as he would a mate. Had she been in human form, she would have reeled at how soon the declaration of their mating came after naming her warrior, but as wolf, with the lingering taste of the deer's fragile life in her jaws and the gentle snowfall all around them, silencing the sounds of the mountains, she couldn't bring herself to care.

Mate, warrior, lover, female.

She could be all these things when she was wild and none of those roles conflicted. She wasn't bound by humanity's silly constructs. She simply was.

The warmth of the packmaster's fur brushed against her as he marked her. He nuzzled against her in a gentle, almost reverent caress.

This isn't real, she reminded herself.

All the same, she leaned into his touch, soaking in the feeling of his warmth against her, his scent all around her, the heat of his breath against her throat, all the things she'd longed for for years but had never been able to have and never would. Not really. Not given freely without stipulation or duty or demand.

As he eased away from her, the scent of him forever lingering on her skin, her brother let out an approving howl followed by the chorus of the other elite warriors. She wagged her tail and pretended to be pleased despite the ache in her chest.

They chased rabbits, deer, and even bears that night, taking and eating their fill, and as the last of the moon slipped into day, Sierra slunk away, veering off from the rest of the pack and distancing herself until she was alone. Once she was separated from the pack, she shifted into human form, huddling naked and freezing with cold beneath a pine, and there for the first time in years, Sierra cried hot tears that cut through the cold mountain snow.

Chapter 16

MEET ME TONIGHT.

Sierra stared at the words, scrawled in Maverick's truncated script followed by the location. It'd been a long day. She'd spent more time than she'd intended helping Blaze reposition the cow cams in the calving shed, so they could keep an eye on the few pregnant mothers who'd bred outside the usual calving season. Most of the afternoon, she'd been up on a ladder next to the shed's rafters, only to descend and gracefully land one of her boots in a fresh cow patty, much to Blaze and Dakota's amusement.

After she'd wrangled Randy, who'd taken a particular interest in Naomi's mare of late, into his pen, she'd returned to her cabin on the far side of the compound before placing Elvis in the small coop she'd built for him on her back porch. It was only then that she'd found the note slipped underneath her door. She glanced down at the words again. A mixture of excitement and nervous relief twisted in her gut.

It'd been over two weeks since she and Maverick had run wild, and if she'd fooled herself into thinking something had changed between them, the time since would have corrected her. Other than several elite warrior meetings, Sierra hadn't seen the gruff packmaster. She'd known his role kept him busy with long hours that bled into long days, but still she'd anticipated seeing him more as they drew closer to the official announcement of their engagement. Before the incident in the cave, the council had been clear that if they allowed her to be promoted before they mated, her and Maverick's pending engagement announcement and wedding date had to be chosen before the month's end. Not that him marking her hadn't already said the events were soon to come, just without official words.

It wasn't until the two-week mark passed with no contact from him that she suspected he was avoiding her. Sure, she had her position now, the most important aspect of their bargain as far as she was concerned. But the council wouldn't let them off the hook that easy. Her continued appointment was contingent upon their marriage—and if they didn't fulfill the request by the month's end, it'd all be for naught. So when his note arrived, the confirmation that he'd keep his word about *all* their arrangements gave her an unexpected sense of relief.

Later that evening, as she headed out to meet him, she locked her cabin door behind her before her foot slid across something movable atop her doormat. She glanced down. Another note. Maybe a change in location? Maverick's initial message had instructed her to meet him at the training gym of all places. Perhaps he'd had a change of heart? She picked up the folded paper, its surface now dusted with dirt from the edge of her boot. Brushing it off, she unfolded it only to let out a frustrated curse.

Another hate note. Not a message from Maverick at all.

She didn't even glance twice at the vitriol before she ripped the paper in two. Whatever asshole was still leaving these, when were they going to take a hint? She wouldn't be intimidated.

Twenty minutes later, she stood alone amid the equipment in the training gym, all thoughts of the hateful note forgotten. This late, most of the packmembers would be in the woods or sleeping if tomorrow was their turn on the ranch's chore rotation. The sound of the gym's heater buzzed in the background, filling the empty space with a constant vibrating hum. He couldn't possibly be planning any "lesson" for them in here, could he?

She leaned against the far wall, waiting, until suddenly a rough hand grabbed her. Before she knew what was going on, she was wrenched backward *into* the wall. In an instant, the stark fluorescent lights of the gym disappeared, and she was engulfed in darkness. A large hand clapped over her mouth.

"Sierra," Maverick grumbled, causing her to still.

Through the darkness, she blinked, allowing her eyes to adjust. Adrenaline pumped through her. She'd been prepared to lash out against what she'd thought was an attacker. Not that there seemed to be much room in this dark space for a fight if the way she bumped against the wall so easily was any indication.

"Where the hell are we?" she rasped, catching her breath from the scare.

"The tunnel."

"Yeah, like that explains anything."

He grunted his agreement. "There are passages, hidden corridors, pathways, all around the ranch in case of emergencies."

She quirked a brow. "And is this an emergency?"

"No," he grumbled. Some dark emotion flashed in his eyes. "But for discretion."

Discretion.

The low growl in his voice promised exactly what kind of discretion they'd need.

With her senses adjusting, she deciphered his outline in the darkness. He filled the small space even more thoroughly than she did. The tunnel ceiling skimmed below the top of his head, forcing him to duck to fit inside. His wolf eyes glowed with anticipation.

Sierra cleared her throat. "I wasn't certain you would keep our deal after..."

Some dark emotion flashed in his eyes. "I'm a man of my word."

Before she could push further, he clasped her hand in his, gently leading her farther into the darkness, away from the glowing square outline of the hidden door.

"Are we going to your secret lair?" she joked.

"Yes."

"What?"

Maverick chuffed a short laugh. It was as close to a chuckle as she'd heard from him in a long time. She couldn't remember the last time he'd joked with her.

"To the packmaster's quarters," he clarified.

She followed him down a series of dark tunnels, weaving and curving until finally they reached another glowing outline of a door. He pushed it open and stepped through. Though the lighting was dim on the other side, the contrast from the complete darkness of the tunnel caused her to shield her eyes.

Stepping through the entry, she lowered her hand and surveyed the room before her. A large office greeted her, decorated in dark, mahogany wood and with coffered ceilings nearly identical to the public office he kept near the command center. At the far end of the room, an open doorway led into a bedroom.

He closed the hidden door behind, the sound carrying with it a finality that signaled they were truly alone. He led her into the bedroom before he turned toward her again. Alone like this, the expanse of his king-size bed between them like an unfilled promise, she felt the weight of all their unspoken words.

She wanted to bridge the gap, close the distance between them, but she didn't know how. She trailed a hand across the burgundy top sheet. Egyptian cotton with a high thread count. The sheets were folded with methodical perfection. She could bounce a quarter off them.

The drawn-out silence grew unbearable.

Sierra gave an awkward smile. "I don't think I've been past the foyer of your apartment."

Maverick swallowed, his Adam's apple giving a sharp lurch. "No, you haven't."

From his clipped, tense tone, she gathered her mistake.

The foyer.

The only time she'd been there had been…

Without meaning to, she'd immediately brought up the elephant in the room. She was fumbling this. "I meant I'm interested in seeing where you live, that's all…" She hesitated. "Where we'll live after…"

After their wedding night.

Time was running out for them to announce a date, and in the meantime, per their arrangement…

She released a long breath. *There's nothing between us*, she reminded herself. *There can't be.*

He'd been clear about that from the start. That Rose hadn't been his choice didn't change that, didn't mean he hadn't loved his late wife, and certainly didn't mean he had any feelings for *her*.

She reached for the door beside her, adjacent to the one they'd come in. Exiting seemed like her only strategy at this point, and she was desperate for a change in subject. She turned the handle to open the door. "Does this lead out into the rest of the—"

Suddenly, his hand was over hers as he slammed the door shut. In this position, he had her caged between him and the doorframe. This close to him, alone in his bedroom, she felt the heat radiating from his body. She stared up into the dark shadows of his face. She could practically feel the tickle of his beard against her chin, like when she'd kissed him. What would it feel like to run her fingers through the coarse scruff across his cheek? For him to pin her flush against this door and kiss her? She'd wrap her legs around him, bury her hands in the long strands of his hair. Her nipples tightened.

Down, girl.

Whether he smelled her arousal, she wasn't certain.

Reaching around her, he twisted the lock on the door before he pushed away from the doorframe again. "We'll move you into the opposite side of the apartment after the wedding. Until then, you're welcome in here, so long as that door remains closed."

She adjusted the hair tie at the end of her braid, a nervous habit. "What's behind the door? Your *actual* secret lair?" She gave a nervous laugh, hoping to lighten the mood. Maybe he'd joke with her again?

But to her disappointment, all she saw there was the same grumbly packmaster he'd become over the years. No hint of the playful young man he'd once been. "That's the family wing of the house."

The family wing. A knot twisted her in stomach. Of course. He didn't want her in the part of his home he'd shared with Rose. Not yet anyway...

The chasm between them widened. Apparently, there was no getting around this conversation. "Maverick, about what happened in the caverns—"

He cut her off. "All the more reason our terms need to be clear moving forward."

"Terms?" She blinked. That hadn't been what she'd expected at all. She'd been about to tell him that she—

"No attachments. No love, and this ends after our wedding night." The decisive command in his words cut through her. "We'll live our separate lives after that."

"I see." It was all she could manage to say at the moment. She'd known what she'd seen in the cave didn't change anything, but still, she'd hoped...

For tonight, he'd whispered. Even then on the mountainside, he'd been clear it couldn't be more than that. She just hadn't wanted to believe it.

"For the sake of the pack, my judgment can't be clouded," he continued. "There can be no repeats of what happened in the cave. It could cost lives. So whatever happens between us in this room *must stay* in this room, and no matter how real anything between us may feel, we both need to be clear that it isn't. Understand?"

When she didn't immediately answer, he growled.

"Sierra?"

It was the tone he used when she was treading dangerous territory, pushing him too far.

"I understand," she whispered. "What happened in the cave doesn't change anything." She swallowed, hard, the silence between them stretching. "For you."

"Sierra," he breathed, the word was laced with subtle warning.

But she wouldn't back down. For her, the cave had changed everything. Somehow it lessened the hurt that singular decision had caused her. She'd felt the pain of his rejection deep in her bones for the past ten years, the pain that even if he did someday choose her, she'd always be second. Second choice. Second fiddle, and until now, due to her gender, second class. But she recognized how selfish that was. She couldn't resent him for not returning her feelings. He didn't owe anything to her. There hadn't been any promises between them, only friendship.

A friendship she'd buried.

And whether he wanted to or not, she needed him to hear this. "I know just because your and Rose's marriage was arranged doesn't mean that you didn't love her, that you don't *still* love her." Sierra spoke around the lump in her throat, the hurt from his rejection caught in her windpipe, making it hard to breathe. "I was home on leave when she passed, you know, so I know you loved her."

The mourning howls still echoed in her memory. That was what their kind did when they lost a mate. Against all better logic, they shifted into wolf form and howled, prowling the mountainside in search of a lost love they'd never again find. Those keening howls had haunted her. She hadn't slept well for weeks. None of them had.

"Sierra," he warned again.

She pressed on. "I know what we saw doesn't change anything between you and me."

He swore, turning to face the opposite wall, his head cradled in one of his hands as he rubbed his temple. Another stretch of silence passed as she watched him, shoulders tense and writhing.

"I just wanted to say I'm sorry," she breathed.

He rounded on her then. "I don't want pity, especially not from you. Rose's death is on my hands. The blood of *every* member of this pack is on my hands. Don't ever forget it." He cut her words short as if he couldn't bear what she'd been about to say. "The past is the past, Sierra."

"I know," she nodded. "I know, but with the air cleared between us, I thought maybe we could be…" She hesitated, thinking of the memory she'd had in the cave. Of him, standing over her, smiling. So much younger. So much more…carefree. "I thought maybe we could be friends?"

Friends. Maverick felt the tension in his body coil. The idea of being friends with Sierra sounded as torturous as this arrangement of theirs was proving to be. He patted his back pocket, where the list she'd given him still remained. He hadn't been able to bring himself to read it. Not without risking everything. It'd been burning a hole there ever since. He could think of few things worse than re-creating the intimacy of friendship that'd once been between them. Not when they were already planning to tread dangerous territory.

He growled at the thought. No. Friends was not something they could ever be again.

"Fucking virgins with a riding crop… Is that what friends do?" He meant the question to be as brusque as it sounded.

She frowned, even as a blush painted her cheeks. "Don't be crass."

He huffed a near laugh, drawing closer to her. "There's nothing about our arrangement that isn't crass." He crossed the room to stand directly in front of her, the heat of their bodies mingling.

She stared up at him, those delicious bee-stung lips of hers drawing into that damn impertinent pucker. "Fine. Then yes. For us, yes. That's part of what being friends means," she challenged.

He didn't try to hide the aroused growl that rumbled in his throat. "I don't have friends. As you pointed out, these days I'm…" He searched for the word she'd used.

"Frustrating? Stubborn? Surly as hell?" she offered.

He frowned, which he guessed only proved her statement. "Grumpy," he supplied. "I believe that was the word you used." He'd tossed that description around in his thoughts so many times since. Admittedly, he'd even tried to force himself to smile since then, but it had backfired when Blaze had asked him why the hell he kept trying to grimace in the reflection of the pack's computer screens.

She shrugged as if the word was of little consequence. "Well, grumpy or not, you do have friends. My brother at least."

He waved a hand in dismissal. "He's the exception that proves the rule."

"The other elite warriors?"

He shook his head. "They don't count. They're forced into proximity with me."

She let out an annoyed huff. "Well, *we* were once friends, and I..." She glanced toward the floor, refusing to look at him as she hesitated. "If we went back to that, I just think it would make life easier on us both."

"Friends." He rolled the word around on his tongue.

As much as he liked the sound of that word on her tongue, it brought her too close for comfort. Too close to *him*.

"Friends." She nodded.

He wouldn't agree to it. Not a chance.

A devious grin curled his lips. "I've never had a friend I wanted to fuck more."

She inhaled a sharp hiss. The sound sent a thrill of pleasure through him. He enjoyed shocking her, watching her lips part on a quick intake of breath.

But she recovered quickly, squaring her shoulders and offering a handshake despite the flush of pink creeping down her throat. "Do we have a deal?"

He ignored her outstretched hand in favor of brushing a wayward strand of hair from her cheek. What he wouldn't give to see her hair down. Wild and free, cascading down her back as he claimed her. His cock stiffened.

"Are you certain you want this?" he countered. Not friendship, but the heat that was between them. Gently, he traced a single knuckle across the curve of her cheek.

Instinctually, she leaned into his touch. "Yes," she breathed.

She was so responsive, aware. Perfection.

His jaw clenched. "Then your next lesson begins now."

Chapter 17

Easing away from her, Maverick crossed the room to the bedside table as he began to disarm. Blades, guns, utility belt. He dropped them onto the table with an audible *thunk* before he stripped off his shirt. He could feel her eyes on him, smell her arousal. She wasn't unaffected. That made two of them.

"Any questions?" he grumbled.

"Why did you wait so long since…last time?"

He nearly laughed. In truth, he'd had to stop himself from going to her on more than one occasion. It'd been so long since he'd been with a woman that he'd wanted to be certain he could restrain himself. "In seduction, anticipation is everything."

One of the floorboards groaned behind him as she moved. It wasn't like him to be so open, but he wanted her to feel safe, comfortable. Protected. Full-grown woman or not, if he was going to deflower his friend's sister, it was the least he could do.

He heard her hesitation. The deep breath followed by a moment's pause. "Will it hurt?"

He flicked on his gun's safety and placed it on the table. "There are ways I can make it more comfortable for you. You'll feel pressure, stretching, but then it should start to feel good, pleasurable."

She forced a nervous laugh. "You say this like you've been with so many virgins before." There was a hint of insecurity in those words. He heard it in the quiver of her voice.

"As you said, when I was younger, your brother and I were cut from the same cloth." He turned toward her. "But I'm not going to take your virginity, Sierra. Not until our wedding night."

"You're not?" She frowned as if her innocence was a nuisance.

He cast her an amused grin. "So eager?" he teased.

She lifted her chin. "I'm not ashamed of my desires."

His grin only widened. Of course she wasn't. "Good. You shouldn't be." Unbuckling his belt, he watched as her gaze fell there, both innocent and curious.

A dangerous combination.

"If we're not going to…" She swallowed. "Have vaginal intercourse," she said, choosing such a sanitary phrase that he had to fight back the amusement that twitched at his lips. "Then what are we going to do?"

He dropped his belt to the floor. "In your words, *other things*."

"Oh." Her hand flew to her lips and stayed there. But her eyes gave her away. They roamed over his torso, tracing the lines of the dark tribal tattoos there.

Fuck. This woman was dangerous.

Innocent yet aroused. Vulnerable yet strong. She ignited his desire until he felt alive with it, like a damn glowing beacon. He'd lived in the dark for far too long.

"Should I take my clothes off now?" she whispered. Using both hands, she stroked the tip of her braid, the golden strands threading through her fingers.

"No," he growled.

"No?" Her blond brows shot up. "Why not?" There was a hint of exasperation in her tone.

She was getting impatient, but that little spark of defiance was everything he craved. That was how he enjoyed her most. Not a meek, mild virgin, but the fierce, dangerous woman she truly was. He grinned. He'd make her dangerous, mold her into the kind of woman who didn't just ask a man for pleasure. She'd demand it, because she deserved it and so much more.

"If we're not going to have sex and you don't want me to take off my clothes, what *are* we going to do?" She placed her hands on her hips.

"I think you'll agree that your clothes didn't get in the way the last time I pleasured you."

She crossed her arms over her chest with a huff, drawing his attention to the swells of her breasts. His cock gave an eager throb. He saw right through her. She wanted to be desired, to feel *wanted*, and clearly, he needed to give her a taste.

Slowly, he prowled toward her, backing her up against the wall as he planted his hands beside her head. "I didn't say I wouldn't have you naked and beneath me."

Her eyes flew to his and locked there.

"I don't want you to take your clothes off, because *I* want to take them off. Piece by damn piece, and any red-blooded cowboy would feel the same."

She reached for him, but he captured her wrists, pinning them above her head. "No," he growled. "If we're going to make it through this, there need to be rules."

"Rules?"

"Unless you want me to take you now against this wall with little restraint like the wolf I truly am." He feared what her answer to that might be.

She smiled, soft and warm. "You say you're more wolf, but when you touch me, it's with a cowboy's sure hands."

He released her from where he had her pinned, and she lowered her arms.

"I touch you, but not the other way around. Not unless I give you permission. Understood?" he said.

"Why?"

When he didn't answer, she frowned. "Is that an order or a request?"

"That's an order, warrior."

"As my packmaster or my friend?"

"Both."

A spark of challenge flared in her eyes as she looped a single finger through the belt loop of his jeans.

He let out a warning growl, but that didn't deter her.

She leaned forward, their noses no more than a hairsbreadth apart. "Yes, Packmaster," she whispered, the hint of a coy grin curling her lips.

His cock stiffened, and it took every bit of willpower he had not to take her over his knee, leaving her ass rosy and pink before he drove into her. She'd remember it with each bounce in the saddle of that damn horny gelding of hers.

Oh, she was dangerous alright. Deliciously so.

He wanted to take those rosebud lips and claim them, but if he tasted her again when they were alone like this, nothing but the howling Montana wind whistling outside the window to keep them company, he wouldn't be able to hold himself back.

Pushing off the wall, he eased away from her, placing some much-needed distance between them. "On second thought, perhaps it's wise if you do take your own clothes off."

Her eyes flashed to her wolf. "Is that an order?" She quirked a brow in challenge.

With her standing there, near the edge of his bed, that deliciously tempting spark in her eye, he couldn't contain the aroused growl that escaped his lips. "Yes," he purred. "Get on the damn bed, warrior."

Turning toward the window, he parted the curtains and stared out into the dark Montana night. The cold winter winds whistled and howled. The mountainside was blanketed with several feet of snow. From behind him, he heard the quiet swish of her clothes hitting the floor, the rustle of the sheets as she crawled onto the bed.

"Maverick." Her voice was tentative, uncertain.

His name on her lips was like a siren's song. He let the curtain fall back into place as he turned toward her.

A sharp hiss of breath tore from his lips. She was gorgeous. His eyes feasted on her, tracing every curve and dip of her smooth skin as she lay in the low lighting of the room, sprawled nude across the bed. Free from the sports bras she wore, her breasts were fuller, curvier than he would have anticipated from how she hid beneath her baggy athletic clothes. Muscled abs led down to a wide swell of feminine hips and the delicious curve of her ass that caused his cock to stiffen in need. His mouth watered as his gaze fell to the patch of trimmed blond hair nestled between her legs.

As his gaze lingered there, a gentle blush highlighted the spattering of freckles on her face. The wide alertness in her eyes was a reminder this was new territory for her. She was watching his every reaction with rapt attention. But despite that, she didn't try to cover herself or hide her body. She wasn't ashamed. She was powerful, breathtaking, strong.

"Beautiful," he purred.

His hands clenched into fists as he struggled to remain by the window. He didn't dare move. If he did, he would cross the room in three quick strides and spread her legs wide before him. He'd bury himself deep inside her tight core, and it wouldn't take long before he'd spend himself. His release would come hot and quick.

But he couldn't allow that. He wanted to pace himself. Savor this moment.

Savor her.

He'd wanted her for too long not to.

Hands curling into fists, he reached out and gripped one hand on the curtain, using the material to anchor himself. "Spread your legs," he ordered. It was the tone of voice he reserved for when he expected compliance without question.

To his pure, delicious agony, she listened. She spread herself wide for him, that swath of blond curls parting to reveal her rosy pink folds. From where he stood, he could see up the length of her body to where her head rested on the pillow.

"You look…" She hesitated, her voice dropping off as her gaze roamed over the tension in his body, the raw desire in his face. "Hungry," she finally whispered.

The muscles in his throat clenched as he swallowed. His cock strained against his jeans, erect and eager.

Christ. If he expected to control himself, he needed to make this quick.

A low, aroused growl escaped his throat. "Touch yourself, warrior."

Her lids popped wide before she blinked at him in confusion. Much to his disappointment, she closed her legs and pushed to sitting on the bed. "What?" There was a skeptical growl in her words.

But at the very least, her change in position gave the growing ache between his legs a reprieve. "You heard me. I want you to touch yourself."

From the hint of frustration cinching her brow, she wasn't pleased with him...yet.

"I thought you were going to teach me how to pleasure a man."

"I am."

"And how are you going to do that if you don't let me touch you and if you don't..." She paused, as if she wasn't certain if her next words revealed too much. "And if you won't touch me." There was a hint of hurt in her voice, and he hated that he'd been the one to put it there.

Slowly, he released his death grip on the curtain and prowled toward her. Leaning over the end of the bed, he supported the weight of his torso with his hands as he drew close to her. "I want to touch you, Sierra. I want to touch every inch of you, and it would be one of the great honors of my life to have you touch me." He reached out and cupped her chin in the palm of his hand. "Don't ever doubt that."

Her quick intake of breath as he slid the rough pads of his ranch-worn fingers over her skin thrilled him. "But if you expect me to teach you, we're going to do this my way. Understand?" He released her, straightening to his full height.

Pulling her bare legs up to her chest, she watched as he returned to the window, glancing out into the dark night.

"I just don't understand how I'll learn if we don't—"

He cut her off before she could undo him even more than she already had. "We will. Just not tonight."

"But—" She started to protest.

He faced back toward her. "Any man worthy of you will care more about your pleasure than his own. If you expect to know how to please a man like that, you have to be familiar with your own body."

He had her attention now. She was hanging on his every word.

"You're going to pleasure yourself, and I'm going to watch so I can see what you like, see what makes you moan." He braced his forearm on the wall, leaning against it. "So then next time, I can do all those things to you. So *I* can be the one who makes you moan."

Her blush deepened, and she looked away as if to hide her embarrassment. "You already did that in the stables."

A smirk curled his lips at the reminder as he let out an aroused grumble. "That was only the start of all the things I plan to do with you."

Her gaze flew to his and locked there.

"Trust me, warrior," he said. "Please?"

Her breath hitched. He could see it. "I don't think I've ever heard you beg for anything."

At that, he nearly laughed, as close to the sound as he'd come in some time. "I'd beg on my knees if it got you to let me see that pretty, pink pussy again," he growled.

Her cheeks flamed, even as she smiled in satisfaction. He'd given her a glimpse of the sort of power she held over him, over any man who asked for her consent, and from her wide-toothed grin, she reveled in it. "I'm not used to you talking this much," she whispered.

"Most of the time, I won't, but when we're alone..."

When they were alone, he planned to lavish her with endless dirty talk.

"I have a hard time using just my hand," she admitted. "I usually use a toy."

"A toy?" He quirked his brow in amusement.

"A vibrator," she clarified. "It's shaped like a tube of lipstick, so it's inconspicuous. I keep it in my bedside drawer."

The thought of her using a sex toy on herself as she imagined her most private fantasies caused his balls to ache in anticipation. "We'll get to toys later. For now, I want to see what you'd do if it were just you, all alone. No assistance."

She nodded, but he wanted, needed, to have her clear permission. "Are you certain you want to do this, Sierra?"

"Yes." She didn't so much as hesitate. "Yes, I want this."

A low, aroused growl rumbled from his throat. "Good. Then spread your legs, warrior."

She nodded, leaning back on the bed again. As she did, she paused, holding her weight on her elbows as she opened her legs. "Maverick?" she called to him.

He grunted in acknowledgment as his gaze roamed over her. She was more relaxed now. So open and comfortable in his presence. When he met her eyes, his breath caught.

"I do trust you," she whispered. "I wouldn't have asked you to do this if I didn't."

Her words humbled him, immediately sparking a sharp ache of longing in his chest. Lord, if he didn't wonder every day what trust, what intimacy could have been between them.

If only...

He cleared his throat, lowering his head and raking his fingers through his hair to mask the pain in his expression. He may never be able to explore the complex emotions between them, but he could explore her, her body. At least until their wedding night...

"I said, spread your legs, warrior." His words were a harsh command, but she obliged him like any good soldier would.

Lowering herself onto the mattress, she trailed a hand over the curve of her own breast, the taut pink nipple puckering with each brush. Slowly, her hand trailed lower, nestling in the soft pink folds there and probing until she located her clit at the apex. As her fingertips connected with her most sensitive flesh, a soft groan of pleasure escaped her.

Maverick felt his knees buckle at the sound. His hand shot out, gripping the curtain again for support. At this rate, he'd shred the damn things before the evening was done. "Open your legs wider."

She spread her knees further, so he could see every illicit detail of her actions. She traced her index and middle fingers around her clit. Her touch was soft, tentative, as if too much too soon would have been overstimulation. He'd guessed as much from their earlier encounter. She was so sensitive.

As her fingers circled, he bit his lower lip, salivating like the wolf that he was at the sight of the glistening moisture that now coated her fingertips. What he wouldn't give to lap up that wet heat with his tongue. She'd taste like sin as he pleasured her with his mouth.

But her movements were still tentative, nervous.

"Don't hold back," he growled. "You're braver than that."

She took the bait, rocking her hips forward, her eyes meeting his in challenge as her fingers dipped inside her wet folds, probing as she cried out. Her eyes flashed to her wolf.

"Fuck," he swore, biting his fist hard enough that even in human form, his wolflike canines nearly pierced his skin. His other hand white-knuckled the curtain, but he could only restrain himself for so long.

Unbuckling his jeans, he gripped the hard length of his cock, pumping and working the head that nearly crested the hem of his open fly. The thick girth rubbed against the material as a bead of moisture coated his tip.

Fuck, she was a delicious sight. Utter perfection.

He watched with total attention as she edged closer. She liked to increase speed and pressure, then slow, denying herself for a brief second so that each return was more blissful and intense. She was getting close. He could see that, but she wasn't quite there yet. He let out a pleasured groan as her back arched against his burgundy sheets and she pleasured herself harder, faster. But at the sound of his own pleasure, her closed lids shot open, finding him instantly.

The desire that flared in her eyes nearly sent him over the edge. "I want to see you," she whispered, her gaze falling to his open fly. From the fire in her eyes, she knew exactly what she was doing to him, and she lived for it.

She could bring the most powerful wolf of their kind to heel with a single sentence.

He knew what she meant, but he wanted to hear her speak the words aloud. "Say it."

"I want..." She let out a pleasured moan. "I want to see how hard you are for me."

He grinned as he slowly shook his head. "Not tonight, warrior."

Her frustration with him flared again. But the way she pleasured herself—denial, anticipation—was the name of the game, and he intended to draw her pleasure out if she let him.

But to his surprise, he'd made one fatal mistake.

She held the power here.

Not him.

"I'm not sure I can finish without you," she said. She stuck out her lower lip like some saucy little minx rather than a shy virgin.

This woman was dangerous. Pure fire.

She rocked her hips back and forth, probing her folds and kneading her clit as she pegged him with a sultry, heavy-lidded stare. "I need you, Maverick," she whispered.

"Sierra," he growled in warning.

She knew exactly what she was doing, and he wasn't certain he could bear it.

Not without losing himself.

She wiggled lower on the bed, her breasts swaying with the

movement before she bit her lower lip and delivered her final blow. "Please, Packmaster," she pouted.

"Fuck," he swore, releasing the length of his cock and prowling toward her.

In one swift move, he gripped her by the hips, pulling her down the length of the bed until her ass was positioned at the edge of the bedframe. He dropped to his knees, burying his face between her legs. Within seconds, his tongue was on her clit, circling and caressing as he ate her.

Christ, she tasted like honey on his tongue. Pure sweetness. She cried out, bucking against him as he held her in place and feasted on her. Her orgasm came hard and fast, shaking her whole body. A flood of delicious moisture coated his tongue as he felt her legs over his shoulders vibrate with the ecstasy of it.

When she finished, he released her. Gently pulling back as he used his tongue to lap the remnants of her pleasure from his trimmed beard.

She let out a long, contented sigh. "I didn't know I could finish so…" Her voice trailed off as she relaxed into the bed with a satiated moan.

"Quickly?" he offered.

"Thoroughly," she corrected. "I felt it in every inch of my body." Her eyes were still heavy lidded, beckoning him. She reached out to touch him. "Thank—"

"Your lesson's through for tonight," he said. He tried to sound cold and distant, but it underscored his pain. He couldn't look at her. Not now. Not when she had that hint of hopeful promise in her eyes.

"Maverick—"

He nearly winced at the sound of his name on her lips. Everything he wanted from her was laced in that single word. Closing his eyes, he kissed her gently, a sweet brush of his lips against hers. Forcing himself to open his eyes, he saw all the hope that lingered there. It killed him. Slowly, he cupped her chin in his hand, gentle and reverent. From the surprise in her eyes, he was more tender than she'd ever expected. "Go home, my beautiful warrior," he whispered. He brushed his thumb over her jaw before he turned away from her so he didn't have to see the hurt on her face. He returned to the window. The wind had stopped howling. Instead, a silent layer of snowfall sprinkled over the pastures. Not enough to stick.

Not permanent.

He heard the creak of the mattress as she eased from the bed. The quiet shuffle as she put on her clothes. The silence stretched between them. The twist of the doorknob signaled her exit. He waited for the sound of the latch clicking shut as she walked away.

But it never came.

"Maverick," she said. Her tone was quiet, softer than he was used to. "About what I said in the stables…"

He shook his head, still refusing to look at her. He knew exactly what she was talking about. "Think nothing of it." He tried to dismiss her, but she didn't take the bait.

She waited a long beat before she said, "I don't think you're a monster."

He nodded. "I know."

She inhaled an audible breath. "Then why did you—?"

"Because I wanted to, Sierra."

"Oh." That single word carried more emotion than he wanted it to. "It's just… A monster doesn't touch a woman as tenderly as you do."

On that final word, she left, leaving him alone in the empty guest bedroom, staring out as the dark Montana sky coated the mountains with cold.

Chapter 18

SIERRA WOKE TO THE SOUND OF SOMEONE RIFLING THROUGH her closet. Ears pricked to the slightest movement, she lay still. Slowly, her hand inched toward the blade on her bedside table. A strong hand clamped over hers. Her eyes shot open.

"You missed our morning run." Cheyenne stood over her, wearing her favorite workout clothes as she tapped the watch on her wrist. "Six a.m. sharp. It's already almost eight thirty." Which meant it was well past sunrise, and Cheyenne wasn't the only invader in her room.

"Told you she'd go for her blade before she smelled it was us." Dakota sat at the end of the bed, watching as another equally petite she-wolf raided Sierra's closet.

"Maeve." Sierra sat up with a smile as the other she-wolf rushed over to pull her into an embrace, a surprisingly tight one. It'd been months since she'd last seen her friend, since Maeve had unexpectedly run off with one of the pack's sworn enemies, who was an enemy no longer.

"What are you doing here? Is Rogue with you?" Sierra wrinkled her nose in distaste, and Cheyenne fought to stifle a snarl at the mere mention of his name.

Releasing her, Maeve waved a hand. "Oh, who knows. We live like nomads. You know how he is. He'll make an appearance when we least expect it, probably at the wedding in a week."

Sierra's brows shot up. "The wedding?"

"Your brother already marked her two weeks ago." Dakota grinned.

Mae's eyes went wide with surprise. "He did?"

"He did more than that." Cheyenne leaned over to Sierra,

sniffing her in a way that was more wolf than human. "You reek of him. No wonder you missed our run. You already had a workout last night."

Sierra lifted her arm and sniffed her shoulder in a move that was far from ladylike. She hadn't had a chance to shower after last night, and even though she'd changed clothes, her skin still smelled of his scent. Hell, she couldn't smell any more like him if she'd been pregnant with his young, and considering they hadn't gotten that far, there was no possibility of that. She'd have to wash his scent off. But that wasn't important now.

"What do you mean the wedding is only a week away?" Sierra snarled, drawing all the attention in the room as she cut Mae off. According to their agreement with the council, she and Maverick only had little more than a week to announce, but they hadn't discussed the particular date yet.

Her friends fell silent, all of them exchanging concerned glances.

"Maverick and I haven't talked about a date yet."

For a moment, the other she-wolves didn't move, before suddenly her three friends burst out laughing.

"Oh, he's in for it now." Dakota cackled.

Mae shook her head. "What is it about alpha males that makes them think they'll never meet their match in a female?"

Cheyenne shrugged. "You'd think they'd have learned by now."

Sierra let out an exasperated huff. "What in the world are the three of you talking about?"

Dakota and Mae exchanged glances before Mae spoke. "With most of the pack still here from the ceremony, Maverick announced this morning that the wedding would be next week. The pack is buzzing with excitement..." Her voice trailed off, but Sierra knew what that meant.

The wedding was in a week, and thanks to the fact that her fiancé was the packmaster, he would get his way, despite her not having been so much as consulted.

Her hands clenched into fists. That bastard. This was what he considered friendship? She'd thought they'd made progress last night. She'd thought…

Oh, there would be hell to pay.

Mae clapped her hands together. "Now, you have an appointment with this lovely human bridal store in Seattle in a few hours, and if we're going to take the pack's helicopter there, we need to be out on the landing pad in an hour."

Sierra shook her head. "I will not be going to any bridal store today."

Mae made a pout face. "Why not?"

Sierra stood, crossing her room before she closed the door, not that closing it or even *locking* doors seemed to keep any of her packmates out. They'd always been this way—noisy, intrusive, overly involved, unaware of personal space or boundaries—and yet they were her family, which meant she wouldn't want them any other way.

Sierra leaned her weight against the now-closed door before she met the eyes of her friends one by one. "What I'm about to tell you cannot leave this room."

Thirty minutes later, she'd finished disclosing the details of her and Maverick's negotiations and encounters, save for the bit with the riding crop and the finer details of the previous evening, for Maeve's sake.

When she finished, Cheyenne let out a long whistle.

"And the plot thickens," Dakota said.

"My brother is a thick-headed moron." Mae scowled as she stamped a foot.

"I can't say I disagree," Sierra said.

"So what are you going to do?" Cheyenne asked.

"The only thing a warrior can do," Dakota answered, a mischievous sparkle in her eye as she cast Sierra a grin only a best friend would understand.

"Wage war," the two women said in unison.

Cheyenne and Maeve cast them both grins. "I'm in," Cheyenne said.

Sierra raised a brow. "Maeve?"

Mae shrugged. "Just so long as I get to help bridal shop with you for the wedding, no one is better at annoying my brother than I am."

There was a lightness in his chest he hadn't felt in years. Maverick stood at the entrance of the corral, inhaling a deep drag of cold mountain air. The cool sensation that filled his lungs felt like the first full breath he'd taken for some time, though considering he'd been thrown off the wrong end of a horse more than once in the past hour and had the wind completely knocked out of him, there might have been a reason for it.

"Easy, easy." The sound of Dean's voice cautioned from behind him.

Maverick turned away from the blue mountain views in the distance and back toward the paddock. Dean was in the pen with the Beast now as Malcolm watched. As soon as the pack had gotten wind that Maverick's new horse, who they'd all less than affectionately taken to calling the Beast, was damn near as untrainable as that monster of a mustang Wes called Black Jack, it'd become the latest point of challenge and amusement on the ranch to see who— if anyone—could tame him.

Thus far, Maverick had been bucked off more times than he could count, and that was only once he managed to get close enough to the animal. Most times, he was practically chased out the gate. Hell, not even Wes, who despite his darker nature had a way with horses, had fared well. Now, after he and Malcolm had been run off as if the horse were more bull than steed, it was Dean's turn to give it a go, not that he appeared to be faring much better.

Dean wasn't more than two feet inside the gate, his hands lifted in front of him in surrender as he inched toward the Beast. Beast stamped his front leg several times, the heat of his breath clouding his nostrils against the chilled Montana air like he could breathe fire.

"Easy now," Dean muttered again. He dared inch closer, but that was apparently one inch too close for Beast's liking.

The mustang charged, sending Dean leaping over the paddock gate within seconds. "Shit," the cowboy swore.

Maverick cracked an uncharacteristic grin as he chuckled.

"Told you it wasn't just my grimace that pissed him off." Malcolm crossed his arms with more than a hint of satisfaction. It was more joy than Maverick had seen the Grey Wolf executioner exhibit recently. As the wolf solely responsible for dealing with any enemies of war and the few unsavory characters the pack maintained as prisoners, Malcolm dealt firsthand with the worst of their kind, and he had the matching disposition to show for it. For their enemies, he was the sure-footed assassin they feared would find them alone in the dark.

The darkness he harbored had only seemed to grow in the past few years—ever since they'd lost Bo, Maverick's second-in-command before Wes had come along. Since then, Malcolm had never quite been the same.

"Clearly," Dean shot back. He glanced toward Maverick and frowned at his hint of amusement. "You're in a good mood for a man whose horse is being a total asshole."

Maverick grunted in response, refusing to pursue the conversation. He wasn't about to go into detail about how he'd spent the previous evening. When he'd woken come morning, he'd felt a keen ache in his chest at Sierra's absence. He hadn't been aware of what he'd been missing, the connection with another wolf. He hadn't been with a woman since he'd lost Rose, and even with his late wife, their time together had been amiable yet…different.

Nothing like the constant ache of longing he felt in his chest now, the joy and anticipation of wondering when he'd be alone with her again. He leaned too close to the paddock gate, causing Beast to snap at his hand. He drew his palm back with a grumbled curse, the snap of the horse's jaw serving as the reminder he needed.

"I can always return him to the breeder. If he's this ornery, there was likely something wrong from the start. Maybe a lame mare or an overly aggressive stud." As the Grey Wolf front-of-house director, it was Dean's duty to deal with all the various human breeders, suppliers, and nearby ranchers. For all intents and purposes, to human outsiders, he was the face of Wolf Pack Run.

"You think they'd give you a refund?" Malcolm asked.

"Likely so. I make most of them uneasy." Dean shrugged. "Makes getting my way a cinch." *Them* referring to the humans he regularly dealt with.

"Being a wolf will do that," Maverick grumbled. There was a reason he rarely left the ranch, save for business trips to the subpacks and adjacent shifter clans. In the human world, his wolf set most creatures on edge. As alpha, him more than most.

"Works to our advantage." Malcolm circled the paddock, watching Beast with narrowed eyes.

"So you want him or not? If he can't be trained, he's a money pit in feed and care that ain't worth the cost." Dean lifted a brow.

Maverick watched the horse, assessing. Beast raised up on his hind legs in frustration. His dark eyes flashed. He'd had enough of being caged. Maverick understood the feeling.

Shaking his head, he turned away from the animal. "Not yet. Give him more time to settle."

Dean opened his mouth to suggest otherwise, but the sound of one of the pack's old pickups drew near, bringing their conversation to a halt.

The truck pulled to a stop outside the stables. The driver's side door eased open with a loud creak, and Blaze emerged. Instead of the typical Carhartt that most of the packmembers on the ranch sported, Blaze wore a black leather jacket with a Stetson and a T-shirt imprinted with the words *Hide your daughters*.

Maverick let out a displeased grumble.

A moment later, Dakota exited the passenger's side. She was never far behind where Blaze was concerned.

"Blaze, care to try your hand at taming the Beast?" Dean hollered from across the paddock. He knew full damn well that if anyone tried to get in the pen again today, they'd likely be on the wrong end of that mustang's powerful hooves.

Blaze barely cast a glance in the horse's direction. "No, thanks. I tame the beast several times a day and always before bed. The pack psychiatrist says it's good for my self-esteem."

Dean let out a bark of a laugh, and Dakota shook her head as they walked toward the stables. "We're looking for Peaches," she offered in explanation. "She needs her insulin shot."

No surprise there. Blaze's decrepit and surly cat had had one foot in the grave for a number of years. Maverick could hardly believe the thing was still happily breathing.

Dakota followed Blaze toward the stables. "Brace yourself, Packmaster," she called over her shoulder before she and Blaze disappeared into the barn.

Before Dakota could elaborate, the passenger's side door to the truck swung open again as Sierra emerged from the truck.

"You could have at least put the seat forward for me," she yelled after Dakota before muttering something under her breath about best friends her ass.

Then she turned toward him. The full sight of her hit him like a punch to the gut.

He'd seen her hundreds, thousands of times before, and the attraction between them had always been present, but this was different, because now he'd memorized every soft curve, every delicate slope of her skin. He knew what she looked like when she came, knew the sounds she made when she moaned. He could practically taste her on his tongue, and fuck, if that wasn't more dangerous than any enemy he'd ever faced.

She headed straight toward him, her braid a flyaway mess from the whistling Montana wind, but all he could think about, all he could focus on, was how he wished he could untie it. He'd set all those blond locks free for his fingers to explore and caress.

"I have a bone to pick with you." She marched up to him before planting her hands on her hips in that defiant way that made him equal parts frustrated and hungry...for her. "We need to talk." Sierra drew closer, lowering her voice so that beneath the wind, only he could hear her.

His cock stiffened in response. He nearly swore as it did. *Fuck.* She smelled of him. Not simply as if she'd been near him, but she smelled *of* him. Like a mate.

"You agreed we were going to be *friends.*"

He shook his head. "I agreed to no such thing, warrior."

She bristled. "You may as well have. Then I wake up this morning to find you announced our wedding date without me, *and* you've given Maeve free rein to plan everything? Do you know how much tulle will be involved?"

He quirked a brow. He wasn't even certain what tulle was. "You wanted to plan it?"

"Hell no," she swore. "I could care less about any of it," she sniffed.

He had a feeling that wasn't the full truth.

"But I didn't appreciate spending several hours with Maeve forcing me into *dresses.*"

He'd never seen Sierra wear a dress a day in her life.

"I should have been consulted."

"It was strategic." He leaned closer, lowering his voice. "We had to announce the date for the council anyway, and an event of this size presents a unique opportunity. With all our allies present on the ranch as wedding attendants, we'll be able to discern which of them..." His voice trailed off, leaving the implication evident.

"Which of them wants you dead," she finished.

He gave a curt nod.

"Be that as it may, I want a small wedding."

At that, he did laugh. "I'm packmaster, Sierra. There's no such thing as a small wedding."

She gaped at him. "So I have no say in this?"

He grunted in mild acknowledgment, which only seemed to ignite her.

"This is what you call being friends?" She jabbed a finger into his chest twice until unexpectedly, her palm flattened. She blinked at the hand resting on his pectoral as if she wasn't certain how it had ended up there, then quickly removed it. But the brief feel of her touch was enough. For once, he didn't have to care that they had an audience. She was his fiancée after all.

He eased closer to her, wrapping his arms around her back and pulling her against him. She let out a small *eep* in surprise, bracing both hands against his chest, but didn't protest. Leaning in, he brushed his lips against hers as he whispered. "I warned you being with me wouldn't be easy. As packmaster, there're rules, expectations, pack needs."

Her eyes narrowed. "This isn't about who's out to kill you. Sure, it will serve that purpose, too, whatever ridiculous plan you've devised, but this is about keeping me at arm's length, pushing me away."

He couldn't bring himself to answer.

She'd dove straight to the heart of it.

"I should have consulted you. Forgive me?"

For a brief moment, her features softened. As they did, he swooped in for the final blow. He claimed her lips, reveling in the way she melted against him, despite the other packmembers around them. A few catcalls from Dakota and a low wolf whistle from Dean brought him back to himself. He broke the kiss between them, and that wouldn't escape her notice. Slowly, Sierra opened her eyes, blinking up at him with a dazed stare and swollen, just-kissed lips. He couldn't help the satisfied smirk that tugged at his lips. Like it or not, he knew how to disarm this particular warrior instantly.

Coming back to herself, she blinked a few times before those plump, delicious lips of hers pulled into a scowl at his little display. "Friends don't fight dirty," she accused.

"No, they don't." He held her gaze for a long beat.

They would never be only friends, even though they couldn't be anything more.

Gently, he released her.

"Kissing is against the rules of a fair fight," she said.

"Good thing I don't fight fair, warrior."

"You did before."

Before.

Back when they'd been young. "You forget that even back then, we were always trying to one-up each other."

Her fingers fluttered to her lips, lingering there as if she could still feel the brush of his kiss. As she started to walk away, a frustrated glare sharpened the lines of her face. "This is war."

Chapter 19

MAVERICK HAD KNOWN SIERRA'S REVENGE WOULD BE SWIFT, but what he hadn't anticipated was that it would be early. Ungodly early. Before sunrise to be exact.

The sharp sound of a rooster crowing pierced his ears, jolting him upright in his bed. *What in the blazing fuck?*

He swiped the sleep from his eyes, flopping back into the sheets with a growl as another shrill crow bounced off the walls of his bedroom. Eyes still shut, he winced. The noise was too close to his head to be from outside.

Daring to crack one eye open, he glanced at the clock. 4:00 a.m. Too early for even the most incessant of the ranch's fowl to be urging them all awake, which meant...

Another earsplitting crow followed by a pair of snapping fingers two inches from his face forced him eyes to open.

"Rise and shine, Packmaster." The sound of Sierra's voice proceeded the third—and what he would ensure would be final—crow, considering he had every intent of butchering the bird, as he took in the sight before him.

Sierra stood over him, dressed and ready for the day, that damn rooster perched on her upper arm. From the bright, doe-eyed look she gave him, she was well rested and almost...chipper? As if most of the pack hadn't just gone to sleep only hours before.

Their kind still tended toward being nocturnal like the true wolves they came from. Thus, they kept a fluctuating schedule on the ranch of who worked which sunrise hours. It was at night when the pack truly came to life.

Angry Sierra he could handle, but chipper?

She was up to something obviously, and he wasn't certain he

wanted to know what was making his bride-to-be chipper at this goddamn hour, but he had an unfortunate feeling he was going to learn—and soon.

She snapped her fingers in his face again. "Come on. Out of bed." *Snap. Snap.* "Chop, chop. This wedding isn't going to plan itself."

When he grumbled, she lifted her arm, where that damn pigeon of hers was perched. He knew it was a rooster, but from the way the thing was perched, it could have been a fucking parrot for all he cared. All he knew was that the crowing was going to stop.

Now.

Sierra lifted a finger, threatening to prod the bird again, but Maverick let out a low, feral growl. "Make that damn bird crow one more time, and I'll eat him and all his cousins for breakfast."

Sierra grinned, satisfied she'd provoked a response from him. "Look at you, pretending to be the Big Bad Wolf like you're not one of the biggest softies on this ranch," she teased. "You're like a big, grumpy cat when you wake up. It'd almost be cute if you weren't so snarly."

"And why exactly are you waking me up at four o'clock in the fucking morning?" He'd been up late finalizing the plans to flush out the traitor in the pack, alongside Colt, Austin, and Blaze. He'd thought it strange when Sierra had ducked out of the meeting early. He should have realized then she was up to something.

Sierra crossed her arms over her chest, the rooster shifting its perch from her arm to her shoulder. "Thanks to you, we have less than a week to plan this wedding, which means there's work to do."

Maverick groaned, rolling over and attempting to shield his eyes from the overhead light with his arm. "Didn't I put Maeve in charge of that?"

Wedding planning was decidedly not on his to-do list. He had more important things.

Meeting with the council. Running intel. Strategizing the staged attack at the reception. Brooding.

"You *did* put Maeve in charge," she said, interrupting his internal to-do list, "and according to her, we have things to do."

What sort of things did one plan for a wedding? He'd never participated in planning his own. When he and Rose had married, everything had been planned for them. "Getting your dress?" he asked.

This time, it was her turn to growl. "Hell no. I'm not wearing a dress."

"Like hell you're not." He sat up in bed, the twisted sheets placed precariously over his bare hips. "If I have to wear a tux, you have to wear a dress."

Truth be told, it was less about fairness and more about the fact that he'd been looking forward to the novelty of seeing her in one.

"It doesn't matter. According to Maeve, today we're going cake tasting."

He wrinkled his nose in disgust. "Cake tasting?"

She placed her hands on her hips. Somehow, *she* seemed to be growing exasperated with *him*. "Yes, cake tasting, and you know how I feel about you repeating everything I say."

He ignored that last comment. "Unfortunately, warrior, you'll have to taste cakes without me. Today I'm supposed to meet with—"

"Don't try to wiggle your way out of this one, cowboy. I already had Maeve clear your schedule." She pulled his Stetson off the end of the bedpost where he'd hung the hat and tossed it at him.

He ducked out of the way of the wayward hat, catching it with one hand. Even half-awake, his reflexes were sharp. "My sister isn't in charge of my schedule."

Okay. This time, he heard it. He did sound grumpy, even to his own ears.

"She is now that you put her in charge of the wedding."

He released a short huff of a sigh. He was starting to recognize what a ludicrous idea that'd been. His sister had never listened to him, even before she'd run off with that criminal bastard she now called her husband. Let alone when she was in cahoots with the other females of the pack, Sierra included.

Sierra clapped her hands. "Now, you heard the King, Packmaster," she said, her tone giving the more exulted of those two titles to the chicken. She grinned with clear pleasure to be ordering Maverick around for once. "It's time to get up. The ranch chores won't do themselves, and we need to be at the bakery by 8:00 a.m. sharp."

He growled.

"Off you go now, Elvis." Still ignoring Maverick's protests, she bent forward, brushing at Elvis's spindly legs and urging him to hop from her shoulder to the floor. As she did, the bend and wiggle move treated Maverick to an ample view of her cleavage not too far from his face.

Despite the weather, she was wearing a fitted black tank top underneath her open jacket. Considering the matching yoga pants she sported, she'd clearly just come from her morning workout. The tight black material, so unlike her usual wardrobe, had to have been a gift from his sister. The word *bride* was emblazoned in looping cursive rhinestones across the curve of her breasts. He knew her better than to think Sierra had chosen rhinestones for herself, though the woman *did* dot her *i*'s with hearts.

He thought of that damn list burning a hole in the pocket of his work jeans. He still hadn't had the courage to open it. He wasn't certain he could handle the knowledge it entailed.

Finally, Elvis hopped off her shoulder with a flap that sent several feathers scattering onto Maverick's bed. As Sierra straightened, her eyes grew wide, fixating on the sight of his erection now tenting the sheets. "Apparently Elvis isn't the only cock demanding attention this morning."

The appendage in question gave an eager twitch. He swore.

Her and those damn puns.

But if it was war she wanted, and this was clearly her first strategy, then two could play at that game.

He leaned back onto his pillows in a long, languorous stretch, thrusting his hips forward, which only caused her eyes to grow wider. The sheet pulled taut across him. He let out a deep-throated groan as he released his stretch. He scratched a hand across the scruff of his beard before he ran his tongue over the length of his teeth.

He knew she was acutely aware of everything his tongue did these days.

"Well, warrior, if I'm at the mercy of your command today, then tell me"—he gestured to his erection beneath the sheets—"are you going to take care of that?"

She sputtered. "I…" She gaped at him, seemingly unable to answer.

He let out a harsh bark of a laugh, more amused than he'd felt in years as he threw back the sheets and stood. Their kind wasn't shy when it came to nudity, but this close and with him erect…

Sierra let out an adorable *eep*, both her hands flying to her mouth to stifle her gasp at the sight of him standing naked and aroused before her.

He flashed her a grin, dropping his voice to a low, purring growl. "Why so quiet, warrior?"

She stammered. "You…you sleep in the buff?" she finally managed to get out.

Gripping the base of his length, he gave his dick a slow, steady stroke. "I find it makes taking care of my *morning duties* easier."

She inhaled a sharp breath, watching him with wide-eyed attention. There was desire and more than a hint of curiosity in her eyes alongside her obvious shock.

Releasing himself, he eased closer, leaning down to lay a quick kiss on her cheek before he whispered in her ear. "Don't worry, warrior. I'm more than confident that with a strong, independent woman like you as my wife, we'll split those chores equally."

He stepped away from her, leaving her still sputtering as he headed toward his shower.

When he reached the sink, he splashed some cold water on his face before her voice carried to him from the bedroom.

"Maverick?" she called, more than a hint of frustration in her tone.

"Mmm?" he responded.

"How in the world is it going to fit?"

The sounds of his deep chuckles echoed against the porcelain tile.

If Maverick had thought the arrival of Sierra and "the King," which she insisted he call the damn bird, in his bedroom at the ass crack of dawn was the only weapon she had in her arsenal, he was sorely mistaken. After he'd showered and dressed, she'd forced him to traipse out to the cold of the truck and assist her in rounding up several strays that'd wandered away from the rest of the cattle herd before they rode to downtown Billings. The sun crested the horizon as the scenery sped by. He couldn't remember the last time he'd been off the packlands, let alone in the city, even one as small as Billings.

According to Sierra, Maeve had set them up for a cake-tasting appointment at a local bakery, and while he could care less about what food was consumed at the wedding, if any, he went along with the plan. Mainly because Sierra wouldn't hear a word of his complaining. Once he'd finally settled himself into the idea, he toned down his protests for Sierra's sake. Despite her insistence that she didn't care about the wedding, she seemed more than a bit enthused about the whole experience. No surprise there. When they'd been teens, she'd been equally pleased during her Den Freedom, a time in which the pack entrusted the secret of their existence to their young adults and sent them out into the human world to live for a handful of weeks. He hadn't enjoyed his own experience. Period.

He didn't complain too much when the human baker spent the first ten minutes of their arrival openly gawking at the sheer size of him or commenting on how, in her unknowing words, "wolflike" his eyes and teeth were. He didn't even swear too loudly when he accidentally broke one of the pieces of delicate china the hostess had placed in front of him. He'd barely squeezed the damn little handle between his thumb and forefinger, and the thing had quivered beneath his touch before promptly shattering in his hand. It was one of only hundreds of things that day that reminded him of exactly why he never left the ranch.

There was no such thing as delicate china at Wolf Pack Run. When they were in human form, they ate with hearty metal forks and spoons, and that was when they ate in human form at all. He preferred his dinner fresh, in his jaws.

Delicate china be damned.

By midafternoon, he'd had more than his fill of both humanity and cake for one day. Sierra had forced him to eat so many miniature sample pieces that he was certain he'd never been so full in his life. Save for one occasion when he was a young teenager, and he'd stupidly tried to eat a whole buck on his own. The result had left him sick for weeks.

Maverick leaned back in his chair, unable to force himself to take another bite. "I think that's enough," he grumbled as Sierra attempted to shove another sample toward him.

She was laid out against the back of her chair, one hand over the curve of her toned belly. "I'll be lucky if I fit into my dress after that." She rubbed her still-taut abs with a groan.

"So you *are* wearing a dress?" He couldn't resist prodding her.

"Not like you think." She grinned. "Don't sound so pleased."

He pushed away the dish in front of him. "I could care less what you wear. Show up naked for all I care."

She laughed. "You'd like that, wouldn't you?"

And to think, he'd almost started to think she'd been right about them calling themselves friends again. He raked his gaze over her in a heated stare. "I would."

No. Friends they were certainly not.

A blush prickled her cheeks, and she reached toward the tasting menu to avoid his gaze. "If you don't care, why the insistence?"

He shrugged. "You know Maeve. She'd never forgive me if I didn't side with her on this, and if we expect to pull this off believably for the council so we can negotiate with the Execution Underground, we need the right…".

"Optics," they said in unison, which caused Sierra to laugh.

Maverick cracked a sly grin

It'd been so long since he'd heard the sound from himself that when she'd elicited it from him this morning, it'd seemed foreign even to his own ears.

"In any case, being believable won't influence the outcome of the plan in regard to flushing out the traitor."

"It could," he answered.

Over the past several days, the elite warriors, Sierra included, had floated information out into the pack about his and Sierra's post-reception plans. The gossip of the plans would no doubt make its rounds, with all their supposed allies in attendance. Once he and Sierra were alone, with the continuing reception keeping the rest of the pack otherwise occupied, whoever was after him would have a unique opportunity to strike again. Or at least, that was the intention.

Because this time, when they came for him, he would be lying in wait.

Sierra poked at a crumb of cake still on the dish in front of her before quickly popping it in her mouth, drawing his attention back toward her. It had never occurred to him that a man could enjoy watching a woman eat, but he did enjoy it. The look of delight in her eyes as she chewed, the way she sucked the last bit of frosting from her finger. On the rare occasions he and Rose shared a meal together, Rose had been the epitome of polite, delicately nibbling at a salad without ever really enjoying her food as they made minimal conversation.

Rose had been sweet, amiable, kind, but she never would have feasted and enjoyed herself the way Sierra did.

Sierra let out an unapologetic moan, savoring the last morsel. "So good. It was all good. How do we decide?"

His cock stiffened, pressing against the fly of his jeans. The sound of her moan elicited more than a few heated memories, and he had plans for more lessons. Only a few more nights and then he would take her—fully. But he was in no hurry. He knew that he needed to enjoy what time he had with her now.

To make it last.

This is temporary. All temporary, he reminded himself.

Anything else held the potential to cloud his judgment, to make him less effective for the pack like he had been in the damn cave. He couldn't allow that to happen again.

She smacked her lips once in appreciation. "Optics or not, I'm looking forward to it."

"To the wedding?"

She wrinkled her brow. "No, to catching the rat bastard that's selling your life to the highest bidder."

He couldn't help the smile that twisted his lips. "Well, if I can endure this"—he gestured to the empty tasting tray that had hosted all the bite-size cakes—"you can pretend to be ladylike in a dress for a few hours."

"Now you sound like my father." She cast him a disapproving look.

He knew her relationship with her father hadn't been perfect, but James had loved her, cared for her. Maverick knew that without a doubt. "Your father was a good man, Sierra, but old-fashioned."

"He was, but—" Something in his tone must have alerted her. She set down the tasting menu. "I'm sorry. I know it hasn't been long since…" Her voice trailed off.

Since he'd learned the truth about his own father. That the

man he'd thought he'd known, at least from a distance, was a liar, a murderer.

Monster.

When he didn't say anything, she leaned forward, reaching out to place her hand over his on the tabletop, a clear violation of their rules, but he'd let it slip for now.

"I know it couldn't have been easy learning those things about your dad."

He grumbled in response, hearing the words but refusing to look at the pity in her gaze. He didn't deserve her pity. Not with all the ways he'd hurt her years ago, all the ways he'd hurt Rose and countless others. The gruff brusqueness of his tone was unintentional. "The reality of his character doesn't hurt me as much as the pain he caused his victims."

She nodded. "No. No, it doesn't." She was no doubt thinking of his sister, of Jared and Jared's father. "But that doesn't make it hurt any less." She was watching him with those caring eyes of hers.

He shifted his weight in his chair, uncomfortable beneath her gaze. Being on the receiving end of that look did things to him, but that was one of the things he loved most about her. Sierra was fierce in all things. In how she fought, cared, empathized, loved.

Love.

The weight of that word kicked against him like Beast had just bucked him.

Love. Did he love her? No, he couldn't…

He glanced toward her. Those honey-brown eyes stared back at him with such soft tenderness that his breath caught. He once had. That much was certain, but now?

Her thumb traced across the palm of his hand, tender and warm, even though he knew she'd seen some of the worst of him.

Unaware of his turmoil, Sierra gave his ranch-worn hand one final squeeze before she released it. "You're not like your father, Maverick. You're a good man. A stubborn, frustrating one at times," she added, eliciting a small smirk from him, "but a good one no less."

She always knew exactly what he needed to hear, even when he didn't want to hear it.

She pointed to the tasting menu. "Now, which of these did you like best?"

The human baker made her way toward them again, but he waved her away. That was one of the things he didn't care for when it came to humans. They were so...fussy. He leaned across the table as if he were about to let Sierra in on a dark secret. "'Like' is a strong word." He flashed her a grimace.

"Come on. There had to have been one you preferred."

He pointed to a random selection on the tasting menu. "That one was the least atrocious."

Her jaw dropped. "You're kidding?"

"I don't care for human sweets."

"What?" Her eyes grew wide. "Who doesn't love sweets?"

"My wolf can't tolerate them."

Sierra looked horrified. She knew exactly what that meant.

Once he shifted into wolf form, this little rendezvous, pleasant as the company had been, would keep him sick to his stomach for days.

She covered a hand over her delicious lips. "Oh my God. You must think I'm the worst. I promise I had no idea. I just meant for this trip to get on your nerves a bit with how silly it was, that's all."

"You may not have, but my sister sure did."

"Maeve," Sierra growled.

For a moment, she pretended to ignore him, returning her eyes to the tasting menu until finally beneath the intense scrutiny of his stare, she relented.

"Okay, okay. So I may have enlisted her help in getting back at you for announcing the wedding date without consulting me," she admitted. "But I wouldn't have put you through this if I'd known it was going to do anything more than irk you a bit, I swear." She sighed, shaking her head. "I can't believe she'd do that."

"My sister has more in common with that criminal husband of hers than one might think, and she's still angry I knew Jared was the Rogue and didn't tell her."

Sierra nodded. "That was misguided, yes. But you were trying to protect her. That's all you ever do, try to protect us all."

"Sometimes I can't."

The pain in those words didn't escape her notice. A beat of silence filled the air between them as any hint of amusement she had at his expense lessened.

"Maverick, I know we're both only in this marriage to get what we want, but since I'm going to be your wife, I can't help but ask… Did you love…?"

"Yes," he answered, without hesitation.

"So you did love her then?"

Her? The pronoun caught him off guard. He'd thought she'd been about to ask if he'd ever been in love with *her*—not Rose. It didn't matter that he couldn't have her as he wanted to; he wouldn't keep the reality from her, and if she asked him the truth, he would never deny it.

He had to sit back in his chair for a moment to contemplate his response. A few days ago, he likely wouldn't even have answered. He would have grunted at her or, maybe worse, growled.

Already she'd changed him.

Yes, he finally decided. Yes, he had loved Rose, but in a different way that was somehow adjacent to how he felt about Sierra. Things with Rose had been simple, amiable, comfortable. Comfortable had never been what he wanted.

"I'm sure you miss doing things like this with her." Sierra pushed her tea tray away. The comment was filled more with sadness for him than any hint of jealousy.

"No," he said, perhaps too forcefully, too quickly.

The noise drew the humans' attention, and the baker came flitting to their side again, exchanging a few back-and-forth pleasantries before Sierra insisted they needed just a few more minutes to decide. Finally, the hostess scurried away again. Maverick didn't allow the brief interruption to deter him, and from the quirk of Sierra's brow, she wouldn't either.

"No, I don't miss doing things like this with Rose," he elaborated, "because we never did anything like this. Rose and I weren't a love match, but we did spend several years of our lives together, so in that way, yes, I did grow to care for her."

Sierra nodded. Abruptly, the watch on her wrist beeped, causing her to glance downward. "I hate to tell you this after I forced you to eat all that cake." She grimaced. "But we're due at the tailor's in twenty minutes. I'm so sorry."

"You don't need to apologize, warrior." He released a long sigh, pushing back his chair from the small table. "This might make me sound callous, but I don't miss her as much as I miss this." He nodded toward her.

"This?"

He stood as he pegged her with a hard stare, the weight of all he felt for her somehow poured into that single look. "The feeling of not being alone."

Sierra's mouth opened as if she were unable to speak. But he took pity on her.

He leaned down beside her, pointing to one of the options on the tasting menu. "Choose the lemon cake, warrior. It's the most tolerable."

Without another word, he grabbed his Stetson off the table, tipping it back onto his head as he exited the bakery and headed toward the truck.

Chapter 20

SHE'D THOUGHT SHE WOULD HAVE BEEN ABLE TO BETTER PROtect herself—or her heart at least. Sierra sat in the chair she'd been perched in at the tailor's, waiting for Maverick to return from the fitting room. During the brief ride from the bakery, he'd been quiet, distant, but that had dissipated as soon as they'd reached the small shop. An array of varying tuxedo and suit styles filled the hole-in-the-wall store in downtown Billings, and in his Stetson and work jeans, Maverick had stuck out like a sore thumb in the small human-run place.

But it hadn't taken more than a few minutes of the human store owner's wife taking his measurements for the packmaster's own jokes about the size of his inseam to begin. She wasn't used to him joking with her anymore, and the resulting change had her blushing more times than she had in the whole of her life.

She crossed her legs, tapping her foot as she waited for him to parade the next tux choice in front of her. He looked downright delicious in every one of them, even without his Stetson, in a way that was ridiculously unfair in comparison to how she'd looked in some of the more monstrous dresses Maeve had put her in. Although Sierra was enjoying ogling him and this had been her and Maeve's exact plan, to irk him with a bit of harmless fun, her wolf was feeling a bit...itchy.

Too much humanity for one day. Too many small, confined spaces, and not enough fresh mountain air and dirt beneath her feet for her taste, and if she was feeling this way, she was certain Maverick was, too.

He emerged from the dressing room and flashed her a grin, being far better a sport about the whole thing than she'd anticipated. "What do you think?"

Before she could answer, the tailor's wife came over, giving them both a cheerful, tittering rundown of the tuxedo's finer features. Once a particularly wolflike grumble from Maverick had scared her away, he turned back toward Sierra, gesturing down his front. "Well?"

"Why did you go through with the tasting?"

From where he stood modeling the tux before her, the abrupt question caused him visible pause. The cords of his throat tensed. "I'm not sure what you mean." The words were gruff, distant. He turned away from her to adjust his bow tie in the mirror behind him.

She released a long sigh. "Why go along with the whole thing, without much complaint even, when it was only going to cause you trouble in the end?"

It was several moments before he answered.

But when he did, he faced her, meeting her gaze with that intense, knowing look of his. Those pale-green irises were so wolflike even in human form, and there was something sad in them, something that made her chest ache.

His voice was a low, rumbling purr. "Because you asked me to, warrior. Because it pleased you."

Sierra's breath caught before she glanced down in an attempt to recover. She hadn't expected being this close to him. Seeing him smile and laugh again for the first time in years would leave her chest aching, because it wasn't enough. A few days would never be enough.

No love. No attachments. That wasn't what *she* wanted.

He must have sensed the tension in her. "What's wrong?" he whispered. When she didn't answer, he stepped toward her and toyed with the mussed end of her braid. "Sierra?" There was concern in his voice, so unlike what she would have thought him capable of only a few weeks prior. She'd known that beneath his snarly exterior, he had a soft, sensitive underbelly, but she hadn't expected this.

The longing for all the years they'd lost.

"I've been thinking of my mother lately." It was the truth. In part. She'd been wishing her mother were still here to help her sort through these complicated feelings, even though she was grown now. She knew her mom would've understood in the way only a mother could.

But it was more than that.

"I know you miss her." The words were spoken in that rough, graveled voice of his, but the emotion beneath them was soft, tender.

Sierra thought to say more, but at the moment, she couldn't. The words were caught in her throat along with the tears she kept from falling.

Maverick stood by her side, stroking the tip of her braid in companionable silence. All the harsh lines of his face slackened, making him look younger again, less harsh. So much like the young man who once saved her.

A shiver ran through her. She could still hear the sounds of the alarm system, clear as day, the harsh, artificial scream of the siren piercing and rattling her wolf senses.

She was cold, so cold. Having been pulled from the warm comfort of her bed, where she'd been curled up in wolf form, she'd barely had time to shift onto two feet and pull on a thin rag of a robe. She needed to be in human form. It would help mask her scent, her mother had hissed. Her whispers burned fresh in Sierra's ear.

"Don't move." Her hand was clapped over Sierra's mouth.

At sixteen, she knew better than to make a sound, but hiding in the brush of the forest as they were, roused from their beds and nearly naked, freezing with cold, she felt like a pup again—back when her mom used to carry her about by her scruff. The sickly sweet smell of vampire coated the chilled mountain air. All they needed to do was to make it to the bunker where the other civilian women and children were, where they'd be safe.

Her mother's body, though weathered with hints of age, was barely larger than her own, yet she shielded Sierra, as if she wasn't nearly help-less in the face of a vampire threat. They lingered there in the bushes, silent and waiting for what felt like an eternity. Periodically, her mother sniffed the air, scenting out the undead predators in their midst. They were nearby. Sierra could smell them, and she knew her mother could, too. If they stayed here much longer, they'd be found, yet movement risked their detection.

"I'll move first. Stay where you are until it's clear." Slowly, her mother released Sierra from her arms, leaving her feeling more naked and afraid than she had only moments before. She gripped her mother's hand, silently urging her to be careful. Tentatively, her mother eased from their hiding place. There were no bloodsuckers in sight, but that didn't mean that they weren't watching, that they wouldn't scent Sierra and her mother's movement from nearby.

With careful steps, her mother eased out into the open clearing, eyes scanning, ears pricked for any sound, any movement. Sierra's heart pounded in her chest. If they could get beyond here, it would be a mad dash for the bunker. Nearly a kilometer, but if they shifted into wolf form, they would make it. Her mother turned toward her, silently mouthing and beckoning her forward. Sierra started to rise to her feet, and that was when she saw the pair of glowing red eyes hovering in the darkness. "Mom!" she shouted. Her mother turned just in time.

"Run!" she shouted back, shifting into her wolf as she dove out of the way.

Rounding back, she lunged at the vampire, meeting its attacks with teeth and claw. Sierra froze. In her head, she was screaming, urging her feet to move yet not wanting to abandon her mother. To leave her alone. Stay where you are. *Her mother's earlier words etched in her head, contradicting every instinct until it paralyzed her. She watched in horror as blow after blow weakened her mother. Her mother was fierce but she was no trained warrior, no match for the vampire's fangs and silver blade.*

No match for its strength.

Frozen in fear, Sierra felt tears pour down her cheeks.

There was blood in the snow.

A sharp yelp.

Keening.

Sierra closed her eyes, trembling. She couldn't look. She couldn't. Then silence. She stayed there, eyes closed, trembling, for what felt like an eternity, waiting for the vampire to find her, waiting for death to come. But it didn't. Finally, a pair of strong, warm arms wrapped around hers, but not her mother's. Never again her mother's.

"You're safe now, Sierra." The voice was familiar yet foreign.

Maverick. Unlike her mother, he was a trained warrior. Maybe he'd reached them in time. Her mother was likely injured, but she'd be fine. She'd… Safe in his arms, Sierra started to open her eyes.

Maverick pushed a warm hand over her eyelids. "Sierra, don't. Don't look. You don't need to see—"

But he didn't understand.

She had to see. Had to see that her mother was okay. That she…

Sierra inhaled a sharp breath, steeling herself against the thought. She'd never forget the sight, but she didn't need to go back there. Not ever again. Because she didn't intend to remember her mother in the way she'd looked when her blood had painted the mountain snow.

As the memory faded from her mind, giving her little relief, she couldn't help the tears that began to fall. She lifted her gaze toward Maverick. He was watching her with soft, caring eyes, this man who'd saved her, who'd tried so hard to save those she loved time and time again.

Even when he sometimes didn't…

He'd risked himself for her so many times, for all of them over the years, and what had it cost him?

Pain. Anger. Grief.

Feeling as if he had to shoulder it all alone lest he stumble or make an error out of love.

Love is a price I can't afford.

When he'd spoken the words before, it'd angered her, but now they only caused her chest to ache. She trailed a finger over the side of his cheek, through the rough stubble of his beard. He stirred, leaning into her touch. She only had a few days left with him. Only a few days before she feared this soft, tender wolf would return to the dark, angry man she'd come to know, a man who isolated himself, whose quiet rage and fearsome cruelty to their enemies was little more than a shield to protect the softer parts of him.

For once, this man before her, who'd taught her to be strong and brave, wasn't here to save her. For once, she feared she needed to save him, lest she lose him to the darkness again.

He seemed to understand the emotions gripping her, and he chose that moment to gesture to his tux once more as a reprieve. "Well?"

She stood and crossed the room to where he stood. "You look handsome but not yourself." She reached over to where a Stetson hung on a nearby peg. Reaching upward, she placed one hand on his chest. With the other, she tipped the weathered hat onto his head. "I think I've had enough of the human world for now," she whispered. "Take me home, cowboy."

They rode in the truck back to Wolf Pack Run in silence.

They'd barely reached the entry road gate before Sierra threw open her door and shifted into her wolf. Fur bristled and paws emerged as she hopped onto the ground, feeling an immediate sense of relief with the wild, beautiful earth at her feet.

The packmaster wasn't far behind her. He tossed his keys to one of the guards, muttering a few brief instructions about what to do with the truck, and then he was beside her. Shifted into wolf form, he nipped at her muzzle, urging her to come along.

To run with him again.

And she did.

She stayed by him as they raced into the woods, and though he was sick to his stomach several times throughout the evening, she still didn't leave his side. Instead, she groomed his fur with gentle licks, keeping him company all through the moonlit night.

Chapter 21

BENEATH HIM, THE GENTLE SWAY OF TRIGGER SLOWLY NAVIGAT-ing the mountainside did little to ease Maverick's worry. The old mare's bones seemed to grow weary. It was only a few hours till morning, and after spending several days in a flurry of wedding plans interspersed with several lessons with Sierra, tomorrow was his wedding day after all.

Second wedding day.

Adjusting his weight in the saddle, he pulled Trigger to a halt and dismounted. He'd give the old horse a break and make the rest of the way on foot. Releasing a hefty sigh, he made quick work of tying Trigger to a nearby tree. As he did, the old mare let out a concerned whinny, nudging at the back of Maverick's hand as he removed the horse's bit from her mouth.

Be careful, the horse's dark eyes seemed to say. Whether in response to the enemy he was about to face or the turmoil in his own mind, he couldn't be certain. All the same, he gave the beast a silent pat of reassurance before he slipped deeper into the darkness.

Away from his stead, he navigated the rest of the path to his destination. The wind picked up, whistling through the mountain pines as the wooden boards of the church that emerged from the shadows in front of him creaked. The old wooden spire swayed along with the treetops, tipping slightly with each gust of wind. He was several miles off the edges of the Grey Wolves' lands, and the old building felt like an icon to eras past—to train heists and gun smoke and outlaws who claimed each other's lives with the single pull of their revolver's trigger.

A grim grin crossed his lips. Perhaps a past not so distant.

He eased closer. One of the church doors was swinging open

in the night air, alerting him to another's presence. Inside the old building, the leftover pews were cloaked in a layer of dust like a thinly veiled shroud. The floorboards creaked beneath the human intruder's feet as Maverick watched the man standing beside the front pew. From behind, if Maverick hadn't recognized him, the impressive size difference alone would have tipped him off. Thanks to the Execution Underground's training facilities and transformative serum injections, the organization's human hunters rivaled the Grey Wolves' elite alpha warriors in both size and strength.

With quiet, lethal stealth, Maverick approached his enemy. Once he stood directly behind the man, he drew his gun from his holster, only the click of the gun's safety and a creak of the floorboards beneath his feet signaling his presence.

The human stiffened as he let out a long exhale of breath through his nose. "I forgot how thoroughly you live up to legend."

Maverick lowered his Stetson over his brow as the barrel of his gun dug harder into his enemy's spine. The metal scraped against bone. Had he not agreed to peace tonight, the hunter would have never stood a chance.

"Quinn," Maverick growled back in greeting.

His enemy didn't dare move. But that was all too like him, of course. Quinn Harper, wolf hunter and leader of the Billings division of the Execution Underground, was never one to move to rash decisions. The human was careful, calculated, which made him just the kind of opponent worthy of Maverick's attention.

The kind that would strike a wolf in the back before he could blink.

"We had an agreement, *Packmaster*," Quinn said. There was a healthy dose of respect coupled with a hint of amusement in his voice.

Maverick stifled the feral snarl that threatened to escape his throat. Killing Quinn would be easy. Easier than taking a life ever should be. He'd killed fiercer opponents with only his teeth, and considering the tenuous state of their treaty...

But tonight, as always, he would do what was necessary to protect the pack, which meant the hunter would live.

For now.

Maverick slid his gun back into his holster as Quinn faced him. Thanks to Sierra's addition to the elite warriors, the moment he'd known the pack would be secure should negotiations go south, he'd set up this meeting with all due haste. Moonlight streamed through the glass windowpanes clouded with age, and the spired roof above them gave a long moan.

Quinn leaned against the edge of the old church pew. "I'm surprised your pack allowed you to come. A little birdie tells me your Elder Council's been advising against it."

"I make my own rules," Maverick growled.

"So I hear," Quinn answered. His enemy raked an assessing gaze over him before he offered a handshake. "It's been a long time, Maverick. My condolences about Rose."

Maverick grunted in mild acknowledgment, ignoring the hunter's outstretched hand. He would play nice, but that didn't mean he was about to get *friendly*.

Quinn dropped his offered hand as his tone soured. "Long time or not, you intentionally violated the terms of our agreement."

Maverick wouldn't deny it. He leveled a hard stare at his enemy. "You would have done the same." Of that, he was certain. Maverick's eyes flashed to the gold of his wolf, a reminder of the difference between them. "But I have an offer for you."

One of Quinn's blond brows perked up. "I'm never one to refuse a good deal."

"No, you're not," Maverick agreed, and it was that single truth that this whole meeting was banked on. "The Seven Range Pact with the Grey Wolves as their leaders will continue to hunt the vampires and protect your precious humans, so long as the treaty continues."

A scowl twisted Quinn's lips. "That's not good enough. You violated the treaty, changed the terms. I need bodies. You know that."

"I can't allow you to continue hunting the rogue wolves freely, but many rogue shifters—"

"Are unruly dogs," Quinn spat out.

"Live outside pack law," Maverick snarled back. He wasn't about to cede that point to Quinn, even though the innocent among the rogues were few and far between.

He knew better than most that even one innocent life lost was one too many. The recesses of his memory hissed in sharp response.

Maverick gritted his teeth and continued. "Should the Pact determine any wrongdoing among them, anything that harms your precious humans, Rogue and I will hand their punishment over to you."

Quinn shook his head. "I still don't like it. Why honor your agreement with the Rogue? Double-cross the bastard and call it a day. He'd do the same to you."

Maverick wasn't so certain that was true anymore. "I'm a man of my word."

It was the single point that allowed him to look in the mirror each morning. He wasn't about to destroy the one part of himself that still held some integrity. Not even for this.

Maverick leaned forward. Despite Quinn's substantial size, Maverick was still larger than the other man. "We'll both get what we want for our kind."

A smirk quirked Quinn's lips. "Will you? Get what you want for your kind?"

Maverick remained silent, watching Quinn with narrowed eyes.

Quinn traced a finger along the edge of the pew before examining the dust that now coated his fingertip. "I've heard that even if our treaty is reinstated, you have far bigger problems on your hands." He brushed the dust from his fingers.

"What do you know?" Maverick's hand drifted to his holster.

He may have agreed to peace tonight, but with what Quinn was implying, that could change—quickly.

Crossing his arms over his chest, Quinn's eyes fell to the hand that lingered above Maverick's gun before flicking back to his face. "I know things, Packmaster. That's how we've ended up here. The attempt on your life is no secret at Execution Underground Headquarters."

"Did you orchestrate it?" Maverick challenged.

Quinn's grin widened. "Not this time."

Somehow, Maverick knew in his bones that his enemy spoke the truth.

Instinct had never failed him.

Quinn looked toward the church altar in front of them. A large wooden crucifix hung on the wall. Not as old as the church itself, but still dated in its own way. Christ stared up at the heavens above them in agony as Quinn cleared his throat. "If I came for you, I wouldn't dare miss my target. I wouldn't risk your retaliation."

Maverick growled. "If you know anything, you'd be wise to tell me now."

At that, Quinn laughed. "The rumors tell me enough. Monster of Montana now, I hear, and among your own packmates..." Quinn glanced toward the crucifix again. "We may be on the same side for now, but we both know that could change in an instant." He made the sign of the cross over his body. A ritual Maverick had seen humans like him repeat before. "I'll consider your offer."

Quinn moved to step past Maverick, signaling an end to their meeting, but as he did, the hunter paused, lingering next to Maverick's shoulder as Quinn's hand fell to the gun tucked inside his hip holster. "But in the meantime, watch your back, Packmaster."

Sierra trudged out to the stables on foot, tucking her hands up inside her jacket as she went. Her gloves were doing all of nothing to keep her fingertips from freezing, but she needed to get out to the stables all the same. For the life of her, she couldn't remember whether she'd switched on Randy's heat lamp, and she couldn't stand the thought of him being chilled all night. Not to mention Elvis was running low on chicken feed. She'd need to snag some from the storage shed, and well, to be honest, considering it was the night before the wedding...

She couldn't sleep.

She gripped her hands over her biceps, attempting to shield herself from the cold. She and Maverick had spent nearly every night of the past week together. The man was insatiable when it came to *other things*. She still hadn't quite wrapped her head around the blunter language yet, even in her own head. But he was good. Amazing, really, with *other things*.

Things that involved his mouth and her moaning and that insanely skilled tongue of his flicking in that delicious way. He may not have been one for cake, but he never seemed to tire of eating...

Heat flushed her cheeks at the thought.

She'd warned him to stay away tonight under the guise that they couldn't risk being caught together come morning. She'd told him Maeve and Dakota would never let her hear the end of it if her two maids of honor found them in bed together when they'd no doubt arrive at the crack of dawn ready to prepare her with their strange and unnecessary beauty regimens.

In truth, she'd needed the space to think.

But now that she couldn't seem to stop thinking and allow sleep to claim her, she regretted it. The winds whistled and howled through the pastures, ringing in her ears.

As she approached the stables, she glanced up toward the moon, but the gray clouds overhead obscured the view. Inside, her wolf stirred. She hadn't spent much time in her true form the past few days between the wedding plans and her and Maverick's lessons, and she was feeling it.

Slipping inside the stables, she made quick work of grabbing the chicken feed from the storage shed and pocketing it in the satchel she'd brought with her before heading toward Randy's stall. The orange glow of the horses' heat lamps cast the empty stables in a fiery hue, and the click of her boots seemed to echo among the quiet purrs of the sleeping horses.

When she reached Randy's stall, she unlatched the gate. Immediately, Randy stirred from where he'd been asleep, curled up in the bed of hay in the bottom of his stall.

"Just turning on your heat lamp, buddy." She clicked the lamp on, the orange glow instantly lighting the stall. Randy moseyed his way over to her, nudging at her coat and pockets with his nose in search of a treat. She reached in and removed a large carrot from her inside pocket that she'd pilfered from the kitchens.

"You don't deserve it, you big lug." She patted the horse on the cheeks as he wrapped his puckered lips around the carrot. He bit down with an audible crunch. "Wes tells me he caught you mounting Star again," she admonished, referencing Naomi's gentle mare. "I'm just glad we took care of things so there won't be any baby Randies running around in a few months' time, Mr. Hooved Lothario."

Randy crunched away at the carrot in contented ignorance.

Giving the horse one last pat, Sierra palmed the stall gate, shooing Randy back as she started to pull it closed. But as she did, she stilled. Her wolf perked up in awareness, instinct telling her she wasn't alone. A chill ran down her spine. Releasing the gate, her hand fell to her gun in its holster. She'd started carrying one now as the other elite warriors did. She pulled her gun in one swift movement, turning toward her approaching target as she did.

"Shit," a male voice swore.

In the light of the heat lamp, Brent, one of their two newest packmembers, stood at the end of her gun's barrel, his hands lifted in the universal sign of surrender and his eyes wide with alarm.

Sierra swore, lowering her gun and pocketing it in her holster. "Sorry, cowgirls have itchy trigger fingers. You snuck up on me."

In truth, she had more of an itchy trigger finger than usual. Following the insurgent's appearance on the ranch, the elite warriors, herself included, had been running intel on who had orchestrated the failed attack. With their plans for tomorrow in place, the wedding and accompanying surveillance would present a singular opportunity to catch the perpetrators.

Their plan would ensure it.

Thus far, they'd confirmed that both wolves who'd come for the packmaster had been rogues, hired by someone to orchestrate the hit, and tonight, much to her nerves, Maverick would be tying up any lose ends with the Execution Underground. There was little doubt in her mind the human hunters hadn't worked with a rogue wolf—or any wolf, for that matter—to orchestrate the attack. They disliked their species too much for that, plus having Maverick dead and no chance of renegotiating the treaty would have been a disadvantage to them. They needed the Grey Wolves and the Seven Range Pact patrolling the vamps as much as the Pact needed to be protected from the human hunters' policing.

Maverick had insisted he had to meet with the Billings division's lead hunter, Quinn Harper, anyway to tie up loose ends, to—with any luck—renegotiate the treaty and cover their bases. His attention to detail, in all aspects of his life, *other things* included, was quickly becoming evident to Sierra.

Other than a few vague leads that had led them nowhere, their only hint of who was behind the attacks lay in the hope that Blaze would be able to use the AI capabilities of the pack's computers to extract data he'd gathered from the session in the caves. Try as she had, though Sierra recalled more than she had before, the last few seconds before she came to were little but vague details, and the only other lead they had hinged upon the whispered words of a madman.

For the Seven Range Pact.

She'd turned the words over in her head countless times over the last few days, questioning which of their Seven Range Pact allies the message had come from, but none of the theories they'd come up with made any sense. The black bears, the grizzlies, the bobcats, the coyotes, the Canadian lynx, the cougars. Hell, not even their Canadian brothers of the Yellowknife Pack. But one aspect remained clear: there was a traitor in their midst. Someone had helped the insurgent past the pack's guards; that much was certain.

And tomorrow, they intended to flush that traitor out.

Brent cleared his throat, drawing her back from her thoughts. "I saw the stall gate open, and I didn't want its resident to make an escape," he said, glancing down. He was shy, quiet. He scratched a hand over his short-shaved hair.

During her service, Sierra had been used to the wolves in her ranks keeping their hair like that. Now, the style seemed out of place, foreign. But despite her initial opposition about allowing former Wild Eight members into the pack, Wes had been right, at least in this instance. Brent had assimilated well.

"Sorry, I forgot Wes had you working out here with him."

"It's easy to forget when things are going your way."

Sierra turned her head to the side as she examined the wolf in front of her. She wasn't sure what he meant by that. There were bound to be some awkward moments, considering they once were enemies.

"Look, I know we didn't exactly meet on the best of terms"— she'd dragged him in unconscious and in cuffs, after all—"but now that you're pack, we can—"

Another chill ran down her spine as she met Brent's eyes, the same sort of chill she'd gotten two days prior when she'd found yet another hateful note in her mailbox. They'd been worse, more frequent as of late, though she still hadn't told anyone about them because she didn't want their pity or their concern, but the sound of approaching footsteps against the concrete and the face that emerged from the darkness were explanation enough.

Silas stepped forward from the shadows in the opposite direction, forcing her to turn toward him.

Sierra let out a low growl. "What are you doing out here?"

Silas frowned, his gaze flicking over her shoulder. "Chasing the demons away."

Was Silas suggesting...? Sierra turned back toward Brent, only to find that the other wolf had ghosted her upon Silas's arrival. She frowned. No, that couldn't be the case. Brent was more than shy. Maybe even a bit cowardly? Just as well.

The true threat stood in front of her.

She pulled Randy's stall gate shut with the metallic scrape of the iron latch before she faced Silas again. He lingered in the shadows, watching the patch of darkness behind her left shoulder in a way that made her uncomfortable.

"If you have no reason to be out here, then you should head back to the compound." She said this with every bit of authority her position now afforded her. These days, when she made an order, even the males listened, not only out of fear of her but because the position had earned her the respect. The thought instantly soured in her stomach. She knew she deserved her position without a doubt, but somehow her deal with Maverick felt like cheating the system.

Could she ever feel worthy when the pack recognized her worth?

Silas stepped from the shadows, easing himself forward until he came into the full light. "Actually, I do have a reason to be here: to speak with you."

"Whatever it is, it can wait until tomorrow." Sierra moved to make her exit, but he blocked her path.

"It can't wait."

Sierra snarled, forcing her eyes to flash to her wolf. She'd taken the asshole down before, and she could do it again. It hadn't been easy capturing Silas, but once she had, the vitriol that spilled from his lips had promised retribution. She dared him to try her.

"What do you know of the attempt on the packmaster's life?"

Silas's tone was a low, threatening growl, but Sierra refused to be intimidated.

"What I do or don't know doesn't concern you." She moved to push past him, but he caught her by the wrist.

Gripping onto where his hand met hers, she pressed down on his metacarpals, shoving his wrist backward before she pulled her gun for a second time this evening. She pressed the hard length of the barrel beneath his chin and clicked off the safety.

"Touch me again and you'll be buried six feet under before sunrise," she snarled.

The grim expression on Silas's face spread into a twisted grin as he laughed. "Take your aim, she-wolf." He leaned into the barrel, pushing the underside of his chin harder against it. "I've got nothing to lose." Something about the wild gleam in his eye and that wide-toothed grin made her believe it.

She raked her gaze over his features. A shame. In another life that hadn't left him scarred in deep, subtle ways anyone with eyes could see, he might have been handsome. Instead, all she saw there was brokenness.

"Go on then, take your shot," he growled, egging her on.

Had she been her brother or any of the male warriors, she might have dared to, but she didn't need to resort to violence to prove anything—only to protect herself and those she cared for.

With a rough shove of her gun barrel, she pushed away from him. Tucking her weapon back into her holster, she breezed past the stall block. Her business here was finished. She didn't need to linger a moment longer.

"You may have brought the Grey Wolf packmaster to heel, but you might ask yourself who would want to do the same to you," Silas called after her.

She didn't slow her pace until she reached the edge of the forest.

As she did, she shifted into her wolf, the sound of Silas's laughter still ringing in her ears for the rest of the night.

Chapter 22

Human-style weddings were superfluous. Maverick tugged at the bow tie of his tuxedo, mumbling several colorful curses as he attempted to loosen the garment's stranglehold on his neck. It'd been bad enough that he'd been forced to wear the thing a year ago for Wes and Naomi's nuptials, the result of which had sparked a trend of human-style wedding ceremonies among the pack.

When he'd placed Maeve in charge of the wedding plans, he'd known better than to envision something small, but he'd still anticipated something similar to when he and Rose had been wed. They'd had their ceremony beneath the moon at the crest of one of the many ridges plunging down into devastating canyons that comprised the mountain peaks of Yellowstone. It hadn't been small. Most of Wolf Pack Run, the subpacks, even some of Rose's Arctic wolf cousins had been in attendance. But it had been simple and uncomplicated.

This was anything but.

"You look uncomfortable." Colt stood at his side. With his hands shoved into his pockets and that handsome mug of his, he didn't just wear his tux; he looked as if he'd been born in it.

"I *am* uncomfortable." Maverick scowled, tugging at his bow tie again.

"You're not allowed to be." Colt stepped toward him, working to adjust the garment to the correct tightness as any best man should. "Not when you're marrying my sister."

Despite Colt's request to walk her down the aisle, Sierra had been insistent that, brother or not, she was not a commodity that any man could give away. Since Colt wouldn't be tasked with that responsibility, who Maverick's best man would be had never even been called into question.

"I know you're not pleased about it," Maverick grumbled low enough that only Colt could hear.

These days, it wasn't often that he acknowledged that he and Colt had once been brothers, equals. That'd been before he'd been forced to accept the role he'd been born into, before every aspect of his life—his responsibilities, his duties, his family, and his friendships—had changed.

As packmaster, it was his duty to lead without question, and more often than not, that meant casting aside the doubts, emotions, and feelings of others in favor of having confidence in his own judgment. But he refused to allow this to be one of those times.

Colt continued to adjust Maverick's bow tie, moving the material back and forth between his fingers. "I wasn't, at first," he admitted. "I know we don't mention it often, but I still remember what you were like before you became packmaster, and the thought of that same training foot soldier I called a brother, who stole that little subpack she-wolf—Cecelia was her name, remember her?— right out from under my nose and kissed her out in the damn barn no less, gave me a moment's pause."

Maverick cracked a grin. "You never stood a chance with her."

Colt shook his head. "No, I didn't. She clearly had more of a thing for the strong, silent type than a true charmer." He flashed Maverick a wry grin before it soon faded. "You could have told me, you know, how you felt about her."

Maverick swallowed hard. He knew without a doubt that Colt wasn't referring to a passing fling from their boyhood anymore.

"You could tell her, too, Mav," his friend whispered. "I'm no fool. I know you only offered to marry her so she could get her position. But you've been lighter these past few weeks than I've seen you in years. I was there in the cave. Lord knows, after Rose, you deserve a damn bit of happiness."

Maverick gripped the other man's shoulder, the emotion caught in his throat, roughening to an even more graveled pitch than usual. "I made a promise to James, and I intend to keep it."

Colt released Maverick's bow tie, finally satisfied with the fit. His eyes cast to the front row of seats where his very pregnant mate sat. "I know from experience that when it comes to love, you shouldn't make promises you can't keep." He turned his back toward Maverick. "My father's dead. Don't let how you feel for my sister die with him."

Maverick could have left the conversation at that. But something deep inside his chest compelled him otherwise. "Colt," he said, not commander or warrior.

Colt paused, turning back toward him.

Maverick drew close to his friend, lowering his voice even among the loud din of the pack and the other onlookers in attendance. "Even if I did tell her, after what happened in the cave, I don't think it's wise."

Colt let out an abrupt bark of a laugh. "This coming from a man who can ignore that I'm not a true Grey Wolf, that his second is his former enemy, and that his sister is in love with a monstrous rogue wolf of a man and still keep her a part of the pack anyway." Colt chuckled and pulled Maverick into a brotherly hug before shaking his head. "Mav, I say this to you as a friend, as a fellow cowboy, not as my packmaster." Colt clapped him on the shoulder with a large hand. "If you think my sister won't help you lead this pack, get your damn head out of the sand."

At that moment, the wedding music cued, causing the guests to stand at the bride's arrival. Maverick and Colt turned toward the center aisle.

"Good God." The muttered, horrified words came from her brother.

"Holy fuck." That particular gem came from Wes, who stood by Colt's side.

"Pipe down, you two," Maeve hissed, waving her bridesmaid's bouquet in her hands as she shushed them. There was no doubt in Maverick's mind that she'd been privy to all this.

But he knew she wasn't the architect.

No. That blame rested solely on the covered shoulders of his bride.

Wherever she was…beneath it? In it? Under it? He wasn't certain.

Maverick released a long sigh as he shook his head.

Massive layers of the fluffy, itchy material shot out from her torso in all directions. It was everywhere. Jutting from her shoulders. Her chest. Hell, the whole thing expanded in a six-foot puff around her. They could all barely see the woman beneath… Could one even call that monstrosity she was wearing a dress? The music in the loudspeakers played around them, covering the less-than-quiet whispers and gasps from some of the subpack wolves.

Had they known her, they wouldn't have been surprised in the least.

Maverick knew she wanted him to be stunned, to be angry with her. Hell, or at least she expected him to pretend in spite of it all that everything, including her atrocious outfit, was according to plan. But he couldn't.

All he could do was laugh at the joke she'd intended for him. The deep-throated, booming chuckle that came from his belly filled the awkward silence beneath the music. As he laughed, from the tearstained edges of his eyes, he thought he saw her grin.

When she finally reached him, she gazed up at him, large bouquet of roses in hand despite the rooster that was pecking at the excessive rolls of tulle that covered her feet. "How do I look?"

He forced his chuckles to fade. "Radiant," he responded, unable to hold back his grin.

She hit him in the chest with her bouquet. "You mean you're not angry?"

"No," he answered. "I love it."

That didn't seem to be the answer she'd expected, yet she smiled all the same.

"Where's your veil?" Maeve whispered.

Sierra shrugged. "Unfortunately, Randy felt the need to sneeze all over it."

Maverick shook his head. Of course he had.

Her gaze was back on him then, and despite all the tulle she was layered beneath, that easily faded away.

None of the wedding went according to plan. Although Sierra was the one wearing a godforsaken tulle monstrosity, it was Maverick who kept getting his hair caught on various parts of his suit. His sister had insisted he put it in a ponytail at the nape of his neck, and the damn thing kept getting caught on everything. On the buttons. In the bow tie. Hell, even on Sierra when he'd bent down to retrieve Elvis. She'd insisted the damn bird would be the ring bearer, and of course, the fucking parrot had started to choke on one of the ceremonial rings partway through the whole ordeal, causing Maverick to forget the few truncated vows he'd managed to write. That was likely for the best. He'd never been the kind of cowboy who had a way with words.

It was somewhere between him pulling the ring out of the choking chicken's throat and Sierra spouting the diatribe of her own wedding vows about the equality of a man and his wife, interspersed with not-so-subtle jabs about how she expected him not to behave like a stubborn mule, that he realized he was in love with her.

Not in the past. Though he had been then, too.

But now.

He loved her.

Tulle-covered monstrosity and all. He *had* to in order to tolerate all the chaos currently surrounding him without so much as a single growl. He hadn't even blinked when he'd pulled the ring from that glorified-meal-turned-pet's throat. All he'd known was that he couldn't have withstood the inevitable tears she'd shed if the ridiculous thing died right there on the altar.

So yes, he loved her.

It was a goddamn shame that he only now realized he could have stood up and said it just like this ten years earlier. When they'd been interrupted in the foyer, he should have told her father to take his insistence that he marry Rose and shove it.

But he hadn't.

And if his time as packmaster had taught him anything, it was that his actions had consequences. Grave consequences. And this time was no different.

Monster. Rose's harsh accusation pierced through him, but Maverick pushed it aside. He couldn't think of that now. Of her. Or the consequences of his actions. Not tonight.

He wouldn't allow his inner demons to sabotage his last moments with her like this.

Tonight, he would allow himself this, her, and come morn, he would do what was necessary. For both their sakes. And he'd force himself to forget…

That he was completely, madly, inexplicably, and crazy in love with his wife.

Near the end of the ceremony, once they'd exchanged rings per Sierra's request—his in great need of cleaning after being lodged down a rooster's esophagus—they took their blood oath. The rings Sierra had requested were more tokens than jewelry, since once they shifted into wolf form, the rings would end up somewhere on the mountainside before night's end. So when they muddled their way through this part of the ceremony, the only part that was a repeat of what he'd been through with Rose, it was no surprise, considering he'd already realized he was in love with her, that everything about the blood oath with Sierra was different.

Nothing with her *ever* went according to plan, did it?

With Rose, there had been little significance in the moment, other than the finality of knowing that he was entering into a marriage he never would have chosen for himself in the first place. The mark on his palm hadn't left so much as a scar.

But Sierra's would. He'd given her a silver blade for that sole purpose.

"Do you have any last words?" asked Wes, who was both the groomsman and acting as the officiant of the ceremony.

Dakota, who stood directly behind Sierra as her maid of honor, buried her face in her hands as Maeve hissed, "That's what humans say at *funerals*, not weddings."

"Actually, I think that's what undertakers say at an execution, but either way." Blaze shrugged where he stood just behind Colt.

Maverick nodded. "I do."

Sierra glanced up at him from where she stood across from him, waiting for the two of them to grip hands. "Do you mean you'll marry me or that you have last words?"

He lowered his voice, enough so that only she could hear him. "I'm not a man of many words, warrior."

"Except in the bedroom," she whispered.

"You're right." A smirk crossed his lips. "Most of the time, I let my actions speak for me."

Before she could respond, he gripped their hands together, sealing the blood bond between them. An electric pulse the likes of which he'd never felt shot up his arm as he pulled her in to him. He'd never felt such a thing with Rose, but at that moment, he couldn't allow himself to ruminate on what that meant.

He was too busy tasting her lips, toying with the gentle thrust of her tongue against his, reveling in the way she melted into his arms. He poured every emotion he felt for her into that single kiss, like he was a drowning man and kissing her was the only way he could inhale his next breath. Around them, every thought, every movement and sound disappeared, because the whole of his focus was on her. This woman he loved.

His wife.

When he finally broke the kiss between them, he was vaguely aware of the sound of the pack howling, but it was only the whisper that fell from her lips that mattered to him.

"You promised not to fight dirty," she breathed. Her lips nuzzled against the scruff of his beard, but she didn't pull away. Somewhere, in the midst of it all, she'd wrapped her arms around his neck, getting a dash of blood from her still bleeding palm on the whites of his tux.

His eyes flashed to his wolf. "I'm not fighting, warrior." He leaned in, his mouth gently brushing against hers before he kissed her again.

Maverick wasn't certain what happened in the flurry of moments following. Howling. Rice throwing that when he shifted got unfortunately stuck in his fur. Followed by dinner in which he had to dress in his tux again, much to his displeasure, and an array of events. Everything before him became a blur. For some reason, he seemed to have developed tunnel vision, and the only thing that managed to break him out of that tunnel was her.

It wasn't until later that evening when he stood on the balcony of the old abandoned barn they'd converted into a large event hall, a glass of whiskey in his hand, that he finally understood. She wasn't just his wife. She was his mate. And tonight he was going to have her.

And he'd be damned if he was going to wait a moment longer.

His eyes scanned the crowd, searching for her, but not finding.

"She isn't here yet." Colt's voice came from beside him. "Maeve said she needed an outfit change."

"What godforsaken garment does she have up her sleeve now?" Maverick growled.

Wes laughed. "On edge, Packmaster?"

They were prepared for tonight. For any outcome that may come. Bloody though it might be…

"No." In fact, when it came to the plans for outing who among them was out for his life, he was almost calm. The eye of the storm.

What he was nervous about was his wife.

"He's eager." The voice came from the edge of the staircase, which led up into the loft from the bottom of the refurbished barn.

The voice was unfamiliar. Had he been in his true form, his hackles would have raised in alert at the intrusion. Maverick turned to find the unfamiliar man standing at the top of the old wood banister that led to the platform where he and the other warriors had gathered. He held a drink in his hand. From Maverick's guess, whiskey, and from the way the amber glow of the glass matched the man's piercing eyes along with the scent of him, he was wolf shifter.

"Who are you?" Maverick's voice was a low grumble laced with threat.

The other wolf didn't answer. Instead, he pulled aside the material of his suit with his free hand, exposing one of his pectoral muscles. With the tilt of his chin, he gestured to the white wolf-print tattoo against his dark skin. Yellowknife Pack, their Canadian allies.

But the man remained nameless...

"What do you want?" Dean looked the other wolf up and down, the assassin likely assessing how he could dispatch this intruder if necessary. It wouldn't be the easiest task, considering the size of him. Ally pack or not, they didn't know this wolf.

The Arctic wolf raised his glass. "To offer my heartfelt congratulations, of course." He dared take a step closer. A lesser wolf would have been intimidated by Maverick's presence alone, but all of them? Whoever this wolf was, he was either lethal in his own right or he had a death wish. "I also came to request an audience."

"With me?" Maverick asked.

"No," he answered. "With your wife. I'm an old friend."

Old friend? The air escaped from Maverick's lungs as he sized the other wolf up. Was this who Sierra had planned to take to her bed after tonight? When she'd first made the proposal to him, he'd been sure that after he was through with her, she'd never want another man. By now, he was certain that much was true. She melted for him. He'd agreed only because he refused to prioritize his pride over her happiness. If that was what she chose, though he doubted it, he wouldn't stand in her way. Nevertheless, part of him had taken comfort in knowing that following their blood oath, his scent would be permanently on her, and no shifter who valued their life would ever dare touch *his wife* with his scent on her skin.

Not this man or anyone else.

"Like hell." Maverick snarled. "Whoever you are, if you know what's good for you, you'll still stay the hell away from my wife."

At that, the Arctic wolf let out a dark chuckle. "I tried to be respectful, Packmaster. But I think I'll see what your wife has to say about that."

With that, the Arctic wolf moved to leave.

Maverick stepped after him, but Colt grabbed onto his shoulder as he stepped forward. "Leave it, brother. Sierra is loyal to you alone, and she can handle herself." Not to mention, the Arctic wolves of the Canadian Yellowknife Pack were their close allies. It was a beneficial friendship for the Grey Wolves, so whoever the wolf was, he couldn't risk it. Not without going head-to-head with their packmaster, Alexander Caron.

Reluctantly, Maverick nodded. The Arctic wolf had disappeared as quickly as he came. "Are the plans in place?" he addressed the group.

His warriors all nodded. All save one who hadn't made herself present.

It was Dean's low, appreciative wolf whistle that drew their attention from the loud thumping speakers of music.

"Who is that?" Austin drawled.

"Is that…?" Jasper lifted a brow.

Colt growled. "Can the wolf whistle, Dean. That's my sister."

Had she been there beside Maverick in her rightful place like the queen she was, she would have told them all she was her own person, that she belonged to no one, and she would have been right. Radiant, stunning, and beautiful as she was now.

He'd always seen it, but now they all did.

And as long as they were staking claim…

"No." Maverick growled, silencing the rest of them as he set his still-full whiskey on the wooden banister. "That's my wife."

Chapter 23

SIERRA LINGERED AT THE EDGE OF THE DANCE FLOOR, UNCERtain what to do with herself. She'd shouldered her way through dinner, mixing and rubbing elbows with the other shifters of the Seven Range Pact in attendance as was expected of her. But now, despite the overcrowded room around her, she found herself well and truly alone. The music throughout the refurbished barn thumped through the loudspeakers. The dim ambiance coupled with the strings of lights overhead and the writhing of warm dancing bodies of various shifters of all kinds, making the inside of the old building appear more like a western-themed dance club than somewhere the pack had used to store old hay.

Sierra clutched the glass of champagne in her hand like a vise. Even in the low heels Maeve had chosen for her, she still felt wobbly, unsteady. She'd never been a fan of not having her feet firmly planted on the ground. Especially not tonight.

There was too much at stake.

Her eyes scanned the crowd, searching for Maverick, but her groom, her husband—she cringed slightly at the thought of that word—was nowhere to be found.

"A bride should never be left alone on her wedding night." A cool voice sounded from beside her. She turned toward its familiar source. She hadn't heard that northern cadence in quite some time.

"Rock." She'd known him once formally as Amarok, his true name from Inuit heritage, but after years serving alongside him in MAC-V-Alpha, the Americanized nickname seemed to suit the Canadian Arctic wolf better now. She was used to it.

He nodded. "The one and only."

She wasn't certain whether or not to take a step back. Rock

was a friend in the sense that she'd once trusted him with her life, allowed him to wage war alongside her, but they weren't in the service anymore, and Rock was not the kind of wolf someone wanted to show up unexpected. She'd seen that firsthand in battle.

"I'm surprised you're here."

He cast her a dark smile. "I don't look half-bad in a tux."

"Apparently." Sierra nodded. Her gaze raked over him. He did look handsome. Devilishly so. She would play nice, but she hadn't seen him in years. Could she still trust him as she once had? He wasn't pack after all. "Why are you here?"

"To help you."

"Help me?"

He drew closer, towering over her with that lean, lithe frame of his. With his dark hair pulled away from his face, it highlighted the sharp lines of his cheeks. "A little birdie tells me you're interested in proving yourself as an elite warrior, and I happen to have information that might be useful to protecting your packmaster."

After an evening spent rubbing elbows with the pack's snobbiest of diplomats, all of whom she subtly surveyed in anticipation that one of them was out to kill her husband, she'd perfected her I-couldn't-be-less-interested-but-will-pretend-to-be-nice voice. Every woman she knew had one, and she was starting to think that, as packmaster's wife, it would become one of her superpowers. "Is that so?"

He raised his glass. The loud music continued to thump around them, silencing their conversation to onlookers.

"If that's true, why not tell my husband yourself?"

He grinned. "Because I make it a habit to help my *friends*, only those I trust. I don't know your husband."

"Which means you don't yet trust him." That, Sierra believed. She shook her head, sipping from the champagne glass in her hand. "I know how you operate because you were once under my command. You don't do anything for free."

"You injure me." Rock pressed a hand to his chest. He stepped around her as if he planned to leave, but before she could stop him, he leaned in close, whispering directly into her ear like the devil himself. "Word on the street is it's not new enemies you need to fear. Old habits die hard." The cryptic words shivered down her spine. "Consider it a wedding present."

She started to turn around to tell the Arctic wolf that former friend or not, she wasn't interested in wedding gifts from the likes of him, but when she turned, he was already gone, having disappeared into the ether of dance floor as quickly as he came.

Sierra shook her head. At a party of this size, she'd likely never find him again. Even if she wanted to. But that wouldn't stop her from searching for her husband.

She needed to find Maverick.

Tentatively, she moved across the dance floor, weaving and navigating around the dancing partygoers. She was stopped several times for awkward congratulations from subpack members and shifters from other clans who she didn't even know. She supposed she was going to have to get used to that, considering she was the packmaster's wife now.

Packmaster's wife.

The more she thought of the title, the more she hated it.

Somehow, she hadn't expected the reality of it to weigh as heavily on her as it did.

She made her way through the crowd. At the other side of the dance floor, she spotted Blaze, alone, drink in hand. Despite the outrageously orange Hawaiian-patterned suit he wore, he was staring out at the crowd ahead of him with a rather grim look on his face as he sipped his beer. Latching on to the familiar face, she made her way over to him.

His brow furrowed as she approached before he gave her a quick, assessing once-over. "Well, look at you." He grinned. "I liked the puffball you were wearing earlier better." He gestured at the slinky white gown Maeve had put her in.

"I'm not surprised to hear that," Sierra said, nodding to the explosion of color that was his matching suit jacket and pants. Maverick clearly had forced him to wear a normal tux—but only during the ceremony. She cocked her head to the side. "Are those...?"

"Palm fronds and pineapples?" he asked. "You bet they are."

She laughed. "You can take the wolf out of SoCal..."

"But you can't take the SoCal from the wolf," he finished for her.

Stepping closer, she lowered her voice. "You'll never believe who just approached me on the dance floor."

Blaze sipped his drink but quirked a brow in interest.

"Rock from our MAC-V-Alpha days."

Blaze didn't so much as blink.

Sierra tilted her head to the side. She knew that look. When most men went quiet, it was an indication that they had something to hide. With Blaze, it was an indication that you were finally getting the full truth from him. She wasn't certain what was more intimidating, the fact that he was so lethal or that he was so skilled at hiding it.

"Rock was here to see *you*," she said. It wasn't a question.

Blaze didn't confirm or deny it.

Her curiosity wanted to know what the two former soldiers were up to. If Rock was here to meet with Blaze, there was a high likelihood he was delivering information, but if the dark look in Blaze's eyes was any indication, she'd best stay out of it.

Blaze was unfalteringly loyal to their pack. Whatever it was, he'd handle it.

And when it was through, even Maverick might not be any wiser.

As if reading her mind, Blaze asked, "Where's your husband?"

"I'm not sure actually. We arrived separately."

Blaze took a swig of his beer. In an instant, the dark, lethal soldier was gone and his usual lighthearted persona had snapped back in place. "Trouble in the marriage already?" he teased.

Sierra let out a short bark of a laugh. "Trouble is the foundation of our marriage."

Blaze shook his head. "You don't have to pretend with me, Sierra. I know the details."

The details?

She quirked a brow. "How do you—?"

That lethal soldier was back again, however briefly. "I know *everything* that goes on on this ranch and a good portion of what goes on outside it, too." When her confused expression didn't change, he leaned closer. "Surveillance cameras are very tiny these days." He made a little pinching motion with his thumb and forefinger to indicate exactly how small. When she didn't appear impressed, he shrugged. "Plus my office adjoins Maverick's, so I... hear things."

Heat filled her face. "Of course." She should have expected as much.

"If you're looking for Mav, last I saw, he was on the balcony with the other warriors, scoping out the perimeter." Blaze tipped his beer toward the balcony overhead.

Of course, she knew logically that was what he was supposed to be doing, but somehow, she'd expected that since it was their wedding night, she'd at least spend the evening with him.

"You *want* to spend the evening with him," Blaze said, instantly reading her face.

She and Blaze had never been close, but like all the pack members, they'd grown up together, shared experiences, and they'd bonded during their years of service, yet he was reading her as if she were an open book. One of his many talents she supposed.

Her brow furrowed. "You can't possibly know that from a surveillance camera."

"You're right. But I know that look." Another swig of Coors to his lips.

"What look?"

"The look of wanting someone who you're not certain wants you back." His gaze flicked pointedly across the dance floor to where Sierra spotted Dakota dancing with another packmember.

She turned back toward Blaze. Her face softened as she immediately realized why he was alone, nursing his beer. "I didn't realize."

Blaze waved a hand in dismissal. "Neither does she obviously."

"I could put the idea in her head, if that would help."

He shook his head. "No. I want her to come to me on her own terms, see me for what I really am. Otherwise, it wouldn't mean anything."

"The friend zone sucks."

He nodded. "So does the you're-supposed-to-be-like-a-sister-to-me zone, though you seem to have gotten past that with Maverick."

She couldn't bring herself to ask exactly how much he'd seen on those security cameras. "Maverick and I are past that, but unfortunately, that doesn't change things."

Blaze laughed. "Of course it changes things. He feels the same way, you know."

"What do you mean?"

Blaze stood from where he'd been seated, wrapping a friendly, conspiratorial arm around her. "He sees you, Sierra. He has from the very start." He paused for a beer sip. "That's why he put your name forth to the council."

"What?" Sierra's attention snapped toward him. "I thought it was Wes or you…maybe Austin," she stammered.

"Don't tell me you're surprised?" Blaze made a face like he was trying to decide whether to be confused or laugh. "You know we all love you and think you're worthy of the position. We'd been waiting for Colt to do it, but when it was clear he was too concerned about how that would look, Maverick beat us all to the punch."

Suddenly, the floor felt even more unsteady beneath her. Even more so with Blaze's weight draped over her shoulders. "I–I thought he'd only approved the nomination. Not that he'd given it."

"He's the one who brought up the idea of appointing you in the first place. He's been your main champion from the start. Not to mention once we found out he needed someone to take his last name and lead the Seven Range Pact if he kicked the bucket, you were always first in his mind."

"What?" Sierra breathed. She'd thought it was only to appease the council. She...

Blaze licked a quick swipe of his tongue over his lips before he followed up with another swig. "Apparently Dakota isn't the only she-wolf warrior who's not very observant."

Sierra frowned. "He never said—"

"Of course he didn't. Pack rules didn't allow him to. You weren't a warrior yet."

"But after..."

Blaze raised a silencing hand. "You know Maverick well enough to know he doesn't do anything for the credit."

Blaze was right. Lately, she knew that more than most.

"But...he had the chance to choose me, years ago, and he chose Rose."

"We were both there in the cave. Like the packmaster of the Grey Wolves *chooses* anything for himself." Blaze lifted his beer toward her. "Congratulations. That's my wedding gift to you." He set down his drink, his eyes zeroing in on Dakota. "Now if you'll excuse me, I have a friend zone to work my way out of, and *you* have *your husband* waiting for you." He stepped forward, then paused. "You look beautiful, Sierra, and from the looks of it, your husband appreciates your new wedding gown far more than I do." Blaze gave a not-so-subtle wink.

Sierra turned to find Maverick rapidly approaching her, looking devilishly handsome in his black tux and dress Stetson, despite the hint of bright-red blood she'd left on the edge of his whites. She had more than a few questions for him after Blaze's admission. She had more than a passing suspicion Blaze had done as much to distract her from probing about why he'd been meeting with Rock. But that wasn't important now. As Maverick approached, she expected him to stop once he reached her, but before she knew what was going on, all questions were lost because she was in his arms, pressed against him, though they weren't even on the dance floor.

Maverick's other hand shot out, catching Blaze by the shoulder before the elite warrior could get very far. The packmaster's order was a feral growl.

"No one dances with her but me," Maverick ground out. "Let it be known."

Blaze nodded as he turned away.

Maverick faced back toward her, still gripping her against him. "What are you doing?" he growled against her ear.

"I'm not sure what you mean, *Husband*." She threw the word at him, because now more than ever, she resented it. Now that it was real. Now that she understood all she'd sacrificed.

Had it been worth it?

She only hoped it would pay off as she planned.

"I didn't mind the first dress, but this?"

She glanced down at the gown Maeve had put her in. The slinky, fitted number was what Maeve had referred to as a mermaid gown, and despite its plunging neckline, which left little to the imagination up front, it had been the perfect choice, because in the back, the sparkling sheer material that trailed behind her was a perfect overlay to hide the small dagger tucked at her back.

"Explain to me what is inappropriate about this dress," she demanded. She'd thought he wouldn't be happy with the first, but then he'd laughed along with her. The sound had been perfection in her ears.

He growled. "The fact that people other than me can see you in it."

She blinked. "You're jealous?"

"Of course I'm jealous. You're *my wife*." Part of her took umbrage with the possessive tone in those words, but another part of her appreciated it, the part that two nights ago had been writhing and screaming his name as she arched against the porcelain tile of her bathroom wall while he pleasured her with his tongue.

She stifled a smile. "It's payback."

"Weren't the cake tasting, the original monstrosity you called a dress, and the vows payback enough?"

She flashed him a coy grin. "Well, if those decisions *had* been payback, they were for announcing the date without me, since they preceded that damn kiss of yours, but no. They weren't payback. I'd already planned those the moment we agreed to get married."

He gave a derisive snort. "Why am I not surprised?"

"Because you know me." She cast him a coy grin. "Better than most these days."

"So whose idea was this then?" His gaze raked over her. Slowly and deliberately. Her nipples puckered in response, and from the aroused growl that rumbled in his throat, he could see that.

"It was your sister's idea."

"What a surprise." The cutting sarcasm in his tone was evident.

"You haven't even seen the best part."

Quirking a brow, his eyes fell to the expanse of cleavage showcased at her neckline. "I think you might be right."

"Your sister says accessories really boost a woman's confidence." She leaned closer to him, whispering with a conspiratorial grin. "And I, for one, feel a thousand times sexier when I have my knife hidden in my dress."

An aroused grumble rose from Maverick's lips. "You minx." He shook his head as he swept his gaze over the full length of her again. "You may be in cahoots with my sister, but she's not on your side as much as you think."

She wrapped her arms around his neck. "How so?"

His large hands shaped the curve of her shoulders, moving

down the sides of her breasts until he cupped her waist. "She's clearly vying to be an aunt soon."

Sierra's breath caught as his eyes flashed to his wolf.

"Because the only thing I dislike about this dress is that you're in it where others can see you, and considering the price my sister withdrew from my bank account in order to purchase it, it's a damn shame it's going to end up on my office floor."

She bit her lower lip.

Before she knew what was going on, he lifted her off her feet and flung her over his shoulder.

She beat two fists hard against his back as she let out a shriek. "You can't just sweep me off the floor like some caveman. We haven't even had our first dance yet."

He growled. "We did dance. Just now. I held you. Music played. That's the end of it."

"Not officially." She laughed as she beat another fist against him, but it didn't faze him.

"I'm the packmaster. In this, I can do as I damn well please."

She wasn't certain she *wanted* to argue with that—not this time—but she needed to.

For his sake.

"We need to follow the timeline. Stick to the plan."

"Fuck the plan," he snarled.

Sierra wasn't certain she'd ever heard him say anything so sexy before, even in all their "lessons" over the past week. She smiled to herself.

He could have carried her with ease across the dance floor, but at her protest, he relented and set her down. "As you wish," he grumbled. He'd do as she asked, but that didn't mean he liked it.

She shook her head. "So impatient. Twenty minutes and then we'll whisk away like we're supposed to." That was the plan, of course.

Over the past several days, the information they'd floated

among the pack hinged on that same information being used as their enemy's means of attack. According to the gossip they'd disseminated, she and Maverick would be leaving at half past midnight to steal away to the packmaster's apartment for the remainder of the night, before they left on their honeymoon tour the following morning. The only part that was true was the departure time and the honeymoon. It was customary for the packmaster to visit the outer subpacks at least once a year, and a honeymoon with his new she-wolf bride who doubled as an elite warrior offered the perfect occasion. With Sierra and Maverick otherwise alone and completely unguarded, the continuing reception would prove as a distraction for all the pack, and it would present ample opportunity for their enemy to strike once again.

But it wouldn't be her and Maverick who would be lying in wait.

Instead, the remaining whole of the elite warriors would be armed and ready inside his apartment, while she and Maverick stole away elsewhere using the underground tunnels. It wasn't a perfect plan, considering neither she nor Maverick were pleased about not being able to catch the rat bastard in their own right and there was no guarantee that whoever came for Maverick would even be the shifter ordering the attacks. But if whoever showed up at the apartment didn't reveal the identity of their enemy, with all seven packs of the Seven Range Shifters present…

Blaze's cameras would.

Maverick grunted in response to her delay. In this instance, she recognized it was a reluctant agreement.

"Until then, we dance." She gripped his hand and pulled him toward her. "Grunt once for yes," she teased. "No isn't an option in this case."

Maverick nipped at her playfully, his wolf eyes flashing. "Dancing is nothing but sex with your clothes on," he grumbled, though he pulled her into his arms all the same.

She grinned. "Then I have no doubt you'll be amazing at it,

Packmaster." This time, she didn't say his title with any disdain. She said it to tease him, to play.

They had plans tonight, plans that involved more than catching their enemies.

And from the feel of his erection pressing against her belly as he held her, they were both highly aware of it. He held her on the edge of the dance floor, gently swaying to a slow-paced country song as the lights dimmed. As they swayed, she rested her head against his chest. If she closed her eyes, it almost felt as if nothing had changed between them in the past ten years, like she'd been here before.

So much so it made her ache for it.

When the song ended, Maverick gently tipped her chin up toward him. "I've been waiting for this for far too long, warrior."

Her breath caught. Something in his gaze made her feel as if he wasn't discussing the events of the evening that lay before them. She cleared her throat, pulling her gaze away from him lest she get too caught up in the romance of the dimmed lights overhead and the gentle sway of his arms wrapped around her. "Twenty minutes won't kill you, though it may kill me."

He lifted his scarred brow.

"I feel like everyone's watching us."

"They are." He shrugged a single shoulder as he swung her into a twirl and then back into his arms again. He was a natural on the dance floor, despite the massive, hulking size of him. "You get used to it."

"That's easy for you to say. When packmembers don't like you, all they do is make up dopey nicknames like the Monster of Montana. When packmembers don't like me, they put nasty notes in my mailbox."

Immediately, Maverick brought their dancing to a halt. "What?"

Reluctantly, she launched into an explanation about the notes she'd been receiving over the past few weeks along with Rock's cryptic warning. With each additional sentence, she could see the rage that radiated off him mounting, and by the end of the dance, the gold of Maverick's wolf eyes glowed with fury as he bared the sharp points of his canine teeth.

"Why didn't you tell me?" he snarled once she was finished.

She knew that snarl wasn't directed at her but toward the threats she'd received.

"I didn't think it was relevant, considering it had started before all this." She gestured to the reception around them. "That aside," she said, cutting him off, "when Rock said 'old enemies,' it set off alarm bells for me."

Maverick's jaw clenched.

"Don't look now, but those alarm bells are being set off again. We're not just being looked at, we're being *watched*." She emphasized the word. "By Silas. Last night while you were meeting with that hunter from the Execution Underground, he confronted me."

"He what?" Maverick growled. He moved to drop his hands from where he held her and move toward the other wolf.

Sierra gripped his biceps—hard. "Maverick," she hissed, "if it is him, you can't do anything until we have proof."

His eyes narrowed and he looked at her as if she'd gone insane. "I'm the packmaster. I don't need proof." He moved to step away from her again.

This time, she caught him by the jacket. "He didn't hurt me. He was just…threatening."

"Threatening is enough." From the look of deadly fury in his eyes, she believed it.

She rubbed a hand over one of his shoulders in an attempt to calm him like she did when she was trying to soothe a scared or feral creature. Goodness, he was large. He dwarfed even her, and she was no wee-miss cowgirl. "Only a little," she whispered.

That didn't seem to matter.

He stepped forward again, and this time, she had to physically block him. "Maverick, you can't botch all our plans in the name of protecting me, and I've already told you. I don't need protection."

He drew toe-to-toe with her, likely the only man on this ranch who wasn't intimidated by her in the slightest. "If he's the rat and I call him out, that will only scare whoever he's working for into a panic, and they'll be forced to strike. Tonight."

She couldn't argue with that. She had to admit it was strategic. Though she knew that reason was only secondary. From the look in his eyes, he was aching for a fight.

"And as for protecting you, you misunderstand," he said.

She placed her hands on her hips. "I think I understand enough. You're treating me like I'm weak. Like I can't defend myself."

"No," he growled. "A real man understands he doesn't protect his woman because she is weak. He protects her because she's important." He eased closer, pinning her in place with that sharp, piercing stare. "*You*, Sierra Cavanaugh, are important to me." He beat a large fist against his chest. "And as leader of this pack and your husband, I'll be damned if I sit by while any man dares threaten the woman I call my own." He pushed past her, headed straight toward Silas.

And to her surprise, she didn't want to stop him.

Chapter 24

MAVERICK FELT MORE RAGE NOW THAN HE EVER HAD IN HIS life. He'd given his trust to the new packmember, if not a small bit of his respect for the way the other man had dared to be so plainspoken with him, and now on an evening that was supposed to be about him and his wife, that same man's action forced him to remember that because of his duty to the pack, he was best off alone. A man like him could never afford weakness.

Even when that weakness was his love for a fierce female warrior...

Silas saw him coming, but to the former Wild Eight's credit, he didn't run. Instead, he watched Maverick's approach with a resigned sort of withdrawal. Like the dog that he was, he knew what he'd done was wrong, which as far as Maverick was concerned was evidence enough.

Maverick didn't stop as he reached the other wolf. Gripping the other man by his neck, he lifted and slammed him into the adjacent wall, leaving Silas gasping for breath. The crowd of guests around them fell silent, and a moment later, the music followed. Each passing moment turned the new packmember's face a deeper shade of red.

But Silas didn't fight. Didn't struggle.

He gripped Maverick's hands against his throat, his eyes flashing to the gold of his wolf.

"Trust and respect. Two things that are easy to lose but the hardest things to get back." Maverick bared his teeth. "Tonight, you've lost mine, mere days after I allowed you to become one of my pack." His grip tightened as he leaned nose to nose with his enemy. "You're not fit to beg at her feet," he snarled.

With one last crushing grip of the other man's throat, Maverick cast him aside, tossing Silas to the floor. Maverick faced away from the other man to find Colt and the rest of the elite warriors flanking him. With one tilt of his chin, Blaze and Austin stepped behind him and dragged the other man to his feet. They'd toss him in the cells for the night.

But as Maverick started to step away, the sound of Silas's gasps for air transitioned into a deadened, flat laugh.

"So that's the end of it then?" Silas called after him. "Blame the first sinful wolf in sight? So like a Grey Wolf. I should've known being your former enemy would put me on a cross tonight."

Slowly, Maverick faced toward him again. Red-faced and thrashing against Blaze and Austin's hold, Silas looked as lethal as the day Sierra had dragged him into Wolf Pack Run. It was a disappointing sight. Had Silas not been such a treacherous snake, a man who'd blazed a trail of dead bodies on his path through hell for most of his life, then in another life, he might have been one of them. Not that his body count would have been any different…

For a brief moment, Silas broke free from Blaze and Austin's hold, casting his arms out to the sides. "Come on now, Packmaster. Put me on your fucking cross tonight."

Maverick wrinkled his nose in disgust. "You're no Christ."

Blaze and Austin pinned the wolf again. This time, he'd be in silver cuffs for the remainder of the night. "You're right," he snapped. "I'm not. You can't imagine the pits of hell I've climbed through just to be able to beg like a pup at your arrogant fucking feet." He shook his head, that demented laugh filling the silence around them again. "Maverick fucking Grey, packmaster of the Grey Wolves, you pompous, arrogant bastard, I'm not the man you want. Not tonight."

If Maverick had his gun, he would have drawn it for the second time in a handful of nights, but he didn't. Instead, the cold metal of a blade's hilt pushed into his open hand. He didn't need to turn to know the identity of the woman who'd given it to him.

He'd once lent her his sword to make her a warrior.

Now she lent him her blade and allowed him to claim her as his wife.

He gripped the dagger in hand, stalking toward his enemy. With his free hand, he gripped Silas by his hair, exposing the skin of his throat as he pressed his blade against it, hard enough to draw a trickle of blood down the other wolf's throat. "Innocent or not, you made your own bed the moment you chose to threaten my life." He'd meant to say *wife*, but somewhere in his unconscious mind, the two words mixed.

Because she was his life. Body and soul.

That was what she'd done to him, brought him back from the deadened, cold life he lived. She was a breath of fresh air into what had felt like a meaningless existence, his sole purpose to live for and protect others. She was the one person who didn't need that protection from him, for whom he could give himself freely. She was his lifeblood.

Even if the life she offered was one he'd never be allowed to live.

A last nod from him and Colt directed some of the pack's foot soldiers to take Silas from Blaze and Austin and drag the Wild Eight wolf off to the pack's cells. Maverick would leave him to rot there. The thought wouldn't even plague him.

He raised his voice, pointing the tip of the blade at those who surrounded him. "Let that be a warning to the rest of you." Turning away, Maverick gazed out toward the crowd without truly seeing any of their faces. "I value her more than my own life, and any threat against her will cost you yours—swiftly."

In this state, that was all they were to him right now—faces without meaning.

Except for her.

He handed the blade back to her, and this time, she didn't stop him when he hauled her over his shoulder. She only let out a small *eep* in response as he stalked from the reception hall, the congratulatory howls of the pack marking them as wolf and wife.

Sierra had never seen him so full of lethal, protective ferocity. It radiated off him in waves—and all in the name of defending her honor. She didn't dislike it.

They left the reception hall in a mad dash, the cold of the Montana winds chilling her instantly as soon as they stepped outside the refurbished barn. Thankfully, Trigger, faithful old mare that she was, had been tied up nearby in anticipation of their departure. As Maverick mounted the old horse, he hadn't said much of anything other than a low grumble of "Get on the damn horse, woman."

Considering his sour mood and the dark look in his eye, Sierra wasn't about to protest.

They followed the plan as dictated, riding out to Maverick's apartment, where one of the foot soldiers waited to return Trigger to the stables. Once inside, they used the hidden tunnel access to reroute from the apartment into the heart of his main office in the compound.

Inside his office, Maverick paced the length of the dark wooden bookcase like a caged animal. He drew open the curtain over the window behind him. The pane was peppered with bits of frost and snow, almost iced over from the Montana cold. Since they finally were alone, he'd turned toward her more than once as if to speak, only to run his hands through his hair in a gesture full of frustration as he muttered yet another string of colorful curses. Cowboy or not, he could put a sailor to shame.

Thank goodness she'd come prepared for this.

If he reminded her of a raging bull now, she didn't want to envision the dark fury in his eyes when she was through with him.

Or maybe she did.

She'd never shied away from taking risks.

Finally, she let out an impatient sigh. "Are you going to pace a hole in the floor, or are we going to have this out? It'll be our first fight as a married couple after all, and as you've said before, fighting has always been something we're good at."

He rounded on her then. "Why didn't you tell me?" he snarled. He let out a low, intimidating growl, but she didn't dare back down.

Her eyes flashed to her wolf, then back to their more human honey-brown again. A sign that as calm as she was, she was equally frustrated. "I could say the same."

For a split second, he watched her with a look of confusion as if he didn't understand before realization dawned over his face. Only a flicker before those prickly, barbed walls he'd built around himself were back in their rightful place, leaving her standing in the emotional rubble left in their wake.

"Why didn't *you* tell *me*?" she accused. "Night after night, we've been together since the lunar ceremony, and not *once* did you feel the need to mention you were the one who nominated me for my position? Or that one of the reasons you needed to marry wasn't *just* to appease the council but so *I* could lead the Seven Range Pact if you were killed? Why? Is it because you regretted your decision?" She knew without a doubt that was nowhere near the truth. She had known that from the moment Blaze told her. Maverick didn't regret his decision. In fact, he'd done everything in his power to make sure all her dreams had come to fruition. She said the words to bait him, to draw him closer.

And it worked.

"Of course not." His response was biting, harsh. He strode several steps closer, advancing on her as she purposefully eased back.

They stood directly in front of his desk. Exactly where she needed him.

"Then why didn't you tell me that it was you who put my name forth?" She jabbed an accusing finger against his chest. "Why keep it a secret?"

His brow furrowed. "I didn't see that it makes any difference."

"Of course it makes a difference," she snapped. Her words were shrill even to her own ears. Like hell it didn't make a difference. Didn't he realize?

It'd changed everything.

His lack of support for her candidacy had been her one safeguard. In the battle strategy she'd been waging to win his heart, that was her pièce de résistance, his one fatal flaw she could use to save herself. She'd been relying on it for the past several weeks to assure herself that in the end, even if he didn't love her like she'd always loved him, she could move past it, carry on with her life.

And now her shield was gone.

He must have realized she was on the brink of baring all her pent-up emotions to him, because he chose that moment to lash out, to push her away. "What do you want from me, woman?" he growled. "I can't give you what you need."

She straightened, holding her head high and standing tall. Weakness would get her nowhere with him. He'd already seen her weak once, and he'd used that moment to raise her up, to inspire her. She owed him better than weak. "I know you won't, which is why I intend to take it for myself."

Without warning, she rushed him, capturing his wrist in her hand and locking the handcuff she'd stored on the garter beneath her dress over it. Riding sidesaddle behind him on Trigger on the way from the reception had given her the perfect position to access it.

He hadn't so much as noticed.

First wrist cuffed, she locked the other end to the latch beneath his desk. Cheyenne was more than handy with a power tool or two, and the fellow cowgirl had been happy to help Sierra install it several days prior.

When Maverick caught sight of exactly what she'd done, the feral snarl that ripped from his throat was nothing short of frightening. "What in the blazing fuck are you doing?" he sneered.

Expect resistance, she reminded herself. Every wounded animal lashed out when they were afraid. She'd gotten more than a fair share of small dot-like injuries on her hand when she'd been caring for Elvis. And this particular king was far more bitter.

She moved toward his other wrist. "Restraining you."

She knew he wasn't going to allow her to do so without putting up a fight. Normally, the animals she brought into her care were considerably more on the cuddly side. Occasional peck of a beak or poke of a feather and all.

When she captured his hand, to her surprise, he didn't pull away. His eyes flashed to his wolf in warning. He didn't stop the growls, though he didn't pull away either. "Restraining me?"

She pegged him with a hard stare. "We had an agreement, Maverick. You said you'd teach me how to pleasure a man, and you didn't fulfill it."

Another snarl. This time, even more wolflike. As if he were seconds away from shifting. "Like hell I didn't."

She laughed. She should have anticipated she might injure his fragile male pride. Men really were the gentler creatures of their species, weren't they? "Oh, don't get me wrong, you've certainly pleasured me. Plenty of times. More than three times just two nights ago, though honestly, I lost count somewhere in the middle of what I think was maybe the second one."

This time, the aggressive sound he made was laced with a hint of arousal.

Which meant she was getting somewhere. She grinned.

She leaned closer. Catching him unaware, with more than a bit of satisfaction, she handcuffed his other wrist to the opposite side of his desk before stepping back to admire her work. He really was a sight, wasn't he? All that writhing male virility bound and chained, the handcuffs that subdued him splaying his chest and arms wide before her, like a succulent present to be enjoyed by her and her alone.

She felt more than a little bit greedy with the pleasure of it.

She heaved a dreamy sigh as her gaze trailed over him, mimicking how he'd taken in her form on the dance floor. "In any case, you haven't held up your end of the bargain, because while you've done plenty of touching me, you haven't allowed me to touch you." She drew close, causing him to strain against the handcuffs like a wild beast. She reached out and gripped the metal of his western belt buckle, hooking one finger into the thin trail of hair that led beneath. "Why?" she asked.

His eyes locked with her. "Which question do you mean, warrior?" Why didn't he tell her he'd put her name forth, or why hadn't he allowed her to touch him? He was purposefully being saucy with her and insolent.

Oh, how the tables had turned.

"Both," she said.

He glanced away from her, staring down at the cuff on his left wrist. "I didn't figure it mattered." The chiseled jaw clenched.

"Bullshit," she accused. "Of course it mattered. I don't believe that for even a second, and neither do you; I can see it."

He bucked against the hold of the chains again with a feral snarl, but doing so only thrust his hips closer to the palm of her hand. "Any man worthy of you will put your pleasure before his own, Sierra."

She believed it, but that wasn't the whole truth. Not in the slightest. "And you accomplished that the very first time. Hell, every night since then. But that's not the only reason, is it? Try again, Packmaster." She threw out his title to bait him.

But he didn't take it. From appearance, he was growing ever more comfortable in the position he was in, or at least he was resigned to it. "I didn't tell you I nominated you because I hadn't thought of it again since then."

"Lies," she hissed. "You can't hide anymore, Maverick Grey. Not from me." She gripped his silver belt buckle in both hands, popping the metal loose as she unbuckled it. He'd changed from his tux into his normal clothes before they'd used the tunnels to come to his office. "I've always known you better than most. Hell, these days, likely better than anyone considering you snarl every time anyone dares draw close to you. I'm the only one persistent enough that you don't scare me away."

As if to prove her point, he growled at her, followed by a muttered curse as she slid his belt from his pants loops and dropped it to the floor, only to start in on the button of his worn ranch jeans.

"I know the reason you didn't tell me, and neither of those are it." She released the button before she pulled down his zipper.

Another curse. Another snarl.

"Then say it," he ground out. He spoke through gritted teeth. The words were filled with equal parts frustration and passion. Exactly what she wanted from him. "Please enlighten me, warrior." The title was derisive, diminutive, but he didn't fool her. He could lash out all he wanted, because she held all the power here, despite his desperate attempts to reclaim it.

"There you go again, growling and snarling like you think it can push me away. But I'm not having it anymore. Not one bit. I know the truth, Maverick. I've seen the soft underbelly you're hiding beneath all the grit, and I won't go back to the way things were before. I *refuse* to *let* you."

Tonight, the permission was hers to give.

And to her surprise, from the spark of pride in his eyes, she was almost certain that despite the frustration he felt, he might actually…enjoy it. Even as it tortured him.

"I know why you didn't tell me," she continued, dropping to her knees as she pulled his jeans and boxers down to the floor. His erection sprang forth, pulsing and hard, leaving him in only his shirt. That would be gone soon, too, if she had her way.

She met his gaze with full confidence. "You're scared, Maverick, because for once in your life, you might have to admit that you love me, too, and that terrifies you."

One didn't catch a man like Maverick Grey off guard by sheer chance.

No.

A man like him required careful planning, strategy, effort.

Confidence.

Yet she'd done it.

For a split second, his prickly exterior faltered, and those feral eyes widened. "You're in love with me?"

As if he hadn't known before...

The denial was strong in this one. She knew he'd seen the hopeful look in her eyes when she looked at him, more than once before, but still, his surprise seemed so...genuine. And he almost seemed pleased, if she dared to let herself think it. "Don't be ridiculous. Of course I am. I always have been, and had you not been so busy trying to protect yourself from being hurt again, you wouldn't be so surprised to hear it." She fingered the hem of his shirt, but she realized she'd backed them both into a corner. There was no way it was coming off over the handcuffs.

To hell with it. She'd buy him another. In one tough yank, she used the whole of her wolf strength to rip the garment in two up the front until he was nude and panting before her, like he was less of a man, less of a cowboy, and more of a chained beast, which from the golden irises of his wolf that stared back at her was more truth than hyperbole...

She rubbed her hands together in anticipation before she straightened the placement of her still intact wedding bodice. "Now, if you've ever loved me, even for just one moment, you'll let me have this." She stepped toward him, placing a hand onto the bare skin of his chest, directly above his heart as she met his gaze. "Please," she pleaded.

Slowly, he eased back, settling into position on the edge of his desk, the jutting length of his cock protruding toward her. He surveyed her, standing in her sultry gown before him as he ran his tongue over the points of his canine teeth. The darkness of his office cast a grim shadow over his face as he flashed her a devilish grin. "Do with me as you wish, warrior."

Chapter 25

MAVERICK LEANED BACK AGAINST HIS DESK, NAKED AND chained, the pulsing length of his cock bared toward her. That was exactly the danger of the power she held over him. As far as he was concerned, she could have her way with him. As long as he was the man she used to take her pleasure.

She watched him with a greedy desire in her eyes that only made his sex jerk in response. "Go ahead," he commanded again, urging her on. "Take your fill, she-wolf."

A hint of fire sparked in her eyes. She'd never been a fan of that term, but now, it seemed to please her. She reached out a freshly manicured hand and gripped the base of his cock. He threw back his head with a curse even as his hips thrust closer to her.

Christ.

The feeling of her small, confident fingers wrapped around the base of him caused his balls to grow heavy with a pleasured ache. Good God, she had the power to ruin him. He'd never be able to be with another.

Not after her.

Slowly, she pumped her hand over the length of him. "You're so hard beneath, but yet the skin here is so…soft," she breathed. The tender nature of that whisper revealed her innocence.

The noise he made in response was part moan, part aroused growl.

No. Not innocence.

There was nothing innocent about this woman, untried as she might be.

She was a she-wolf temptress, a devil in her own right, a danger to any man who dared cross her path, and from the look of hunger and pleasure in her eyes, she damn well enjoyed it.

She gripped and kneaded the length of his cock in her careful hands, her eyes widening as a bead of moisture gathered at the tip.

"Oh." That little sound of surprise on her lips nearly did him in. "Are you...?"

"Close?" he finished through gritted teeth.

He gave a rough shake of his head, unable to speak further, causing several strands of hair to fall from the base of his ponytail. He may not have been ready to finish, but that didn't mean the sweet way she toyed with him and his body—as if *he* were little more than a naughty plaything whose sole purpose was to fulfill her every request—wasn't pure, delicious torture.

She bent down, drawing her face closer as the swells of those full, round breasts pushed against the edge of her wedding bodice. Fuck, they were practically bursting out of it, begging for him to fondle them in his hands.

Hands that she'd chained to his desk no less.

He snarled and bucked against the bindings, but she didn't so much as blink. She was still watching the bead of precum on the tip of his cock with erotic, curious fascination.

"I wonder..." she whispered, tilting her head to the side slightly. Oh no. She...

Before he could stop her, she swooped down, her tongue darting from those delicious bee-stung lips to lick that bead of moisture from his swollen length.

"Fuck," he moaned at the sight.

At his reaction, her eyes grew wide and there was a sparkle of pride there. "You like that?" she asked.

He didn't just like that. He needed it. Craved it.

He needed all of her.

But he couldn't bring himself to speak. Though he didn't have to. The way he was rutting against the bindings that held him, working to break free so he could finally have her, claim her was evidence enough.

She watched him with rapt attention as she ran that delicious tongue over her lips again, tasting the hint of him that remained there. "It's salty like I expected, but also...sweet."

He groaned.

Fuck, this woman would be the end of him.

"I think I want to taste you again," she said.

His cock pulsed, eager, and also weak...

For her. *She* was his weakness.

And his strength.

The response that tore from his lips was every bit as filthy and wrong as the nickname that preceded him. He growled. "Wrap your mouth around my cock again, you little minx, and I promise you when I break free from these chains, you'll have screamed my name in pleasure so many times you'll be hoarse come morn."

Monster of Montana indeed.

She laughed, full and deep. "You say that as if it's a threat, *Packmaster*."

She was a minx. A sexy, chaotic minx.

And he loved her for it.

"For a virgin, it is." He growled, not in malice but in warning.

She shook her head at him as if he were the one who was ignorant. "You misunderstand." She flashed him a mischievous, wry grin, dropping to her knees in front of him like she was at his service despite him being the one who was chained. Her fingers encircled the base of his length. "I won't be a virgin by the time I'm through with you," she whispered.

Christ. She was dangerous. Pure fire.

His cock gave another heady pulse, causing the head to weep. She captured the bulged end of him in her mouth, wrapping her tongue and lips over him as she sucked him long and hard. He thrust against her lips, rutting and writhing like a wild, untamed beast. He could feel his wolf threatening to break free from his chest as he panted and snarled through the mounting pleasure throbbing through him.

As she continued to lick him, suck him, taste him, he lost himself to her, every bit of him shattered to the pleasure he found at the mercy of her hands and mouth. In all his years of seeking an escape from himself, from the dark life he lived, from his duty, his role, the lives he'd taken, he never could have known that a monster of a man like him would have found his refuge in the sweet mouth of an innocent woman.

No, not any woman.

A warrior.

His wife.

Mine.

Fuck, the things she did to him.

As he finally resigned himself to it, to the swirl of her tongue over his tip, to the soft grip of her palm beneath the wetness of her lips, he closed his eyes, throwing back his head with a low, guttural moan.

Instinctually, she must have realized he was drawing close, because she chose that moment to release him from her sweet torture.

Eyes still closed, he heard her smack those gorgeous, swollen lips of hers together like the sound of a wet kiss. He felt her ease back from where she knelt before him as she stood again. "I enjoyed that," she announced. "A lot."

There was little doubt in his mind that she had. She'd let out a pleasured groan or two of her own at the sight of his response. The wilder with arousal he became, the more it seemed to please her. She liked him that way. Unrestrained. Wild. Free.

All the things he'd always longed to be.

She placed a hand on his chest. "Lean back," she instructed, easing him down.

He laid his body across the expanse of his desk, the muscles of his back covered in sweat and heat against the cold wood beneath him. For a moment, he forced his eyes open, staring up at the dark overhead lights. It was only by the light of the fire she'd started in the hearth upon their arrival that he could see them. The orange glow pulsed throughout the room as he heard a rustle of her movement. His wolf ears pricked to the slightest sound.

What more could she possibly ask of him?

His eyes shot up as he heard the unmistakable sound of her wedding dress being tossed onto the floor. Lifting his head, he caught sight of her, standing in the warm glow of the firelight, the soft curves of her nude form only serving to highlight all the muscle and strength beneath that, with his encouragement, years of training had afforded her.

She was exquisite. Breathtaking.

Slowly, she sauntered toward him, prowling like a lioness or the wolf that she truly was. She climbed on top of his desk, straddling him, those golden flecks in her honey-brown eyes glowing with the desire he could smell on her skin.

He'd never seen anything more beautiful.

"I didn't imagine it like this," he purred. "I envisioned you here"—he nodded to where he was positioned—"beneath me."

But equals. Always his equal.

She'd earned that respect from him and so much more.

"It will be easier, more pleasurable if you let me go." He rattled the handcuffs chaining him in place. "Let me pleasure you." He wanted to lift her by the narrow dip of her waist, placing her delicious curve of feminine hips over his face as he buried his tongue inside her sweet, hot cunt. Then she'd be ready for him.

She let out a low, throaty laugh. "Always so eager to take care of others." She rocked her hips back, sliding her slit over the length of him. He moaned. She was already wet for him. Easing forward again, she cupped her hand over his cheek, stroking the coarse hair of his beard. He'd shaved his cheeks around his goatee for the ceremony, but there was already a thick shadow of hair there. Evidence that he was more wolf than man.

"Not a chance, Packmaster," she whispered. She shook her head.

"This is *my* chance to care for you. This time is for me. Please." She met his gaze with a tender, quiet plea. "Let me."

Resigning himself, he nodded in agreement. He knew that even if he wanted to, he wouldn't have been able to stop her from having her way with him, from trying to fix him. He couldn't bring himself to tell her that it would all go to waste. A man couldn't be healed if he didn't want to be fixed in the first place. And as much as he loved her, as much as he wanted this, her, all of it, it *would* all go to waste, because he couldn't allow himself to have her.

Not as he truly wanted.

"I only have one request," he whispered.

She stared down at him with those wide, curious eyes filled with anticipation, her long, blond lashes fluttering with shadows cast by the firelight. "Anything," she breathed. "Except that I release you," she quickly amended with a grin.

She likely didn't realize that what sounded like yet another growl from him was more the gravel of painful emotion now caught in his throat. "Take down your hair for me, warrior."

She smiled at him, coy and sweet, unaware of the pain she brought him.

He wouldn't have traded that pain for anything.

As she straddled him, she untied the white ribbon she'd put in the end of her braid for the wedding night before she gently placed it in the palm of his still-cuffed hand. Threading and combing her fingers through the golden strands, she let the waves of her hair fall down her back and over her shoulders, so long and luxurious that the light tips, bleached even paler gold from the leftover days of summers spent out in the ranch's pasture, brushed over the pink buds of her nipples.

Perfection.

As she bent down, her hair created a curtain around them, forcing him to zero in like they were the only two wolves in the world, and the universe was theirs alone. She kissed him, soft and sweet, before he felt her snake a hand between them, gripping his cock again in a way that made his body blaze with heat. She positioned him just outside her entrance.

"You'll feel pressure, a hint of pain," he warned, "but you'll stretch. Your body will make room and accommodate the intrusion, and then it'll start to feel good...pleasurable."

"My body sounds far more amiable than I am. I'm not very accommodating," she teased.

"I wouldn't have you any other way, Sierra."

At those words, something in her eyes glistened, like unshed tears. But before he could ponder what that unspoken emotion meant, she pressed down on him. The head of his cock penetrated her as she let out a quiet gasp in surprise.

He strained against the handcuffs, rattling the chains. Fuck, he wanted to be free of them. "Are you alright?"

"Yes," she whispered though the words were short, tentative. "I've felt worse than this on the battlefield."

He couldn't stifle the smile on his lips. Of course she had.

His brave, confident warrior. Always the trouper. Never afraid.

Slowly, she eased down further on him, taking his cock inside her inch by inch until with one last gasping thrust, she sank down, burying him inside her all the way to the base.

He let out an appreciative growl. "You're so fucking tight and wet."

"It feels so much...larger than I expected."

"Over time, you'll come to enjoy it."

"If I ignore the stretching, I think I already do." She gave a tentative wiggle of her hips, driving down onto him.

He moaned.

"And I like it when you do that. When you make noises, when you growl filthy things at me." She rocked her hips again, raising up a small bit before driving back down again. It gave him a sense of pride that she felt comfortable enough, free enough with him to experiment.

She repeated the movement again, causing him to groan again. Only this time, louder.

"Oh yes, I like when you do that." He felt her slicken against him. "I like that a lot."

"As do I," he purred.

She braced her palms on his chest, allowing one finger to trace the black curved markings there. He wanted to grip the round globes of her deliciously thick ass cheeks, using the weight of her to drive down onto him. But those damn chains still held him in place.

Time became a blur, minutes pushing into what felt like hours as she continued her sweet torture of him. Each thrust a little more daring, a little wilder and more brazen as she took her fill of him, thrusting down onto the thick girth of his cock with little gasping moans of pleasure. He may not have been able to pleasure her with his tongue in the way he'd originally intended, but he used his mouth to please her all the same, purring and growling a filthy, endless lament of dirty talk, of all the things he intended to do to her if only she'd let him free of these goddamn cuffs.

Finally, when she seemed to have taken her momentary fill of him, she let out a long low moan, trailing her hands through the ends of her hair and gripping her own breasts. They'd discussed in their last "lesson" that while he wanted to make her come more than he cared for his own pleasure, during her first time, finishing from intercourse alone wasn't a realistic expectation for most women. Not without significant clitoral stimulation, a feat that he couldn't manage at the moment, considering she'd bound him to the fucking desk in order to have her way with him.

"I think it's time I let you free now," she declared. She lifted her hips, unsheathing the length of his still-hard cock from inside her as she climbed off him. Pulling open one of his desk drawers, she reached inside to where she'd clearly stashed a small key several days prior.

Naughty. Little. Minx.

He'd realized straightaway she'd been planning this for days, but the key being right inside his desk where he could have easily noticed it at any moment drove the point home. Using the key, she released his left wrist first, stepping behind the desk and out of his reach as he broke free. She wouldn't be out of his reach for long.

"I've had my way with you the first time, and now it's your turn to do as you please the second round. I want the full experience. All of you. That's how I intended it."

He shook his head. She was a madwoman, winding him up like this and releasing him like an animal, giving him full rein to lay siege to her body. "I don't want to hurt you."

"You won't, Maverick." She released the cuff on his right wrist. "I have the utmost confidence in that."

He was up from the desk and holding her within seconds. Pinning her against the bookcase, he cradled her bare ass in his hands as he repositioned himself outside her entrance. He kissed her, hard and deep, his tongue invading her mouth before he pulled back with an aroused growl. Now it was his turn. He slipped inside her, sheathing himself in the wet, hot heat of her pussy with a low, guttural grunt. He intended to torture her, long and slow, as she had him.

"I love you," she whispered. Cupping his chin with both hands, she forced him to meet her gaze. The gold of her wolf eyes shone back at him. He'd believed her when she'd said it before, but this time, it was different. There was enough hope there to break him.

He shook his head. "Please don't say that," he begged her.

"Too late," she whispered back.

He thrust into her, channeling every bit of pain he felt that after tonight, he'd never have this exquisite, amazing, stunning, confident woman in his arms again. And fuck, she loved him.

That only seemed to make it all worse.

"I love you," she said again. This time, a challenge. A dare.

For him to stop her.

She knew he wouldn't.

He thrust again.

"Tell me," she pleaded, stroking her fingers over his cheekbones. "Tell me you love me."

He shook his head again. Of course he did. She had to know it from every day he'd looked at her for the past ten years. He'd always loved her. He'd never stopped. "You know I can't."

Another slow, deep thrust. This time, she cried out.

"Listen to me, Maverick Grey." She pawed at his face desperately, forcing him to look at her and meet her gaze, even though everything in him screamed to turn away—to end this.

It'd already gone too far.

"Listen to me," she hissed. She clutched the sides of his face, hard, as she wrapped her legs around his waist, forcing him to remain in place. "Rose's death may have changed everything, may have broken you, but I won't allow you to *stay* broken. Do you hear me? I won't," she growled. The bottom of her lip quivered as her irises transitioned back to their human form, glistening with unshed tears.

Tears that cut straight through him. Tears that made him loose-lipped and reckless.

He'd do anything to make the sadness in her eyes go away.

He kissed her again, feeling the warmth of those tears now coating the sides of his face. When he released her, they were both panting, fevered with emotion and the heat of their sex. He rested his forehead against hers, their noses touching in a gentle caress, as his lips brushed over hers. For once, he spoke the words of his heart rather than from that place of dark, swirling anger inside him that had become the home of all his pain, his grief.

He brushed his lips against hers. "The only thing becoming packmaster didn't change is that I still want you." He thrust into her again. They were both panting and rutting like the wolves they were as he claimed her. He felt the pressure building inside her, the subtle clench of her already tight cunt around him.

She cried out, whether from the pain or pleasure of it, he wasn't certain. His thrusts fell into a steady rhythm. Long, hot strokes that left them both sweating, aching. She clenched around him, milking his swollen cock until finally he cried out, spilling himself inside her. Ecstasy pure and white hot blurred his vision as he came apart inside her.

She was everything. His pleasure, his pain, his lifeblood.

Artemis. Goddess of wolves. She had to be.

Because he was the most powerful alpha wolf to have ever lived.

Yet it was *she* who held his heart.

Chapter 26

SIERRA STILL COULDN'T REMEMBER EXACTLY HOW THEY'D ended up in his spare bedroom, but when she woke the following afternoon, she was lying in his bed all the same. She twisted about in the sheets, feeling the smooth coolness of the cotton rub against her still-tingling skin. She vaguely remembered him carrying her naked through the tunnels come morning, howling and yelling through a crack in the door that led to the rest of the apartment for all the remaining elite warriors to, in his words, get the hell out.

She hadn't bothered to ask what the outcome of the evening had been in regard to their ally-turned-enemy, for Silas, but she was sure to find out in time, and at the moment, she couldn't bring herself to care. Reaching a lazy hand out beside her, she felt around on the bed for him, but the other side of the mattress remained empty. Pulling the sheet to her chest, she sat up, glancing around the spare room. A hint of sunlight streamed in through the still-cracked door, leading out into the rest of his apartment.

The door he'd told her never to go through.

Clearing her sleep-filled thoughts, she called out for him. "Maverick?"

When there was no initial answer, she tried again.

Silence answered her back, but he had to be nearby. She still smelled the delicious, masculine scent of him lingering in the air, or was that her scent mixed with his on her skin? She threw her legs over the edge of the bed, treading to the bathroom to relieve herself before splashing some water on her face. When she returned, she noticed a spare pair of her clothes and her boots, which he must have retrieved from her apartment, folded in a neat pile on the edge of the bed. Her wedding dress was likely still strewn across the floor of his office and would likely be encountered by Blaze when he went into the control room for the day. At least he could corroborate what had happened between them to the council.

Changing into the clothes, she called out into the silence once more. "Maverick?"

Still no answer.

She peeked through the crack of the still-open door into the hall, but no sign of him. She palmed the handle, uncertain whether she should go through it, even in search for him. He'd specifically asked her not to, but...

Judging by the late hour on the clock, they only had an hour or two to gather their things before they departed for the tour of the subpack lands. They were scheduled to arrive at their first stop in the rebuilt Missoula ranch by nightfall. And...well, to be honest, her curiosity didn't help the matter.

She pushed open the door, walking out into the main living area. She wasn't exactly certain what she'd expected.

But it hadn't been this.

From where she stood, the whole of his apartment was the size of a large penthouse, a whole home tucked away beneath the heart and the center of Wolf Pack Run. She'd seen the foyer of course, once, years ago, and the guest bedroom and adjoining office more than once, but she'd expected the rest of his rooms to be immaculate, a home fit for a king.

Instead, the walls were bare, the bookshelves, the tables. Everything empty. It was as if no one lived here. What should have been the main living room, filled to the brim with books and soft comfortable furniture and pillows, was barren. She ran her hand over an empty bookshelf, and her fingers came back covered in dust. It looked as if no one had even been in here in...

Six years.

Her heart clenched.

Since Rose's death.

As she tread carefully over the creaking wooden floors, Sierra's heart only sank further. Though it had hurt her when he'd married Rose, she didn't hold any ill feelings toward the other woman. Rose had seemed as shocked as they all had, and as Rose's pack-mate, jealous or not, Sierra would never have wished such a dark fate upon her. She'd known that Maverick grieved deeply after her death, but from the looks of things, Rose's death had not only broken him.

It'd shattered him completely.

Each room was like a ghost of what had once been, lingering and refusing to let go of the past. The walls, the fixtures, the flooring. Sierra's heart broke a little more with each step.

He didn't sleep in the master suite. She'd known that. She'd found him more than once over these past few weeks sleeping in the guest bedroom. She peeked through the open door to the master's suite. The room was like a long-preserved homage to the woman who had once lived there. Sierra continued exploring. Finally climbing the stairs, she reached a room at the end of a short hall.

Gently, she eased the door open, and immediately, she regretted it.

He'd lost more than Rose that night…

She inhaled a sharp intake of breath, covering her mouth as tears filled her eyes. She hadn't heard him approach, hadn't felt his eyes on her. But a deep, rumbling growl sounded from behind her, alerting her to his presence.

"Get out." The words were flat, without emotion.

Immediately, she realized her mistake.

She startled, turning to find Maverick standing over her, his face twisted in a look of such deep agony that it bordered on anger.

Her mistake hadn't been her curiosity, her invasion of his private space. No.

Her mistake had been thinking she could somehow heal him,

bring back the man she'd loved when she was young by dragging him out of the darkness and into the light once more.

She ran past him, tears pouring down her cheeks as she left the packmaster, his past memories, and the ghost of an abandoned, unused nursery in her wake.

To Maverick's frustration and disappointment, they still weren't any further on determining who had set out to claim his life. Despite a lengthy stay in the pack's cell, Silas continued to be tight-lipped on the matter, doing little more than repeatedly claiming his innocence. They were no closer to finding which of their allies was truly an enemy than they had been weeks before.

But there hadn't been a repeat attack since they'd locked Silas away.

That didn't mean Maverick had stopped searching...

The next few weeks followed exactly as he'd promised. During the day, he and Sierra toured the outer subpack lands, meeting with the packmembers there and forging relationships that Maverick would have never been able to accomplish from the refuge of Wolf Pack Run. Sierra was utter perfection at the whole ordeal of course, far better than he ever could have been.

She beguiled all the packmates the same way she had him, impressing them with her quick wit and honed skills as a warrior and endearing herself to them with her relatable embarrassing tales of the menagerie of animals she had in her care. He'd never known that the reason she cared for them, these animals that others would have deemed unworthy of love, was because as a girl, in the shadow of her brother becoming high commander and her father's disapproval of her becoming a warrior, she'd once felt the same.

As if she were second choice, second fiddle.

Unworthy.

He'd never known that about her, but he learned, listening to her openly speak about her life, her doubts and fears with all the packmates. He'd even overheard her confide in one of the older male warriors, a wolf who'd served on the council but was so ancient that his time was well since past, that she'd been so lonely of late despite the bustle of the tour that she intended to adopt a three-legged kitten when they returned home.

The thought of her feeling alone when he wanted nothing more than to go to her made his chest ache.

Amid those shared moments at her side, playing newlyweds for all the eyes of the packmates, he could occasionally almost convince himself that everything was as it seemed—that they were lovers, mates, together, happy in their newfound marriage. No, they weren't upset. They were both just a little bit homesick for the ranch and the sprawling mountains they called their own. But it was the nights that brought him back to the cruel truth of reality.

He spent each night alone. No matter what territory they chose to visit or the quality of their sleeping quarters, that was the one thing that remained.

The emptiness he felt without her lying by his side.

As promised, she hadn't come to him since their wedding night. Not even once. In public, she was amiable, caring, if not a little slow to smile, but when they were alone, there was only silence if they even remained in the same room for more than a few moments.

He knew it was for the best, but that didn't stop it from paining him. From eating away at that already dark hole in his chest where his grief resided. That hole only seemed to widen with each passing day.

By the time they returned to Wolf Pack Run several weeks later, the excitement of their marriage had almost been forgotten, considering Belle was overdue to give birth to her pup any day now, which had transformed into an auspicious prediction for the mated couples of the pack.

The sun went down early at this point in winter, and it was near nightfall when Maverick felt Sierra approach from behind him. He didn't hear her or see her; he simply felt her presence lingering there in his shadow.

Like one did a destined mate.

Except their only destiny was to always have an entire pack of wolves forcing them apart.

"Why didn't you tell me?" she hissed.

Unlike their wedding night, the words were full of anger and rage. He'd known they were coming, but he hadn't thought it was wise to warn her of it. It'd be easier this way. A clean break. Or at least that was what he kept telling himself.

When he didn't answer or turn toward her, she clutched the sleeve of his leather jacket, using his shoulder to force him toward her. Her cheeks were flushed with color, whether from the cold wind or rage, he couldn't be certain.

"When did you intend to tell me that the council revoked my warrior status?"

He tipped his Stetson lower from where a hard gust of wind had nearly blown it from his head moments prior. He leaned over the fence of the corral, watching Beast buck about in his pen. He still hadn't even come close to training the bucking mustang, and if something drastic didn't change in a few days' time, he'd be forced to toss in the towel and request that Dean return the horse to the damn incompetent seller he came from.

Unfortunate, but that was life on a ranch.

He leaned harder on the paddock gate as he watched Beast, hoping she'd catch the hint that he wasn't prepared to engage in this discussion. He wasn't sure he'd ever be.

"Well?" she prompted.

He shrugged. "I've known for a few days, Sierra."

"A few days?" she snapped. She brandished the rectangular letter at him, reminding him of the last time she'd come at him with an unfortunate piece of paper.

That fucking list of hers was still burning a hole in his damn pocket. He still couldn't bring himself to look at it.

"If you've known, then you have to have talked to them? Did you tell them it wasn't my fault that the ceremony didn't prove as fruitful as we'd expected? That I wasn't the one to cause the issue?" Her questions flew at him like knives, but he held little defense against them.

He *had* told them. He'd told them all that and more. He'd argued her case until he'd been blue in the goddamn face, but nothing he'd said had seemed to matter. He'd told them it was *his* fault, that he'd ended the genetic memory early and that the only hope they had of finding out the truth hinged upon data Blaze could potentially recover from *her*. He'd tried to explain to them that the whole mishap had nothing to do with the fact that she was female and had everything to do with the fact that he was wildly in love with her.

But it hadn't mattered.

It'd circled back to being about her gender again, exactly as the council had intended it, about how a female couldn't *be* an elite warrior. They'd gotten what they'd wanted after all, him mated, which would likely spark a trend of romance to follow among the packmates, and along with what they hoped would be Belle's successful birth, a surge in the pack's population numbers. The negotiation of the treaty with the Execution Underground had even gone through after a few additional concessions demanded on Quinn's part, securing his place as Pact leader again, and thanks to Sierra's charm, the members of the subpacks had never felt better about his leadership. According to the elders, having her by his side made him seem less intimidating, more *human*…in the loose sense of the word.

"It won't change things, Sierra. They've made up their minds."

"So that's it then?" She bashed a clenched fist onto the rickety corral fencing, which caused Beast to rear up on his hind quarters with an angry whinny. "I give you everything you asked, everything you needed from me, and what do I get in return? For you to support the council's change in decision?"

"It wasn't *my* decision. It's out of my hands."

"Like hell it is." She jabbed her finger, hand still clutching the letter into the center of his chest. "You're packmaster of this godforsaken ranch, of this pack as you've felt the need to remind me so many times before. If you wanted, you could change any part of it, but instead you hide like a goddamn coward behind the pain of a woman, of a child"—her voice softened to a near whisper—"you lost six years ago. Do you think they would have wanted you to be miserable like this?"

He drew to his full height, looming over her, his voice dropping to a low growl. "No one calls me a coward. Not even you." He stepped away from her, considering hopping over the fence into the pen to place the paddock gate between them. He'd rather be in a cage with his fucking brute of a horse than hear another diatribe about how she thought she could heal him. She was already years too late. "I fulfilled my end of the deal. Every fucking agonizing part of it."

"Agonizing?" she asked. Her chin quivered slightly with hurt. Barely imperceptible, but he saw it there. He saw everything when it came to her.

But that didn't stop him from lashing out. From pushing her away.

That was him after all.

Monster.

"Yes, agonizing," he said, his words dripping venom. "I even allowed you to have your way with me so that you could take that knowledge and run off with some other man."

"You're a fool, Maverick. Stubborn as any damn mule on this ranch. There *never* was another man. You have to have realized that by now."

Maverick's breath rushed from his lungs. "What?"

"I never had any intention of another mate. I only said that to get you to realize you could lose me if you kept turning away." She placed a hand on his chest, over his heart. "I love you. It's always been you. I've only *ever* been in love with you, even when I thought you didn't love me. The only mistake I made was being foolish enough to think that I could make you see it."

He stepped out of her reach. "You lied to me?"

"No." She shook her head. "No more than you did to me."

"I don't know what you're talking about."

"Failing to tell me that it was you who put my name forth? Not bothering to ever mention that you hadn't chosen Rose of your own free will? Never telling me about the…the…" Her voice trailed off.

The baby. His child. The one that Rose had been carrying at the time that she'd died.

The yellow walls of that ghostly excuse for a nursery had been the unspoken tension between them for weeks now.

"That aside," she said, "none of that matters. Your lie is more recent than that."

"I have no idea what you're talking about." He turned away from her.

"Don't you?" She stepped back into his line of vision, refusing to let him turn away from her. "Throughout this whole thing, you've said over and over again that you couldn't be with me because of your role, that you needed to distance yourself to protect the pack."

"That's still true."

"Don't kid yourself." She caught his shoulder as he tried to turn away again. "It was never about protecting the pack. It was about protecting yourself. If you don't allow anyone close to you, you can't possibly risk losing them again. So you use that stupid nickname—and now your father's damaged reputation and the duty of your role as an excuse—to paint yourself like you're some sort of monster. But you're not a monster, Maverick Grey. You're a man, albeit a broken and grief-ravaged soldier."

She reached out and cupped his cheek in her hand. "I may not know everything that happened to you and Rose, but don't speak to me about protecting the pack, because I do know this." She stroked her thumb over the line of his chin, through the coarse hair of his beard. So tender it made his chest ache. "You've only been protecting yourself from the start."

He cupped his hand over hers, holding it there. He wanted to lean into her touch, to gather her in his arms and never look back. But couldn't she see?

He'd never be that man.

He couldn't be...

He could never allow himself weakness, vulnerability.

Love.

Not without risking the very people they both held dear.

If Rose's death had taught him anything, it was that he was stronger alone.

Even when that loneliness felt like more than he could bear.

Gently, he guided her hand away from his face. As he did, she dropped it to her side, her face and the hope in her eyes extinguishing along with it.

"I can't," he whispered.

But fuck, if he didn't want to. She had to see that.

Sierra swallowed hard, clearly fighting back tears. She glanced toward the corral, refusing to let him see her pain, but her voice was rough as she spoke. "If you expect to get anywhere with that damn horse, you might start by giving him an inch of freedom instead of keeping him locked in a cage."

"Packmaster." Dean's distant shout sounded from the distance, drawing both their attention. Dean pulled up in the truck, hanging halfway out the driver's side window as he shouted at them. But they didn't need to hear what he said as soon as the sound of the entire pack's excited and worried howls echoed in the distance.

"Belle's in labor," Sierra murmured.

Maverick hopped over the paddock fence, both of them rushing into the bed of the pickup truck. At least on his part, he was grateful for the distraction, because without it, he might have been forced to admit that she was right. He was protecting himself *and* his pack.

He'd never have anything more than that.

———————

Sierra hadn't anticipated the terrified look on her brother's face. Not concern but total and complete terror. Colt had seen some of the pack's most malicious battles, but still he was as white as a damn sheet, his eyes flitting about like a scared, kicked pup at the possibility that he could lose his mate. She gripped his hand in reassurance, but he stared at her, his expression blank as if he couldn't even think straight.

"Austin's in with her now," he muttered. His eyes were wide like he was looking at her without really seeing.

Until Maverick approached.

"Packmaster," Colt breathed. Not Mav or even Maverick, as she'd heard her brother call him thousands of times before when they were in an unofficial capacity. Not even brother.

Packmaster.

That single word held so much weight that she struggled to comprehend it.

Maverick mounted the porch steps to Belle and Colt's cabin, standing before her brother as he gripped Colt by the shoulders.

His eyes flashed to his wolf, steady and reassuring. "She'll be fine, brother. She's strong and a helluva fighter, enough that she's willing to put up with the likes of you."

Sierra released the breath she hadn't realized she'd been holding. In the wake of her anger at him, over the way he continued to push her away, she hadn't anticipated this would be the moment she understood exactly what he was talking about all along. As he gripped her brother's shoulders, steadying his commander and friend with that reassuring gaze of his, she finally saw it.

All the responsibility that'd been pressed down upon Maverick since the moment of his birth.

His mere presence as their packmaster, their ultimate protector, brought back a hint of color to her brother's panic-stricken expression, giving him strength and fortifying him for the hours to come. And hours it was.

The whole of the pack waited for word.

It wasn't until Colt poked his head out from their cabin again and smiled at her and Maverick with a relaxed grin filled with the knowledge that his mate and young were fine that the whole of the pack started to howl again. Maverick threw back his head first. She was quick to follow. All the Grey Wolves joined in as the pastures and mountains sang with their collective celebrations.

Colt beckoned them inside. It was customary for the packmaster and, on this occasion, his wife—the babies' aunt—to be the first among them to greet the newest members of the pack. Belle lay on top of some freshly changed sheets, two babies in wooden bassinets beside the bed and one cradled in her arms nursing.

Sierra rushed to her side, clasping her hands over her mouth as tears filled her ears. "Oh, Belle, they're just beautiful." She stared down at the small babies in their swaddles. "Can I pick one up?" Sierra asked, addressing the gorgeous she-wolf before her.

"Of course." Belle smiled, her eyes tired but happy, as Sierra bent down and cradled one of the warm newborns against her chest. She lifted it to her cheek, marking her scent across its skin and inhaling the scent of him.

This one was a boy, but there were also two little girls.

When she'd had her fill of snuggling the one, she flicked her gaze toward Maverick. Knowing what she knew now, this moment would be harder on him than it appeared to most. But to her surprise, there was no remorse or sadness in his face, only pride and a hint of joy for his friends as he promptly pulled Colt into a tight brotherly hug. Colt's eyes went wide in surprise over Maverick's shoulder.

Sierra wasn't certain Maverick had hugged Colt in years.

Once Maverick released Colt, after a few grumbled congratulations muttered under his breath, Maverick turned toward her.

"Would you like to hold this sweet boy?" Sierra asked, extending the swaddled newborn toward him.

Maverick didn't even hesitate. He cradled the baby in his arms, bringing the swaddled babe to the coarse hair of his cheek and marking the little one as he cooed several soothing words in the Old Tongue.

Sierra shook her head. Monster of Montana…right.

She'd never seen him so at ease, so excited.

One by one, he held each of Belle and Colt's young, whispering to them and marking them with his scent, the scent of the pack, with soft, snuggling strokes that forced a lump to form in the base of her throat. The fact that he'd been robbed of such an opportunity for himself caused her chest to ache.

If it's children you want, I can give them to you. It wouldn't be a problem.

His words from that first night barreled through her. What had it cost him to make such an offer to her when he'd lost so much? Only for her to accuse him of doing it for his own selfish reasons. Yes, he'd been trying to protect himself, but she realized that she couldn't even begin to understand the scope of his grief.

But she could try. She could love him, empathize.

Her part was the easy one.

She could try to understand, even if she didn't like the way he still met her gaze with that sad, pained look in his eyes.

It was sometime later when she found him standing on Belle and Colt's now-empty cabin porch as she finished saying her last goodbyes for the night. Her brother and his mate deserved some rest and time alone with the littlest members of their family.

She leaned next to Maverick on the edge of the porch frame, staring out at the sun setting over the mountains in the distance. Most of the ranch had already gone dark, the last rays of the sun's winter light casting blue, green, and purple hues across the distant edge of the sweeping landscape. She nodded toward the star-coated darkness. "Walk with me?"

He grunted in agreement, which only served to make her smile considering she'd just watched him spend a prolonged time snuggling a small trio of sleepy newborn babies, yet still on the exterior, he was that same stern, grumbling grump of a man.

They walked for a fair distance, headed in the direction of her cabin in companionable silence, before finally to her surprise, he was the one who spoke.

"I didn't react well when I found out she was pregnant."

She didn't need to ask to know that he didn't mean Belle.

"When we're surprised, sometimes we say things we don't mean and—"

He stopped walking. "No," he said, cutting her off. "That's the problem. I meant it."

She slowed her pace, coming to a stop beside him. They were only a few yards from her cabin now, her porch and the painted green swing on its hinges within sight, thanks to her wolf eyes. Tentatively, she gripped him by the arm and led him toward it, sitting down beside him and cradling her head against his chest.

"I know you regret it," she said.

A low grunt. Short. Pained.

They were silent for a long time, listening to the sounds of the window and an occasional hoot from an owl in the forest. The quiet swish of a hare passing through the underbrush.

"Rose knew I wasn't in love with her. At least, not in that way. Not at first. I did come to care for her over time, but I was up-front with her. We both knew that our marriage was arranged, but we agreed that for the sake of the pack, we'd try to find a small bit of happiness together."

She nodded, watching the way the warmth of his breath swirled in front of his face as he spoke. She was grateful he'd had that, at a time when she'd been so caught up in her own hurt that she'd abandoned him and turned away from their friendship—at a point when he likely needed her.

"We were never ecstatic about one another, but we fell into a sort of comfortable companionship. I thought that was enough for her. It seemed as if it was. We'd never discussed children. As far as I knew, she'd been taking precautions against it, carefully timing her cycles throughout the month and the shifts of the moon."

For females of their kind, that was the only way. Human birth control wasn't exactly effective on them, considering their bodies metabolized it within only a few hours. But the fact that pups were rare blessings, more common among mated pairs, kept most unwanted pregnancies at bay.

"I'd just returned home from a long night against the Wild Eight. It was when Wes was still their packmaster, and as you know, prior to my now brother-in-law, Wes was one of my most formidable enemies to date."

She nodded, rubbing a hand against his chest in encouragement.

"When she sprang the news on me, I didn't know what to say. I knew we'd have to have children eventually to produce an heir, but I hadn't expected for it to happen then. When she told me, all I could think, all I could feel was anger. Anger at the fact that it was never Rose I'd wanted to have a family with." He turned toward her. "All I could think about was you, how it was supposed to have been you I called my mate."

Sierra couldn't have fought the tears that began to fall from her eyes even if she tried. "Maverick—"

"No." He shook his head. "Let me finish, and damn it, don't you dare apologize to me, warrior. Let me say my piece," he growled.

She didn't push him further.

"I said things, hurtful things, about how I'd never wanted her or the babe. Things that later, once I'd had time to process, I didn't mean, though I'd meant them in that moment. I may not have loved her as I love you, but I cared for her all the same, and I did love the child we'd created together. But in that moment, all I could think about was how a child made it all so much more permanent, how after the baby's birth, things would never be the same, because even if Rose and I ended, I couldn't have ever been with you. Not in the way I envisioned.

"I left Wolf Pack Run then, against my better judgment. But my head was clouded. It took days for me to cool down. Since we hadn't been trying to conceive, I foolishly felt betrayed, manipulated. But that wasn't the case. In her own way, Rose was just trying to create a small bit of happiness in the otherwise dark space that was our marriage, and I'd spit on it. So when she called me a monster, she was right. I deserved it. I deserved every one of the hurtful words she had to throw at me, because I'd done the same. I'd cast the first stone.

"I meant to apologize. When I returned to Wolf Pack Run, I spent a whole week putting together that nursery for her—for the baby—to apologize. I'd been reluctant before, but I wanted to show her that I was beside her now, that I'd be willing to let go of everything I thought my life *should* have been and embrace the little bit of happiness I could make out of my real circumstances. But I didn't get the chance before the vampires came."

Sierra rubbed a gentle hand over his chest. She'd been home that night. On leave from the MAC-V-Alpha for a few days when the alarm bells had rung.

"You have no idea the guilt I harbored after her death for ever wishing to be free of her. She hadn't asked to give up her life for the pack any more than I had, but now she and the baby were gone. They'd been targets because of me, because of who I am, and I realized my true mistake. It wasn't in thinking I could be happy with Rose. It was in thinking I could ever find happiness in the first place. That's not who I am. The pack comes first in all things, which makes me a terrible mate and a beastly monster of a man to boot, and if Rose's death taught me anything, it's that a packmaster is best off alone, when he doesn't open himself to the weakness that comes with loving someone."

Love wasn't a weakness. It was a strength. She wanted him to see that, but until he found that answer on his own, they'd be empty words. She rested her head on him again, leaning into his hard, masculine weight on the opposite side of the bench. They stayed like this for a long time, her giving him the space to breathe, to feel and remember, until finally she cleared her throat. "Do you know why I wanted to become a warrior?"

The question seemed to catch him off guard. He stroked a hand over her hair, gentle and relaxed. This time, the grunt was longer. A sign of encouragement. She understood it as clearly as if he'd said, *Go on*.

"I'd wanted to be one from the time I was a girl, mainly because my father had forbidden me from it, but by the time I realized that was the sole reason, I'd already spent so many years telling everyone that's what I was doing that it seemed too late to change course."

"Too late?" He chuckled. "You couldn't have been more than a teen."

She shrugged. "In any case, I did eventually find a different reason, around the time that my mother passed. It sounds crazy but at first after she died, I was…angry with her. For moving from our hiding place, for risking herself for me, for not fighting harder, being better prepared, you name it." She shook her head. "But there was a moment when I finally realized I was just hurt that she'd left me behind, that she'd died and I was still here. And then I started to admire her. The courage and bravery it would have taken to try and protect me like that, even though she had to have known that she barely stood a chance. I promised myself then that I'd always try to be brave and courageous like she was."

She lifted her head, positioning herself beside him as she wrapped her arms around his neck and tugged him into an embrace. "And then there was you."

Me? his lifted brow seemed to say. She nearly laughed at how thoroughly she was coming to understand those quiet, grumbling expressions of his.

"You were so powerful, so brave and fearless that I felt like if I stayed that vulnerable, that weak, I'd…I'd never be worthy of you." She inhaled a deep breath. "Everything I am, everything I've become is in part because of you, because I've been fighting to not be that weak, cowering girl anymore, fighting for you to see me. I love you, Maverick Grey, and I have since I was a girl, and no silly promise about no love or attachments is going to change that." She pulled him closer, resting her forehead against his as he'd done when they'd been in his office. "Please say something," she whispered.

Gently, he cupped the side of her face, bringing her lips toward his. "You don't have to fight anymore, warrior. I see you. I see every part of you." He kissed her then, a kiss that let all his quiet actions speak louder than the words he still couldn't bring himself to say. Their tongues mingled and danced, both of them drawing closer. It didn't matter how long he held her. It would never be close enough.

And then he made love to her. They spent the whole of the night together there on that bench, exploring each other's bodies, the heat of their wolves warming them from inside out despite the cold winter winds. They didn't say anything to each other through those quiet hours, because somehow, she realized, they didn't have to. They understood each other perfectly.

In a way that only friends who'd also once been enemies could. They knew all of each other's flaws, fears, doubts. It was all laid out between them.

When the last remnants of night faded into morning, it wasn't until she heard Elvis crowing from his heated cage on her back porch that she realized their time was about to come to an end. She stirred in his lap, waking from what had been a comfortable half sleep as they had lain together on the swinging bench, thoroughly sated.

"Packmaster!" His title was shouted again off in the distance.

He let out a soft groan as he pulled the blanket he'd retrieved from inside over her.

"I'm starting to realize why your long days extend into long weeks." She'd learned as much during their tour and in the following days. "You never seem to be able to catch a break."

"Duty always seems to call at a time that's…" His voice trailed off as he buried his face in the crook of her neck, kissing his way up the length of her skin. She moaned and he let out a rumbling purr in response. "Inconvenient," he finished.

"Packmaster!" The shout came again. This time, closer.

"Go," she said, urging him off her, though she instantly regretted it. "I'll be fine."

He nodded before he turned and shifted into his wolf, lifting his pile of clothes from the ground with his teeth and dragging the garments along with him as he ran off to meet Blaze's shouts in the distance.

She knew for certain he wouldn't be returning anytime soon.

With a level of resolve she didn't realize she had in her, she'd accepted it. Maverick Grey was his own man, and he was never going to be fully hers. She couldn't heal him. She couldn't make him realize he was better off with her by his side than he was alone, because he was all the things she'd accused him of and more.

He was the Monster of Montana. Her packmaster. Her friend. Her husband. A grief-stricken widower.

All of it.

And she couldn't ask him to change, flaws and all.

Not if she truly loved him.

And she did. She loved him with every ounce of her being.

Which meant she had a choice to make.

He'd already made his, and as much as it hurt, she refused to be second any longer. She couldn't make him call her a true mate. She couldn't make him defy the council. No more than she could make him love her, though she had more than a passing suspicion he did, even though he'd hesitated to say it.

No, the choice she had to make was how she would handle his decision.

Pining away at the side of a man who refused to have her?

Or claiming her life as her own?

It was the *only* choice that was left to make.

Fortifying herself, Sierra inhaled a deep breath, entering her cabin to dress before she trekked out to the pack's nearest truck. The key got jammed in the ignition, and from the frost they'd been getting, it took her a couple tries to get the engine to turn over, but it finally did.

Once the truck was started, she drove into downtown Billings, parking outside the nearest recruitment office. She waited more than an hour before one of the recruitment officers finally unlocked the door. The moment he did, Sierra barreled inside, catching the human soldier by surprise.

"Can I help you?" he asked.

She nodded. "I need to speak with Colonel McGinnis."

The recruitment officer furrowed his brow, but he sat behind the desk and pulled the phone toward him all the same. Perhaps she'd set him on edge. That was often the case when humans came into her presence.

The human raised a brow. "And to whom exactly am I speaking?" He looked skeptical, intimidated by her eagerness.

She swallowed the lump in her throat as she removed her fake human ID from her wallet along with her former MAC-V-Alpha ID, though the card would never identify her as such, not to someone this low in the ranks. MAC-V-Alpha didn't exist on paper. "My name's Sierra Cavanaugh, and you can call Colonel McGinnis and tell him that I'm here to reenlist."

Chapter 27

"You need to see this."

Maverick stood over Blaze's computer, one hand on the back of Blaze's leather office chair and the other planted firmly on the control-room desk. Ever since he'd found Blaze searching for him throughout the compound, the elite warrior had launched into a long-winded explanation with far too many tech and military terms for even the most intelligent of cowboys to understand.

Maverick grumbled. "In plain English."

Blaze's fingers had been flying across his keyboard for the past thirty minutes, replicating the process he was attempting to demonstrate as he droned on. Meanwhile, his mouth had also unfortunately been going a mile a minute. In the reflection of the several large monitors, Maverick could see where Blaze's current particularly apropos T-shirt read *I can explain it for you, but I can't understand it for you.*

"In easy-to-understand terms…" Blaze said, pointing down to his shirt with a pointed You-may-be-packmaster-but-I'm-the-brains-of-this-operation look. "I cracked the code." Blaze jammed his finger onto the final enter key, and a moment later, a distorted video popped up on the screen.

Maverick watched with narrowed eyes. The quality was fuzzy, blurred considerably, but he could make it out enough to see vague forms, shadows. "Is that a she-wolf?" he asked.

"I think so." Blaze nodded.

The video played out, allowing them to see through Sierra's eyes as she had when she'd been alone in the genetic memory. The duration was no longer than two minutes. Sierra had described what she recollected to them in detail more than once, save for the last few seconds that had faded away. The last few seconds when the pack's female ancestors had joined in a haunting, howling chorus. The screen finally went blank.

Maverick ran a hand over the coarse hair of his chin with a quiet shake of his head. He'd hoped if they were able to access the footage, it would be illuminating. But seeing the last few seconds play out only wrought more confusion.

"We need to show this to Sierra," he said.

When they found her, Sierra was driving up to the compound in the truck from who the hell knew where.

"Where have you been?" Blaze asked before Maverick could get a word out.

Sierra shook her head. "It doesn't matter now."

Ten minutes later, they stood in the control room, having replayed the video over a dozen times. Sierra was shaking her head, pacing about the room, muttering under her breath as she racked her brain. Maverick watched her with more than a hint of pride, this intelligent, fierce female he had the fortune of calling his wife, even if they both knew that they couldn't continue like this. He'd decided as much when he'd been inside her, making love to her on the porch swing last night. This had to end. For both their sakes.

"For the Seven Range Pact. For the Seven Range Pact," Sierra repeated like a mantra, shaking her head and unable to make sense of it.

"What does that have to do with the genetic memory?" Blaze asked.

Sierra shot him a hard look. "Everything. It's the only solid clue we have. We can't hinge all our hopes on deciphering a few seconds of symbolic, blurred footage our ancestors thought might be relevant. The fact that the pack has survived so long with this being one of our main intelligence tactics is a miracle."

"The ceremony is helpful, but it's not the *main* tactic," Blaze said defensively. "What do you think I'm doing in here all day and night?"

Maverick tended to agree with them both on that front. Too much emphasis was placed on the ceremony, particularly by the elders of the pack, and considering the council's decision to exclude Sierra for an act that had been his own doing, he understood the sharp bite of her rage.

Sierra waved her hand, causing Blaze to fall silent again as he spun his desk chair back toward the screen. "Something's just not adding up." She glanced toward Maverick, those honey-brown eyes pinning him in place. "Are you certain that's what the first attacker said?"

Arms crossed over his chest, he gave a firm nod. There was no doubt in his mind. The attacker's message had been clear.

"For the Seven Range Pact. For the Seven Range Pact," Sierra repeated.

Blaze groaned. "It's pretty obvious what 'for the Seven Range Pact' means, Sierra." Within seconds, he had a dictionary pulled up across the computer screen. "'Intended to, belong to, suiting the purposes or need of, or...'"

"Because of," Sierra shouted.

"What?" Blaze asked.

Maverick eased from where he'd been leaning against the control-room wall toward her. From the look in his brilliant warrior's eyes, she'd realized something. "Sierra." The rumble of his voice seemed to draw her attention back to the room.

"The word 'for' has two meanings. That first night, when the attacker said, 'For the Seven Range Pact,' they didn't mean on the Pact's behalf. They meant 'For the Seven Range Pact,' as in *because* of them, because of what the Pact has done, because it exists, because whoever is doing this already views the Pact as their enemy. We made an error; the attacker was never an ally. They were *always* an enemy. Rock warned that our enemy wasn't new but an old one, and what other shifter enemy could it be than..."

"The Wild Eight?" Maverick asked, following her line of thinking. He shook his head. "Silas and Brent were the last at-large members. Since we've had Silas in holding, the attacks have stopped. You think he wasn't acting on anyone's order but of his own accord as a means of revenge?"

Sierra nodded. "Potentially."

"Does an innocent man often escape from his cell?" Blaze asked, a hint of concern in his voice.

Maverick and Sierra turned toward Blaze's security monitor. Sure enough, on the screen Blaze had just clicked to with the image of the pack's cells, Silas was nowhere to be found.

"Fuck," Maverick roared.

Before he could get another word out, the door to the control room flew open, and Dean charged in. "Packmaster."

Maverick didn't need to hear another word. He knew in an instant from the dark look in the elite warrior's eyes that he needed to come with him. *Now.*

Sierra and Blaze followed, and minutes later, they stood on the steps of Sierra's porch above a bleeding and wounded Cheyenne. From the bloodied knife flung by her side and the pressure Austin was applying to her abdomen to stop the bleeding, it was easy to ascertain what had happened.

"Cheyenne." Sierra fell to the other warrior's side, clutching her hand.

It was then that Maverick noticed who stood lurking in the porch shadows.

Silas.

Maverick drew his blade, charging the other man and pinning the wolf against the wooden frame of Sierra's cabin door. He shoved the point of the blade into the other wolf's throat. "I showed you mercy. Now your death will be mine." Maverick drew back his blade.

"No." Cheyenne let out a pained groan from where she lay bleeding, drawing Maverick to a halt. Her face grew more pale by the second, but she was still conscious. She drew in a sharp gasp of air. "Wasn't him. I let him out."

"What?" Sierra gripped the other woman's hand, drawing her attention back toward her as she brushed back the tendrils of Cheyenne's blond hair, the locks matted to her forehead from the sweat soaking her face.

"Hand me the gauze," Austin ordered Dean, who was standing beside his medical kit, as Austin began packing Cheyenne's still-bleeding wound.

"Came to warn you. Not Silas. Brent," she panted.

"Brent?" Sierra muttered. She glanced up to where Maverick held Silas at the point of his dagger to watch the other wolf's face. "When you came out into the barn that night, you weren't threatening me... You said you were..."

"'Chasing the demons away,'" Silas snarled from where the point of Maverick's blade still lingered at his throat. "I know Brent well. I was certain he was up to something, but who among you fucking Grey Wolves would believe a former Wild Eight?"

With a reluctant shove, Maverick released him.

"Came here to warn you," Cheyenne rasped at Sierra again. She let out a wet, painful-sounding cough. "Brent came from behind. Thought I was you. Not Mav. *You*."

Sierra cast Maverick a concerned look as realization dawned on them both.

He had never been the target.

She had been.

"Where is he?" Maverick snarled. He'd flay the bastard alive for daring to look twice at her. Threatening his life was grounds for death. Threatening hers? He'd torture the sick fuck slowly, only to allow him to heal and then repeat it again...

For him, Maverick would know no mercy.

At that moment, Austin shooed Sierra back. Having slowed Cheyenne's bleeding, he scooped her into his arms as he headed toward their medic center.

"He likely wants retribution for you capturing him." The sound of Silas's voice grated on him, and Maverick rounded on the other wolf again. Silas may have been innocent of these crimes, but he'd still failed to be forthright with his packmaster—fully honest.

Once more, Maverick's blade was at his throat. "Where is he?"

With several touches, Blaze accessed the pack's security cams on his phone. "He's in one of the trucks."

"Where's he headed?" Maverick snarled at Silas.

The Adam's apple of Silas's throat jumped, though his eyes didn't betray a hint of fear in the face of Maverick's blade. "By my guess, likely headed to the old Wild Eight clubhouse. It's abandoned now, but—"

Maverick didn't need to hear another word.

Releasing Silas, he caught Dean's gaze. He pointed toward his own wolf eyes and then toward Sierra. "Don't let her out of your sight," he ordered. Maverick tore from the porch, headed toward the other spare truck.

But Sierra wasn't far behind him. Gripping his wrist, she stopped him. "Like hell you're going to leave me behind."

He didn't have time for this foolishness. Maverick's eyes flashed to the gold of his wolf, and he bared his teeth in a feral growl, in their world, a direct order to stand down. But she wasn't having it.

Her own eyes flashed to her wolf as she bared her teeth and let out a snarl of her own. She wasn't intimidated by him in the least. "This is *my* fight. Not yours. Cowboy or not, you're not leaving me standing here in your dust as you ride off into the fucking sunset. We do this together or we don't do this at all."

They held each other's gaze for a long beat, both too stubborn and bullheaded to back down. But when it became clear this was what she wanted, Maverick forced his eyes to shift back to their human form and staked his blade at her feet.

Fighting by his side was where she belonged.

The old Wild Eight clubhouse had long since been abandoned. Inside the run-down building, the walls had been tagged by graffiti, and only broken-down bits of furniture remained among the layers of dust. Sierra eased inside, not knowing exactly what lay ahead of her. As she did, one of the floorboards let out a loud creak.

She stiffened in anticipation of her enemy's onslaught. But it didn't come. Slowly she eased in farther, inching forward as she held tight to the hilt of her blade. Finally, she crossed the threshold into the old house's foyer.

And then he was on top of her.

Brent lunged at her from the darkness, springing onto her back to knock her to the ground, but she was ready for him. She gripped him by the wrist, using his momentum against him and throwing him over her shoulder. The move brought them both rolling onto the floor of the small space. In a flurry of fists and punches, she met him blow for blow, refusing to back down. As a male of their species, he rivaled her in strength, but he was no match for her skill.

As their brawling roll ended, he came out on top. He slashed his dagger down, and she was forced to block it with her arm. Her own dagger dropped from her fist as his blade sliced against the skin of her wrist. She let out a sharp hiss as a warm trickle of blood coated her sleeve, but she didn't falter. With him on top of her, he thought he had her pinned in place. That he held the advantage.

Not a chance.

Knocking him sideways with a twist of her hips, she brought her knee up between them, aiming straight for his groin. He seized in pain, giving her the split second she needed to leverage his weight against her leg and kick him off her. He fell backward as the heel of her boot collided with the center of his face. From the sharp snap, she'd broken his nose.

Yet he was still clutching his groin in pain. "Cheap shot," he groaned.

She lifted herself up. "You men think your balls are so fucking great, but they're your biggest damn weakness."

There was a blade in his hand, but hers lay on the floor between them.

He could have come at her again, but they'd be hand to hand in this small, enclosed space. He must have realized it wouldn't be a favorable outcome for him, because he snatched her blade and scrambled like the spineless coward he was, running farther into the abandoned house in search of a larger space.

Jumping to her feet, she barreled after him, finally cornering him in what appeared to have been an old billiards room. Brent stood on the far end of a worn pool table. The smooth green felt had been ripped around the edges.

"What you gonna do without your blade, you nasty Grey Wolf bitch?" He held his blade in one hand and hers in the other, laughing at her as blood poured from his nose into his mouth. His teeth were already coated red with it, his demented grin even more insane.

"A lot more than you can." She had him cornered, and he knew it.

At that moment, the side entrance to the gaming room flew open and Maverick prowled inside, his own blade in hand.

"Oh look," Brent sneered. "If it isn't your packmaster come to your rescue."

Maverick snarled, his golden wolf eyes pulsating with lethal intent. He stalked toward Sierra, planting a kiss on the top of her head before he turned his attention back toward Brent. With both Maverick and Sierra surrounding him, there was no chance of Brent making any escape.

"As easy to catch as you were last time." Sierra grinned.

"Suck me, you ragged bi—"

"Speak to my wife that way again, and I will bury my blade in your trachea," Maverick growled. He was inching closer by the moment, and Brent didn't stand a chance against him. "I'll never understand why you'd choose your own death over a life at Wolf Pack Run."

"I know why," Sierra said.

Brent's gaze narrowed on her, the color of his face burning with rage.

"Humiliation."

The red in Brent's face deepened. If looks could kill...

"That's why he had to hire rogue wolves to go after me, because he was too afraid."

"Shut your mouth, you viper-tongued c—"

"Can't you see, Maverick?" she said, speaking over Brent.

The knuckles of Brent's fists turned white where he clutched the blades, but he wouldn't dare move with Maverick so close to him. Not without a bit of bait.

She drew closer to the edge of the pool table, within reach of Brent as she drove in her final blow. "Brent's a weak, spineless coward after all. He couldn't stand the thought that he'd been bested by a woman—that he was so pathetic, he couldn't even find a beta mate."

Brent lunged across the pool table, his rage making him sloppy.

Maverick grabbed the other wolf, hooking him under the arms and hauling him back with the whole of his weight until his blade pressed against his throat.

"You're one to talk," Brent snarled. "You let him fight your battles for you now, you worthless flake?"

Sierra shook her head. "No, but he's a great distraction, isn't he? I knew if he wasn't here, a chauvinist pig like you wouldn't have let me get a word in edgewise."

Brent snarled.

"There's only one thing I *will* let him do for me. I wouldn't be a proper cowgirl otherwise." She reached behind her, removing the revolver Maverick had slipped into the back of her jeans as she cocked the hammer back and aimed straight at Brent's head. "I'll let him slip me a gun in the midst of a knife fight."

She didn't hesitate to pull the trigger.

The shot rang out, harsh and clear. Their enemy crumpled to the floor, released from Maverick's arms in a now-dead heap.

Maverick grumbled, wiping some of the blood spray from his face. "You could've warned me you didn't intend to let him linger for long."

"I only delayed to verbally castrate him like he deserved." Sierra rounded the pool table as she stared down at her enemy's corpse. Her nose wrinkled in disgust and her lips pursed in displeasure. "That was far too easy."

Maverick grunted. "It always is." He nudged Brent's still-fresh body with his boot.

"As long as I don't have to clean up, I'm good." She tucked the gun into the back of her jeans again. "Next time, do you really have to come with me though? Other than to get my two cents in, you really were unnecessary."

He let out an amused chuckle. "No," he said, the hint of his laugh fading. "But if you choose to still be my wife, there will be a next time," he warned.

There was little doubt in her mind.

"I'm more than prepared for it." Turning away from the bloodshed, she headed toward the opposite exit from which Maverick had arrived, prepared to return to the ranch in her victorious state. "What I don't understand is why he brought us off the packlands all the h—"

"Sierra!"

Maverick saw the rusty old trip wire only seconds before she opened the door. His body flew back from the force of the explosion, knocking him to the ground as the sound of the blast rang in his ears. The inside of the building pulsated with the fiery orange glow of the now-lit ceiling beams as the last shrine of the Wild Eight went up in flames. A thick layer of smoke clogged the air, choking him. The broken glass of the game-room windows was littered across the floor, and he felt a trickle of blood run down his temple from where one of the shards had cut him. But he didn't hesitate.

"Sierra," he ground out, calling her name as he dragged himself to his feet amid the rubble. His eyes fell to the floor on which she lay—bleeding.

No.

Maverick rushed to her side, eyes dazed, as a myriad of thoughts shot like rapid fire through his head. Rose lying in the middle of the mountainside, a trail of bloody pawprints from before she'd shifted back into human form in her wake. The filthy scent of bloodsucker in the air. The pool of crimson at her neck. The matted bits of earth clumped in her hair.

He'd lost her. Slowly. He'd been too late. Far, far too late. And it could happen again. He could be back in that dark place again.

There was no sound in his ears but the ringing of the blast. Time blurred, seeming to move in slow motion as he carried Sierra from the wreckage. Next thing he knew, they were in a strangely familiar white room, the smell of antiseptic stinging his wolf nose and the glare of fluorescent lights stinging his retinas. Someone moved to pull her from his arms.

He snarled in response, baring his teeth.

A flash of brown skin and even darker curls. Austin in front of his face. His packmate was shouting something at him, but for the life of him, he couldn't hear it.

All he knew was he couldn't leave her side, couldn't allow them to take her, because if he was absent, if he wasn't with her, death could claim her.

Minutes. Hours. Days.

He wasn't certain how much time had passed. His vision was clouded. All he could see was her laid out in the bed, attached to machines.

"Packmaster. Packmaster."

Someone was yelling at him again, but the sound was muffled, distant, as if the speaker had been held underwater.

He understood the feeling of drowning, of having the life sucked out of you and not being able to draw breath. He'd been drowning since the moment he'd seen that fucking trip wire. The voice drew closer. This time harsher, more guttural.

Wes.

Or was it Colt?

He'd didn't give a fuck.

Whoever it was, they were hauling him away from her side. Using every ounce of his strength that remained, he thrashed against them. They couldn't take her from him. He couldn't lose her. He couldn't. Something sharp in his throat caused him to still as he fell into darkness. The next thing he knew, the ringing in his ears turned into a steady...

Beep. Beep. Beep.

He cracked an eye open, thinking only to stop the steady beeping sound before...

"Sierra," he growled, forcing himself up, only to be shoved back down again by the pain in his side and a large imposing hand.

"Be still." The voice was familiar. This time, he was certain of its owner.

Colt.

"She's fine, Mav. She was out of the hospital within less than forty-eight hours. It's you who's been under for well over a week."

His head was throbbing, the vein in his temple punching him with each beat of his pulse. He grumbled. "Me?" He hadn't even begun to think of himself until this moment. Every moment after the blast was a blur.

Save for the terror he'd felt at the idea of losing her.

"Sierra took the brunt of the initial trauma that's for certain, but you know her, she's a fighter. With Austin's help, she healed quickly. You, on the other hand, refused to leave her side, and after over thirty-two hours at her bedside with a chunk of a pool table leg embedded in your abdomen, by the time we finally realized you'd been wounded, too, you had an infection. Austin had to stick you with one of the horse tranquilizers before we could get you to leave her."

Maverick let out a long groan. "Is she here?"

Colt hesitated. "No, brother."

"Where is she?"

"She left."

At those words, Maverick's eyes shot open, though the glare of the overhead lights still pained him. "What?"

"Once it became clear that you would be fine and it was just a matter of waiting for the infection to clear, she left."

Maverick's brow furrowed. "Where to?"

"MAC-V-Alpha." Colt pulled up a chair beside him, the loud scrape against the tiled floor making his pulse race. "Apparently, once you made it clear you didn't intend to defy the council for her, she said she only had one choice for her career. She reenlisted."

Which meant he *had* lost her.

Just not in the way he expected.

"Did she say anything?"

He wasn't sure he wanted to know the answer, but he asked the question anyway.

Colt was quiet for a moment before he finally said, "When I asked her why she was leaving, she said you'd know. She said our father was right and that you actually didn't want a *real* wife, whatever that means."

A vise grip constricted Maverick's chest as he fought hard to swallow the dark emotions blocking his throat, but it was no use. He knew exactly what those words meant. Everything had been wrong from the start. Not that he'd chosen to marry Rose. That was behind them now. But that in every move he'd made since then, he'd pushed Sierra away. He'd chosen the pack, himself, his duty, everything over her. It didn't matter that he'd given her the position she wanted—at least temporarily—or even that he'd been the one to nominate her. When he refused to stand up to the council, he'd shown his true hand. He hadn't done anything to fight for her or for what she wanted.

He'd done it for the good of the pack.

And for a woman who'd been told she was second to all— her brother, her father, the male elite warriors—for her whole life, he'd committed the worse kind of sin. It didn't matter that he loved her.

He'd never chosen her in the first place.

Her wants, her desires, her needs.

Isn't that what you're doing? Using me as a means to an end?

He hadn't realized it at the time, but he had been. He'd been so blinded by duty to the pack and his drive to protect himself that he'd become the very thing he'd been running from. And in the process, he'd lost her.

Chapter 28

RECOVERED AND HEALTHY AGAIN, OVER THE COMING WEEKS, Maverick tried to tell himself it was for the best that things had ended between them like this. That though he'd never meant to hurt her, the pain of that hurt would keep her away, make her see that as much as he wanted to put her first in all things, when it came to his role, he couldn't. Love would make him weaker, vulnerable, and he couldn't risk vulnerability when he had a responsibility to the pack.

It was long past noon, the early evening sun fading over the mountains, casting shadows across the ranch. The snow had settled in to stay, a constant, packed layer coating the ground as the last of autumn had long since faded away. They still had a few months of cold to endure before the first buds of spring made their way. Maverick leaned on the paddock fence, panting and sweating. He'd been in the pen with Beast on and off the whole damn day, and still he hadn't so much as gotten close to saddling the wild mustang.

"You can't stand to be caged, can you?" he mumbled at the horse.

Beast let out a frustrated huff in response.

If you expect to get anywhere with that damn horse, you might start by giving him an inch of freedom instead of keeping him locked in a cage.

Sierra's voice had come to him so many times over the past several weeks that it'd become a game. What could he do? What situation could he put himself in to evoke the sassy tone of hers so clearly in his memory? It was a poor excuse compared to having her by his side, but she'd made her choice. Any dream he'd had of them had gone out to pasture. Or so he kept telling himself...

It's better this way. Best for the pack.

That was his mantra, but deep down, he'd never truly believed it. Not then or now.

But it was enough to hold him together most days. He couldn't change what he'd done, the choices he'd made.

Cursing under his breath, he started to head toward the barn to finally call Dean and throw in the towel, but he only managed two steps before he paused.

What could it hurt?

Rounding to the far side of the paddock, he watched Beast, angry and feral in his pen, huffing and stomping his foot with every step he made. His dark eyes flashed. No, it couldn't hurt. Taking her advice, Maverick threw open the gate, but to his surprise, the horse didn't immediately shoot out it. He held it open, gesturing for the horse to go.

"Go." The horse didn't move. "Go on now. You're free."

Slowly, tentatively, the horse inched toward the gate. Then suddenly, with the last few steps, he shot forward like a live wire. Beast galloped out into the open expanse of the pasture, running at full speed. The animal truly was a sight. Fast. Wild. Free.

Maverick climbed a rung or two of the paddock gate, watching the horse as he let out a triumphant whoop in relief. It didn't matter that the freedom wasn't his own. It was a sight to watch. The horse ran until he was little more than a pinprick in the distance. Dean wouldn't be pleased about having to track him down on the outskirts of the ranchland, if they even so much as bothered, but at the moment, Maverick couldn't bring himself to care.

With a deep sigh, Maverick stared up at the wide Montana sky, inhaling the fresh air for several minutes. Once he'd had his fill, he climbed down from the gate. Pushing the thing closed, he snapped the latch, but as he did, he heard the sound of running hooves against the frozen ground. He turned to find Beast, trotting back toward the gate, any hint of the fury in the animal's eyes long since gone.

Maverick couldn't help himself. He laughed low and long as Beast came right up to the gate. The horse stopped several feet away. Clearly, he would no longer bite the hand that fed him, but he wasn't ready to be friendly yet either. Still, it was impressive and unusual all the same.

Maverick let go of the gate, easing forward to try to approach the horse, but as he did, the edge of his back pocket caught on the splintered wood of the gate, and something fell from his pocket. He glanced down at the folded paper that had fluttered onto a patch of frozen grass.

Sierra's list.

He hadn't been able to bring himself to read it during the time they'd spent together. Too afraid he'd go wild with lust—or more specifically, love. But now, with her off retraining for MAC-V-Alpha in the foothills of North Carolina, what harm could it do?

Bending down, he picked up the list and unfolded the page. To his surprise, the folds were looser than he'd anticipated, and from the way he didn't get even a bit of resistance from the page, he realized the list wasn't new, it was aged, which meant she had to have written it when they'd been young, or at least years ago—and it wasn't an homage to all her deepest sexual fantasies either.

It was far worse.

> I want a man who will treat me with kindness and compassion. A man who will always put me first. I want a man who will respect my needs and desires, who asks permission, who waits, who protects me because he loves me, not because he thinks I'm weak. I want a man who will kiss me under the stars, and lend me his weapon, and champion my skill with a sword, all in the same breath. I want a man who is man enough to stand by my side.
> Man enough to take my breath away.
> Man enough to call me his equal.

Underneath her treatise, she'd written a short list of possibil- ities, but every single name had been crossed out except for one she'd underlined and circled, beneath which she'd written and dated ten years prior.

I want Maverick Grey.

Maverick clutched the list in his hands. He couldn't remember the last time he'd shed a tear. Had he done so at Rose's funeral? He didn't know anymore. But with Sierra's love cutting through him and all his grief, he couldn't help himself.

The Grey Wolf packmaster dropped to his knees and wept.

Chapter 29

MOST DAYS, SIERRA DIDN'T WEEP. MOST DAYS, SHE COULD manage to make it through the constant deluge of thoughts about him and not crumble to pieces, but today was unlike most, because today, she thought of him, and to her surprise, she smiled.

She stood on the steps of Rogue and Maeve's North Carolina mansion, glancing out over the Blue Ridge mountains. He would've hated the view here, grumbling and saying it was nothing comparable to the Montana mountains she called home. That was Maverick after all, always grumpy. Had he been here, she wouldn't have allowed him to even get started on the fact that his sister and his criminal brother-in-law had to distinguish between mansions in more than one state, when he was the most powerful packmaster in existence and only owned one home, but that was a thought for another day.

Another day when she didn't feel the sting of his absence so keenly.

She wrapped her hands around the mug of hot chocolate Maeve had brought her, the outside of the porcelain serving to warm her hands. She needed it, considering she'd spent most of the day in wolf form tromping through the woods across the couple's vast property. As far as she was concerned, a day well spent.

The only way it would've been better would've been if she'd spent it with him. She could almost feel the low vibration in her belly as she heard him say, "Sierra."

She turned, expecting to find it was only her memory, but instead, he stood there, Elvis pecking at the ground behind him. She dropped the mug of cocoa, immediately spilling the warm liquid all over the wooden patio.

The scarred side of his brow furrowed. "You can wield a sword twice your size but not a mug of cocoa?" he grumbled, picking up the mug that had clattered near his feet.

"Most men would start with hello."

"I'm not most men." His eyes flashed to his wolf.

No. He wasn't.

He was packmaster of the Grey Wolves, and she'd never forget that. He'd made certain.

His eyes surveyed her, not aroused—yet—but lingering. "You look different."

She didn't bother to respond. She crossed her arms over her chest to hold herself together. "What do you want, Packmaster?" She hurled his title at him like a weapon, and to her surprise, he flinched.

But he recovered quickly. "I've come to negotiate a treaty."

"A treaty?" Her mouth dropped open.

And to think that for a moment she'd thought…

"A treaty with you," he amended.

"A treaty with me?"

The edge of his lips quirked into a wry, teasing grin. "Repetition, warrior."

She didn't have it in her to bristle against it.

"Clearly, the war between us hasn't worked out too well," he continued, "so I thought I'd come to make amends."

She let out a haughty huff. "And demands, I'm certain."

He shook his head. "No demands."

Now, he'd *truly* caught her off guard.

"Only war reparations." He eased closer, and reaching into his coat pocket, he removed a small bundle of papers. He untied the string that bound them first before reaching for her hand at her side.

She let him.

Gently, he lifted her palm and pressed the first paper into her fist. "This is the document detailing the dissolution of the Elder Council."

Her jaw dropped. "What?"

"I'm not even close to finished with my groveling yet. I've only just begun. With your permission, I'd like to finish?"

Her eyes grew wide. With her permission? For a moment, she remained frozen before she finally found it in herself to nod.

Another paper pressed into her hand. "This is a pack law detailing there will be no discrimination based on gender for any position open within the pack."

Her breath caught.

"This is the document changing the laws of primogeniture to ensure that both firstborn males *and* firstborn females can become packmaster."

Sierra couldn't bring herself to breathe, though her heart was beating a mile a minute.

"This is the document allowing for our mate separation, the first of its kind. A divorce, as it's worded here."

"Divorce?" Her voice was shriller than she'd anticipated. "You're groveling with divorce papers?"

He swallowed, hard as if he didn't want to think about that particular option for too long. "That one is only valid if you sign it, if you so choose. Of course, I want to be married to you, I always have, but considering the whole marriage-of-convenience thing and you having to marry me to get your position, I didn't want to assume…"

"Naturally." She nodded. "Go on." There were still more papers in his hand, though what they could represent, she couldn't imagine.

He inhaled a deep breath, starting again. Another paper pushed into her palm. "This is the document reestablishing the council, but this time, not an Elder Council but a Peer Council with equal representation of all various genders and ethnic groups, including representatives from all the subpacks."

Her head was swimming with so many emotions that she was starting to feel dizzy.

"And this," he said, pressing the final piece of paper into her hand, that damn smirk on his lips setting a fire deep in her belly as he met her gaze, "is the letter detailing how that same council unanimously, of their own accord, voted for you to be named as an elite warrior with my full support and title backing the nomination."

Sierra cradled the pile of papers in her hands, staring down at them in awe before she glanced back up at him, tears pouring down her face. He'd done it. He'd placed her wants, her needs and desires before all other duty and kept his promise.

He'd fulfilled every point on her list and more. She smiled. A small part of her had always known he'd eventually come through, as long as she could pull him from the darkness long enough for him to get used to the light.

"Please say something."

She sifted through the papers, shuffling them until she removed the one about divorce and ripped it in two. "I don't need this."

A low grunt. An appreciative one. "I was hoping you'd say that."

"But there is one thing you've forgotten to do, Maverick."

"Anything, everything you wish."

Deep down, she knew that this time, he truly meant it. She tucked all the papers in her back pocket, adjusting his Stetson before she cupped her hand over the rough stubble of his cheek. "Tell me you love me, cowboy."

He didn't hesitate. "I'll do more than that. I promise you, Sierra Cavanaugh, that not only will I love you for the rest of my long life, but I will learn from my mistakes. I'm stronger with you by my side."

She loved the sound of those words on his lips. Deep, and throaty, and pure male. "Say it again."

A low, aroused grumble vibrated from his throat. "I love you."

He kissed her forehead.

"Again."

"I love you."

Her cheek.

She didn't need to continue with her demand.

"I love you."

Her chin.

"I love you."

The tender skin of her neck.

"I love you."

Then her breasts, and yet still he drew lower.

Desire burned through her as he dropped to his knees, his head now level with her breasts as he continued to inch further downward. She knew exactly where that delicious, filthy mouth of his was headed. Skilled wolfish tongue included.

"I can't wait for you to return home."

From MAC-V-Alpha. She sighed. Neither of them would have to worry about that.

"Maverick," she said, stopping him before he managed to lose him—and herself—to the pleasure that came whenever he was in between her legs.

"Mm-hmm." Part grumble. Part purr.

"There is one more thing I have to ask for."

He quirked his scarred brow as he gazed up at her.

She could get used to the idea of him staring at her with those gold wolf eyes from beneath her for the rest of her days. "I'm coming home sooner than expected, and the elite warriors, well, all the pack's females for that matter need to be given long maternity leaves."

His brow furrowed. Clearly that hadn't been what he'd been anticipating. "Maternity leave?"

She nodded. "Yes, maternity leave. My reenlistment to MAC-V-Alpha isn't happening after all. I told them I couldn't, because I–I think I'm going to need it." She placed a hand over her belly, where when he'd said she looked different, she was grateful he'd been too tactful to point out that instead of the flat abs of a warrior, she'd begun to sport a subtle, gentle curve.

He kissed her there, inhaling her scent, likely in search of the smell of the future pup beneath before he threw back his head and howled. To her surprise, the whole of the woods and mountains seemed to answer him, echoing back the sounds of the forest and the howls of their pack as if they recognized he was their king.

And she was his queen.

"Sierra Cavanaugh, packmastress of the Grey Wolves, I know you've already married me and I've asked you this more than once, but would you do me the honor of being my wife—truly—no caveats or restrictions?"

"You didn't ask, you demanded. Though this time's clearly different." She smiled. "Yes, I will, with one small exception." It may not have been a pun, but at the moment, it was as close as she could manage. "As long as you don't lose that wicked, sinful grin and you'll still be the Monster of Montana for me when we go to bed each night."

And to her complete and utter joy, at that, Maverick threw back his head in a full-throated laugh.

*If you can't get enough of Kait Ballenger's
red-hot shifters, read on for a look at the next
book in the Seven Range Shifters series*

WILD COWBOY WOLF

Coming soon from Sourcebooks Casablanca

"YOU NEED TO LET THIS GO, BROTHER." MAVERICK'S SHARP COM-mand cut through him.

Blaze tipped his Stetson low on his forehead, fighting to mask the frustrated snarl which tugged at his lips. His eyes changed to his wolf's. He couldn't let it go. He'd tried. More than once.

Refusing to turn and look at the packmaster, he slowly straight-ened to his full height from where he'd been standing, stooped over his desk. The muscles of his biceps ached with tension. Blaze flexed, rolling his shoulders like a predatory animal as he tried to release the stiffness there. But it was no use. The want for violence still lingered.

Inside, his wolf clawed at him.

For the past two hours, he'd been holed up here in the security office at the center of the Wolf Pack Run's ranch compound, fin-gers pounding across his keyboard in a frenzied rage. He hadn't been able to stop himself. Since the moment he'd seen movement in the darkness near the pack's borders on his phone's security stream, he hadn't been able to think of anything else. Command. Protect. Serve.

Kill, if necessary.

De Oppresso Liber. He'd been trained for it.

Only to find himself at yet another dead end.

Blaze snarled. *Fuck.*

"It doesn't work like that and you know it," he growled over his shoulder at Maverick.

As if in answer, one of the wall monitors in front of him glared blue through the darkness, enough to sting against wolf retinas. Maverick let out a grumbled curse, but Blaze didn't so much as blink. With a quick stroke of his finger on the keyboard, the screen went black before he turned toward the packmaster.

Closing the office door behind him, Maverick flicked on the dim overhead light and pegged Blaze with an all-too-knowing stare. From the dirt on his jeans, the Grey Wolf packmaster been out in the stables and now, standing amid all the pack's security monitors, the fellow cowboy wolf warrior looked out of place. Maverick was the fiercest the pack had to offer, but as alpha, he was also a testament to their lineage, a legend born of their true nature. Like most of the pack, that meant that even in human form, he was still sensitive to blue light and not fond of human technology.

Blaze, on the other hand, had been forced to adapt, change, camouflage. Whatever it took. Years ago that was exactly what Maverick had asked him to train for—burying the truth.

He'd gotten a bit *too* good at it.

Blaze leaned against the edge of his desk.

"Where's Kieran?" Maverick asked, referring to the young wolf who was *supposed* to be in the office tonight.

Blaze shrugged, as if he didn't know.

Maverick growled.

Blaze rolled his eyes and released a short sigh. "I sent him home."

"Call him, damn it." Maverick pointed an accusatory finger at Blaze. "You're supposed to be off duty."

"We're having a pissing contest because I'm doing *extra* work?" Blaze raised a smug brow.

Maverick frowned. "Don't get cheeky with me, Blaze."

Blaze cast him a wide, intentionally cheeky grin. "I wouldn't dream of it."

Maverick swore and shook his head with a frustrated grumble. "It's been over nine months since the reception, since Amarok's warning."

"I know."

"You're not going to find anything."

Blaze nodded. "I know."

"Yet you've been poring over those damn screens every goddamn chance you get."

"And?"

Maverick didn't take the bait. Not this time. "And if they were going to attack by now, they would have."

Blaze shook his head. "You don't know that."

The movement he'd seen on the forest cams tonight had turned out to be little more than a deer. But the thought of what *could* have been had still sent him prowling through the more unsavory corners of the Dark Web in search of information again.

For something. Anything. A lead.

Whatever it took to keep them all safe.

To keep his secrets hidden.

Maverick let out a disapproving grunt. "I understand your drive to protect the pack, but you can't run yourself into the ground while doing it."

"*You're* lecturing *me* about work-life balance?" Blaze snorted. "That's rich."

Maverick growled again. "Cut the jokes, warrior. I say this as your alpha, not as your friend." The packmaster purposefully held his gaze for a long beat. "Let it go."

Blaze refused to look away. "I can't."

"You will." Maverick placed his hand on the door handle.

To Blaze's surprise, Maverick was the first to look away.

Blaze smiled an unamused grin. "You asked me to go to Russia, Mav, and I did. You don't get to choose how I behave now that I'm back. Not as long as I'm doing my job."

Maverick hadn't been there. For all the experience, bloodshed, and battle the Grey Wolf packmaster had seen, Russia would always be worse.

Blaze knew because he'd relived it every goddamn night for the past four years.

"I know what you saw there was—"

"Don't," Blaze warned. The feral snarl in his voice was barely contained.

Maverick didn't know the half of it.

Turning away, Blaze cleared his throat and sat down in his desk chair. The dozen monitors covering the wall offered multiple views of Wolf Pack Run, the Grey Wolves' sprawling ranchlands, and the bordering Custer-Gallatin National Forest. This time of night, with most of the pack shifted and in true form, the woods were alive with their howling. The compound, on the other hand, proved quiet.

"If you start being too mushy instead of grunting all the time, hell might freeze over. Montana doesn't need any more snow." Blaze grinned over his shoulder.

Maverick didn't so much as laugh.

Typical.

"There're more important things on the table at the moment." Maverick's voice held more than a hint of concern.

Blaze rotated his chair back toward the packmaster.

"Josiah called today. One of the subpack members out in Bozeman hasn't come home."

Blaze shook his head and turned back toward the security monitors. "Big surprise. They shift, then disappear on a long hunt and lose all sense of time out there. Must be nice to have so few responsibilities. They always turn back up."

"This one *hasn't*. Not in over seventy-two hours."

Blaze hesitated from where he'd been about to start typing again. A chill ran through him. That long with no sign of a pack-mate *was* unusual, even in the subpacks.

His mind quickly scanned over the list of possible foul play. Their treaty with the human hunters of the Execution Underground had been recently restored, providing the Grey Wolves immunity while still keeping their agreement with the rogue wolves in place. The last of the Wild Eight had also recently been wiped out, the only remaining members having been incorporated into the Grey Wolf Pack. That left the bloodsuckers.

But the vampires hadn't attacked the outer subpacks since the Missoula massacre nearly two years earlier, and it was only recently that they'd seen a resurgence of movement among them closer to Billings and here at Wolf Pack Run.

Could it be…?

"Don't let paranoia rule your instincts, brother," Maverick said, cutting the thought short. "I need you to look into it."

Blaze nodded. "I'm smart enough to do both." He powered up the monitor again and placed his hands on the keyboard.

Maverick crossed the room in two quick strides and clicked the monitor back off with a sharp grumble. "You're *smart enough* to listen to your alpha. You *won't* do both. That's an order."

Blaze lifted a brow in surprise and laughed. "Look at you. Since when have you learned to power off a computer?"

The Grey Wolf packmaster could kill a man as soon as look at him and never struggled to operate any of the ranch machinery, but when it came to computer technology, he was nearly illiterate.

Maverick crossed his large arms over his chest with a frown, the black-banded tattoos of his packmaster's markings writhing along with the movement. Despite his usual grumpy demeanor, for a brief moment, he looked sheepish, if a bit embarrassed. "Sierra taught me." Maverick cast Blaze a smirk.

His new mate.

Blaze smiled. "So you really *are* going soft?"

"I mean it, Blaze." Maverick's grin fell and his lip curled in warning again.

Blaze expected the frustration. It was the concern underneath that he couldn't handle.

"Yeah, I know." Blaze waved a hand, brushing him off. "I'll take care of it. You have my word. But you're late to a meeting."

"There's no keeping secrets from you." Maverick shook his head. "Especially not when it has to do with Dakota." Maverick cast him a pointed look.

Blaze grunted in acknowledgment. He didn't want to have this conversation, even with Mav.

The packmaster's brow only inched higher, waiting.

Blaze ran a hand through his hair and released a long sigh. "That obvious, huh?" He slumped lower in his desk chair, tilting his head back as he scrubbed a hand over his face.

"No one ever called you subtle, Blaze. The only one who doesn't realize is her."

"Good." Blaze ran his tongue over his teeth.

"You could tell her, you know," Maverick said.

Blaze shook his head. "It's better this way."

Maverick scoffed. "I don't think even *you* believe that."

"Would you have told Sierra on your own?" Blaze's eyes flashed to his wolf, and he gave the packmaster a warning stare. "I don't have anything to offer her."

"You offer her yourself. That's all you need, warrior."

"I lost all sense of myself back in Russia." Blaze twisted back toward the computer.

"Then rebuild, damn it." Maverick fist's thumped hard against the doorframe. "You can't let your enemies win, Blaze."

Blaze released a long breath. He hesitated for a long moment, choosing his words carefully. "You weren't there, Mav… They go for families first, loved ones. There're no survivors. *Ever.* I can't put her in harm's way like that. If they decided to target her because of me, I wouldn't be able to protect her. If something happened to her..." He swallowed. "I wouldn't—"

"Perhaps *she* should be the one to make that decision," Maverick said, sparing him from the more gruesome details. "She's a fierce warrior. You're making excuses. She doesn't need you to protect her and you know it."

Blaze shook his head and let out a low whistle. "Sierra really *is* softening you."

At that, Maverick smiled. "Consider it." He turned to leave. "There's been no movement since Amarok warned you. Let it go."

The packmaster was already halfway out the door before Blaze managed to speak again. "Maverick."

Maverick grunted in acknowledgment.

"Just...promise you'll keep the extra patrols and drills in place like we talked about."

For a long moment, Mav didn't respond, until finally, he nodded. "If it'll help you sleep at night, warrior, you have my word."

Blaze cleared his throat again. "Nothing helps me sleep, Packmaster."

"I know." Maverick's voice was grim as he started to close the door. "That's what concerns me."

About the Author

Kait Ballenger hated reading when she was a child, because she was horrible at it. Then by chance she picked up the Harry Potter series, magically fell in love with reading, and never looked back. When she realized shortly after that she could tell her own stories, and they could be about falling in love, her fate was sealed.

She earned her BA in English from Stetson University—like the Stetson cowboy hat—followed by an MFA in writing from Spalding University. After stints working as a real vampire a.k.a. a phlebotomist, a bingo caller, a professional belly dancer, and an adjunct English professor, Kait finally decided that her eight-year-old self knew best: she's meant to be a writer.

When Kait's not preoccupied with writing captivating paranormal romance, page-turning suspense plots, or love scenes that make even seasoned romance readers blush, she can usually be found spending time with her family or with her nose buried in a good book. She loves to travel, especially abroad, and experience new places. She lives in Florida with her librarian husband, two adorable sons, a lovable mangy mutt of a dog, and four conniving felines.

Readers can connect with Kait via her newsletter by signing up at kaitballenger.com or chatting with her on social media: facebook.com/kaitballenger or Instagram @kait.ballenger.

Also by Kait Ballenger